lost in dreams

AN ALTERED HEARTS NOVEL

Published by Barbour Publishing, Inc., P.O. Box 719, Uhrichsville, Ohio 44683, www.barbourbooks.com

Our mission is to publish and distribute inspirational products offering exceptional value and biblical encouragement to the masses.

Member of the
Evangelical Christian
Publishers Association

Printed in the United States of America.

lost in dreams

AN ALTERED HEARTS NOVEL

by Roger E. Bruner
with Kristi Rae Bruner

BARBOUR
PUBLISHING

chapter one

Act 1

"Kim! Look out!"

Aleesha's scream almost gave me a heart attack as it split the early afternoon lull and reverberated throughout the Skyfly Departures Terminal at San Diego International Airport.

Before I could figure out what I was supposed to look out for, my feet started sliding gracelessly across the floor. Was this one of those California earthquakes I'd heard so much about?

But how could it be when I seemed to be the only object shaking or moving?

As I teetered and tottered to maintain my balance, I felt like a pedestrian who'd stepped on an unexpected patch of icy sidewalk. . .and never stopped sliding.

I didn't have a chance to think about protecting the arm I'd broken in Mexico a couple of weeks earlier. I was too concerned with not breaking my neck this time.

Just as I stopped skating out of control and started regaining my stability, I made the mistake of shifting my weight the tiniest bit. That motion offset my center of gravity just enough to make both feet shoot out from under me. Although Aleesha had gotten close enough to grasp my unbroken arm, she couldn't hold on to it.

I wish I could say her valiant effort served as a parachute slowing my fall, but truth be known, I probably more closely resembled a jumper whose chute has failed to open.

From a speeding, out-of-control vertical position to

splattered flat on the floor in 3.353 seconds. That would be a new record for any accident-prone eighteen-year-old. It was for me.

"Ow." *Good girl, Kim. No cursing. God cured you of that in Santa María.*

I sat up and wiggled back and forth a time or two to make sure my most important body parts were still working. I focused on the expressions of concerned passersby to keep from having to look at Aleesha's laughing face.

As much as my body ached from the fall, this accident didn't match bashing my head on a rock the first night in Santa María or breaking my arm the next day when I caught my toe in the cuff of my flared trousers and fell off the first rung of a short ladder. This spill had probably only added a bruised bottom—not a broken one—to my ever-lengthening list of minor mishaps.

Although I was too sore, too shocked, and too aggravated to blush with embarrassment, I could feel that same quantity of blood flooding the surface of my face with righteous anger.

"Stupid kids must've dropped dice or marbles on the floor," I said under my breath, half-afraid their parents would overhear and cuss me out for stepping on their children's toys. Parents could be strange the way they defended careless children. But only their own.

I ought to know. Mom and Dad spent long years doing that for me before forcing me to take some responsibility for myself. Unfortunately, the lessons had been slow, painful, and not altogether successful.

I looked around. No parents in sight. No kids, either. *Thank You, Lord.*

What was I sitting on, though? It felt familiar. Like. . . pebbles.

Giggling for all she was worth, Aleesha pointed to the

washed-out looking denim tote bag that lay collapsed and lifeless on the floor beside me. Before leaving the village five hours earlier, I'd filled it about a third of the way with pea-sized pebbles.

I'd planned to hand them out when I told the youth group at church about my mission trip. Our youth director, Pastor Ron, would appreciate the idea, even if no one else did.

Besides that, authentic Mexican pebbles—I wouldn't have to admit I hadn't bought them—were cheaper than bringing everyone souvenirs. As if I'd had that kind of money. Besides, I hadn't been anywhere that sold souvenirs.

Except for the airport, that was.

I had it all worked out in my head. I would talk about trusting God when minor things went wrong and seemed more serious than they were—I'd had plenty of recent experience with that—and I would illustrate by talking about the pebbles under my blanket the first night in the village.

I looked in the bag. Nothing.

I turned it inside out. Not one pebble. . .or one speck of pebble dust. Not even any regular dust. The bag couldn't have been emptier.

What it did have, though, was a triangular flap where two intersecting seams had torn—each one maybe two inches long.

Okay, so maybe I hadn't quite overcome a lifetime of carelessness during my stay in Santa María. I should've known better than to fill that denim tote with ten times as many pebbles as I needed. Each one had looked so tiny by itself. And what an idiot I'd been, making it twice as heavy as I could carry comfortably with my good arm.

My good friend Neil had offered to help me with it—bless his heart!—but I figured anybody as scrawny looking as him wasn't apt to be much stronger than I was. Besides, I'd already loaded him down with my other stuff. None of the other 143 team members had brought four suitcases of items they didn't need.

Fortunately for Neil, I'd left as much stuff in Santa María as I could. Skyfly Airlines might legitimately charge me for an excess number of bags, but they couldn't claim my luggage was overweight.

Not this time.

I'd half-carried, half-dragged the denim bag across the street and bumped it up onto the curb to get it into the building. Because my left arm was already killing me, I decided to try pushing the bag with my feet.

My shoes had a *slight* point, though, and I *might* have pushed my cargo a little harder and faster than necessary. Truth be known, after making very little progress urging the bag forward with gentleness, I developed a good working rhythm kicking it with all my might.

I didn't notice the hole in the tote or the pebbles leaking out like spring water dribbling down a rocky mountainside. Then an extra good kick sent the bag scooting ten feet ahead of me, turning the dribble into Niagara Falls and carrying me along with it.

Okay, so I should have noticed the bag getting light, lighter, lightest. I couldn't have kicked it that far otherwise.

But I hadn't caught on yet. I thought I'd simply perfected my technique.

So much for pebble-based preaching. Once again, God had used a Kim-tastrophe to teach me a lesson. He just hadn't revealed yet what it was.

"You looked silly trying to prance on those pebbles, girl," Aleesha said somewhere between the chuckles and the guffaws. "I'll have to teach you to do that right."

Her black face radiated the joy of her relationship with a Savior whose friendship meant even more to her than mine did, and that's saying a lot. Our biracial sisterhood worked beautifully because Jesus was the most important person in my life, too.

I was *trying* to make Him most important, anyhow. Especially after going on this mission trip and being reminded once more that the world didn't revolve around me.

"I could've done a fancy dance on those pebbles of yours," Aleesha said as she reached down to help me up. "Come on, girl. Let's get moving before the cleanup crew follows the pebble trail, catches up, and blames me."

I gave her a playful frown and then glanced back over my shoulder. She might have been teasing about blame, but two fellows with huge brooms and tiny dustpans were closing in fast. They were still maybe forty-five yards back, though. I couldn't tell at that distance if they looked angry or just disgusted, and I didn't plan to stick around and find out.

I looked at Aleesha and held an arm out. *Pull me up, would you?*

"No, girl." She snorted. "Not that one."

I lowered my broken arm, and she rolled her eyes and shook her head. She might as well have added, "*You dodo.*"

But she wasn't like that.

I held up the other arm, and she grasped it firmly. She was nonstop giggles as she uh-ed and oh-ed, pretending to struggle hard to pull petite, lightweight me to my feet. We stepped carefully to avoid any remaining pebbles and then took off running in the opposite direction from the pebble sweepers.

I had no idea what Aleesha meant about doing a "fancy dance," but I didn't doubt her dancing abilities—on pebbles or anywhere else.

"Anybody. . ." She looked at me and hesitated. "Anybody who's halfway coordinated, that is, can dance on a good, clean surface. And any uncoordinated fool—nothing personal, girl—is certain to slip and fall on an unstable one."

I shrugged. She had me pegged accurately, even though I couldn't imagine where she was going with this monologue.

"But if someone can prance or dance on a loose surface"— she stopped to look back at the pebbles that had led to my, uh, downfall—"a layer of those little roly-poly critters, for example, she must be. . ." She paused and finished her sentence in the exaggerated, dignified tone of a famous actor-to-be. "She must be exceedingly talented." A grin lit up her face. "Like me."

I looked at her with all the doubt I could muster. After two weeks of listening to her make the impossible sound not only plausible, but effortless, that was tough. I waited for her to laugh, but she didn't.

"So," I said, "you're saying African-Americans like you can prance on pebbles better than skinny white girls like me?"

We both giggled. No two people could have had more fun coming up with outrageous, nonexistent racial differences.

"Not at all, my dear Miss Kim. I'm saying we folks of color only prance on pebbles when no one else is around. We wouldn't want word to get out that a few of us are just as uncoordinated as you."

I smirked.

"Girl. . ." Her face softened the way it did when she was about to say something especially meaningful. Her dark brown eyes peered into mine as if she was looking for something, and she smiled as if she'd found it. "I was just messing with your head about 'prancing on pebbles.'"

I smiled.

"Physically, that is," she said. "But my dad talks a lot about something he calls a 'Season of Pebbles.' He says all Christians have them sooner or later, and I believe him."

"Huh?"

I'd never heard of a "Season of Pebbles," and Aleesha's

reference to her father as an active, ongoing presence in her life caught me off guard. She'd barely mentioned him before. So much for thinking I'd outgrown all of my racial stereotypes.

"The worst troubles, problems, and challenges in life. . . they're all pebbles that can make you fall. They're peskier than real ones, though. Peskier, more dangerous, and almost too numerous to count at times. During a time of prolonged difficulties—"

"A 'Season of Pebbles'?"

She nodded. "Those pebbles are there, ready to trip a Christian morally, emotionally, and spiritually. So 'prancing on pebbles' means 'depending on God to stay upright.'" She paused, apparently giving her explanation additional thought.

"More than upright, though. *Prancing* suggests forward motion. No matter how unbalanced you feel. So to take it to a deeper level, 'prancing on pebbles' means demonstrating the real meaning of 'Victory in Jesus.'" She began humming the familiar hymn.

"Like overcoming my problems in Santa María, you mean?"

"Kim, as irritating as those things were, they were nothing compared to what I'm talking about. You never came close to falling there."

She smirked, and I chuckled.

"Well," she said, "except for the time you actually fell down."

"I'm not expecting anything major to happen for a while. No pebbles for me. I think God's going to let me rest up from Santa María and live a normal life for a while."

"I hope you're right, girlfriend," she said as we hugged good-bye.

chapter two

*C*ome on, Mom. Answer your cell phone.
    I was exhausted. My mother couldn't pick me up soon enough. She thought Atlanta's Hartsfield International Airport might have a cell phone waiting lot where people could park and stay in the car until a newly arrived friend or family member called to say she was waiting. That was supposed to lessen the congestion at Hourly Parking, not to mention saving the picker-upper a bit of cash.

Great idea.

Mom, I'm dying to tell you all about my trip. You won't believe how much I've changed. I've really grown up.

After spending the last of my change on a handcart, I piled it high with my four suitcases—and that well-worn denim tote bag a teammate had given me in Santa María. I'd have to use the bag for my object lesson instead of the lost pebbles. Unable to see around my pile of luggage, I kept my eyes on the overhead sign pointing to Passenger Pickup as I worked my way through the crowd.

Okay, Mom, I'm ready and waiting. I'd tell you that if you'd just answer. So where are you? Don't tell me you were wrong about the cell phone lot and you had to find a place in Hourly Parking. Dad will really razz you about that.

Maybe I'd help him. That could be part of my "learn to get along better with Dad" campaign. Wouldn't that surprise him?

Or—more likely—shock him. Mom and I usually sided with one another in disagreements with Dad.

I hoped I could stay awake until she got here, though. Sure, I could put the passenger seat back and sleep the whole way home if I wanted to. Mom would understand. She'd probably expect it.

But I had too much to tell her. I wouldn't be able to sleep. Not for a while.

Mom, I've matured so much since you last saw me. My two weeks in tiny Santa María have changed me totally, and responsibility is my new middle name. Isn't that great? And won't Dad be thrilled to see the positive changes?

I snapped my fingers. I knew what I could do. Offer to drive. Mom hated Atlanta traffic, especially at and near the airport. Consideration like that would blow her mind. Of course, she'd realize I wasn't in any shape to be behind the wheel of a car, but she'd appreciate the thought nonetheless. Yes, I'd offer to drive home.

If Dad hadn't surprised me by changing my flight to a nonstop, I'd probably be killing time at Dallas/Fort Worth now. He'd sounded genuinely disappointed about not being able to drive Mom to the airport, but he didn't think he should postpone today's meeting with the president of the university.

Getting an appointment with Dr. Cutshaw sometimes took days, even for a tenured English professor like my father, and Dad's need must have been too important to risk a delay. I hoped they were discussing something good. Something that would please Dad. He needed more joy in his life.

Learning how much he looked forward to seeing me was sweet, though. I'd never seen much of his affectionate side until I called home about my broken arm. After that, he left several voice messages saying how much he loved me. Not only had I saved them, but they'd also already made me cry eight or ten times.

Today.

Dad and I were going to get along great now. I could feel it. How could God fail to bless such a righteous undertaking as drawing my family closer together?

Mom, come on. My calls keep falling through to voice mail after the fourth ring. You can't be on the line with somebody else, or I'd get your voice mail greeting on the first ring. Isn't your phone working? Or has my phone flaked out?

After my phone sat around unused for two weeks in an area so remote it couldn't find the time or a roaming signal, I wouldn't have been surprised to discover that the hot sun had baked its fragile little insides. Hmm. But I wouldn't have reached Mom's voice mail greeting if that had happened.

If I tried calling Dad, I could ask if he'd heard from Mom, but I didn't know what time his meeting was, and I didn't want to chance interrupting it. He was always too preoccupied to think of turning his phone off or setting it on vibrate. No need for me to make Dr. Cutshaw aware of that shortcoming.

I grinned at myself. I was learning to be more thoughtful. That was part of the new me. I'd have to tell Dad I'd purposely avoided calling him, even though I hoped he'd notice other aspects of my maturing without my having to wave a flag in front of his face.

From the windows facing Passenger Pickup, I didn't see any sign of Mom's Honda Civic. The rain was so heavy I could barely see the street. Although I'd overheard a couple of people talking about a thunderstorm, I hadn't heard any rumbles. A heavy-duty building like the terminal must do a great job of keeping the outside noises outside.

I guess the storm slowed you down, huh, Mom? I'm glad you're being extra cautious in this horrible weather.

She always allowed extra time for the unexpected, though. Still, the drive from home took an hour-and-a-half to two hours at best. Anything could have delayed her. Accidents— weather like this was apt to result in a number of fender-benders—sometimes blocked the interstate for hours.

I didn't leave a message the first three times I called. Hadn't Mom told me a million times that retrieving voice mail while driving was almost as dangerous as texting? But when my fourth call went to voice mail, I started talking at the sound of the beep.

"Mom, it's Kim. I thought I'd say that in case you've forgotten what my voice sounds like, even though I just talked to you this morning. I'm waiting just inside the baggage claim area. Let me know when to come outside. Be careful in this rain. I love you, Mom."

By then, I was so tired of standing—or maybe just tired period—that I set several of my nearly empty suitcases on the floor and angled my cart so I could climb on top and face the window. Maybe that wasn't the most dignified thing I'd ever done, but who cared?

People sometimes called me Miss Priss or Miss Prep, but they never accused me of being dignified.

The rain had let up some, but every car in sight still had headlights on. I leaned forward and pressed my nose and forehead against the glass. It felt pleasantly cool, even though the outside air would be hot and muggy. After all, this was Atlanta in early August.

I closed my eyes for a minute.

I hadn't suffered jetlag flying to San Diego, but flying west to east. . .Aleesha had told me that would be bad. As usual, she'd been right.

I don't know how long I'd been dozing in that awkward position, but I was barely awake when my phone started playing "Amazing Grace." Mom. That was her favorite hymn, so I'd made it her ringtone.

"Mom?" I said as I tried situating the phone against my ear. "I'm so glad to hear from you. I was starting to wonder. Where are you?"

"Kim?" a male voice said. "Kim Hartlinger?"

chapter three

The sound of a man's voice coming from my mom's cell phone number wouldn't normally make me fall off a luggage cart. No matter how responsible and conscientious Mom was in every other way, she was a complete failure when it came to keeping up with her cell phone. She'd been lucky so far. Uh, blessed.

She hated the word *lucky* as much as I did. We agreed that Christians shouldn't believe in luck. And God had blessed each of her phone losses with an honest finder who called to let her know it was in safe hands. I knew that from firsthand experience.

Because I always had my phone on me and didn't ignore her calls the way Dad did—he spent hours at a time in another world, one where he wasn't apt to notice his phone ringing— Mom finally broke down and entered my number in her phone book as her primary emergency number. Her ICE—In Case of Emergency. Besides, she knew I wouldn't tease her about losing her phone. . .again and again and again.

But I fell off the luggage cart this time. Sort of.

While answering my phone, I started climbing down. But I didn't realize my weird position had cut off the circulation to my feet and legs, leaving them too numb to support me. In fact, I didn't discover it until I crumpled to the floor and saw my phone go flying. My thinly padded bottom would probably be more than just sore after landing on it so hard twice in one day.

"I'm sorry," I said while scooping the phone up and putting it to my ear again. I was surprised it was still working.

"I dropped my phone." No point in admitting I'd fallen and sent the phone sprawling. "What did you say?"

"Are you Kim Hartlinger?" His voice sounded intense.

Although sirens howled in the distant background, I didn't pay much attention to them. After all, this was Atlanta. The big city. Something was always going on here.

"Where did she leave it this time?" I sat on the floor pounding the feeling back into my feet.

At least this call explained why she hadn't answered my calls. She didn't have her phone. But why was she so late? Had she wasted time she didn't have trying to find it?

"I beg your pardon?" The caller sounded confused. "This is Kim Hartlinger?"

"Yes, sir, this is Kim. So you've found my mother's cell phone? I asked you where she left it."

The man didn't answer for a moment. The sirens sounded closer now. I wondered if he was on the way to an emergency.

"In her car. She was apparently holding it when. . ."

chapter four

How the. . . ? I swallowed the curse word. I felt guilty for even thinking it.

But how was I supposed to find the interfaith chapel when the tears ran off my face like the Mississippi River overflowing its banks at flood time? A policewoman was supposed to meet me at the chapel. She would give me details. . .

Details about the accident. About Mom's condition. She would tell me if. . . I couldn't let myself think it.

Some guy emptying garbage cans had given me easy-to-follow directions to the chapel. At least they'd sounded easy, but I couldn't see well enough to walk. Tears clouded my vision and limited my visibility to probably less than 5 percent.

God must have been guiding my feet, though. I managed to ease my way from the middle of the busy walkway to an out-of-the-way spot without running into anyone. As soon as I felt the wall's coolish tiles, I pulled a packet of Kleenex tissues out of my purse. Neil had given them to me that morning while translating Rosa's letter. Had God told him I would need them again this soon?

The officer on the phone had sounded kind. Gentle. Concerned. But he hadn't wasted time getting to the bottom line. Mom had been in an accident. It was serious. Life-threatening. She was on her way to the hospital. He refused to speculate about her condition, but he was obviously afraid she might not—*no! I won't let myself consider that.*

I tried not to think about the other thing he'd told me. "She was apparently using her cell phone at the time of the accident."

Why had she been using her phone while driving? And in such horrible weather at that. The very thought of it freaked me out.

"She wasn't trying to answer one of my calls or listen to my voice mail, was she?" I asked myself repeatedly while dabbing my eyes with tissue after tissue. Surely not. Not as much as she preached against cell phone use while driving.

She knew better.

I used up the rest of the tissues before resorting to the sleeve of the red sweatshirt I'd bought just hours ago at San Diego International. I'd smiled to myself when I first spotted it. It was pizza sauce red, although I couldn't tell what brand.

But I wasn't smiling now, and "just hours ago" seemed like a lifetime. I'd talked to Mom before I left San Diego. She was so looking forward to seeing me. . .to hearing all about my trip. Now I didn't even know if she was. . .still alive. The world wasn't big enough to contain all the tissues I'd need if she wasn't.

And nothing could keep my stomach from churning mercilessly each time I asked myself, *Is it possible I'm responsible for Mom's accident?*

I barely noticed people staring at me. Most of them rushed on by the way people do in an airport. One lady stopped and came closer, though. She looked concerned. . .like she really wanted to help.

But her Vietnamese features—especially her hair and face—were so similar to Mom's that I had to turn and face the wall. Under the circumstances, I couldn't deal with someone who reminded me that much of Mom.

It was like confronting a ghost. Had God sent this woman as a sign that Mom was dead? Or that she wasn't?

Those dark eyes undoubtedly reflected the ton of kindness and understanding she felt for an older teen who was bawling her eyes out against the tiled wall of a busy airport, but I could only see my mother's face, criticizing me for my thoughtlessness.

Why had I kept calling Mom after discovering the weather was so bad? Why had I insisted on leaving voice mail? Why hadn't I simply waited for her to arrive—no matter how late?

Deep inside, I wanted to verbalize a prayer, but when I closed my eyes, I knew the Holy Spirit would have to accept the uncontrollable moaning that meant, *Heavenly Daddy, make Mom be okay. Don't let her. . .*

I couldn't say it. Not even in prayer. I couldn't face the possibility that Mom was. . .gone.

The Vietnamese woman spent several minutes patting my shoulder lightly. Every once in a while, she spoke words I might have recognized if I'd let Mom teach me her heart language. If Mom. . .survived, I'd beg her for lessons. I hoped it wasn't too late to learn more about the Asian half of my heritage.

Before my Good Samaritan moved on, she reached in her purse and took out a purple handkerchief. It looked clean and had a freshly ironed smell. I tried to smile when she gently pried open the fingers of my left hand, placed the handkerchief in my palm, and closed my fingers around it.

I couldn't smile, though, and I hated my inability to explain why. I hoped she understood that I didn't always act this ungrateful.

When I opened my hand and looked at the handkerchief, I found a tiny wooden cross inside. An angel had attempted to minister to me, and I'd rejected her. At least I felt like I had.

I stared at the wall through tear-bleary eyes. I felt like beating my fists against its hard, unforgiving surface, but that wouldn't help me find the chapel.

"Kim? Kim Hartlinger?"

The voice sounded familiar. I turned around to face a stylish black woman in her early thirties. She wore a smart-looking Skyfly Airlines uniform and a photo ID. I stared hard through my tears.

Mirages only appear in the desert. They never happen in airports, do they?

chapter five

M rs. Adams?" I didn't try to hide my amazement. . .my disbelief. "Penny?"

A miracle like this would have been beyond my ability to hope or pray for. Who but my precious Heavenly Father would do such a thing on my behalf simply because He loved me and knew how badly I needed help?

"Kim," Penny said as she opened her arms for a hug. I probably shocked her by burying my face in her shoulder and breaking out in fresh tears. She'd seen me frantic before, but not this far out of control.

I wouldn't have made it to San Diego in time to join the team a couple of weeks before if she hadn't exerted her authority as a Skyfly supervisor to get me on an early-enough flight out of Dallas/Fort Worth after I missed my scheduled flight.

Penny's unexpected appearance today relieved my concerns so much I didn't think to ask why she was in Atlanta. I just cared that she was with me. As a Christian, she'd undoubtedly go out of her way to help me again. Especially now that she realized I was major-league upset.

I lifted my head from her shoulder and tried to speak, but I couldn't get any further than "I. . ." for crying.

Her face revealed the same kind of compassion I pictured Jesus showing the sick people who came to him for healing.

"What's wrong, Kim?" Her concern was real. Her voice revealed a genuine desire to help.

I dried my eyes with the purple handkerchief and blew my nose before answering. "An auto accident. My mom. Just a little while ago. She may not. . ."

Her smooth face wrinkled, and her eyes narrowed and clouded with mist. "I am *so* sorry." She pulled me into her arms once more. The warmth of her hands on my back—the tender strength—reminded me of the hugs my mother. . .used to give me. "I'm here for you, baby."

Although I was preoccupied with worry and the beginnings of guilt—were those two of the "pebbles" Aleesha had cautioned me about or perhaps the whole bagful?—I would never stop thanking God for Penny's undivided attention. What a blessing to have the assurance that she had moved me to the top of her priority list.

"You need help." A statement, not a question. I didn't respond. "What can I do first, Kim?"

"The chapel," I managed to say between sniffles. "Must get to the chapel. Somebody. . .policewoman. . .meeting me there. Will tell me. . .if—"

"Whoa, Kim," she said as she caught me and guided me to a nearby seat.

"You're too wobbly to walk. I'm getting you some transportation."

I nodded. At least I assume I did.

Before I knew it, she was talking into her portable phone. . . and her words were coming out over the public address system. "I need a wheelchair at the Skyfly counter." She gave me a quick once-over. "Make that a wheelchair, a bottle of cold water, a wet washcloth, and a box of tissues at Skyfly. Please hurry."

She repeated her announcement before turning to me again.

"Where are your suitcases, Kim?"

I shrugged. For all I knew, they were still in or near the cart. But where that was, I couldn't say. I wasn't sure where I was.

"Don't worry. We'll find them."

"They're almost empty this time. No bricks." That's what

Millie Q had accused me of carrying to San Diego. Under different circumstances, I probably would have laughed. But these circumstances were the wrong kind of different.

Before I knew what was happening, Penny was wheeling me through the airport and talking on the phone with airport security. "How many suitcases?"

I held up four fingers, and she relayed that information to the security people.

"Tan?"

I nodded.

"Two large, two extra-large?"

I nodded again.

Although Penny was careful not to run into anyone, she didn't waste any time rushing me to the chapel. If I'd been in better spirits, I might have teased her about whether she intended to have a second career as a female NASCAR driver.

After wiping my face and blowing my nose, I reclined my head slightly and draped the white cloth over my eyes. Although it felt pleasantly cool, I was more concerned about not having to watch people staring back at me as we made our way through the airport. Before long, I quit caring.

Stress can make a girl aware of the strangest things. One of the wheels on my wheelchair suffered from a significant nick. Or maybe a long-dried-on lump of gum. Either way, I seemed to be riding on a highway that needed repair. Bumpety-smooth-bumpety-bumpety. Bumpety-smooth-bumpety-smooth.

When Penny stopped, I uncovered my face and wiped my eyes. Even so, they couldn't have burned much worse if some sadist had poured a ton of salt in them. So I wiped them again while she opened the chapel door. Holding it open with one foot, she wheeled me inside.

The only other person in the small chapel was a middle-aged

woman—mid- to late-thirties. Her police uniform didn't flatter her figure. She—who did the policeman who called from Mom's phone say would be meeting me? Officer Dawson?—stood up and turned around.

She took forever coming to greet us. I wouldn't have been in a rush to tell me her news, either. Once I saw her close-up, the tension in her face scared the daylights out of me.

"Miss Hartlinger. . .Kim." Looking into my eyes, she took my hand without shaking it. I looked at my feet. "I'm Officer Ellen Dawson."

I didn't make any effort to acknowledge her greeting, but looked up again with fresh tears already clouding my vision. She was still holding my hand—ever so gently— the way Mom. . . would have done.

Like when she knew something I didn't know. Something she didn't want to tell me. Something that would upset me to hear.

"No! Mom can't be. . ."

Officer Dawson glanced over my shoulder at Penny, who had begun massaging my shoulders. Tears were forming in the policewoman's eyes, and I heard Penny sniffling behind me.

She quit rubbing my shoulders and took a firm hold. As if she needed to hold me in place to keep me from falling apart.

"I've called your father," Officer Dawson said. Duty must have required her to get back to business, no matter how unpleasant. "Mrs."—she strained to read Penny's ID—"Mrs. Adams, can you take care of Kim while Mr. Hartlinger goes to the hospital to identify. . . ?"

I screamed as if my heart was full of demons, and the chapel echoed with sounds I'd never known I was capable of making.

chapter six

I hadn't been inside a funeral home since my grandmother died, and I could barely remember that time. Even though her estate helped fund my mission trip to Santa María, she and I had never been close. Truth is, I didn't know her well enough to love or miss her.

Dad never told me how he felt about his mother's death, and I never saw him cry. Not even at the funeral. I might not have known much about grief, but that "stiff upper lip" attitude struck me as odd.

Perhaps even cold. But my dad could be that way at times.

Everything was different this time, though. The deceased was Dad's wife and my mother, and I'd never seen him look so dragged out and pathetic. His weak, haggard appearance was not just heartrending, but downright scary.

Not that I'd ever thought of Dad as strong—or weak. I'd never known him that well. Not emotionally. But I was determined to do something about that now.

If I ever got over my own grief—I couldn't imagine that would ever happen—I'd do everything I could to close the gap between Dad and me. I would take good care of him and show him how much he needed me. How much we needed each other. Mom was gone, but neither of us had to feel helplessly alone.

Still, the thought of playing cook, laundress, and maid to my father made me feel far older than eighteen. The idea scared me almost senseless. Had I really matured enough to take my mom's place in meeting Dad's day-to-day needs? How could I hope to run the household the way she had? Could God give me enough patience to put up with Dad's peculiarities?

On the way home from my life-changing experiences in Mexico, I thought I could do anything within my power to build a better relationship with Dad.

But now? I felt as helpless—as powerless—as he looked and acted.

I stood as far back from the casket as I could. Wishing I could hide in my own little broken world, I stared at the cheapy watch I'd bought on the way to Santa María—now wasn't the time to have my cell phone out—and wished everyone would go home and leave me alone. But wishing didn't keep people from finding me, no matter how little I felt like talking with anyone.

With anyone but Aleesha or Betsy Jo, that was.

But Aleesha had gone home to Baltimore. She wept with me over the phone when I called to tell her about Mom's death. She offered to come be with me, but I told her she didn't need to.

I could have kicked myself for not saying, "How soon can you get here?"

And Betsy Jo? I didn't know where she was. Even though I'd been home from Santa María more than forty-eight hours, I hadn't heard from her. Not even a text message.

Because we'd been best friends almost since birth, her avoidance seemed out of character. If my grief hadn't made me so self-centered, I might have worried that something was wrong with her.

Then again, Mr. Snelling didn't mention her when he stopped by to see Dad and me the night of the accident. He came over after midnight because he saw our lights were still on. His concern had been genuine. And obvious.

Although Mrs. Snelling had already gone to bed, she sent

her condolences. At least we felt confident of their support.

Their support. But not Betsy Jo's.

I hated making comparisons, but after growing so close to Aleesha in Mexico, I couldn't help wondering if she hadn't become a better best friend than Betsy Jo. Aleesha wasn't just *a* good Samaritan.

After drooling once more over the gorgeous flower arrangement she'd sent, I concluded she was the *only* one.

I wished some of the other teens had come to visitation. It's not like they had to look at Mom's body. They couldn't have, in fact. In spite of the airbag's futile attempt to protect her, the accident had disfigured her face and upper body so horribly that Dad wouldn't even let me see her.

The mortician had done his best to reconstruct her basic features, Dad explained before insisting that I'd be better off remembering Mom the way she looked the last time I saw her. I begged him to change his mind, but he wouldn't, and he went along with the funeral director's recommendation to keep the casket closed during visitation.

Nobody should see Mom looking like that. Everyone should remember her the way she'd looked in life.

Although I made Dad promise to take a picture of Mom in the casket and show it to me when I turned twenty-one, the frustration was overwhelming. I just wanted to go home, bury my head under the covers, and hope I'd awaken to find that the events of the past few days had all been an unspeakable nightmare.

Maybe I'd wake up and find myself still sitting on top of the luggage cart at the airport.

Why did people say such irritating, thoughtless things to the bereaved? Didn't they know not to resort to useless clichés?

Aleesha had been different, though. When I told her not to

come, she'd said, "But I want to. I love you."

That was all she said, because she knew she didn't need to say more. She didn't need to elaborate. She cried with me on the phone, and that said it all. Aleesha wasn't the kind of girl who cried about unimportant things.

During the first hour of visitation, I must've heard "What a terrible loss" twenty times. Those people sounded like they were talking about *their* loss—not mine. *Who gives a rip about you people? I just want my mom back!*

I remembered a poem I'd memorized years before.

> *"When you give up*
> *Something you love dearly*
> *And do it willingly,*
> *They call it a sacrifice*
> *And pat you on the back.*
> *When something you love*
> *Is taken away from you*
> *And you have no choice,*
> *They call it a loss*
> *And pat you on the back."*

Those words hadn't made sense at the time. Now they did. At least a dozen older ladies said, "She was still so young. . ."

Maybe she'd seemed young to them, but she was—she had been—old enough to be my one and only mother.

Eight people—maybe ten—said, "Your mom's at home with Jesus now." A few said, "Our loss, Terri's gain." Several of them had almost sounded jealous because they weren't the ones to leave this broken earth. One woman actually admitted feeling that way.

Her honesty had been so refreshing I smiled at her. In agreement.

Although I'd only heard, "I don't know what the choir will be like without Terri" three times so far, most of the choir members hadn't made it over to my little corner yet. I was bound to hear that lament plenty of times more.

In spite of their best intentions, I wanted to scream, *"The choir? I don't know what my* life *will be like without Mom— period."*

I lost count of the people who said, "Let me know if I can do anything for you."

Their offers sounded kind. Sincere. But I didn't want nonspecific help. And none of them could have done what I needed most and brought Mom back.

Maybe I shouldn't have felt so resentful, but most of those offers came from people who could have helped without making us ask for it. After getting to know Dad better the past several days, I felt positive he would agree with me. Neither of us was apt to request anyone's assistance.

That's why I grinned big-time when someone handed me a large index card neatly printed with her name, address, phone number, and e-mail. Even Twitter and Facebook. Her offer was generous. "People have brought you lots of food," she said. "That leaves you with lots of dirty dishes. I'll pick them up, wash them, and return them to their owners for you. If I don't hear from you in a couple of days, I'll give you a call."

Almost immediately after that, while still basking in the thoughtfulness of her offer, I heard the most thoughtless comment of all. From each of two different people at that.

"I know how you feel."

Not "I can imagine how you feel" or "I can't imagine. . ." or "I don't want to imagine. . ."

Even if those two women had actually lost a parent in an auto accident, I'll bet they didn't have any reason to feel guilty about it.

But I did.

chapter seven

I need to ask you some questions about the accident," the policeman said half an hour before the funeral service. Great timing. . .grrr.

When he opened his notebook—*why haven't you told us your name, sir?*—I scooted closer to Dad. Although I wanted him to put his arm around my shoulder, he didn't. So I took his hand in mine. Our hands were closer to the same size than I'd realized.

His eyes opened wide. My display of affection must have really caught him off guard.

"We need each other, Dad," I whispered as quietly as I could. The policeman, a stranger to both of us, didn't deserve to share that special moment, but we couldn't control that.

Dad squeezed my hand, and I started crying. Never overtly affectionate, he'd just done something warmer and more loving than I could ever remember him doing before.

"Mr. Hartlinger. . .Ms. Hartlinger," the officer said, keeping his eyes on his notebook instead of making eye contact with either of us, "I'm sorry about your loss."

Oh, yeah? Then why have you come here today right before the funeral service?

"This won't take but a couple of minutes."

I'd seen some of the ancient *Dragnet* series reruns, and this guy had that emotionless Sgt. Joe Friday "Just the facts, ma'am" tone down pat.

He started reading from his notebook. "Mrs. Hartlinger was apparently going at a high rate of speed when she hit a slick spot on the highway, jumped a drainage ditch, and smashed into a nearby tree. She died instantly."

As thankful as I was Mom hadn't suffered, his deadpan—ugh! what a choice of words—description made the accident seem all too real. Unnecessarily so.

"Her cell phone was in her left hand—"

"Terri is. . ." Dad caught himself. "She was right-handed. So she held her phone in her left hand when she was using it."

The officer scribbled something in his notebook. I couldn't imagine what Mom's handedness had to do with his investigation. In fact, I had no idea what this investigation was all about, anyhow, but I wasn't about to prolong an already-agonizing conversation by asking.

"Does she always talk on the phone while driving?"

Does? Present tense? Yeah sure, mister. But only if they have phones and cars in heaven.

"No," I said before Dad could answer. "She didn't. . .she wouldn't let me do it, either. She said it was against the law."

The officer smiled at me. His need for dental work reminded me of Millie Q at Dallas/Fort Worth. I wondered if she would have seemed more sympathetic than him. Probably not.

Is that what this is all about—gathering statistics about cell phone usage and fatal accidents?

"We checked with your wireless carrier—"

Dad cocked his head.

"She was listening to voice mail at the time of the accident."

What? You mean she might have been listening to my message when she lost control of the car?

I'd considered the possibility before—I'd fretted myself nearly sick over it—but now that I had a reason to take my fears more seriously, the muscles of my face tightened and the perspiration started dribbling down my forehead into my eyes. A major headache struck like an unexpected bolt of lightning, and I could only imagine how red my face had turned.

I thought I'd pass out, but I didn't. I thought I might throw up, but that didn't happen, either. Although the amount of acid that shot upward into my throat might have been small, it gagged me so much I started coughing. I couldn't stop for a number of minutes, and the leftover taste of bile was indescribably bitter.

I unwrapped a stick of gum as fast as I could, rolled it up, and threw it in my mouth. The sweetness neutralized the bitterness a little bit, but not enough. I hoped I could find a bottle of mouthwash—or at least a breath mint—before the service started. Maybe Pastor Ron had something in his office. Or Senior Pastor Cecil in his.

I had no idea whether criminals suffered remorse for their crimes—or how much—but I couldn't imagine even the most penitent criminal suffering more guilt than I was. After all, I'd killed my mother by leaving that voice mail, and I couldn't undo the damage or bring her back.

No one would ever prosecute me for my "crime," though. No one would need to. I'd spend a lifetime punishing myself.

The cop tapped his pencil against his notebook.

"Mrs. Hartinger—"

My mom is dead. Don't you even care enough to pronounce her name correctly? "Hartlinger," I said. I didn't try to hide my aggravation. "With an L. Terri Hartlinger."

He glanced at his notebook and shrugged. "Yeah, Hartlinger. Sorry."

If his tone was any indication, he didn't mean, *"I'm sorry I mispronounced your mother's name."* Just, *"I'm sorry you noticed, and I wish you hadn't said anything about it."*

"Was"—he checked his notebook before trying to pronounce it again—"was Mrs. Hartlinger in the habit of exceeding the speed limit? From the testimony of several witnesses and the physical evidence, we place her speed at about seventy-seven. That's twelve miles over the limit for the road she was on. Drivers using cell phones sometimes accelerate without realizing it."

I wanted to say, *"So you plan to give her a posthumous speeding ticket? How about arresting her for trespassing on the property where she landed and giving her another ticket for littering by leaving her car and body there?"*

But I bit my tongue and answered him as calmly as I could. "Mom was a conservative driver." Dad seemed relieved to have me answer so many of the cop's questions. "I don't know about speeding up while on a cell phone, but she normally stayed under the speed limit. She was coming to pick me up from the airport, and she must have been running late."

Officer Unknown scribbled a few more notes.

"We sometimes teased her about being a slowpoke," Dad said. Although he was super-clean-shaven today, I couldn't help noticing a single teardrop colliding with a single piece of stubble and splitting in two. "We often had trouble making her go the speed limit."

"Oh." He jotted a little more in his notebook. "What about her other driving habits?"

Dad and I looked at one another.

"What do you mean?" I don't recall which of us asked.

"Did she drive one-handed very often? Did she have much experience driving on wet pavement? Things like that."

"Officer," Dad said with a degree of patience I couldn't have faked nearly as convincingly, "my wife was an experienced driver and a good one." He glanced at his watch. "If you have more questions, they'll have to wait until after the funeral service. And the burial."

Long after. Like years from now.

Officer Unknown must have caught me looking at him

resentfully. He looked me in the eye and frowned. He knew. I could tell.

That unfeeling policeman who'd never bothered to tell us his name might not have written it down in his little notebook, but he knew I'd killed Mom.

chapter eight

I got up to answer the doorbell. The number of visitors had been trickling down, although neighbors and church members still kept us well supplied with food. The lady who'd offered to wash those containers had seriously underestimated what she was in for. She'd already picked up dirty casserole dishes twice.

I looked through the peephole. Betsy Jo. Finally. . .

Ordinarily, she and I would have hugged the instant she walked in the door, but neither of us made an effort to. It almost seemed like she was staying out of hugging distance on purpose.

"Kim. . ." Betsy Jo couldn't look me in the eye. We sat down at opposite ends of the sofa. She cleared her throat. "How was your mis—?"

"You must be Betsy Jo Snelling," a grinning Aleesha Jefferson cut off what sounded like an inappropriately timed question about the mission trip. "I've heard *all* about you, but— if we're going to become friends—I'm calling you *Jo*. Life's too short to say *Betsy Jo* every time." She shook her head playfully—as if flipping her short haircut this way and that.

I knew what she was thinking. *Southern girls and those two-part names.* I often laughed at that myself.

Betsy Jo apparently missed the sarcastic overtones, though. She wasn't any better at catching subtleties than Aleesha was at avoiding them, and I could tell Aleesha was just warming up.

I couldn't blame her, though. She'd shocked the daylights out of me by showing up for Mom's funeral after all. I'd expected Betsy Jo to come, yet she hadn't. No wonder Aleesha had spoken some harsh words to me about my supposedly best friend's lack of support.

"Who are—?"

"I'm Aleesha Jefferson. You've heard of me?" As if Aleesha were already a famous actor. She'd given me grief one time for saying *actress*.

I thought I'd crack up. Jo—I followed Aleesha's lead about shortening Betsy Jo's spoken name—wouldn't have known anything about Aleesha yet unless she'd come to see me and learned about the trip.

Aleesha reached out for a handshake—she must have concluded Jo wasn't a high-five kind of girl—but Jo didn't reciprocate. So Aleesha reached down and fist bumped her. She didn't let people ignore her unless she *wanted* them to.

Jo's frown could have frozen the entire Atlantic Ocean. Instantly.

"Kim and I became close friends in Mexico." Aleesha emphasized the word *close*.

Jo squinted at her and then looked at me. A question mark shadowed her face. Although this encounter with an outgoing stranger had obviously shocked her, I wondered if there was more to her reaction than that.

So I remained silent and waited to see what would happen. Aleesha was in control of the conversation. She had no choice. Since she'd been the only one talking so far, she just kept on going.

"I hadn't been home from Mexico but a few hours when Kim called to tell me about her mother's accident."

"Aleesha cried with me over the phone," I said, hoping to force Jo to say something about Mom's death. "She offered to come down from Baltimore immediately to help any way she could, even though she'd only just gotten home herself.

I thanked her, but told her not to bother. As you can see, she loves me so much she ignored me."

Yeah, Jo. I told Aleesha I didn't need her to come because I'd have you to lean on. What happened?

"Kim was on the phone with me again when your father stopped by to express your parents' condolences. Kim, you said Jo wasn't with him, right?"

Aleesha's bite was as sharp as her memory. She wasn't about to let Jo get away with her failure to behave like a best friend.

"I was. . .busy." Jo looked away.

"Busy?"

A theater-and-drama major, Aleesha was going to make a knockout actor. From her cross-examination of Jo, I was already looking forward to her becoming a humongous success in some lawyer show.

"Actually," Jo mumbled, "I was asleep." I could barely make out her last word.

"Ah, I see." I could almost see Aleesha loading word bullets into a verbal pistol. "It was late, and you must have gone to bed before your parents learned about Mrs. Hartlinger's death. That was what time, Kim?"

I scratched my head, more for effect than anything else. "Seems like Dad called the Snellings around suppertime."

Aleesha gave Jo a *"so?"* look.

Jo looked at the grandfather clock. "I went to bed early."

I expected Aleesha to say, *"That early?"* but she didn't. "You've been busy every minute since then?"

Oh, Jo, you don't know what you've gotten yourself into. . .

"I. . .my cell phone is broken."

"Your job has kept you too busy?"

"I don't have one. Not exactly."

"Then the housework you do for your parents has taken up

all of your time?"

"I do clean the litter box. Sometimes."

I almost laughed. I wouldn't have accused her of lying, but I couldn't picture her doing that. Actually, didn't their cat stay outside? *Jo, do you know how ridiculous you sound?*

Aleesha looked at me and rolled her eyes. I couldn't blame her. Jo's excuses were pathetic. No matter how much her failure to offer timely support had hurt my feelings, holding my laughter in was nearly impossible. I couldn't remember having laughed once since Aleesha and I giggled together in San Diego about my spilled pebbles.

"I see." Aleesha faced Jo and put on her most serious look. "Those things make a difference, don't they?"

No actor could have done a more convincing job as a lawyer cross-examining an unresponsive witness. And Jo didn't have anyone to object to Aleesha's line of questioning. I almost felt sorry for her.

Almost, but not quite.

"All of the phones at home are broken, too?"

Jo stared at her feet.

"Oh, but didn't Kim tell me you live just a few houses away?" Aleesha paused, but Jo didn't respond. She wiped both palms—I assumed they were sweaty—on her jeans. She couldn't have looked more frightened if someone had been pointing a semiautomatic at her head.

"A couple of blocks away," I said. For all the good it would do Jo, Aleesha still needed to play fair by using accurate facts.

"Ah. That's different. Tell me. . .has the Health Department quarantined your family? You know, kept them inside because they're contagious." The room was pin-drop quiet during Aleesha's dramatic pause. "No, your dad made it here several days ago. Have *you* been quarantined?"

I put my hand in front of my mouth. That changed the

sound of my snicker to something between a gulp and a cough.

Jo looked at me with *"Do I really have to put up with this?"* written all over her face. The border drug war that made her mama keep her home from the mission trip would have been safer than a sarcastic Aleesha. Once more, I was tempted to feel sorry for her, but instead I raised my eyebrows as if to say, *"You brought this on yourself, you know."*

Aleesha broke into a deep belly laugh without warning.

"You'll have to forgive me, Miss Betsy Jo Snelling," she said in what anybody but me might have mistaken for the beginning of a real apology.

Nobody would have mistaken her meaning when she continued, though. "I'm just a poor, ignorant person of color trying to understand how white best friends treat each other. I think I have it now."

Jo looked more deflated than the denim tote bag after leaking its load of pebbles. She might not have caught the full implications of Aleesha's put-down, but she understood enough to turn a glowing red.

"Excuse me," I barely managed to say before speeding from the room. "Back in a minute." I couldn't hold my laughter in any longer.

When I reentered the room five minutes later, I was amazed to see Aleesha and Jo sitting side by side, talking like two normal people. Like people who got along with one another. Jo looked up at me.

"I'm sorry, Kim. I was just explaining to Alice—"

"That's Aleesha, my dear Miss Jo."

"Yes, I was telling Aleesha how much your mom's death has upset me. That's why I couldn't face you until now. I kept thinking, '*What if my mama died? Or my papa?*' That's all I've been able to think about since I heard about Terri. I've just kind of gone crazy thinking about it."

I cringed at hearing her refer to Mom by her first name. That didn't used to bother me, but now it seemed disrespectful.

"I've really let you down, and I'm sorry. Please don't hate me."

She and I hugged. Not the kind of hug I'd expected. The kind I'd gotten from Penny. . .and from Aleesha. It didn't remind me of my mother.

No, girl, I don't hate you. I'm trying to understand you, but you're not making sense. All I know is I needed you and you didn't come. Do you expect your talk of going crazy and your whiny apology to comfort me now?

Although Aleesha has been the best of friends for less than three weeks, she's put her whole life on hold to come a lot farther than a few blocks to minister to me.

Jo, I admit it. I resent your unconcern.

"Uh, no. . .no, I don't hate you."

chapter nine

Jo's visit had been awkward, and I was glad she didn't stay long. That was a first, considering we practically used to live at one another's houses.

"Aleesha, I'm afraid I need to brush up on Rob's lessons about forgiveness. I shouldn't resent Jo the way I do."

"You and me both, girl. You remember what I told you about detecting the *smell?*" That was her special way of describing prejudice—or at least a strong intolerance. Her clenched teeth formed an unmistakable frown. "Jo reeked of it."

"She. . . ?" What could I say? Even I had wondered about that.

"She wasn't one bit happy to see one of. . .*us* in your living room."

I sighed, shook my head ever so slightly, and waited for her to continue.

"Girl, when you and I met at orientation, I could tell you hadn't been around many of us permanently well-tanned individuals. Sure, you had a few innocent misconceptions about us, but at least you didn't have that smell. I couldn't detect a lick of prejudice in you."

I smiled.

"So Jo really is"—I couldn't make myself say the word *prejudiced*—"that different from me?"

How could she have been prejudiced without my knowing it? She'd never spoken badly about any group of people that I could recall. Of course, I'd never seen her interact with anyone outside our own little group, either. But had that been by choice or lack of opportunity?

Aleesha was probably right, though. She had an uncanny knack for figuring out what people were like on the inside. She'd sure pegged Geoff right, even though he eventually did a one-eighty.

"If you'd seen the look in her eyes when she first saw me, you'd—"

"She hadn't met you before. She didn't expect to see you. Strangers make me uneasy, too. Especially when I don't expect to see one in a familiar setting."

I didn't want Jo to be guilty of prejudice. Maybe I still owed her a bit of my loyalty, but attempting to defend her—even slightly—over an issue like this seemed almost. . .wrong.

I could say anything to Aleesha, so I did. "Don't tell me you expected Jo to say, '*Oh goody! Here's a strange African-American in Kim's living room. Won't she make a fine second-best friend?*'"

Aleesha cackled, and I laughed for the second time since Mom's death.

"Maybe she's watched too much television, you think?" she said. "Color television. Not enough basic black-and-white."

Laughing felt great. I hadn't had any disturbing thoughts about Mom for at least two minutes now.

"How do you think she's going to feel when she realizes that you've become my best friend now? Or at least a co-best friend?"

Oh, drat. I might as well admit and accept it. You and I have more in common now than Jo and I. We've shared some of the most meaningful events in our recent lives. Although I can't blame Jo for pulling out of the mission trip, my experiences have changed me in ways she can't appreciate or understand because she wasn't there.

"She'll be thrilled at having me for a new friend, of course."

Aleesha belly-laughed. "Not hardly, huh, girl? As skinny as you are, you sure there's enough of you to go around?"

Although she liked to tease me about being skinny, I knew—this time—she was questioning whether I could maintain two best friendships. Especially if one best friend was highly, uh, intolerant of the other.

I wasn't worried about Aleesha, though. Her expectations were realistic. What had she said to Geoff in fun that time? *"Call me whatever you want to as long as you do it with a modicum of respect, boy. Even if you call me 'that fool black girl' just do it with respect, and we'll be fine."*

Before I could tell her I didn't know how far I could spread myself in opposite directions, the front door opened. Dad had a bundle of important-looking documents under his arm. Legal papers, they looked like. I wondered if Mom's will was there. I'd never seen it.

He smiled, leaned over, and gave me a peck on the cheek. "Hello, Kimberly. . .uh, Kim."

Wonderful! Mom's death hadn't formalized him again after all. She and I had worked hard to break him of calling me by my full first name. Calling me Kim now was a special tribute to her memory.

I couldn't keep from hopping up and hugging him. Although he'd acted too numb to pay special attention to me the day Mom died, that changed almost immediately. Aware that he wasn't the only one suffering a huge loss, he'd reached out to me more and more—both to offer and to accept support. The perfect start for a new-and-improved relationship.

We hadn't discussed guilt, though.

"I'm sorry, Aleesha," he said. "I didn't mean to ignore you. How are you?"

Although he extended his hand to shake hers, she slapped his palm in a playful "gimme five" instead. Aleesha enjoyed confusing people, and she was good at it. As dignified as Dad could be—almost stuffy at times—his reaction was beyond my ability to guess.

He laughed. Shocker.

Dad, what is Mom's death doing to you? I like it.

Then a pang of guilt hit me. I shouldn't attribute something good to something so horrible.

"You're always fine, aren't you?" Dad asked Aleesha. Something unusual tinged his question. Not jealousy. Something more like. . .wistfulness.

"I'm fine now, thank you, sir. But, no, I'm not always fine."

I wondered if she was thinking about her father's Season of Pebbles. Probably just as well she didn't say anything about it now. No need to make Dad dwell on his loss anymore than he already was. We would survive the coming weeks and months—it would require a humongous dose of Jesus' help— but I wasn't sure how victorious we'd feel.

"Plenty of things get me down," Aleesha said to Dad. "Like the way Jo—"

"We've started calling Betsy Jo 'Jo' now, Dad." I grinned at Aleesha.

"Like the way she didn't come to see Kim until today. People who mistreat my friends upset me more than people who mistreat me."

"What a remarkable attitude," Dad said. "And you're only eighteen?" She nodded. "You're positive?" He winked at her.

"Positive. But this attitude comes from nine years as a Christian, not eighteen years of life. Living by faith has turned me into the mature, modest young lady who stands—"

"Who's seated. . ." I giggled.

"The one who sits before you today." She smiled as she turned to glance at me. "Kim's been learning to care more about other people, too." *Thank you for pointing that out.*

"She started developing that attitude working with the migrant kids at your church's House of Bread, but it became part of her lifestyle in Santa María. You would be proud of her unselfishness there."

Go, girl! Tell Dad how much I've grown up.

His eyes brightened. "Kim and I haven't had much chance to discuss her mission activities yet. . ."

"Or much of anything else," I added. I wanted—I needed—to talk with him about Mom. I suspected he wanted that, too. Maybe I was wrong, but I thought we'd both been afraid to broach the subject.

He put his arm around my shoulder. "That will change now, won't it?" he said as I snuggled into his shoulder—much as I'd done with Neil on the bus and with Penny Adams after receiving word of the accident.

"Be sure to ask her about the litter cleanup and her reading of the Gospel of Luke. In perfect Spanish, at that." Dad's eyes opened in surprise. He knew I'd studied French all the way through high school. "God was definitely in charge of that. But don't let the cat leak out of the denim bag. . ."

I giggled, and Dad gave both of us the weirdest look.

"You've got a wonderful daughter, Mr. Hartlinger."

"Call me Scott, please." He must have seen my eyes pop wide open. Jo tended to refer to him by first name, but no other teen had ever dared to address him that way. "No more Mr. Stuffy for me." He looked at me and winked.

Dad, what's gotten into you? You're not the same person you were when I left for San Diego. This new you is great, but did you pay one bit of attention to what Aleesha just said about me? Has Mom's death left you partially deaf? This is so weird. I might have expected you to become bitter or more withdrawn, but you've become Mr. Nice Guy. . .with a new hearing problem.

"No can do, sir," Aleesha said. "I often use my great acting skills to keep my elders from discovering that I'm not always polite and respectful. That I'm human, in other words. So I'll demonstrate by addressing you as *Mr. Scott.*"

"Fair enough. And, Kim. . ."

"Yes, Dad?"

"What Aleesha said about you in Mexico sounds amazing. I want to hear every detail."

My word, Dad. Not only do you still hear fine, but your listening skills are a trillion times better, too.

The three of us talked about the mission trip for hours. He and Aleesha were still talking when I went to bed. I couldn't stay awake any longer.

If I'd known what my night was going to be like, though, I would've forced myself to stay awake.

chapter ten

Dawn, Kim. . .time to get up. That rubbish isn't going away by itself."

I rolled over toward the voice. Was I back in Santa María? No, wait. The rubbish cleanup was over. And so was the reading of *Lucas*.

I yawned a couple of extra times between normal yawns, but I couldn't open my eyes quite as wide as I'd been opening my mouth. I couldn't have felt more worn out if I'd just completed a day of rubbish cleanup in Santa María.

Aleesha knew me too well. She waved a mug of coffee under my nose. Mmm. That opened my eyes. Then I sat up so she could hand it to me.

"Thanks." I cradled the mug in my hands and passed its steaming scent beneath my nostrils once more. Real coffee like this would taste a lot nicer than the coffee candy she'd shared with me my first morning in the village. It would have more caffeine, too.

Another yawn escaped before I could take a sip. "What time did you go to bed, Aleesha?"

"Haven't been there. Didn't have time." She made a clucking noise with her mouth that sounded remarkably like a horse's clop. I had no idea what that was supposed to signify.

My clock read 8:37. That must've been a.m. I hadn't gone to bed until 10:15 the night before and felt too dragged out to have slept around the clock.

Thanks for not really waking me up at dawn the way you always did in Santa María.

"You haven't been to—?"

"It's all Mr. Scott's fault. Your dad's a great talker."

My dad? Aleesha, you're a big talker. Yes, maybe even a "great" one. But Dad? Dad the professional introvert? Maybe you're right, though. He's been coming out of his shell a bit this week, and he shocked the daylights out of me last night by being such an interested listener.

He asked question after question about my adventures in Santa María, and each answer seemed to inspire two new questions. This new him seemed to have improved both his talking and his listening skills.

What could have caused a change like that? Surely not Mom's death.

"Don't look so shocked, girl. You just need to know how to wind him up and start him ticking. That part is easy for me. Stopping him is something else. We talked all night, until"—she glanced at her watch—"approximately 8:35, to be precise."

Approximately. . .precise? I refused to let myself giggle.

I wanted to make a smart-aleck comment about who couldn't stop whom, but she barely stopped talking long enough for me to open my mouth.

"Don't tell him I said anything"—she lowered her voice almost to a whisper—"but we spent a lot of time talking about his feelings. Don't let that cheery exterior fool you. He's hurting plenty, too."

I closed my eyes for a moment.

"Why did he share his feelings with *you*?" I hoped I didn't sound jealous, but I couldn't take back my question then. "Instead of with his own daughter, I mean?"

"Because he knows you're hurting, and he doesn't want to make you feel worse."

"Worse?" I must have spoken louder than I realized, because Aleesha shushed me before I continued. "We've been supporting one another. We should bear one another's burdens. Like a Christian, uh, father and daughter."

"That's exactly what I told him. But Mr. Scott said you weren't up to dealing with his problems. He explained that you'd overreacted to the plight of the migrants when you worked at the House of Bread. According to him—and he admits he's no psychologist—you almost had a nervous breakdown over things you had no control over."

"I. . ." I sighed. "I can't pretend that's not true. I was concerned about complete strangers then, but this is something in my own family."

"Uh-huh. And don't you know that proves his point, girl? If you got that upset about strangers' troubles, how would you react to your dad's?"

"I. . .know better than to react that way again. Don't you think my experiences in Santa María strengthened me both spiritually and emotionally?" She didn't say anything at first. "Please, Aleesha." I pled with my eyes as well as my voice. "What's going on with Dad?"

"Girl, I have mixed feelings about telling you this, but Mr. Scott didn't ask me not to. I can't stay here forever, and he needs your help as much as you need his."

I hugged her.

"Here goes. He has this crazy idea that Miss Terri's death is his fault."

"What? That's—"

I didn't realize I'd gotten too loud again until Aleesha put her hand over my mouth. For all the sense that bit of information made, Aleesha might as well have told me the sky was falling.

"He should've postponed his meeting with Dr. what's-his-face and driven with Miss Terri to Atlanta to pick you up."

"Why? What difference would—?"

"He would have been in the driver's seat. So the accident

wouldn't have happened."

"That's crazy, Aleesha. What makes him so sure of that?"

"Crazy or not, he's convinced it's true. Reason or no reason. That's not something you can talk a man out of believing once he's got it in his head."

How can Dad be responsible when I'm the guilty party?

"There's something about this I still don't get," I said. Aleesha aimed a puzzled look at me.

I shrugged. What good would it do to confess my crime to her—to explain that Dad couldn't be guilty because I was?

Aleesha caught on that I wasn't going to explain. "It was so sad." She paused to wipe her eyes. "You know what Mr. Scott kept saying over and over?"

Unsure whether I wanted to know, I barely shook my head. A twister like the one that destroyed Santa María had gotten loose in my brain, and it wasn't leaving any of my thoughts and feelings intact.

"He said, 'If I'd been driving, Terri could have answered her cell phone safely. Then none of this would have happened.'"

No, Dad. It wasn't you. It was me. If I hadn't phoned Mom. . .if I hadn't left voice mail, she'd still be alive. It's my fault, not yours. And you'll hate me for it if you find out. I can't let that happen.

"Uh." That involuntary grunt made its way to the surface from deep within me.

"Girl! What's wrong?"

"I. . ." Did I dare to reveal the truth? I could barely hear myself thinking over the pounding of my heart. I needed to tell someone, but. . .no, I couldn't. "It. . .it's nothing."

I looked away. Aleesha knew my statement couldn't have been further from the truth. Even unsubtle Jo would have caught on. I hoped Aleesha would lay off now instead of pushing for the truth.

She changed the subject. *Thank you, Lord.* "You must have been dreaming something awful last night."

I nodded slightly and closed my eyes tight for several seconds. But I couldn't shut out the memory of what had kept me awake almost all night.

"I could hear you all the way downstairs," she said. "Sounded like you were thrashing around, maybe wrestling with the devil. I didn't think you were winning. I came upstairs to make sure you were okay. Bedcovers were everywhere but over you, and you were, well, you were lying in a pool of sweat."

I've never believed a person can be held accountable for her dreams. The dreamer has no control over plot, theme, or characters. She can't specify the setting or influence the dialogue. Neither can she determine whether dreams are good, bad, or indifferent.

Most dreams are neutral, I suppose, and we forget them almost as soon as we wake up. If we remember them that long. Even the most vivid dreams—good or bad—don't remain with us long.

But last night's dream had been different. The nightmare was so vivid that just thinking about it now made me start trembling and sweating all over again. I hoped Aleesha wouldn't notice.

Attacking me with relentless fury not long after I went to bed, this nightmare terrified me so completely I fought to stay awake for fear I might dream it all over or—worse still—have it continue from where it had left off. The sleep that finally took control of my body did nothing to erase my fears, and I felt wiped out now.

Aleesha and I could discuss anything—no holds barred—but I wasn't sure I wanted to share the details with her. Not if it required me to relive what I feared I'd never forget.

Aleesha could almost read my mind, though. . .or my body language. Far too accurately.

"Girl"—her tone was somewhere between compassionate and frustrated—"if a problem bothers you so much you can't talk about it with your best friend—or even your second-best friend—that's a sign you really need to discuss it with somebody."

Aleesha's father was a psychiatrist or psychologist at a Christian counseling center in inner-city Baltimore. No wonder she was so good at reading people and knowing just what to say. She'd probably learned how to do that from her father, even though she'd once claimed that her psychobabbological savvy wasn't as good as her medical knowledge, which—though iffy—was better than mine.

If father and daughter were as much alike as I suspected, they probably practiced on each other. In spite of the seriousness of my quandary, that thought nearly made me smile.

"Do you want the door closed?"

I nodded.

"You know that dream I had on the bus last week when we were leaving Santa María?"

"The one about heaven?"

"You remember how joyful and encouraging it was?"

"It gave you hope for the villagers' salvation and made you decide to major in Spanish. Nothing special about it that I can recall." White teeth gleamed from ear to ear, and I shook my head at her playful, understated commentary.

I welcomed that brief moment of levity.

"If that dream was a ten-plus on the scale of worthy and wonderful dreams, last night's dream was a minus one-million. It was horrible. I'll never forget it."

Aleesha sat down on the bed and took my hand. "What I said a minute ago. . .don't tell me if you don't feel up to it." Her sensitivity was a welcome relief.

"Thanks, but you were right. I *do* need to talk about it." Aleesha nodded almost imperceptibly. "When I heard that Mom had her phone in her hand at the time of the accident, I was like, 'Mom, you didn't lose control of the car because you were trying to answer one of my impatient calls, did you? Or because you were listening to my voice mail?'"

Aleesha's lips parted slightly. Her eyes focused on mine. She was listening with head, heart, and spirit.

"I can't be sure about that, of course, but the possibility that it's true has been tearing me up."

Aleesha looked like she wanted to say something, but she didn't interrupt.

"I was doing a fair job of not dwelling on it until that dumb cop talked to us just before the funeral. He said the cell phone records showed she'd been connected to voice mail at the time of the crash."

Aleesha looked as if a clichéd feather would have knocked her over.

"The guilt has gotten a million times worse since then. I haven't been able to get it out of my head. To somebody else, this might sound as crazy as Dad feeling responsible. It's not crazy to me, though, and I can't rationalize my way out of feeling guilty."

"And that's what your nightmare was about?" She spoke in a softer tone of voice than usual.

I nodded.

"In the dream, I was waiting for Mom at the airport, but it was San Diego International part of the time and Dallas/ Fort Worth the rest. Never Atlanta. I called her every thirty minutes and left voice mail each time until I filled up her voice mailbox. I was nasty and impatient. 'Where are you? Hurry up. I'm sick of waiting.'

"Two days passed, and I hadn't heard from her once. I was still at one of the two airports, living off pizza, killing time by finger painting on my sweatshirt with pizza sauce, and dozing while I lay across the laps of four sleeping passengers who were also waiting for someone to pick them up.

"Then this big bruiser of a policeman—he bore an uncanny resemblance to Millie Q—waltzed up to me with his handcuffs open. 'Kim Hartlinger,' he said, 'you're under arrest for the murder of your mother.'"

Aleesha grunted. Tears glistened. Telling her the nightmare was tough on me, but hearing it was obviously tearing her up, too.

"'My mother's not dead,' I told him, jerking my hand away before he could cuff me. 'She's on her way to pick me up. She has to drive across the whole country, you know. She'll be here any minute now.'

"'Have you checked your voice mail recently?' he asked. I pulled out my cell phone and punched a few buttons. 'I have one message.' 'Listen to it,' he said. I did."

I couldn't continue. Aleesha blotted my face with a tissue and then slipped wordlessly into the bathroom. She returned with a wet washcloth and proceeded to wipe my face. That helped. But only physically.

"You don't have to tell me the rest," she said. "It must be horrible."

"I need to finish, Aleesha," I said in a more insistent tone of voice than I normally use. "The voice message was actually a recording of the accident. The sounds of skidding. Landing. Crashing into the tree. Glass breaking." I hesitated and then lowered my voice. "Mom's groan at the instant of her death.

"Then the policeman said, 'If you hadn't phoned her, she'd still be alive. We're only going to charge you with involuntary manslaughter, though. We know you didn't mean to kill her, but that doesn't change the fact she's dead now. Shame on you!'"

Aleesha and I were both blubbering by then. There's no better word to describe it. We must have made more noise than we realized, though, because Dad came bounding up the stairs—sounding like he took two or three at a time. He knocked and then opened the door without waiting for a response.

Aleesha glanced at me as if asking permission to explain. I mouthed *okay*.

"Bad nightmare," she told him. "Horrible nightmare."

That was the last thing I heard.

chapter eleven

I don't know what happened to me, but when I came to, Dad was hovering over me like a mother robin that sees a predator coming too close to her little ones.

"Are you okay, Kim?" Dad said. He kissed me on the forehead. "You—what's the current word?—you zoned out for about ten minutes."

No matter what I'd experienced, I felt slightly more awake than before. I didn't hurt anywhere, and I didn't feel faint, dizzy, or nauseated. Concluding that I must be all right, I nodded at Dad's question.

"I thought you might have fainted, but Aleesha said you must have just fallen asleep again. She told me a bad nightmare kept you from sleeping well last night. You looked pretty lifeless just to be asleep, though."

I wrinkled my eyebrows in a questioning look.

"Aleesha checked your temperature. It was normal. So was your pulse. We couldn't determine any other symptoms. But I was so worried I told her I was going to hand-carry you to the ER if you didn't come out of it soon."

Worried? If your quick breathing, trembling hands, and the ghostly look on your face are any indication, I think 'scared to death' is a more accurate description. Even though I hate seeing you this concerned over nothing, it makes me feel good.

He looked past me at the sweaty, crumpled sheets. "How did your linens get pulled out like this?"

He started urging one very uncooperative corner of the fitted sheet back into place, but it kept slipping off. Since

Aleesha didn't have any trouble with the side she was working on, she came around and fixed his side, too. She gave me her *"Men!"* smile.

Dad's question had just been another way of expressing his concern. He probably remembered from my early childhood that I usually woke up in the same position I'd gone to sleep in. Restlessness and crumpled bed linens weren't the norm for me.

"How. . . ?" I said, fishing for an explanation, "Uh, I had a bad dream."

After he nodded two or three times, I remembered he already knew that. "So you wrestled your covers off while you were dreaming? Don't feel you have to hold back. Aleesha explained that your dream was. . .serious."

I sighed. I didn't want to discuss this with my father. Especially now that I knew he was wrestling with his own guilt—we were flip sides of the same coin.

"Uh, it was a terrible nightmare," I said. "Worst one I've ever had." I hoped I wasn't sounding defensive or elusive, although I was probably both. I quit talking. I'd said all I could safely say.

"Aleesha wouldn't tell me what you dreamed about. She said it was personal, and I don't want to pry. I wish you felt comfortable telling me, though. I'm here to help."

"Dad. Daddy. . ." I threw my arms around his neck and clung to him the way I probably hadn't felt comfortable doing in years. "I know you want to help, but I. . .I'm not sure I ought to explain why I can't say any more."

"Please. If it's that important, you need to share it."

Hmm. Sounds like somebody's been talking to Aleesha. Or the other way around.

"But I don't want to hurt your feelings, Dad."

How could I soften the blow? What I said had probably

hurt his feelings. At the end of the longest and most painful five minutes of trying to figure out how to explain diplomatically, I was no closer to a safe, satisfactory answer than when I started.

In the meantime, Dad stared at me as if I were the fuse on a stick of dynamite, burning and ready to explode any second. How could I assure him it wasn't like that?

I had to say something, though. Increasing his anxiety level by delaying any longer wouldn't be right.

"Daddy, I love you so much." Safe beginning. "I love being with you. . .and talking with you. Last night was the greatest." *I'm sorry, Daddy, but you asked.* "But it hasn't always been that way. Until Mom's death, you were always so. . .preoccupied. Teaching. . .church activities. . .reading and studying. I'm proud of you, your career, and your responsibilities at church, but."—*do I have to tell you?*—"you haven't always seemed sufficiently accessible."

At least I'd said, "haven't seemed" and not "haven't been."

But that hadn't helped. If the stricken look on his face was any indication, I'd punched him hard in the stomach of his conscience. I'd so wanted to avoid that. I couldn't have felt like a worse daughter if I'd slapped him in the face. So I skip-skipped to what I hoped would make him feel better.

"You're not like that anymore, though. You've changed so much. I like—I love—this new you." Although he wasn't quite smiling, I could see his facial muscles starting to relax. "But the changes have come so quickly. Almost overnight. I don't know how to react to them yet. Not completely. That's why I can't tell you the specifics of my nightmare."

Dad's breathing was almost back to normal, and his face had regained most of its normal color. "I hope that makes sense to you, Daddy."

"I'm probably saying this all wrong, Kim. A doctorate

in medieval literature isn't apt to make a man an expert at expressing his feelings. What I'm trying to say, though. . .we still have the rest of a lifetime for correcting past mistakes."

A statement like that from some other middle-aged man might have sounded a tad cheesy, but the tears in his eyes supplemented the message he'd attempted to express in words. I just hoped *his* lifetime would be longer than Mom's.

Dad kissed me and walked to the door. He turned back.

"Kim, I never realized how much I loved you until you got on that plane for San Diego. I prayed for you many times daily. Then when you called about the broken arm. . ."

I could barely speak. "You sounded like you were glad to hear from me when I called. And those messages you left. . ."

"I love you, Kim."

He nearly sprinted back to the bed, and we threw our arms around each other. In my failure to be more responsible, I knocked him in the head with my cast—how I looked forward to getting rid of that thing in another month or so—but that didn't appear to faze him.

"I love you, too, Daddy."

Once we heard him reach the bottom of the steps, Aleesha closed the door again and sat down beside me on the bed. I'd fiddled with the fitted sheet during the tensest part of my talk with Dad, and one side had pulled loose again. She looked at it and shook her head.

"Miss Kim," she said in the kind of quiet, formal voice that sometimes made me uneasy, "you know I'm not always diplomatic."

Although I giggled at her understatement, she continued in a serious tone. "I've never seen anyone sleep as soundly as you did a few minutes ago. Mr. Scott didn't tell you that both of us tried to wake you. You groaned without responding. At first I thought you might be having that nightmare again."

Her eyes began twinkling. Was she about to transition from serious to silly?

"You were obviously still alive, though, and that was a good thing. I only brought enough dress clothes for one funeral, and I didn't think I'd fit into one of those preppy outfits of yours. I'm too tall."

Too tall and too well filled out.

She paused. The twinkle was still there, although she hadn't smiled yet. I kept staring at her. Surely she didn't expect me to laugh at such a horribly tasteless joke. She wouldn't have intentionally hurt my feelings for anything. Yet Mom's funeral was barely over, and she didn't seem to take it seriously anymore. What was with her?

Then she added, "Besides that, only one funeral per visit is permitted."

That comment might have been equally tasteless, but it broke the tension. I cracked up. In my mind's eye, I saw Aleesha driving home to Baltimore after Mom's funeral, pulling into the driveway, and then backing out again without going inside. Just so she could return for my funeral in strict adherence to some silly rule about only one funeral per visit.

She winked at me. Something about the way she'd told those two jokes made me realize she'd probably been testing my emotional reflexes rather than trying to be funny. I doubted that she'd found them anywhere close to normal.

"As Mr. Scott pointed out, your only detectable symptom was sleep far too deep to be normal. You obviously heard us shouting at you. But it's like you were fighting to remain asleep. I don't know what's normal for you at home, but you never slept that way in Santa María. So we left you alone and waited for you to wake up on your own."

I crooked one eyebrow as I searched her face for further clues. What was she trying to say?

"I wish you could talk to my papa," she said. "I'll bet he could figure this out."

Your papa the psychiatrist? So now you think I'm nuts?

She must have seen my grimace. "No, Kim, you're as sane as I am."

I really cracked up then—I'd never known anyone who acted crazier than Aleesha—but she couldn't have remained more completely straight-faced. *Okay, girl, so that wasn't supposed to be a joke.*

"Kim, I'm no psychologist, but I wonder if your strange little nap was purely physical."

Maybe her statement should have shocked me. Maybe it should have made me resentful or angry.

But it didn't.

I'd just started wondering the same thing myself.

chapter twelve

A leesha, didn't you say west-to-east jet lag is worse than east-to-west?"

She squinted at me as if trying to figure out the reason for my question. "Uh-huh."

"And didn't you say jet lag doesn't necessarily hit the hardest the day after travel?"

She nodded ever so slightly without releasing her squint.

I hoped my desperation wasn't showing. "And it can last for days?"

"Go ahead, girl. Spill it."

"I'm so tired today I can barely wiggle. I don't feel like getting out of bed. Truth be told, I just want to go back to sleep."

"Mmm."

"Mmm, what? Is that jet lag or not?"

"Could be. Or the aftershock of Miss Terri's death. You haven't had much of a chance to unwind, and things won't be normal for a while—"

The tears started spilling out. "They're never going to be normal."

"You're right," she said as she put her hand on my shoulder. "Not like before, anyhow." She paused and gave me a once-over. "Girl, you're zoning out again now. Go on back to sleep. I'm going downstairs to do some cleaning, but I'll be quiet."

"But I'd planned on doing that. I wanted to show Dad I can do just as good a job as Mom at taking care of him."

Aleesha looked at me with an expression that said, *"Your intentions are good, but you don't know what you're talking about."*

That made me even more determined to prove myself to Dad.

"Kim, baby, if you're suffering jet lag—or any kind of lag—you may not feel much like housecleaning for a few more days. You go back to sleep and let me do it this time. I'll gladly give the job back to you when you feel better."

I fell asleep so quickly I thought I was dreaming when she said, "I'm going to keep my eye on you, girlfriend. Whatever this is, it *isn't* jet lag."

chapter thirteen

I refused to acknowledge my fears the next time Aleesha talked to me about my constant fatigue, but I couldn't ignore Dad.

"Kim, more than two weeks have passed since your mom died. Jet lag doesn't last this long."

I looked at him through half-closed eyes. He'd waited until early afternoon to come upstairs to talk with me, hoping I'd be awake and alert by then.

But I wasn't, and the lack of energy was bugging the daylights out of me. I couldn't keep pretending nothing was wrong.

"Aleesha explained that you've wanted to take care of me. . . to do the housework, the cooking, the laundry."

"I do, Daddy." If I sounded as feeble as I felt, I didn't sound very confident.

"That's a wonderful, responsible attitude. I didn't expect you to provide that kind of help, and I'm proud of you. Hopefully you'll feel up to taking on some of those chores soon. Not all of them, though. A man should help out around the house, too—be he husband or father—and I've been irresponsible that way until now."

Wow! Even middle-aged adults were capable of making major changes.

"But you're not up to it now. That's why Aleesha has stayed longer than she originally intended. She didn't want to desert us when we needed her help."

Unable to sort out or verbalize my jumble of emotions, I smiled to acknowledge my appreciation.

Dad looked uncertain about how to proceed.

"She's enrolling at Dogwood University here instead of carrying through with her plans to attend Howard University. She'll stay here for at least this semester. I pulled a few strings to get her in at this late date."

No matter how dragged out I felt, my heart sparkled at that news. I hoped my face did, too.

"You're probably wondering why she changed her plans at the last minute. . ."

"You said. . .she didn't want. . .to desert us."

"That's just part of it," he said. "I asked her to stay. She'll earn room and board and a little spending money doing chores around here. We needed someone to help, and she was available. You understand, don't you?"

How could I fail to understand that my new best friend would be living with us for a while? Despite the fact she'd be doing the very things I wanted to do for Dad, why wouldn't I be thrilled to have her around? Still, a teeny-weeny part of me was jealous that he'd already grown so dependent on Aleesha.

But I didn't have the energy to dwell on negative feelings.

Or on prayer, either. Maybe I didn't feel up to talking with God the way I had in Santa María, but I bathed in the belief that He loved me and would take care of me. Even so, on those rare occasions I could pray without falling asleep again, I kept asking Him if this fatigue problem was just another part of that Season of Pebbles Aleesha's father had told her about— one that had started with Mom's accident.

"Kim?"

"Huh? Yes, Daddy?"

"I thought you'd fallen asleep."

"I was actually thinking for a change."

"That sounds dangerous."

Although his teasing made me feel loved, no amount of playfulness could hide his concerns. That's why he'd insisted on taking me to our family doctor, Dr. Holly.

But I didn't want to think about that now.

"Daddy, I'm glad you asked Aleesha to stay."

"And I'm glad you're glad." He smiled. "I was afraid you'd be disappointed about having someone else do the things you want to do for me."

Disappointed? You've turned into quite a diplomat, too. You know the right word is jealous.

"Baby girl"—my eyes popped open at hearing him call me by a pet name, probably for the first time ever—"we need to find out what's wrong with you and get you well again."

"I told you I probably just picked up some kind of bug in Mexico." I wasn't trying to argue, but I didn't want to admit how worried I was.

"Dr. Holly doesn't think so, Kim. You took shots for everything before going to Santa María, and she's tested you for every disease Mexican tourists come home with. Most of the tests are back—all negative. She doesn't expect the rest to be any different."

I sighed. I could have told him that, but I didn't want to believe it.

"You ate packaged foods and drank bottled water. No chance for contagion there. Were any of the villagers sick while you were there?"

I sighed again. He knew the answer without my having to tell him again. We'd had this discussion before. Several times. But I loved him for exerting so much effort to find a solution.

"No." I didn't have the strength or the heart to argue. I knew what was coming next, and the thought of it brought bile into my throat. When it went down again this time, I barely noticed the bitter aftertaste.

"Dr. Holly wants you to have more tests. She'll probably refer you to some specialists, too."

I groaned. Not because the tests might hurt or be unpleasant, but because I grew hopelessly tired and weak whenever I had to walk farther than the distance from my room to the bathroom. The last time I'd gone anywhere with Dad and Aleesha, they had to lug me home between them just to get me inside. They probably looked like they were carting home a prodigal drunk.

Dad listed some of the tests Dr. Holly had ordered. Most of the names were meaningless to me. But one tickled a few hairs of curiosity.

"Sleep apnea?"

"Yes. Or some other sleep problem. Dr. Holly wonders if sleeping the way you did in Mexico has somehow affected your ability to get the rest you need from your sleep now."

"Huh? How do they test for that?"

"You go to sleep."

Hmm. I might be able to handle that one.

chapter fourteen

Jo was sitting on the front porch when Aleesha, Dad, and I got home from Dr. Holly's office.

After several months of nonstop lifelessness, I'd just received the final diagnosis—four separate diagnoses along with Dr. Holly's, that was—and I wasn't the least satisfied. Neither were Dad and Aleesha. We learned that the only thing our family doctor and four renowned specialists could agree on was that none of them knew what was causing my fatigue.

One of them had removed my cast, though. My right arm—weak as it was from disuse—might have been the only normal part of me. Or at least the healthiest part.

At least they'd ruled out leukemia and every other life-threatening disease under the sun. They saw eye to eye on the symptoms, but not the cause.

At first, a specialist in teen medicine thought it was mono, but Dr. Holly had already ruled that out. Then the specialist considered fibromyalgia, but I wasn't suffering muscle aches. So he concluded my problem was anxiety and depression and prescribed adult-strength medication.

Another specialist suggested chronic fatigue syndrome, but he couldn't be sure until my condition remained unchanged for six months. If that was the problem, it might last the rest of my life. Not what any normally active girl of almost nineteen wants to hear.

The sleep study had been soundly conclusive. That was, I slept soundly through the night with electrodes stuck to various parts of my body while a technician monitored everything from heart rate to body twitches to eyelid movement on a computer in another room.

In the morning when they woke me up—with great difficulty—I talked with both the technician and the doctor. Not a sign of sleep apnea. In fact, neither one of them had ever seen anyone sleep more soundly. According to the computer, I should have felt wonderful. But I didn't.

Good thing I didn't have a recurrence of my nightmare that night.

The fourth and final specialist said what I'd half-expected all of them to say. "It's in your head. Go see a psychologist or maybe even a psychiatrist." He probably thought me crazier still for requesting a referral to a Christian, but he did it.

And Dr. Holly admitted she was still as baffled as she'd been when we started. Probably more so.

Dad and I had planned to talk about the referral to the psychiatrist or psychologist—I never could remember which was which—when we got home, but the discussion would have to wait until Jo left. Dad went inside, leaving Aleesha and me to deal with Jo. The autumn temperature was brisk, but refreshing. Jo's unexpected visit would probably be brisk, too— she never stayed long—but I had little hope that it would prove refreshing.

"Hey, guys!" she said with a smile. She looked me up and down. "You look like you've lost your best friend." She laughed.

You're referring to yourself, Jo. Or don't you know that? You've known about my fatigue problem all along, but you haven't shown any concern about it. You may not want to believe this problem is real, but I guarantee you I didn't dream it up to get attention. If this is the best you can do as a best friend. . .

Why expect this visit to be any different from the two or three she'd made since fatigue took over my life and squashed the daylights out of almost everything that made my life enjoyable? Too exhausted to keep making excuses for her, I would have been just as happy if she'd stayed home. She'd perfected the art of doing that.

I remembered too well how her parents—mostly her mama—made her cancel the mission trip at almost the last minute because they were afraid of Mexican drug wars, even though they were nowhere close to Santa María. . .or to Ciudad de Plata, our original target city. I couldn't blame Jo for that.

But I couldn't believe Jo's mama kept her from visiting me. If she'd thought I was contagious, she wouldn't have let Jo come at all. And no matter what, she wouldn't have forbidden Jo from calling, texting, or Tweeting me.

So I accepted Aleesha's assessment. Only her ongoing presence in our household explained Jo's ongoing absence. If she allowed prejudice to keep her from supporting an old friend and accepting a new one, that was unfortunate, but I was powerless to change her heart.

Only God could do that, and He wouldn't do it unless she was willing.

Aleesha had been using my car while I was incapacitated, and I'd begun wondering if Jo checked for its absence before coming over. None of her previous visits had included Aleesha.

Frankly, I hoped Aleesha's presence would drive Jo away this time, too. I had too much on my mind, and her visits hadn't been very uplifting, anyhow. As strange as it might sound, she made me think about some of the things I'd heard divorced women say about their ex-spouses. Things like *"I grew up, but he didn't"* or *"We grew apart"* or *"We just didn't have anything in common anymore."*

I couldn't accuse Jo of failing to grow up any more than I could claim to be completely mature. I wouldn't achieve that goal until my next birthday.

We had grown apart, though. Maybe because we didn't have Santa María in common when we should have. We'd done everything together in planning for it. Everything from filling out applications to getting shots to buying those dual-language Bibles that turned out to be Spanish-only.

But when Michelle Snelling made Jo drop out, that left me on my own. Not having my favorite little guardian angel nearby to protect me from myself had seemed disastrous at first, but it turned out to be a good thing. Jo's absence helped me to integrate into the team better than I would have if she'd been there, and I learned to rely more fully on God.

When I told Jo about my experiences on the trip, she reacted the way I'd expected. Half-fascinated, half-envious. My reaction to the project change made her laugh, but she could barely believe the part about my reading to the villagers in perfect Spanish.

Although she'd expressed some pleasure about Rosa's conversion, she didn't act thrilled about it. Maybe I'd been wrong to expect her to care deeply about someone she should have gotten to meet, but didn't.

On one of Jo's visits, I was about to ask her to run home and get her Spanish Bible so I could give her a sample of my pronunciation skills.

But Aleesha got home first. "Hey, girl," I said. "How was—?"

"Whoops!" Jo said as if she didn't care about interrupting me. "I need to go home."

What had happened to the old Jo? What besides us growing apart, that was? I could live without any more visits like those, and today's wasn't likely to be any better despite her cheery greeting.

Cheery? Perhaps *stupid* would be a more fitting description of joking about losing a best friend. Then again, maybe she didn't realize how she'd sounded. Oh, great, here I was making excuses for her again.

Yet she did sound different this time.

Jo stood up. "Kim, you look exhausted." She guided me to the rocking chair she'd just gotten up from. "What did you find out from the doctor today?"

She sounded deeply concerned. Like the Jo I used to know and love. If she kept this up, I might yet enjoy her friendship again, but I wasn't going to make any quick and easy assumptions about that happening.

"Four doctors—"

"Five," Aleesha said, keeping an eye on Jo as if watching a mosquito that was hovering too close. "Don't forget Dr. Holly."

"My family doctor, four specialists, and a ton of tests have determined that I'm not dying."

"Praise the Lord!" Her sigh of relief was almost as loud as the sound of cars going by. Her mouth curled into a cautious smile.

"That's the *good* news," I said with a weary grin. The visit to Dr. Holly's office had worn me out. Then I snorted at the thought of that. I *lived* worn out.

Jo's eyes narrowed and her mouth twisted in concern. Yes, maybe the old Jo had returned. "The bad. . . ?" she mouthed.

"The *bad* news is they don't agree about anything. One thinks I'm depressed and prescribed some potent medication. Another thinks I may have chronic fatigue syndrome, but he won't be sure for another six months. The third one says it's not sleep apnea, and the fourth has referred me to a fifth specialist—a Christian psychiatrist."

Or was he a psychologist?

"And what do *you* think it is, Kim?" Hmmm. Not even Aleesha had asked me that.

Did I dare to admit to my two best friends that I *knew* what it was?

God was using my guilt to punish me for killing my mother.

chapter fifteen

Although I'd told Aleesha about my guilt feelings months earlier, I hadn't talked with her about them since. If she suspected that I was not only harboring, but nurturing those negative feelings, she didn't say anything.

So I dodged the issue in responding to Jo's question. "Your guess is as good as mine. I'll take the antidepressant, and maybe I'll go see the psychologist, too."

"Psychiatrist," Aleesha said. Why couldn't I keep those two straight?

Jo bent over and hugged me. Old times were back. That's what I wanted to believe, anyhow.

"Alice, uh, I'm sorry. Aleesha, how are you doing? I didn't mean to ignore you. I understand you've become indispensable around here. Like a member of the family."

I couldn't deny that Jo's words were amazingly friendly. Accepting. Approving. And highly unprejudiced.

But I still had a slight suspicion that—regardless of her choice of words—she preferred thinking of Aleesha as a servant and not a family member.

"Only until Kim is up to taking over. I'll teach her all of my housekeeping tricks, and then Mr. Scott will be so pleased he won't even notice it's not me anymore."

"Not unless he looks at the person doing the work," Jo said.

Strange comment. I decided to try something. "He still won't be able to tell. He's color-blind, you know."

Ahhh. . . Jo wasn't able to squelch a major frown. Hitting below the belt might not have been fair, but I found out what

I wanted to know.

So Aleesha had been right about Jo all along, and the restoration of a good relationship between Jo and me wasn't apt to bring her any closer to a friendship with Aleesha. I wondered why she'd bothered pretending to be nice to Aleesha. Probably to gain my approval.

And it had almost worked.

During those rare times I could focus enough to pray, I asked God to convict Jo of her prejudice—or could it just have been a strong dislike?—and to make ours a genuine, three-way friendship.

Although Jo came over more frequently after that—she no longer tried avoiding Aleesha—I couldn't see any improvement in their relationship. I really had to bite my tongue the time Jo said, "Aleesha, why don't you run out to the kitchen and get Kim and me something to drink?"

That superiority mentality angered and frustrated me, but Aleesha—future star of stage and screen—took control of the situation and appeared to have a great time doing it.

"Yes'm, Miss Jo."

Despite Aleesha's distaste for the racially derogatory aspects of *Gone with the Wind*—something she'd made me self-conscious about in Santa María when I told her *GWTW* had always been my favorite book and movie—she was playing the subservient Mammy role with style and sarcasm for Jo's benefit. So Jo would benefit from the lesson Aleesha wanted to teach her, that was.

"Would you gentle white folks prefer a soda, milk, coffee, iced tea, or water? And would you prefer sugared or unsugared drinks? I can run to the store if you want something we don't have."

How Jo could have missed the sarcasm, I'll never understand.

"Maybe I'll whip up a nice cake for you. . .from scratch," she said. *"And serve it unbaked,"* she mouthed to me, *"complete with eggshell fragments."*

Jo couldn't see what Aleesha was doing to her. No matter how much I felt like laughing—Jo deserved every bit of Aleesha's put-on Uncle Tomfoolery—I almost felt sorry for her.

Aleesha could take care of herself, but Jo? Uh-uh. She was no match for Aleesha.

Before I could intervene, Jo announced, "No cake, but I am in the mood for a homemade milkshake. Aren't you, Kim?"

Jo, you don't know what you're asking for. . .

"Sure 'nough, Miss Jo. I just need to run out back and milk the cow first so the ingredients will be as fresh as you deserve."

Jo actually laughed at that, but she didn't appear to notice that Aleesha was laughing even harder.

"Miss Kim, your dad does have an ice cream maker, doesn't he? Not one of those fancy electric ones that do all the hard work for you, but one I can hand-crank until I'm satisfied with the results."

"Sure. There ought to be one of those in the kitchen somewhere. Just check the cabinets. Or maybe the pantry. I'd help you if I—"

"No, Kim," Jo said. "You just stay where you are and rest. I'm sure Aleesha can find it."

I had no idea whether we owned an ice cream maker of any kind, but Aleesha had payback in mind, and I could hardly wait.

"Chocolate or vanilla, Miss Jo?"

"Surely you know chocolate will make my face break out. . ."

Bad mistake telling her that, Jo. She'll probably load your vanilla shake down with chocolate.

"Could you just bring me a cola, please?" I said. "A diet cola, that is. With caffeine." Since I was trying to set a good example, I smiled and said, "Thank you, Aleesha. That's very thoughtful of you. You don't have to do this, you know."

Okay, maybe I overdid it a tad, but I wanted to give Jo one last chance to avoid the consequences of her attitude. Unless she changed her mind about the milkshake and began treating Aleesha like the equal she was, she was in for big trouble.

"One vanilla shake, one diet cola—with extra caffeine—and one belly laugh coming right up," Aleesha said as she left the room.

"Belly laugh?" Jo asked me. "What's that? Some kind of mixed drink those black people drink?" At least she hadn't used the n-word. I would have kicked her out for that. "Your dad doesn't keep alcohol in the house, does he?"

I couldn't resist. "*He* doesn't, but *Aleesha* does the grocery shopping now. I don't know what all she buys. Dad doesn't check the receipt. No telling what she's chugging down in the kitchen right now."

Jo looked flabbergasted. I knew some Christians drink. Even some of the folks from church. But she didn't. Her mama didn't want to disillusion her.

Aleesha did a lot of banging and clanging in the kitchen. Practicing to kill Jo, I suspected. Or at least to torture some sense into her. And Jo probably thought Aleesha had gotten drunk that quickly. She'd been within smelling distance of alcohol even less than I had, and that's saying something.

After twenty minutes of killing time rather than Jo, Aleesha came back. Whatever she'd done to that shake, it looked perfect. I almost regretted turning one down. At least she would have made mine edible.

"I made this shake extra special, Miss Jo," Aleesha said. "So don't you go hurting my feelings by failing to drink every single drop of it. You understand?"

I'd seen less ferocious looks than Aleesha's on two grizzly

bears in the zoo fighting over a piece of raw meat, but I'd never seen as strange an expression as Jo's while forcing that shake down.

Aleesha smiled when Jo handed her the empty glass and then belched loudly.

"I have a little bit left in the kitchen, Miss Jo. Shall I fetch it for you?"

Jo couldn't respond, though. She was too busy running for the bathroom.

I didn't think Jo would ask Aleesha to play servant anymore. And I thought I'd go crazy waiting to ask Aleesha what she'd put in that milkshake.

chapter sixteen

As soon as Jo left the day we received the various diagnoses, Dad and I met in the living room.

"Don't you want to join us?" Dad asked Aleesha. His acceptance of her as a member of the family couldn't have been a more complete contrast to Jo's rejection. "We need to make a decision about going to the psychiatrist."

I wasn't ready for her response, though. "Mr. Scott, I appreciate the invitation, but I have some unfinished homework. A project deadline is coming, and the end of the fall semester is just around the corner. I'm already reviewing for exams."

Although those things were true—the 4.0 GPA she had at midterm proved how seriously she took her studies—they were undoubtedly excuses. She must have thought Dad and I could handle a few things without her help.

"I don't know what to think, Kim," he said after Aleesha made her way upstairs. "I can't imagine what in your head would affect your body this way."

Although he produced a feeble grin, I knew he wasn't trying to be funny. We'd discussed my condition enough for me to know he favored *any* kind of help that might restore me to normal health. Anything short of a voodoo witch doctor, anyhow, but not necessarily exclusive of a faith healer. Concern for a family member could broaden the scope of any well-educated man's faith.

"In my head. . . ?"

How was I going to handle this? I couldn't say anything about feeling guilty for killing Mom. I didn't know whether he'd moved past his own guilt or not, but I was afraid his loving acceptance of me might change completely if he knew what I'd done. I couldn't live with that possibility.

"Mom's death," I said in a near-whisper, hoping he wouldn't ask for specifics.

"You've never lost anyone close to you, have you?" He knew I hadn't, but I shook my head anyhow.

"Your grandmother's death didn't upset you nearly as much as it did me."

He'd never said anything to me about his mother's death. I shook my head again. "I didn't know her very well."

He remained quiet for a moment. "I've spent so much time grieving over your mother's death I've sometimes overlooked its effect on you. I'm afraid it's hurt you more than I've realized."

I nodded, and then we met in a hug.

More than you can realize, Dad. If only I could tell you what I've been going through. . .but you wouldn't understand.

How could you? I don't understand it myself. I mean, what normal teen feels overwhelmed by guilt over her mother's death because she called her mom while she was driving in bad weather? That's irrational. It's. . .

It's just plain crazy.

chapter seventeen

I didn't look forward to seeing Dr. Lancaster, but at least he was a Christian. That established an immediate and significant bond. Almost as much of one as his assurance he wouldn't tell Dad anything we talked about.

I was so sick of lifelessness that I didn't try to hold anything back. My words rushed like water from a collapsed dam. I talked about everything under the sun and a few things farther out in the solar system. He probably learned more about me during our first session than he knew about patients he'd been seeing for years.

Those shrinks on TV always ask questions to probe their patients and make them understand themselves better. Dr. Lancaster didn't have to. I asked questions and then I answered them myself.

We ran out of time before I got around to telling him what was wrong with me, though. I don't know why I didn't start with that unless I wanted to make him feel he'd accomplished something worthwhile by the time he finally pulled that information out of me.

Ha-ha!

I started there on my next visit, though. Talking with someone who had nothing to gain or lose by hearing the truth proved amazingly easy. The truth as I saw it, anyhow.

"Dr. Lancaster, I can tell you what's behind my fatigue problem."

"You don't say?" Nice, noncommittal response. The response of a professional listener. Probably only a few of his patients had ever attempted to diagnose their own problems. And only a handful of those people had been spot-on right.

But I was one of them, and I knew it.

"What I can't tell you is how to cure it. I'll leave that up to you."

There. Letting him handle that part should make him feel good.

He raised his eyebrows and cocked his head in an unmistakable *I'm listening* posture.

"I told you about calling Mom while I was waiting for her to pick me up at the airport. . ."

He'd taken notes in a small notebook at our first meeting— he probably filled two of them and was wearing an elastic wristband today from all the writing. No notebooks this time, though. He was using a laptop. As much as I'd said at session one, he must have realized he couldn't keep up with me a second time without typing.

"What I didn't tell you. . .Mom had her cell phone in her hand when they pulled her out of the car."

Dr. Lancaster stopped typing and looked at me. He'd probably heard just about everything during his lengthy career—he was even older than Dad—but I'll bet he didn't expect to hear that. He opened his mouth, but I kept going before he could speak. Not that I meant to be rude, but I had to finish before I lost my nerve. I wondered if this was anything like confessing sin to a priest.

"According to cell phone records, she'd connected to voice mail just before the accident. She must have been listening to my message when she lost control of the car."

He wrinkled his brow. His eye twitched. I didn't know the meaning of those motions in body language, but my story must have gotten to him.

"I killed her, Dr. Lancaster. I might as well have. If I hadn't called when I knew she was driving in horrible weather, none of this would have happened. If I hadn't left voice mail, she'd still be alive."

I don't know what I expected him to say, but he surprised me by *not* saying what I would have said to someone in the same predicament.

Not something corny and unbelievable like *"You can't blame yourself."* Not, *"But you needed to get in touch with her."* Not, *"She made the decision to answer the phone, not you."* Not even, *"You can't be sure that being on the phone made her lose control of the car."*

I'd already tried convincing myself of all those things. Asking, receiving, and accepting God's forgiveness hadn't helped as much as I'd expected. Otherwise, I wouldn't have been sitting in a psychiatrist's office spilling my guts in an effort to overcome my fatigue.

"Kim, you believe your feelings of guilt are the cause of your fatigue?"

"What else could it be?" Judging by the faraway look in his eyes, my response must have stumped him. When he didn't respond, I asked playfully, "Would you feel more comfortable talking about something else?"

That brought him back to earth.

"I'm sorry, Kim. You reminded me of a former client who experienced problems similar to yours."

"What happened to her? How did you solve her problem?"

He turned away instead of responding. When he looked at me again, sorrow had replaced his normally emotionless expression. "You may want to change psychiatrists, Kim. I'm sure one of my colleagues can be more objective."

Huh? What are you talking about? You've told me I remind you of someone you've helped. Just answer the question, will you?

"So how did you help her?" My persistence might have irritated him, but I couldn't stand getting this close to a solution only to have him babble on about something irrelevant. Something that made no sense.

"Kim, I. . .didn't take her guilt feelings seriously enough. She. . .died. Before I could help."

A little part of me died then, too.

chapter eighteen

Although Aleesha started to open the front door for me, I didn't want her to treat me like an invalid. So I pushed her hand away from the knob and opened it myself.

"Dad," I said in my most-energetic-but-still-pitifully-weak voice. "Dad. . . ?"

"Maybe he's, uh, occupied," Aleesha said before closing the door behind her. Her diplomacy amazed me at times. Especially compared with other times.

I would've looked for him, but collapsing on the sofa took all the energy I had. I thanked God daily that at least I no longer felt like sleeping all the time, and today had been one of my more wakeful periods.

"I'll check on him," she said. I didn't object.

A couple of minutes later, she was back. "Sounds like he's on the phone. Maybe with Dr. Lancaster. . ."

"Could be," I said. "I gave him permission to talk with Dad as long as he doesn't reveal what I feel so guilty about."

If Aleesha's wrinkled brow and scrunched eyebrows were any indication, she was as curious as I was about what my shrink might be talking with Dad about. But before we could speculate about it, the door to Dad's home office opened, and he joined us in the living room.

"Welcome home, Kim. . .Aleesha." He kissed and hugged me before hugging her. I still couldn't believe he'd kept all this warmth and affection bottled up inside for so many years.

"That must have been some session you had with Dr. Lancaster." He smiled.

The good doctor must have been true to his word. Dad wouldn't be smiling now if he'd learned about my crime. He'd start blaming me for Mom's death, too, and I couldn't live with that.

"I suppose so," I said. I hated to sound cautious, but Dad might have found out something I didn't already know. That possibility made me uneasy.

"From what Dr. Lancaster just told me, today was a breakthrough session. He's never seen anything like this so early in counseling, and he's been practicing for sixteen years." He looked older than that. Especially at the end of today's session.

Dad must have been waiting for me to respond. I wasn't sure what to say.

"He didn't tell you what my problem was, did he?" I had to know that before I could say anything else.

"I didn't ask, and he didn't offer. I knew he wouldn't. . .and I knew you'd tell me whatever I want to know."

Need to know? Maybe. Want to know? No way.

"Daddy. . ." I squirmed a bit on the sofa and started playing with one of the holes in the afghan. Mom would have gotten after me for stretching it. That thought was enough to make me stop.

I couldn't force myself to sit still, though.

"I told him"—*how much can I safely tell you?*—"I told him I've been feeling really guilty about something."

Aleesha cleared her throat and shifted her weight. She hadn't forgotten about the things I couldn't tell Dad. I knew she was praying for me.

His face grew a huge, instant crop of worry lines.

"Don't worry." I forced myself to smile. "It's nothing illegal." *Not in the usual sense, that is.* "Nothing immoral. It's just too. . .personal to talk with you about." *There. That's the truth in a safe nutshell.*

"Would you have been able to talk with your mother about it?"

Boy, did that one catch me off guard. As horribly as I missed Mom, I hadn't thought that much about not having her around to talk my problems over with. But after what Dad said. . . ? I broke out crying, and he held up both hands. . .in immediate surrender.

"I'm sorry, baby girl." He put his arm around me, and I leaned into his shoulder. "I didn't mean to pressure you. Dr. Lancaster agrees that this guilt is responsible for your fatigue, I assume?"

"Yes. Probably, anyhow. He wants me to stay on the antidepressants, though. He thinks they'll help some—"

"You seem more energetic now than when you left to see him today."

"Maybe, but I've got a long way to go. Dr. Lancaster said emotionally induced fatigue isn't easy to fix." I decided not to mention the patient who'd committed suicide.

"He indicated that to me, too."

A slight smile curled upward from the corners of my mouth. Dad had just given me the opening I'd been waiting for.

"Daddy, I've 'fessed up now"—*as much as I'm going to, anyhow*—"so what else did he tell you?"

Aleesha leaned forward, her ears more closely resembling a pair of satellite dishes than I'd noticed before.

The three of us must have talked for a couple of hours after that. As bushed as I'd felt initially, I found the prospect of getting better exhilarating. No matter how long it might take.

The most important part of our conversation—Aleesha didn't mind participating in this one—had to do with Dr. Lancaster's recommendation of a complete change of scenery. As soon as humanly possible. It wouldn't heal me, he'd said, but getting away from everything that reminded me of Mom could only help. New sights, new sounds, new smells would help me accept the fact that Mom's death wasn't the end of my life.

For the first time since arriving home from Santa María, I realized I'd unwittingly become the center of attention once more. I'd planned to help out at the House of Bread again— outside myself. And I'd planned to start college and start my study of Spanish in earnest—in preparation for helping others.

But I hadn't even been up to giving a report on my trip to the youth group at church. That hurt.

"You know what, Kim?" Dad said "Maybe we shouldn't stay in this house. It's pretty big for just you and me—"

"And your loving second daughter," Aleesha chimed in. "The one her pale twin sister put in a basket and left floating on the Nile for eighteen years. Amazing what that kind of sunshine can do to a girl's skin."

I cracked up. Dad stared at her. Speechless. He was quite fond of Aleesha, but he sometimes found her unpredictability a bit, uh, unsettling.

"A little joke, Mr. Scott," Aleesha said. "Please don't start thinking of me as a permanent member of the family. If I stay here forever, I'll start fading. Cheshire cat style a la *Alice in Wonderland*. Slowly losing all my beauty. Like Kim's suntan in midwinter."

I'd enjoyed a couple of good laughing bouts since Mom's death, but I don't think I'd laughed this hard since cutting up with Aleesha at San Diego International. It didn't just feel good; it felt great. And why not? Laughter was a healthy reminder that there was hope for me yet.

But that didn't answer the question about the house.

"This place holds a lot of memories, doesn't it?" I asked. "I've seen those pictures you took while it was being built. And when you first moved in. "

Truth be told, I didn't have strong feelings one way or the other about the house. I didn't want him to do anything he might later regret, though, especially if he did it only for my sake.

"Mmm." He sighed. *Okay, so you don't want to sell the house.*

"Do you want an apartment or a condominium?" he said.

So you do *want to sell the house? Okay, I'll tell you what I think.*

"If we were to sell the house"—I was proud of being so grammatically correct in this discussion with the live-in English professor who'd always enjoyed correcting my mistakes—"I'm sure we'd want a condo. That way we'd still own our home."

Dad tried to hide a frown, but he didn't do it fast enough to keep me from seeing it.

"I was thinking you might prefer an apartment, Kim. No upkeep."

Just say it, Daddy. You'd *prefer an apartment.*

"I don't want a condo if you don't," I said. The cliché about "lying through my teeth" ricocheted from one side of my brain to the other and back again.

"And I don't want an apartment if you want a condo," he said. "After all, the purpose of moving is to provide a change of scenery for you. . .a chance to escape any lingering memories that might hold you back. No need to move into an environment you're not fond of just because it's different."

Good point.

"Hold on, you two," Aleesha said before she started chuckling. "This isn't a tennis match, and both of you need to come out winners."

Dad looked at me, smiled, and shook his head. I winked at him.

"You have a better suggestion, girlfriend?" I said.

"As a matter of fact. . ." She reached into her purse—one that had room for everything but the kitchen sink—and pulled out a folded sheet of paper. Maybe two.

"Check this out. . .fresh e-mail from Mr. Rob."

"Cool!" I wondered if that announcement had brightened my smile as much as it lifted my spirits.

"Mr. Rob. . . ?" Dad said. "He was your—"

"Our senior project lead in Santa María," I reminded him. "The older fellow."

He snapped his fingers and nodded.

"Okay, older dude and younger dudette," Aleesha said before Dad and I could say anything else, "do you want to hear this or not?"

"Please!"

"'Aleesha, thanks for letting me know about Mrs. Hartlinger's death. I wish I could have been there for the funeral. I'm glad you could stay with Kim and her father for a while. I know you've been a big help. It can't be easy for—'"

The doorbell rang, but before anyone could answer it, Jo stuck her head inside. "Am I interrupting anything major?"

Since it was Aleesha's e-mail, I thought she should decide. "Is it okay?" I mouthed.

She shrugged. Even though Jo had behaved better lately, Aleesha insisted that she still had some of "the smell." But at least she conceded that it wasn't as strong as it had once was.

"You want to come in and sit down, Jo?" Maybe she was giving Jo another chance, but she didn't sound very enthusiastic about it.

Jo plopped down at the opposite end of the sofa from me, making me bounce. At some more appropriate time, I'd have to tease her about gaining weight.

"You can read Mr. Rob's message for yourselves later," Aleesha said without giving Jo any of the backstory. "But here's the nutshell version. He's helping to build housing for people to stay in while they visit friends and family members in a prison that's located in a remote, mountainous area in California. Some local churches have raised enough money for the materials, but not enough to pay for the actual construction. Sound familiar?"

She grinned.

"Why can't those people just stay in a hotel or a motel?" Jo asked.

I'd wondered that, too. I was glad she'd been the one to ask, though. If the question turned out to be dumb, I'd prefer that she look stupid and not me. Then I laughed to myself. I hoped I didn't really feel that way.

"Several reasons, Jo." Much to my relief, the question didn't appear to upset Aleesha. "First of all, when I say 'remote, mountainous area,' I mean thirty or forty long up-and-down miles from the closest town. With the price of gas now, people can't afford to make that commute two or three times over a long weekend. That's not counting the unnecessary exertion and the amount of visitation time they'd lose by spending so much time on the road."

"That would be a shame," Dad said. I nodded.

"Furthermore," Aleesha said, "the people we're talking about helping can't afford to stay in a motel or eat every meal out. They need a simple room with little more than a bed, a toilet, a sink and a shower, and a small refrigerator and microwave—and it has to be cheap and close to the prison."

"Oh, wow. . ." I sat forward on the sofa, anxious to hear more. I was already hurting for these people.

Dad, Aleesha, and Jo began staring at me with amazed looks on their faces, but I didn't realize at first they'd noticed how much perkier I was acting. Although that change had taken place almost instantaneously, it took me a few minutes to see it in myself. Aleesha gave me a thumbs-up before she continued.

"In many cases, they're visiting the very people who used to be the family breadwinners. Incarceration of husbands—and sometimes of grown sons—has left a number of unskilled women in desolate condition. Many families that used to live comfortably are on welfare now."

"How horrible." Jo might have had her prejudices, but she still had a heart.

"So," Aleesha lowered her voice to a near-whisper, "can you imagine these women trying to visit their sons or husbands when their financial situation is already working against them?"

I was in tears. I forgot about my guilt—at least for the time being. Same about my fatigue.

"Does Rob need help?" I asked. Dad and Jo narrowed their eyes at me and then looked at Aleesha.

"Mr. Rob pointed out that Christmas vacation is coming up, and he thought we might have some time on our hands. He also pointed out that doing something for people in need is the same as doing it for Jesus."

Everyone remained silent for a moment. "So you aren't the only one he's invited?" Dad said to Aleesha. *Go, Dad!*

"He told me he could use five or six people, but he'd settle for—let's say—three or. . .four."

Four? I looked around the living room. Uh. . .the one, two, three, four of us?

"He knew about Terri's death," Dad said under his breath. "He wanted to come." He might have been talking to himself, but we could hear him.

"That's what Aleesha said," I said in a near-whisper. "And he sent flowers."

"He also knows about Kim's fatigue problem," Aleesha

said. "He said to be sure she comes. Getting away from here and helping meet somebody else's needs might rejuvenate her." She looked at me. "I don't think he realizes how incapacitated you've been, though."

Rosa's daughter, Anjelita, came to mind. That little eight-year-old had done wonders in Santa María with only an arm-and-a-half. She didn't think of herself as handicapped or incapacitated. She'd inspired me with her ability to find a way to do whatever needed doing.

I could view this challenge either of two ways. I could keep giving in to my current limitations, or I could return to California and trust God to enable me. Which would it be?

Everyone was staring at me. At least it felt that way. I could almost hear Aleesha thinking, *"Will you stay down there where circumstances have landed you or get up and let God help you prance on those pebbles?"*

What do You want me to do, Lord? I'm not making any more trips without checking with You first. I could almost hear Him laugh and say, *"This is a no-brainer, girl. Go for it."*

I must have startled everyone in the room when I yelled, "Amen!" at the top of my lungs. Like Dr. Manette when they freed him from prison in Dickens's *A Tale of Two Cities*, I felt like I'd been "recalled to life."

chapter nineteen

I feel great," I'd said after Dad, Jo, and Aleesha got tired of staring at me for my unexpected gush of energy that evening. "I feel like turning somersaults."

"Uh," Jo said, "I wouldn't try that if I were you. You almost broke your neck trying to do those in gym class."

The room filled with laughter. Aleesha's was the hardiest, and she and Jo actually smiled at one another. Maybe that smell would disappear yet. And maybe Aleesha would quit sniffing so hard.

"You know what?" I said. "Don't bring my supper to the sofa. I'm coming into the dining room." I hadn't eaten at the table in months.

"If you feel *that* strong now," Dad said, "why don't I take you all to a steakhouse to celebrate?"

And what a celebration it was.

My prime rib and fries with cheese and bacon might have weighed me down—as did three mugs of Shirley Temples and a huge ice cream-covered chocolate chip cookie—but I still felt plenty peppy. Maybe the extra food had helped. I hadn't been very hungry or enjoyed eating during the time fatigue had controlled my life. I'd lost a pound or two—maybe more—and I needed every one I had and then some.

But the topic of heading west to help Rob build his hostel didn't come up during dinner. I didn't think of it again until we got home and settled down in the living room again. For once, I was sitting up on the sofa and not lying down.

"Okay, gals and respected older guy," I said, "when do

we leave for California?"

"Rob said to come during Christmas vacation," Aleesha said. "Mine starts the first week in December."

Jo shrugged. I wondered if she was worried about the cost. Since she wasn't in school or working—I had no idea what she did with her time—money should have been the only possible thing to keep her from going.

Drat! The only thing but that doggoned overprotective mother of hers.

Dad looked at me with those washed-out blue eyes of his. How often I'd been thankful I didn't inherit them. He looked like he was trying to stay afloat on an emotionally turbulent ocean.

"Kim, I thank God that you feel so much better now. I—"

"I do, Dad. I've already prayed about this trip"—*just don't ask me how many seconds it took*—"and I believe God made me better just so I could go. I could almost hear Him saying, 'Go for it, Kim.'"

His lips and eyes twisted the way they did when he opposed something—or at least questioned its wisdom. "I wish God would say something to me about it, then. It's not that I don't want you to go. . ."

I wanted to finish the sentence for him: *I want all of us to go.*

"Dad, it's not just me. Rob invited all of us because God wants all of us. We're a team."

Jo shot me a questioning look.

"Yes, Jo. You, too."

She smiled, although she still appeared uncertain.

"Kim," Dad said, "I wouldn't hesitate to say yes if you were well." He must have seen the look on my face. "I know. You think you're well now, and I can't discount today's miracle— there's no other word for it—and the effect it's had on you."

"What, Dad? You don't think God's miracles are good enough to last?"

Oh, my word! I had *never* spoken to my father like that, and the look on his face was a mixture of shock and. . .and of what? Had I totally turned him off, or had I gotten through to him in spite of thoughtless, unintentional disrespect?

"Daddy, I'm so sorry. I shouldn't have said that."

"You're forgiven if I am."

I crooked my eyebrows.

"I was wrong, too. Faithless, anyhow. You really believe you can handle a trip like this?"

"If my fatigue comes back, I'll just sit around and supervise everyone else. I'll be the highway worker who stands there watching everyone else work hard."

Aleesha howled. When she laughed that hard, nobody could resist joining in.

"Baby girl, I still have reservations."

Jo jumped in. "What kind of father would you be if you didn't?" Aleesha gave her a thumbs-up. I wondered if Jo was thinking about her mother's overcautiousness, but now wasn't the time to ask.

"We can live on my income alone, Kim," he said. *Huh? What's that got to do with this?* "We'll miss your mother's when it comes to some of the extras, though." I twisted my eyebrows in curiosity. "She paid for your car. I couldn't have bought you such a nice one on my income alone."

No! Are you saying we'll have to cut back on extras without Mom's income? Is this trip an extra we can't afford? What about the money you inherited from your mother? Did my trip to Mexico use up all that was left of it?

Lord. . . ?

"At the same time," Dad said, "your mom had better-than-average life insurance coverage through her job, and it pays double for accidental death. I had a similar policy on her. Bottom line: We have enough money to do this trip."

I looked at Aleesha and Jo. Could they afford it?

Dad must have seen my concerned look. "All four of us, I mean. I think Terri would want that."

Only the deafest of our neighbors five blocks away could have failed to hear the whooping and cheering.

We had plenty of planning to do, though, and I made mental lists off and on all night—how wonderful to be so awake for a change. And I felt wonderful the next morning, too. Wonderful and energetic.

Thank You, Lord.

But one thing kept bugging me.

chapter twenty

I wondered if things would be warmer in California. The relationship between Jo and Aleesha, that was. In spite of what I'd taken as good signs last night, Aleesha let me know privately that she wasn't enthusiastic about having Jo come with us. I hoped that wouldn't affect the success of the trip.

"You ready, girl?" I asked as Dad and I got ready to head over to the Snellings' house.

"I'm not coming with you," Aleesha said.

"Huh? How come?"

"What if Jo's parents have the smell, too? I don't want to be the reason they say no."

Dad must've heard her. "I've known the Snellings forever. They aren't like that."

But Aleesha refused to change her mind, so we went without her.

Dad rang the Snellings' doorbell. I stood there shivering and thinking.

"Scott, Kim, what a surprise." Mr. Snelling ushered us into the living room, and Dad and I sat down without waiting to be invited. That was how it's supposed to be at a friend's house, wasn't it?

"Where's Michelle?" Dad said.

"Oh, she's"—he shook his head—"uh, I don't know." He acted like he didn't care, either, and that shocked me. I'd ask Dad about it later if I remembered to.

"I understand you're feeling much better now, Kim," Mr. Snelling said, his words ending in a huge smile. I'd never felt comfortable calling him Josh, even though Jo had always called my parents by their first names. Behind their backs, anyhow. "I'm glad."

The degree of warmth in his voice told me *"I'm glad"* meant *"I couldn't be happier."* As much as Michelle Snelling liked to talk and as much as she had to say, he—maybe I'd do an Aleesha and refer to him as *Mr. Josh*—had probably had lots of practice keeping his comments short.

He called Jo in from the kitchen, and the four of us enjoyed a few minutes of small talk.

"I've been helping Papa out at his insurance agency," Jo said.

"Oh, yeah?" *So that's what you do in your spare time. And you didn't think I'd be interested in knowing that?*

"Two or three days a week. Sometimes more."

Aleesha's opinion of Jo would probably shoot up a couple of notches when she learned that. She thought Jo was lazy, and defending her was a struggle because I often felt the same way. I usually blamed her inactivity on her mama's "smother love," though. Mrs. Snelling was afraid something would happen to Jo if she went anywhere to do anything worthwhile. She never seemed to consider the possibility of that something being good—either for Jo or for someone else.

"It isn't a real job, though. Papa would be glad to enlarge his agency to *Snelling & Snelling* when the time comes—"

"But I want Betsy Jo to do what God wants—and what will give her the greatest satisfaction."

I wondered if Mrs. Snelling would be happier keeping Jo safely behind a desk—or maybe inside a safety deposit box—than letting her take chances by following God's leading.

"Anyhow," Jo continued, "I asked to help Papa so I can get my feet wet. You know? Even unpaid work experience looks good on a résumé when a girl has never held a job."

That kept us talking for a while about how a young adult

can't get a job without experience or experience without a job. When the conversation lulled, Dad reached into his jacket pocket and pulled out the familiar two-sheet printout.

"Josh, I want you to hear something. This e-mail came from Rob White, Kim's supervisor in Mexico. Settle back. It's not short."

The two men laughed, but Jo and I just looked at each other. What was so funny about that? Must have been a man thing.

"It's worth hearing, though," he added.

We'd told Jo last night not to say anything to her parents about this mission trip. She was to pray about it and let Dad deal with her parents.

I watched Mr. Josh's face while Dad read the message aloud. I didn't need to be a genius or a body language expert to see how much the idea excited him. He was grinning and nodding so enthusiastically by the time Dad reached the end that I half expected him to ask to go, too.

He didn't say anything, but I could picture those clichéd wheels spinning off their axle. Dad allowed him another minute of silence.

"Josh, I want to take Jo—uh, Betsy Jo—with us during the holidays. We'll be gone a couple of weeks, but she'll be strictly supervised, and we'll keep her safe."

I hoped he would add, *"No Mexican drug wars that far north of Sacramento"* for Mrs. Snelling's sake, but he didn't.

"She should have gone to Mexico," Mr. Josh said. "I told Michelle repeatedly that Betsy Jo would be safe, but she wouldn't listen. She doesn't. . .listen."

If he was trying to hide his resentment toward his wife, he was doing a lousy job of it, to use a word I intensely dislike. Were he and Mrs. Snelling having marital problems? I'd never thought about whether they seemed happy together, yet I suddenly realized how blessed we were to have this conversation in Michelle Snelling's absence.

Dad remained silent. I think we both knew Mr. Josh had left some important things unsaid. Things he probably needed to talk about with someone.

I looked at Jo, and she wore a more miserable hangdog look than I'd ever seen before. Which was she more worried about— her papa's feelings about the trip or her parents' marriage?

"Betsy Jo. . ." He looked at his daughter. "Jo? I like that." She smiled. "Do you want to go on this project?" From his tone of voice, I could tell he just wanted to hear her say it.

She threw her arms around him and kissed him. I was almost in tears.

"We'll pay her way," Dad said.

"Thanks, Scott, but no. We'll pay. That won't make up for keeping her from going to Mexico, but it'll make me feel better."

"You're sure?" Dad knew the Snellings weren't poor, but they weren't as relatively well-off as we were. Especially now that we had an unspecified amount of life insurance money in the bank, somewhere in the mid–six figures if my guess was anywhere close to right.

Mr. Josh laughed. "That Rob White. . .when he refunded Jo's money, he sent her a little note. 'Hope you can use this on a *safe* mission trip, Betsy Jo. I'm looking forward to meeting you then.'"

I started to say something, but Jo and I looked at each other and broke out crying. If Aleesha had been with us, she would have been bawling the hardest. That note was *so* Rob. It's no wonder he'd become my second father at a time I wasn't at all close to Dad.

Dad kept opening and closing his mouth. He narrowed his left eye as if puzzling over something. *What are you so hesitant to say?*

"Josh. . ." *Go on, Dad.* "What about Michelle?"

Jo and I stopped blubbering. I don't know about her, but I think I stopped breathing.

"She doesn't get a say in this. She's already said too much—for too long."

Dad's eyes opened wide. I wouldn't have known how to respond, either.

"Jo," Mr. Snelling said with a smile on his lips but sadness in his eyes, "here's the way I see it. You're eighteen. You're free to go wherever you want whenever you want. You don't legally need your mother's approval or mine."

Why did that statement sound so bittersweet?

chapter twenty-one

Act 2

Being away from home felt wonderful. Intoxicating. The way I assumed intoxication made a person feel, anyhow. I'd never touched alcohol and didn't plan to start anytime in the next eighty years. Life was crazy enough without it.

Although my plane seat didn't compete with the comfort of our living room sofa, I had an advantage over my co-travelers. Far shorter than even the shortest of them, I invited Dad and Aleesha to stretch out and use some of my unneeded foot space. Unfortunately for Jo, she sat across the aisle from Dad, where my free space wouldn't help her.

Even though I'd closed my eyes, I couldn't sleep. I was thinking about *A Tale of Two Cities* again. It had made a profound impact on me in the tenth grade. What teenaged girl in her right mind wouldn't be moved to tears by that *"It is a far, far better thing that I do than I have ever done"* ending when Sydney Carton chooses to die in Charles Darnay's place?

The idea may have sounded Christlike, but it wasn't. Just the opposite, in fact. Jesus lived a sinless life, but Sydney Carton hadn't even lived a good one.

I'd been planning to reread that book when I got around to it. But now that I was sufficiently alert to start an intensive study of Spanish, I'd have to put Dickens on hold awhile longer. Maybe I could get a copy in Spanish when I became fluent enough.

Some parts of the story came back clearly. One in particular. Even though the authorities released Dr. Manette from the Bastille—physically—the severe emotional problem that resulted from his traumatic imprisonment held him an even more horrendous kind of prisoner for a long time after that.

Would this trip to California free me from my guilt problem—or just make me forget about it for a while?

"Kim, wake up," Aleesha said. Her whisper was far gentler than the way she was manhandling my newly recovered arm and so quiet I could barely hear her over the roar of the plane.

"Huh? What?" I mumbled, only to find Aleesha's hand over my mouth. Quadruple that *Huh? What?*

"Hush, girl. You don't want your father to hear."

No! I'd drifted off and had a nightmare. . .while sitting between Dad and Aleesha on the flight to Sacramento.

"Mr. Scott has headphones on, so he probably didn't hear you. I didn't think you would want him to know."

She was so right. As concerned as Dad was about my ability to make this trip—he'd kept asking how I felt up till boarding time—he might send me home again as soon as we landed if he found out I'd had another nightmare.

Lord, nightmares are bad enough, but please don't let my guilt feelings result in severe fatigue again. Not until after this project, anyhow.

That would be worse than the broken arm, although I didn't doubt that God could still use me. Somehow.

"Same one you had months ago?" Aleesha said. Although she was still whispering, her eyes were tense with worry.

Quick glance. Dad appeared to be sound asleep.

"Not exactly," I whispered back. "A continuation of it."

Aleesha narrowed her eyes.

"They threw me in jail after convicting me of involuntary manslaughter. A group of rough-looking inmates asked what I was in for. When I told them, 'Murdering my mother,' they dropped back with terror on their faces and anger in their eyes.

"Questions flew at me from everywhere. 'Was she mean?' 'Did she take away your beef jerky?' 'Did she make you wear clothes that were far out-of-style?' 'Did she ask you to do the dishes?'

"'None of those things,' I told them. 'She was the most wonderful mom in the world, and I miss her terribly.'

"I explained the circumstances surrounding her death. The more I said, the harsher and meaner their looks grew. They were obviously planning to gang up on me and give me what I deserved. I didn't know what that would be—not specifically— but it would be horrendous. Somehow, I knew it would involve my hair. And its color.

"Then I heard a still, small voice say, 'Kim, this is how I punish foolish young adults who disobey my "Thou shalt not kill" and "Honor your father and your mother" commandments. Especially when they do both at the same time.'

"They grabbed my cell phone—I'd made the mistake of telling them about the voice mail recording of the accident from the original nightmare—and handed it to a guard. I don't know what they said to him, but before I could blink back the tears, the sounds of the accident began playing over the public address system. At top volume.

"Over and over again. Throughout the night. If I dropped off to sleep, my big bruiser of a cell mate woke me up and said, 'Hartlinger, here's something you need to hear. . .'"

Just telling Aleesha about the nightmare wore me out. Was this a sign of my fatigue coming back?

Please, Lord, no!

Aleesha suddenly put her finger against my lips and nodded ever so slightly toward Dad. Although his eyes were still closed, the headphones dangled from his neck and his head inclined a bit more in my direction than before. He might as well have been wearing a sign that said, *"I'm awake and trying to listen without being obvious."*

Have you heard anything yet? If so, how much?

The part about listening repeatedly to the recording of the accident would have been bad enough, but if he heard about me confessing my crime to the other inmates, he'd discover my real problem. I broke out in a cold sweat at the very thought of him blaming me and treating me the way I deserved.

What would he say if I asked, *"Daddy, how much did you hear?"*

He might pretend he hadn't heard anything. But if we turned around and headed home again as soon as we landed in Sacramento, I'd know he heard too much.

"Aleesha," I said in what I hoped was my normal tone of voice, "I wonder if we'll meet any inmates while working on this project." I didn't wait for a response. "I hope so. I want to share my testimony with some of them."

"You and your desire to evangelize. . ." Although Aleesha shook her head playfully, she wore a major smile. She cared as much about people's souls as I did. And about them living the best possible earthly life, too.

"It's important," I said. "I want my life to touch other people in a positive way."

"To be Jesus to them—His hands and His feet? Like in that song the team sang in Santa María?"

"Exactly. If the opportunity arises, nothing's going to stop me from witnessing."

"Amen," Dad said. "That sounds like a plan."

He hadn't said that in a *"You're going home, baby girl"* tone of voice. So I quit worrying about what he might have overheard.

I stayed awake for the rest of the flight. Dwelling on my nightmare. Drowning in guilt. Dreading Dad's finding out. Thoughts like those were enough to keep me wide-eyed awake.

Good thing. I wouldn't have dared to dream again before we got to California.

Dad might have heard more the next time.

chapter twenty-two

Dad, Jo, and Aleesha waited near the carousel for our luggage to come around, and I went looking for Rob. Although we spotted each other almost immediately at opposite ends of the baggage claim area—he was wearing the same plaid shirt I'd first seen him in—working our way through the crowd took forever. From the way he hugged me, observers probably assumed we were a grandfather and granddaughter who hadn't seen one another in years. The problems I'd been experiencing made our four-month separation seem an eternity.

"How many suitcases today, Kimmy?" he asked with a wicked-looking grin.

Lord, please don't let the other team members start calling me Kimmy while I'm here.

"I only brought one tractor trailer with me," he said with a laugh. "But that one is towing a second trailer. Will that be big enough for all of your luggage?"

I pretended to count suitcases on the fingers of both hands. "Maybe." I grinned. "Sure. I'll have you know I only brought one suitcase this time, and it's small and light. I have construction clothes and little else."

"What? No trunk full of makeup?"

"If you look more closely, you'll notice I'm wearing only a small amount of makeup. And I'll have you know it fits nicely in my purse, thank you very much."

I stuck my tongue out at him. Four weeks earlier, I wouldn't have felt up to this kind of give-and-take.

"Did you bring any pebbles to bed down on and to drop on the sidewalk when you want to go skating?"

Aleesha! You told him about that?

And to think teasing had once been the last thing on Rob's mind. He would probably have preferred to shoot and skin me at orientation. Truth be known, our relationship couldn't have gotten off to a much rockier start. But God didn't let things stay that way.

"You bring a sleeping bag this time?"

"Your e-mail said to, didn't it? I read that message as soon as it came and followed your instructions to the letter." I started digging in my purse. "Want to see my checklist?"

He shook his head, and I blew a raspberry at him.

He held his chest, pretending to have a heart attack. My failure to see—much less to read—several crucial messages before leaving for Mexico had created a world of unnecessary problems. I couldn't blame him for not letting me live it down—in a good-natured way, thank goodness.

"So where are we sleeping this time, Rob? And where's the rest of the group? How many of us will be working on this project?"

"You'll be staying. . ." He stopped in mid-sentence when he saw Aleesha, and the two of them hugged like long-lost family.

"Mr. White. . ." Dad said as he shifted a suitcase from his right hand to his left.

"You must be Mr. Hartlinger," Rob said, extending his hand to Dad.

"Scott, please. Mr. Hartlinger was my father."

"Rob, if you don't mind addressing an older fellow by his first name." Rob was maybe fifteen or twenty years older than Dad.

The two men laughed politely, and we girls rolled our eyes in amusement.

I'll never understand why two men meeting for the first time have to act so formal, but that seems to be typical. In my book, having to ask the other fellow to lighten up is just plain weird.

No sooner did Rob look at Jo than his eyes lit up.

"And you must be Betsy Jo. I'm Rob." His face bore that confused look of someone who doesn't know whether to shake hands or hug someone. "Oh, fiddle. You remind me of my daughter when she was your age."

With that, he gathered her into his arms in a grandfatherly way. Although she looked a little flustered at first, she didn't protest. By the time he released her, her uncertainty had morphed into a major smile.

"Rob, you can call me Jo."

"Jo? Kimmy never referred to you as anything but Betsy Jo, but I'm not too old to break the habit—eventually, that is."

Dad's face wrinkled as he mouthed, *"Kimmy?"* I caught his attention and rolled my eyes. When he and I were alone, I'd explain that Rob had given me that nickname in Mexico and I hadn't had the heart to object. Back then, I was a lot closer to Rob than to Dad.

"Are you folks ready to roll? Anybody need to visit the little construction workers' room while we're still in civilization?"

In civilization? Surely this work site wasn't as remote as Santa María.

The four of us shook our heads. We'd already taken care of business.

"We have quite a drive ahead of us," Rob said. "We start on I-80—I forget if it's marked north or east, but we're actually going northeast—and then we head north on 395 for a good little way."

Dad shook his head. That information apparently meant

nothing to him. "I'm glad *you're* driving," he said.

"Oh, but I'm not." He pulled out his cell phone—actually, the satellite phone he'd bought in San Diego—and punched in a speed dial number. "Graham O'Reilly is chauffeuring us today."

"Graham O'Reilly?" I said. "Is he one of the kids on the project team?"

Rob chuckled a couple of times and then started laughing harder. Every time I thought he'd finished, he started all over again. "Graham is a few years older than me, and I don't think he feels like a kid anymore. He doesn't act anything like one, as you'll soon discover."

Okay.

"He isn't on the team. Not exactly. In fact, the four of you and I are *it*."

"Wha . . ?"

"Huh?" Aleesha and I said almost simultaneously.

"We had a good-sized crew for two weeks, and they got almost everything done They went home a couple of days ago. We didn't want you to come for nothing, though, so I had them leave you the painting. Inside and out." He let that sink in. "And I've saved a special job for you, Kimmy." He winked at me. "My crew failed me in one way and one way only." And there he stopped.

Come on, Rob. Spit it out before I die of curiosity.

Rob couldn't have missed the impatience on my face. "They failed to clean up their mess, and there's a mess of it. Anyone for litter cleanup? Kimmy?"

Everyone else laughed, but I felt my face glowing. I don't know why. The litter cleanup campaign in Santa María had been a major success. Although I'd only been able to use one arm, Anjelita and her little friends, other team members, and even the older villagers all pitched in.

At least my cast was off now and I could use both hands and both arms, although my right arm was still a little tender and a lot weak. During my bout with fatigue, I hadn't needed to use it much, and when I did, it balked like a rubber band that's stretching almost to the breaking point.

"Don't worry, Kimmy," Rob said. "We're all pitching in. We won't paint until we're done with cleanup. We have wheelbarrows and dumpsters, and you won't have to worry about what lies underneath."

Thank You, Lord.

"You have—what's her name again? Anjelita?—little Anjelita's necklace on, I see. It's beautiful."

"I practically never take it off," I told him. "It helps keep my memories of Anjelita alive." I was always extra careful not to lose or damage it. Since the tornado hadn't hurt it much, though, I doubted that I could.

By that time, we'd arrived at Passenger Pickup. Within two minutes, a large, blue passenger van with *Wash Me* written in the dust on the side panel stopped in front of us, and an old fellow got out and opened the back for our luggage. I didn't see his face until Rob introduced us.

A few years older than you, Rob? This guy looks ancient. Or maybe even older than that.

"Folks, this is Graham O'Reilly."

Mr. O'Reilly nodded just enough to avoid appearing rude. He looked like he would've preferred to remain anonymous.

"Graham's a real quiet fellow, so don't be offended if he seems to ignore you. He probably will. He's a good man, though, and he works hard at what he does."

Uh, okay. But was Mr. O'Reilly. . .was Graham a Christian? I needed someone to share my witness with to make this project an evangelistic mission trip.

"Luggage in?" Rob said.

"Check."

I could barely hear Graham's voice. That was the first word I'd heard him speak, so I didn't have much to go by, but he sounded like he was almost afraid of the sound of his own voice. Strange.

"Passengers aboard?"

"One-two-three-four back here," Dad said. "You and Graham make six. Check."

"Everyone buckled in?"

A chorus of "checks" echoed back.

"Let's head on out, Graham."

"Hey, Rob," Jo yelled to the front seat.

"Yo?" Boy, did a California response like that sound strange coming from somebody Rob's age.

"How did Graham get to Passenger Pickup so quickly?"

"He parked in the free cell phone lot."

That answer hit me like the proverbial ton of bricks. Why couldn't Mom have made it to the cell phone lot at Hartsfield International instead of having that accident? And why ask myself that when I was the one who kept her from getting there?

I happened to glance at the driver's inside rearview mirror and saw Graham staring back at me. I could tell from his expression that he'd noticed my guilty look.

Noticed and recognized it.

chapter twenty-three

I can't say that the Welcoming Arms Christian Hostel reminded me of Santa María even in its degree of isolation. After all, we were still in the United States, not Mexico. The van had chugged its way up rugged mountain terrain rather than gliding across land that was pond-surface flat.

We rode on smooth, paved roads the entire distance, and we could see them winding their way out of sight beyond the hostel and the prison property opposite it. The final, bumpy, dirt road to Santa María—if one could properly label a rutted, overgrown footpath a road—had ended at the village.

The cashiers at the two service stations where we'd stopped both spoke English. Maybe not the most cultivated English I'd ever heard, but without any trace of a Spanish accent. No translator needed there.

Although the two towns closest to the hostel seemed like villages compared to home, they were Atlanta compared to teeny-tiny Santa María, which—to the best of my knowledge— had no neighbors within who knew how many miles. Between the border and the village, I'd looked for road signs to *any-where* and hadn't seen even one.

The hostel didn't have Anjelita, Rosa, or any of the other villagers I'd fallen in love with and read Scripture to. It also didn't have well over a hundred teenaged team members who'd learned to love and accept one another and to work together.

The hostel just had Rob and Graham, and Rob didn't live in this part of California. I had no idea where Graham called home.

I wasn't sure what his function was, either. Although he was wiry—probably stronger than he looked—I couldn't imagine him helping with the heaviest part of the construction. Besides, Rob had said Graham wasn't exactly part of the team.

He hadn't exaggerated Graham's quietness. If Graham and I ever chanced to hold a conversation, I knew which one of us would do most of the talking.

Maybe all of it.

The hostel wasn't the huge multistory structure I'd envisioned. Rob and his volunteers had apparently worked from "paper napkin plans" similar to the one he'd drawn up for Santa María. But instead of building individual cottages, he'd combined a number of them—I couldn't tell how many—in a U-shaped, motel-style, single story structure with the open end of the U facing the highway. When I peeked inside one of the units, the trash made me flash back to Santa María.

The hostel had a similar rustic feeling. Santa María had been too far from civilization to have electricity or plumbing. The hostel had plumbing, Rob said, but no electricity. Not yet. The local power company hadn't come out to make the necessary connections.

My mind wandered for a split second. Why not just run an ultralong extension cord across the road from the prison? I giggled at my silliness. The prison buildings were set pretty far back from the two-lane road, so the extension cord would undoubtedly have to be longer than anything I'd ever seen. And someone would surely protest the secular State of California's providing even temporary power to a religious project. One final giggle gurgled to the top like a lone bubble.

Rob looked at me. The twinkle in his eyes said, *"Our little Kimmy hasn't changed a bit."*

Our job, he explained while showing us around, was

to paint the hostel inside and out and to prepare it for an occupancy-licensing inspection.

"Very impressive," Dad said after completing the tour. "People visiting the prison can't complain about the distance they have to go. Looks like the facility's right across the road. They can walk."

"If they want to," Rob said, "but that entrance road you see is probably a mile, mile-and-a-half long."

"I wouldn't mind walking that," Jo said.

"Hope don't. Either way."

Huh? Had Graham actually spoken? And why had he said that? Strange words in strangely incomplete sentences from someone I already considered the ultimate in strangeness. Maybe "the ultimate mystery" would describe him more accurately.

"One good thing about this location," Rob said. "Buses come by here five days a week—one in each direction. Some days that's just about all the traffic this road sees. That and people who work at the prison."

"So visitors won't *need* a car once the hostel opens. . ." My words were more of an observation than a question.

"We expect more visitors because of that," Rob said. "Warden Jenkins is highly supportive of the hostel. His church is one of the sponsors."

"You're not giving up your day job to manage this place, are you?" Dad asked. Rob returned Dad's grin.

"I've retired so I can do volunteer construction full-time. That's what I felt God calling me to do."

Murmurs of approval all around. "And my dear wife is glad to have me out of her hair for several weeks at a time." Exuberant clapping and cheering. "When she doesn't come with me, that is. Sometimes she does."

"As for management, that's what Graham is here for. He'll evaluate the applications—it would be frustrating to give one of these spaces to someone who doesn't need it. Especially if that kept someone needier from getting in. He'll also collect the token amount we charge—ten dollars a night—and keep an eye on things for us. We don't want to padlock the microwaves and little refrigerators in place, but we're realistic. Some of the visitors probably deserve to be in *there*." He nodded toward the road. "Not over here."

Nobody spoke. I thought about the biblical account of Adam and Eve and the fall of man. Even after two thousand years of Christianity, mankind's depravity seemed to keep spiraling downward. Maybe that's why I took personal evangelism so seriously.

I couldn't save the world, and I couldn't return mankind to the Garden of Eden's pristine condition. The Fall had resulted in death and decay, and I couldn't reverse that, either. But maybe I could save a few individuals from hell, give them hope for the future, and help them live a more meaningful earthly life.

Nothing was more important to try doing.

"So where are we sleeping?" I said. Although the answer was obvious, I wanted to make it official.

"We have a dozen units here," Rob said. "All unheated. I've settled into one of them, but the rest are up for grabs. Everyone can have his own."

Aleesha stared at him with a reproving look.

"Or *her* own."

Aleesha's face relaxed into a smile.

"*Its* own." He stuck out his tongue at her, and she smirked.

"Personally," I said, "with a prison this close by, I'd just as soon have a roommate."

"Me, too," Jo said.

"Me, three." Aleesha's affirmation completed the vote.

"Hmm. You can probably cram three sleeping bags into one unit, but you'll have to clean the litter out first. Not that you're in any danger, of course. There's a reason for the lack of trees here and across the road. No place for escapees to hide."

I shivered. I couldn't speak for Jo and Aleesha, but Rob's reassurance didn't make me feel a bit better. Now, if he'd explained that Red Cedar Correctional Center—at least the state had named it after my favorite wood—had never had a breakout, I might have felt slightly better.

If he noticed my reaction, he didn't say anything about it.

"I know teenage girls. I've raised a couple of them myself." Aleesha gave him *the look* again.

"With some major help from my dear wife Patricia, of course."

"Otherwise, they would have been motherless from the time they weren't conceived," Aleesha pointed out. She loved picking on Rob and sounded like she'd practiced some since summer.

"Almost suppertime," Rob said.

What? We don't have electricity. Are you going to feed us like you did in Santa María? Cans and packages of prepared food? My stomach shuddered at the thought.

"Kimmy"—Rob must have seen my look of despair—"don't worry. I didn't forget the beef jerky."

My eyes brightened, but Dad shot me a strange look. Had I failed to tell him about falling in love with jerky in Mexico? I mouthed back, *"I'll explain later."*

"Seriously, though, we keep a generator running— "

"I don't hear anything," Jo said. Up till then, she'd been standing around looking bored. Or maybe just tired. I was. And there I was, making excuses for her again. It seemed different now, though.

"Smart girl," Rob said. Jo beamed. "I brought a small solar-powered generator that makes no noise whatsoever. So we won't have to totally relive the powerlessness of our Santa María experience. It—"

"We had the power of the Holy Spirit, though," Aleesha said with a grin.

"Be good, girl," I said. "You know what the man means."

Rob smiled before trying again. "It won't power the whole hostel, but it's big enough to power Graham's place. He has a full-sized stove and refrigerator. I'll leave the generator as his backup."

Full-sized? I must have twisted my face in surprise.

"Kimmy, you wouldn't expect our resident manager to live in the same kind of room the visitors occupy, would you?" He didn't wait for an answer. "You've seen the shape of the hostel. Graham has a good-sized apartment—the whole bottom of the U, in fact."

Oh, of course.

"He deserves it."

Oh? And what makes this strange old man so deserving?

chapter twenty-four

Supper was great. Graham deserved that full-sized oven, anyhow. He'd put a huge pan of lasagna in to bake as soon as we arrived at the hostel, and it tasted as wonderful as it smelled. We all had seconds. Little piggy me had thirds. I was still making up for those months I didn't feel like eating, even though I'd already regained the lost pounds.

After supper, we settled as comfortably in Graham's little living room as six adults could do. Unlike the visitor units, his place was already tidy, furnished, and homey-looking.

Not only had he cleaned the construction rubbish out of his apartment, but he'd also already given it one coat of paint. That amazed me, for I hadn't changed my opinion about his having limited strength. Driving to the airport that day instead of being free to give his place a second coat of paint must have frustrated him, though, if what appeared to be frequent frowns of resentment were any indication. Then again, maybe he just didn't like us.

Because Graham would receive little actual income for managing the Welcoming Arms—the sponsoring churches had provided the name as well as the funds for construction materials—Rob had set aside a reasonable-yet-still-modest amount of money for decorating and furnishing the apartment to Graham's taste. Everything looked and smelled brand-new but Graham himself.

I couldn't understand why someone that close to the end of his earthly life—someone who'd made it a lot further than Mom, anyhow—hadn't accumulated any furniture of his own.

Or much of anything else, apparently.

He did have an excellent collection of books, though. Many of them were Christian fiction. They looked well worn. So did the Bibles and commentaries that filled a shelf of their own. Okay, so he was probably already a believer and not in need of evangelizing, but I'd still make sure.

He didn't have a TV, and that seemed odd. But why should I be surprised? I hadn't turned on the television since Mom's death. When I'd been alert enough to do anything but fall asleep again, I read and listened to music.

A man like Graham living alone had to have a cat, though. Sure enough, I found a litter box in the bathroom.

As I was exiting—the bathroom, not the litter box—a cat barely out of kittenhood scooted between my legs and made for her facilities. As mysterious as Graham was, I wasn't surprised that his cat was midnight black.

Because of the time difference between coasts, it was still early. At the hostel, that was. But we the newly arrived were already yawning and stretching because it was bedtime at home, and we'd had a long day of travel.

"I'm sorry to have to keep you folks up past your bedtime," Rob said, "but we need to have a team meeting. I'll keep it as brief as possible."

"That means we'll be done by midnight if we can just keep Rob from praying," I said before Aleesha could make a similar dig.

"Does that mean you'd like to start us off in prayer, Kimmy?"

"Sure."

I took a deep breath before praying for our health and strength, God's guidance in completing our task, the inmates in the prison, and the friends and family members who would be staying here. I prayed for a good night's sleep, and I actually refrained from giggling when I prayed for God to keep us awake long enough to complete the meeting.

My amen came less than two minutes after I started praying. Others echoed mine. I could have been wrong, but I thought I heard Graham's voice.

"First order of business," Rob said. "We don't have the same sense of urgency in finishing the hostel we had in building Santa María's cottages. Nobody's going to be any worse off than before if we don't finish while you're here."

"How long has the prison been here?" Dad said.

"Many years. And this hostel has been needed that long, too."

Dad *mmm*-ed.

"All that to say—"

"We told you he was long-winded."

Aleesha got her licks in that time, and we all laughed. Everyone but Jo. I hoped she was just tired. She didn't seem to be getting into the spirit of things. I hoped she didn't regret coming.

"Hmm," Rob said. "I forget where I was. I'll have to start over."

We laughed, hissed, and booed. Even Graham's frown curled slightly upward. Not into a real smile, but close. Kind of.

Jo's expression remained closer to a frown, though.

"Okay, folks, short version. Breakfast is at seven thirty. A hot meal—with real coffee. We'll have a prayer and devotional time after that and then start cleaning out the construction rubbish at a reasonable rate of speed. Think you can handle that, Kimmy?"

I nodded. It sounded like Rob was trying to make things as easy on me as possible. Of course, he didn't know how much better I was doing. Not counting the nightmare on the plane, that was. He would probably have been even more considerate if he'd known about that. He was the kind of man who'd do anything to keep me from suffering a relapse.

"You okay, Jo?" Rob said.

Hmm. So I wasn't the only one to notice her apparent disinterest.

"I guess." She might have meant for her words to sound positive, but her tone of voice distinctly said, *"No, and don't bother asking."* That shocked me.

"Maybe we should cut this meeting short," Rob said.

Nobody protested. But then Rob kept on talking.

Jo had that same hangdog look I'd seen earlier. Something was wrong. But could I get her to tell me what?

chapter twenty-five

When I first woke up, I couldn't remember where I was. I had a hazy recollection of Rob suggesting that we stay in Graham's spare room—at least until we could clear enough rubbish from a unit of our own to lay our sleeping bags flat on the floor. This way we'd have heat and access to a shower. The units would remain unheated until the electrical hookup took place in another ten days or so.

Rob invited Dad to room with him in the unit he referred to as "my home away from home." I wondered what they'd find to talk about. Dad had never been one to enjoy small talk about sports and cars, and two mature men like them certainly weren't going to sit around and talk about women. Other than their own wives. . .

Would Dad cry on Rob's shoulder about Mom? He had to still be grieving. It had only been four months, and I was. Grief and guilt were doing a real number on my insides. I'd begun gulping antacids down like candy and trying to keep Dad from noticing.

I looked around the room without getting up, but my roomies had already left. Gone to breakfast, maybe?

No, my watch read almost eight thirty, and we were supposed to have breakfast at seven thirty. Why didn't they wake me? I'd give somebody some painful grief if she—no matter which she—kept me from getting at least two cups of steaming hot coffee. Although I was hungry enough, food wasn't at the top of my priority list.

At least I felt rested. Great, in fact. And no dreams that I could recall. Not that I would have forgotten another nightmare.

When I stood up—still with no noticeable fatigue—I noticed a piece of paper beside my sleeping bag. Wondering if it was a note or a piece of trash, I stooped down to pick it up. I rocked back and forth a time or two trying to maintain my balance and almost fell on my bottom.

Flashback to the pebbles at San Diego International. Minus the pebbles. Flashback to falling out of the cart. Minus the cart. I might have gotten over my fatigue, but I hadn't grown coordinated overnight.

I rolled back on top of my sleeping bag with the paper in hand.

Mr. Rob—Aleesha must have written this—*told us not to wake you. He wants you to be at your peppiest. Leftover breakfast in the kitchen. Go outside and listen for work noises when you're ready.*

If that didn't make me feel I'd been unnecessarily pampered, I don't know what would. But how could I fault my friends for loving me and wanting to take care of me? Especially when my fatigue problem wasn't that far in the past, and not even I could be 100 percent sure it would stay away.

And to think I'd questioned my dad's faith.

The smell of fresh coffee led my nose—followed by the rest of my body—straight to the coffeemaker on the countertop. The carafe was huge—and still half-full.

Mmm. Hazelnut. Or was it southern pecan? I loved those nutty blends, even if I couldn't keep them straight.

Next to the coffee was a box filled with a donut assortment. Before I could grab the first chocolate donut hole I came to, I saw another note—this one taped inside the box top.

You only get a hot breakfast at 7:30. Or you can fix one yourself.

Smart alecks. How did they expect me to eat at seven thirty

if no one was going to get me up?

I'd show them. Maybe I was dangerous in the kitchen, but I wasn't helpless. Not as long as a fully charged fire extinguisher hung within easy reach. That's the first thing I made certain of before getting started.

Splattered batter from earlier—it hadn't fully dried yet—decorated the griddle that perched on the stove's largest burner and the stove surface as well. Looked like Graham had fixed pancakes. Hmm.

I opened the fridge.

Sure enough, I found a huge stainless steel mixing bowl containing enough batter to feed a small army. I grinned. *Small army* described our team more accurately than any other term I could think of on an empty stomach. A covered plastic container was full of those big sausage links I liked so much, and—glory be!—they were already cooked.

I'd show those jokers I could fend for myself, but first I downed a cup of coffee and swallowed half a donut hole to tide me over while the griddle heated. The results were worth waiting for, even though our family dog might have turned her back on the non-sausage part of my meal.

I'd purposely overlooked the additional note that read, *The price of cooking your own breakfast is washing everyone else's dishes.* Humph! Was this Rob's idea of coddling me? Did he think scrubbing that much cookware was a softer, easier job than cleaning up construction rubbish? I'd show him.

But before I could make a clean getaway—pun definitely intended—he cleared his throat and walked into the kitchen. Smiling at me, he pointed to the note. "You didn't see your first assignment of the day?"

I rolled my eyes in protest, but his stern look sent me to the sink, which was already half-full of slightly sudsy water. It had gotten obnoxiously lukewarm from lack of recent use. I ran some more hot water in the sink, squirted a few additional drops of detergent under the spray, and swished my hands around until the suds looked inviting enough for a bubble bath. Doing dishes in the hottest available water and not scrimping on detergent were two sanitary procedures my mom had successfully pounded into my head.

"We're like the New Testament church," Rob said. "You have to work to eat. Unless you can't, of course."

So much for coddling. What a relief to have Rob treat me as normal.

"You missed out on part of our discussion last night," Rob said. I narrowed my eyes in curiosity. "You fell asleep on the sofa, Kimmy. You should have seen us trying to brush your teeth for you. We'll show you the video sometime."

Unable to figure out if he was teasing, I licked the roof and the sides of my mouth before touching the back of my teeth with my tongue. I could still taste breakfast, but not last night's highly garlicky lasagna. Maybe they really did brush for me.

"Thanks, I think."

"You were definitely zonked when we zipped you into your sleeping bag. That's why you're still wearing yesterday's clothes. The girls didn't want to wake you up to change you into nightclothes."

Hopeful that Rob was teasing but fearful he wasn't, I looked down. Nope, same clothes. Flashback to both my first night in Santa María when I slept in my travel clothes and the second night when he and Aleesha gave me a dose of codeine medicine without waking me up.

"What'd I miss, Rob?"

By that time, he'd grabbed the dish towel and was drying as I rinsed.

"You remember that the warden really approves of this hostel?"

I nodded and yawned. Simultaneously. And loudly.

"Did I mention he belongs to one of our sponsoring churches?"

I nodded.

"I wouldn't be surprised to learn that he's also one of the main contributors."

I nodded again.

"He's invited us to come over and hold worship services every evening you're here."

My eyes opened wide.

"He really wants us to come."

My heart started bouncing around out of control. Like popcorn kernels going crazy in a bag in the microwave. "We'll go *inside* the prison?"

Rob laughed. "Warden Jenkins is a great guy, but he's not about to let his inmates come outside and sit on the grass like your English teacher probably did sometimes in high school. Not even for Christian activities. Inmates are referred to as *insiders* for a reason."

Oh. . .yeah. I could only imagine what kind of dumb look I must have had on my face.

"So, what will we do there?" I pretended to be calm, but I thought my stomach was going to erupt any second. "What specifically, I mean?"

"You sing, don't you, Kimmy? That's why you brought that karaoke box to Santa María. Right?"

"I don't have it here, though." My courage was slipping away fast. Sing for prisoners? Uh, insiders. And what would they do if they didn't like my singing?

"I'm sure they won't care if you sing a capella. Warden Jenkins has been trying to get somebody to donate a piano for that meeting room, but no success so far."

I sighed. Mom's piano sat at home unused. Neither Dad

nor I played. Of course, shipping it to California would probably cost twice as much as buying a new one locally. Uh, if one of the towns nearest Red Cedar was big enough to have a music store, that was.

"The prison has some well-worn hymnbooks," Rob continued. "So you won't need to worry about whether they know the words."

"Oh, you want me to lead *them* in singing?" That sounded better. Safer, anyhow.

"The men would appreciate some solos, too, I'm sure."

"The. . ." I almost choked on my gulp. "The *men?*" *This isn't a. . .?*

"You thought this was a women's prison?" He smiled. "Afraid not."

"Are there any hard-core offenders here?" I gulped again. "Like murderers and rapists and people like that?"

He nodded without smiling. "Possibly." He was quiet for a few seconds. "Probably."

"I. . .I don't think I can do that, Rob." I was trying to ignore the still small voice that kept saying, *"Oh, yes, you can. Where's that spirit of faithful obedience you demonstrated in Santa María?"*

"You believe in personal evangelism, don't you, Kimmy?" His voice was kind. Encouraging. "Witnessing to the lost? Sharing your Christian testimony?"

Play fair, Rob! "You know I do, but—"

"Many of the guys are already Christians, Larry Jenkins says. But he's cautioned me that some of the men only pretend to be believers. They'll do anything to get out of their cells for a while. Even sit through a Christian worship service." He hesitated. "This won't be a captive audience, even though it is."

I probably disappointed Rob by my failure to laugh at what he probably meant to be a cute crack, but I couldn't let myself get sidetracked. Not while I still had major misgivings.

"You. . .you aren't going to ask me to preach, too, are you?"

He shook his head. "Some of the insiders come from very conservative backgrounds. Very conservative as in they wouldn't permit a woman to preach to them. You'd feel comfortable giving your testimony, though, wouldn't you?"

I nodded. These guys would think it was tame, though. For men like them, I would've preferred having a Saul/Paul conversion story. Something that would knock their socks off and show them God can forgive anything. Something like, *"Four months ago, I murdered my own. . ."*

That thought jolted me into reality. I'd murdered Mom all right. God had forgiven me, but I hadn't forgiven myself. I didn't think I ever would.

"You can read the Bible. . ." Rob must have wanted me to understand how much I could do at the prison.

"Of course. In English and in Spanish. Even if I don't know what it means in Spanish."

"And you can listen. . ."

"When I'm not busy running my own mouth." I'd almost forced thoughts of Mom out of my head for now, and my confidence was growing, although not very fast. "But. . ."

"Kimmy, you're not doing this by yourself."

"Sure, I know the Holy Spirit will enable me, but—"

"You're part of a team. Remember?" He looked like he was trying to suppress a smile. "The five of us will be there—Graham has his own reasons for not going—and each of us will play an important role. We're still working on Jo—maybe she'll do Bible reading and testimony—but Aleesha will sing, too."

No! She's so good. Nobody will want to hear me after hearing her.

"But mostly she's going to do dramatic readings and monologues."

My sigh of relief made the dish towel billow like a ship's sail on a blustery day.

"Your father has agreed to preach."

Huh? My dad, preach? I almost smirked when Rob said that. Of course, Dad was a university English professor with a doctorate. Maybe a couple of them. He was also a sincere, Bible-toting Christian. But would those things qualify him as a preacher?

Then I thought about what I'd learned in Santa María. The only qualification for anything God asked was faithful obedience. What was that saying? Something like, *"God doesn't call the qualified; He qualifies the called."*

Still, what if Dad's mild-mannered temperament carried over into his public speaking? I couldn't imagine those rough-and-tough insiders politely ignoring a speaker they found disappointing. *Boring* was probably high on their list of don't-you-dares.

And was Dad up-to-date on political correctness? Would he say something he thought was innocent and get us all into trouble? How much motivation would these insiders need to beat us up or to. . . ?

I don't think Rob noticed that I'd started trembling.

Of course, death might not be that bad. Dad and I would make a premature trip to heaven, reunite with Mom, and live not just happily ever after, but eternally so. My responsibility for Mom's death wouldn't matter anymore. In fact, we wouldn't remember any of the bad from our earthly lives.

Yes, death might be a good thing, although I wasn't very comfortable imagining what dying might feel like. Especially at the hands of a group of rowdy insiders at a place like Red Cedar Correctional Center.

But we'd have armed guards protecting us, wouldn't we? Heavily armed. And wouldn't the insiders be handcuffed? For that matter, wouldn't we hold the services in the passageways between the rows of cells? Where the insiders couldn't reach us. . .unless we stepped close enough for a strong arm to grab an unsuspecting victim through the bars.

Me, probably.

My anxiety gave way to panic. That scenario might not have matched the one in my second nightmare, but it came close enough to make me start trembling uncontrollably.

Was this God's punishment for what I'd done to Mom?

chapter twenty-six

Rob asked Jo to help him clean out one unit. "I want to get to know you better."

Graham, on the other hand, announced his plans to give his apartment a second coat of paint that day, starting with the room we'd slept in.

Mister O'Reilly, if you enjoy being a loner, that's fine with me. But if you don't want us staying in your apartment and sharing your bathroom, why don't you just say so? You don't have to exterminate us with paint fumes as if we were two white rats—because I had only a tinge of Mom's coloration and no Asian facial features, nobody ever thought of me as half Vietnamese—and a black one.

Dad was working on a unit by himself, leaving Aleesha and me to work together. We'd picked the unit that most appealed to us—the one in the right-hand corner of the U, adjacent to Graham's apartment. It seemed like the safest one. We would move our sleeping bags and suitcases in as soon as we de-junked it.

What a difference from the churchyard cleanup in Santa Maria. That rubbish—up to two feet deep in places—had consisted of unknown materials, many of which were awkward, unpleasant, and even potentially dangerous to handle.

But at the hostel, we only needed to remove leftover materials, distinguishing between the "still usable" and the "beyond all hope"; to pick up spilled nails and put them in a bucket for future use; to rescue any hand tools that might still be lying around; and to sweep up. No one would have believed how deep the sawdust was; walking through it was like toeing my way through sand at the beach.

After doing all of that, we'd brush off the walls—the ceiling, too—with a wide, long-handled broom and sweep the floors again. Only then would the unit be ready to paint.

"You'll probably want to clean out all the units before doing any painting," Rob told us; but since his comment had only been a suggestion, Aleesha and I proposed an alternative plan.

"Why not paint as soon as we finish cleaning each unit?" she said.

"That way," I explained, "the rooms won't get dirty again before we paint them."

Rob nodded. We couldn't fool him, though. "Besides, it'll give you a welcome break from cleaning up."

I winked at him.

"Great idea, Kimmy, but you're missing a step." I shot him a questioning glance. "I left a step out in describing your job duties, I mean. I need to teach you to look at these units the way the building inspector will. Hopefully, you'll catch little things that need fixing before he does. Once a unit is inspection-ready, you can paint it. You'll need your keenest eyes and your most critical, judgmental spirit."

Good thing we're not inspecting people. That assignment wouldn't sound very Christlike.

He spent a good hour showing us the kinds of things to look for. I would've taken notes if I'd had any paper on me. I still had the marker Santa María team members had used on my beloved purple cast, but my bare arms wouldn't have begun to hold everything he told us. So I'd have to rely on Aleesha's memory, which was vastly more dependable than mine.

Rob left to find Jo, and we were finally on our own.

"How long do you think this unit will take?" I asked Aleesha.

"Uh. . ." She appeared to be measuring the dimensions of

the unit with her eyes. "Maybe three or four hours to clean up. I don't know how long to inspect."

I'd *hoped* she would say just two or three hours. I *wanted* her to say only one or two, but—even as naive as I was—I knew that was wishful thinking.

"Where do we start?"

"Anywhere." She looked around. "Everywhere."

Working our way in from the doorway made the most sense. We weren't stupid enough to trample over the stuff near the door to reach and remove junk that was farther inside.

"It's like widening the path to the Passover Church in Santa María, huh, girl?"

I nodded, but then discovered she wasn't looking.

"I'm going to start with these sheets of plywood." I tried to find a good place to grasp something that was ten times bigger than me. "They're in the way."

When Aleesha saw me struggling, she started to pick up the other end. "One at a time, girl," she said, chuckling at me and letting the other four sheets fall back to the floor.

I was thankful for her help. I'd forgotten how heavy and awkward even one sheet of plywood was. Once we got the first sheet to the doorway, we maneuvered it onto the wheelbarrow Rob had left outside for us. After watching me nearly dump the load twice, Aleesha pried my hands away from the handles.

She shook her head. "I hope you drive a car better than this, girl." She wasn't smiling.

She pushed the wheelbarrow to the area Rob had designated. He'd hand-painted simple signs indicating where each kind of material belonged. We lifted the plywood off the wheelbarrow and leaned it neatly in place.

After working our way almost to the far side of the room, Aleesha and I stopped for a breather. Although I hadn't been conscious of exerting much effort, I was perspiring. No, as drenched as I was, I was sweating. And this was early winter in the mountains. The temp might not have been freezing cold, but it wasn't the least warm, either.

"You didn't have any nightmares last night?"

I shook my head.

"That's good. I kept waking up and praying you wouldn't."

My parents had probably stayed awake worrying about me a number of times. Like when I was sick with a high fever or out driving by myself after I first got my license. Or out on a date. But Aleesha had gone beyond the call of both duty and friendship. She wasn't just a best friend who'd gone the second mile. She was my sister in Christ, a sister who'd never thought about counting the miles.

I gave her a hug.

"What's that for, girl?"

"Just because you're you, you're special, and I love you."

She didn't just smile. She glowed. "Are you tired today?" She must have wanted to make sure the nightmare on the plane hadn't caused a relapse.

"Exhausted," I said, mustering all the seriousness I could. "I can barely wiggle enough to place one foot in front of the other. Can't you tell?" I gave Aleesha just enough time to frown. "Sleeping so much later than I was supposed to has worn me out completely."

She stared at me for a moment, and then we both started howling. "Tomorrow. . .the right time. . .regardless of. . .what Mr. Rob says," she said, her series of unceremonious guffaws chopping her sentence into pieces. While I wouldn't describe her laughter as totally raucous, I doubted that the hostel had any mice left by the time she calmed down again.

"What do you think about going to the Correctional Center?" I said. I'd put the fears out of my head for a while, but that was like putting bread in a toaster and pushing the lever. It always popped up again.

"About going *to* prison?" Aleesha said, laughing again. "I'd just as soon stay on the straight and narrow, if you don't mind. Being on God's good side is safer than the consequences of straying. Especially *that* far."

I noticed Graham leaning against the doorway and examining a small piece of paper. He appeared to be reading it over and over, and I couldn't help wondering how literate he was. If he read like he talked. . .

Oh, you dodo! What about all of those books he has? He must be a voracious reader.

What was he doing in the doorway, though—eavesdropping? That thought almost freaked me out. Rob wouldn't have placed him in such a responsible position if he weren't trustworthy. That fact should have calmed me down, but it didn't.

A moment later, Graham looked up and saw me staring at him. He disappeared from sight so quickly I almost thought he'd been an apparition.

I was glad he was gone, though.

"You silly thing!" I said to Aleesha. I'd almost forgotten what we were talking about. "I meant how do you feel about *doing* worship services there."

"I've done prison ministry before," she said. "You'll really enjoy it."

Enjoy? Here I am scared to death of even going, and you're telling me I'll enjoy it? Can't you hear my heart pounding its way out of my body?

"Jo's the one I'm concerned about," Aleesha said. "As sheltered as her life has been, she'll probably be petrified." She hesitated. "It won't help that a number of the insiders are minorities—nowhere close to all of them are African-American, though—and I don't have to tell you how she feels about us more darkly colored Americans."

While I kept hoping that Aleesha was wrong about Jo having "the smell," I couldn't pretend that Jo had gone out of her way to interact with Aleesha. If anything, their relationship had drifted somewhere in the direction of mutual tolerance.

I used to believe tolerance was a desirable attitude, but now I believed it was neutral—no more positive than a *C* on a report card. Like the New Testament church God accused of being lukewarm—"neither hot nor cold."

I understood tolerance, though. But what did I know about prejudice?

I'd been in a minority setting only once in my life—one of a handful of white viewers at the well-attended screening of a movie featuring a mostly African-American cast. Although I wasn't scared, I felt extremely self-conscious about my minority status. But I wasn't aware of any hostility.

I couldn't deny that Jo had a problem or that it might have been race related. But I wondered whether it had more to do with Aleesha herself. Could Aleesha's smell-detector make that kind of distinction?

chapter twenty-seven

Graham cooked spaghetti for supper. Was pasta a particular favorite of his? He'd made a number of pans of the previous night's lasagna from scratch and frozen them a week earlier. His spaghetti sauce was homemade, too, and it was the best I'd ever eaten.

Superior—*I admit it, Graham*—superior even to Mom's. Truth be known, though, she'd been better at opening cans and jars than cooking from scratch. But I'd loved her cooking, and I missed it. If I hadn't. . .if I hadn't killed her, I'd still be enjoying it.

When I asked him where he learned to cook like that, he just shrugged. But he actually smiled—just slightly—when I told him he ought to start a cooking school. I told him I wanted to become his first student.

If I was going to take care of Dad when we got home, I needed lessons from somebody.

Although Graham still struck me as a bit strange—and a lot mysterious—he was growing on me. I hefted a quick prayer heavenward asking that I might learn to love and accept him before returning home. I was hesitant to pray that I might also learn to understand him, but God told me—through feelings I couldn't misinterpret—to add that as a postscript to my prayer.

And so I did.

We were about to push away from the smallish table— fitting the six of us there had been a challenge from the get-go—when Rob clinked his glass with a spoon. We settled back and gave him our overly full attention.

"We're scheduled to hold our first worship service at Red Cedar Correctional Center at six thirty this evening."

Aleesha and I had been so busy painting the first unit and cleaning out a second one that afternoon that I'd actually forgotten about the prison ministry. Finally.

My stomach reacted faster than my brain. It jerked, gushing spaghetti sauce upward like oil from a newly drilled well. Fortunately, the journey was both short-lived and incomplete, and everything settled down peacefully again. Unfortunately, it left the most awful taste in my mouth, and I couldn't very well go gargle until Rob finished. That problem was getting old.

"If you looked for Scott this afternoon and couldn't find him, that's because he went with me to make the arrangements. Then I gave him the rest of the afternoon to work on his talk. The warden suggested not calling them sermons here. Sounds too churchy."

"And too long-winded," Aleesha said with a mischievous grin.

"Rob," Dad said, "aren't you going to tell them?"

Rob looked like Dad might have just yanked the rug he was standing on. Or painted him into a corner he didn't want to be in.

What the. . . ?

"Only some of it, of course," Dad said, apparently realizing he'd said something he probably wasn't supposed to mention. "Just enough. . .in case they, uh, notice anything."

Rob's single sigh could have blown out every candle on a hundred centenarians' birthday cakes. Simultaneously.

"I guess you're wondering what we're talking about. . .uh, not talking about," Rob said, examining each of our faces in turn. Although he didn't even glance at Graham, the old man was staring at him. Hard enough to drive nails.

Although Jo, Aleesha, and I nodded, Rob's initial reaction

to Dad's slip kept us from revealing the extent of our curiosity.

"We spent some time talking with Warden Jenkins," Rob said. "He's a Christian brother and a fine fellow. He referred us to Chaplain Thomas, who's been working with prisoners for probably as many years as some of the long-termers have been incarcerated. He's worked at Red Cedar the twenty years it's been in existence."

I scrunched one eye. *What does all this have to do with the price of tea in China, as Mom likes. . .liked to say?*

Rob must have noticed the expression on my face. "Hang in there. You'll see the relevance of this shortly." He reminded me of a movie defense lawyer asking the judge to overrule the prosecution's objection to a seemingly irrelevant question. "When Scott and I went to see Chaplain Thomas, we expected him to be warm and friendly, welcoming of fellow Christians, and grateful for our interest in ministering to these insiders."

Of course. A Christian chaplain would be an idiot not to respond that way.

"Seems we were wrong. Our plans obviously displeased him, and he immediately started spouting off a number of rules and regulations that might have fooled uneducated visitors into thinking they couldn't hold a worship service there. But we knew he was talking baloney. Those regulations had nothing to do with us."

I couldn't have taken my eyes off Rob if someone had yelled, *"Fire!"*

"The long and the short of it is he told us to stay away from Red Cedar. He doesn't want us to meet any of 'his men.' He says some of them are unstable, and he's the only one who can handle them. Outsiders would be certain to disturb them."

I didn't realize how tense Rob's news had made me until I noticed a spot of blood on my hand. I'd hugged myself so tight I jabbed a hole in my arm with a fingernail.

"'So you're not going to be able to come,' Thomas told us. 'Not tonight. Not anytime.'"

Graham didn't seem so strange anymore. Not compared to this Thomas guy. If I'd thought Thomas would be an idiot not to welcome fellow Christian brothers and sisters, I had to wonder now if the man was even a Christian. Wasn't that a job requirement for a chaplain? A Christian one, anyhow. Maybe I should have slapped myself for being so judgmental, but what was I supposed to think about a man who didn't even talk the talk, much less walk the walk? Was he part of the local mission field, too?

"So what did you do?" Aleesha asked.

"We went back to Warden Jenkins. Our report didn't surprise him. He told us he didn't forewarn us because he wanted us to form our own opinions. Objective ones."

"And your objective opinions are this chaplain guy is a creep?" Aleesha said. Her normal smile had morphed into a vicious frown. She wasn't shy about expressing her opinions, and they were usually spot-on.

Rob smiled. "I wouldn't have put it quite that way, but yes." He rubbed his forehead as if trying to massage the next few words out of his brain. "There's more to the story than this, but I've told you all I can. The warden has sworn us to secrecy."

Aleesha, Jo, and I looked at one another before looking at Rob again.

"One more thing, though. The warden wants us to keep an eye on the interactions between Chaplain Thomas and the insiders."

"What. . . ?" Whoever said that spoke for all of us.

"Don't ask. We can't tell you more than that."

I rolled my eyes. *Fine. If you can't trust us to keep a secret, so be it.*

Aleesha caught my eye. I couldn't tell what she was mouthing, but I couldn't have missed her meaning: *Quit fretting. The warden trusts Mr. Rob and Mr. Scott to keep* his *secret.*

I sighed. She was right. She was almost always right, and it got so frustrating sometimes.

"Bottom line time," Aleesha said. "We *are* going to the prison tonight?"

"I'm not," Jo said in a flippant, almost boastful tone. "Graham asked me to help him with something."

Rob narrowed his eyes and looked at her, but he didn't say anything. Not to her specifically, that was.

"The Warden says we're in. As long as he's in charge and Chaplain Thomas works for him, all Christian groups are welcome. Our coming wouldn't be so important, but not even the hostel's sponsoring churches are geographically close enough to do a regular prison ministry at Red Cedar. We'll be in the area for two weeks, and he plans to work us hard."

"If you've had teams doing construction for several weeks," Aleesha said, "why didn't *they* have run-ins with the chaplain?"

"They were doing hard labor compared to you. Because their daily work wore them out so much, I didn't feel I should ask them to do anything extra. I didn't even bring up the idea of prison ministry."

Hmm. Sounds like you want to make sure our trip here is worthwhile.

"Besides that, they didn't have the variety of abilities you four have."

As scared as I'd been of visiting the prison, I couldn't help cheering because God was more powerful than the chaplain's best efforts to keep us away. That, plus we'd get to use our evangelistic skills.

Aleesha applauded, too. She and I were on the same page. As usual.

Rob started passing out papers. "The warden says you need to complete these visitor questionnaire forms before we get there tonight. It normally takes thirty days to get them approved, but he jumped through a number of hoops—I think he had to go through the big boss of the California prison system or maybe the governor himself—to get permission for us to come on such short notice. Without official preapproval."

I gave him a questioning look when I noticed he didn't start completing one of the forms. "Scott and I have already turned ours in."

Oh.

"I don't need—"

"You *do* need, Jo," Rob broke in. "Before you work on your form, you and I are going to have a private conversation about your proposed plans. *If* I let you help Graham—don't get your hopes up about that—tonight's the *only* night you'll do it. You'll be with us every time we go to the prison, and you'll ask me before attempting to schedule any change of activity."

My word! I hadn't heard Rob talk so tough since he threatened to send his own nephew Geoff home from Santa María for destroying the rock garden Anjelita and I had worked so hard on.

"Yes, sir." Although Jo's response sounded humble and contrite, I caught a hint of resentment Rob might have missed hearing. He didn't know Jo the way I did.

I asked Dad for a pen and started filling in my form while Rob and Jo went into the living room to talk. Her face was scarlet when they came back in the kitchen, but she sat down without saying a word and reached for the pen I'd just finished using. As hard as she was bearing down with it, I was afraid she might dig a hole in Graham's new wooden table.

Flashback time again. This time of an unharmonious mission team. I hoped Jo wouldn't do more harm than good by participating in the service.

chapter twenty-eight

It was only 5:40 p.m., and we weren't going to the prison for at least another thirty-five minutes.

"Where are you going, sweetie?" Dad asked as I pulled on my down-filled jacket. I'd never needed anything that warm at home. I probably looked like a mouse wrapped in a king-sized quilt, but I'd bought a larger size than I normally wore so I'd have plenty of room to dress in layers.

I hugged him. I ate up his expressions of affection now, although I still couldn't understand the timing of his transformation from a near-neutral dad to a terrific one. Surely Mom's death hadn't made him happy.

Especially considering what Aleesha had told me about his feelings of guilt. But I assumed he was over that. I had more of a reason to feel guilty than he did. I had no doubt that I'd caused the accident, but he couldn't be equally positive about his ability to prevent it.

"Going for a little walk," I said.

"You want some company?"

I hated to turn him down, but I needed some me-time. "Dad, I'd love for you to come, but I. . .well, I need to do some praying."

"We can pray together," he said. Oh, did he want to come with me! I felt twice as bad as before. "We can prayer-walk Red Cedar Lane if you like."

Great idea. Although I'd heard about prayer-walking, I'd never tried it. But now wasn't the time to start. Not with a partner, anyhow.

"Tomorrow evening, okay?" How could I make things

clear without hurting his feelings? "I need some private prayer time now."

I felt like I'd just kicked a gaping hole in some little kid's intricate sand castle, but Dad pretended to understand. I hugged him again.

"Great idea about Red Cedar Lane, though. That should be a safer place to walk at night than that dark, twisty two-lane road we took to get here."

He smiled.

"Besides, if I'm not back by the time to go, you can pick me up along the way."

"You have a flashlight?" Rob said as he walked into the room. He must have caught the tail end of my talk with Dad.

"Some strange old man e-mailed us and told us to bring flashlights or else," I said with a cackle. "I didn't have the courage to face the 'or else.'"

"Tell him the truth, Kim," Dad goaded me playfully. "I made sure we had everything that was on Rob's list. All you would have packed was jewelry and makeup."

He winked at me, and I zipped and snapped my jacket as loudly as I could in protest. But when I giggled once and then chuckled, he gave me a curious look.

"Haven't you ever wondered what I'd look like fat?" I asked. "I have."

Dad, Rob, and Aleesha were still laughing their heads off when I stepped outside and turned on my flashlight.

The temperature had already dropped—I could see my breath—but my jacket felt wonderful. After looking both ways—I'd bet no cars had passed that way in hours—I crossed the highway and looked down the long, dark, lonely looking prison road. *Red Cedar Lane* sounded too elegant to be the entranceway to a prison complex.

As I commenced my walk—actually more of a casual

stroll—I started thinking about Jo, Aleesha, Graham, and the prison ministry and wondering why our small team had so many relational problems. I'd once taken a short, introductory sociology class as an elective, and I still remembered the basics of an activity that involved drawing solid lines connecting individuals to the members of the group they felt the most comfortable with. And dotted lines for less desirable relationships.

I'd try something like that in my head. My version wouldn't be very scientific, though. Done correctly, the information should come from careful, unbiased observations made over a number of months. I'd have to base mine on limited—and not necessarily objective—observations.

That, and woman's intuition—and mine hadn't finished maturing yet.

A solid line would link me to Dad, Aleesha, and Rob since our relationships were excellent, but my line to Jo. . . That link wasn't as strong as it could be. My link to Graham didn't even merit a line, no matter how I hoped that would change.

Dad seemed to link equally well to Rob, Aleesha, and me. I couldn't tell how he related to Jo. I hadn't seen him make any effort to speak to Graham.

Rob related well to everyone but Jo. He related to Graham better than anyone else did. And Graham related only to Rob.

Or was that entirely accurate? If Graham had asked for Jo's help when he wouldn't say boo to the rest of us girls, maybe they at least had a dotted-line relationship.

Jo seemed to have a dotted line with both Aleesha and me. A limited comfort level with Aleesha made sense, but I couldn't understand why Jo and I hadn't been closer on this trip. I thought we'd reestablished a good relationship before coming, but something had changed.

And even before Rob lectured her earlier, she seemed

unable or unwilling to get close to him. Did she even have a dotted-line relationship with him?

I doubted it.

My analysis was driving me nuts and getting me nowhere. Besides that, I'd told Dad I wanted to pray, and that's what I needed to do. I'd probably walked halfway from the two-lane road to the prison buildings by now, but I still had time. So I started praying.

Aloud. Talking as if another human being was listening helped me experience a greater sense of God's presence. After all, Jesus was both God and human.

"Lord, thank You for this crisp, cool night and all the stars I can see without being able to count them. The lights back home are so bright I can't see them this clearly. Thanks for the reminder that it's Your world, Your universe, and You made it perfect, even if mankind messed it up by sinning. Somebody eventually puts a ding in the new car, but Adam and Eve totaled it before it even left the dealership.

"This mission trip is Yours, too. You called us here to complete the Welcoming Arms Hostel, but I believe You expect more from us than that. I don't have to tell You that our team isn't pulling together the way it should. I don't know what the problem is.

"You know, though.

"Maybe I'm not supposed to know. Or even to try to figure it out. Am I supposed to just do my part and leave the rest to You? I'd love to do that, but I need Your help to quit fretting about our problems. I can't do that on my own.

"And why do I have such an unsettled feeling about Jo? I was thrilled she could come, and her enthusiasm seemed genuine at the time. Yet now that she's away from home, she's a different person. I don't get it. She isn't homesick, is she, Lord? Is it something that simple?

"I don't recall her ever being away from home very often—not without her parents, that is—and that was only for local mission trips. Like to the beach. Come to think of it, she was on the phone with her mother every time I turned around. I've seen her get out her cell phone here, but I haven't heard her talking on it.

"Lord, hold on a second. . ." I pulled my phone from my purse and powered it on. "Whoopsy doodle! No bars. My phone can't find a network to connect to. Is that part of Your plan for these beautiful mountains of Yours—no cell phone coverage? If Jo's homesick and can't call home. . .is that why she's acting so strange? Do You want me to talk with her about that?

"You also know that Graham O'Reilly is another of my concerns. I know, I've been unfairly critical of him. Mostly because I can't figure him out. The reason doesn't matter, though. I'm just sorry about it, and I ask Your forgiveness. I'd ask his forgiveness, too, if he knew how I've felt. I guess he has problems, too, but I don't know if I'll ever be able to talk with him.

"Ha! How right You are, Lord. I don't know if he'll ever be willing and able to talk with me, either. About anything. But if he does, please open my heart. Let me be receptive, and please keep me from being judgmental."

I stopped walking and leaned against the split-rail wooden fence that ran parallel to Red Cedar Lane.

"Speaking of having an open heart and not being judgmental—You know what I want to talk to You about next, don't You, Lord? Please strengthen me and soften my heart and spirit as we do this service tonight. You know how terrified I've been today. Off and on. Part of it's my fear of the unknown. I experienced some of that before leaving for Mexico, but You're the only one I ever told about it.

"This fear is different, though. These insiders are *men*.

They probably haven't been near a woman in years. And some of them may not be petty thieves or white-collar criminals. They may be guilty of violent crimes, and some of them may be lifers.

"You know the figures Rob told me this afternoon. The insiders are almost evenly divided between black and white, with a much smaller number of Latinos, Asians, and American Indians. He didn't think the warden would permit anyone from death row to participate in our services, but he wasn't sure.

"Lord, I'm not telling You anything You don't already know. You know every person in that prison—the staff as well as the insiders. You know their offenses. You know their hearts. You know who already has a right relationship with You and who doesn't. You know who's sincere in professing Christianity and who's just pretending.

"And You know what's going to happen tonight. You know who'll attend the service and how each person will respond. You know our apprehensions. . .okay, *my* apprehensions. You know whether we'll be safe here or whether Dad and I will join Mom in heaven tonight.

"Please fill my tank with high-octane calm. Or should I say low-octane? Remind me that I'm obeying You, just like I tried to do in Santa María. Maybe the problem is I don't feel worthy to be part of this. Not after what I did to Mom. I feel like I belong in there. . .well, in a women's prison, anyhow. I really need Your help dealing with that.

"I feel like I'm slip-sliding on those pebbles again, and I don't know if I'm going to prance or fall. Lord, I'm trying to trust You. I want to be victorious. I'm trying to leave things in Your hands, but it's not easy. . ."

I resumed my walk along Red Cedar Drive and continued praying aloud. It helped. A lot. Maybe I prayed about the same concerns over and over, but at least I ended up with a positive attitude about tonight's prison ministry.

Just then, a voice spoke to me from the darkness—somewhere to my right. Not more than seven or eight feet away, and I could barely steady my hands to focus my flashlight in that direction.

Or would I need to use it as a weapon?

chapter twenty-nine

*L*ord? *That's not You, is it? I don't see a burning bush.*
"You okay. Me here."

"Graham? You scared me to death." The way my heart was pounding, I felt like an atomic bomb had exploded inside my chest.

"Alongside. Whole walk. Keep watch."

It took me a few seconds to interpret what he'd said. "Rob didn't send you?"

"No." He lowered his volume a few more notches from shy-quiet to a reverent near-whisper. "God."

I hadn't expected an answer like that. "Thank you, Graham."

"Thank God." He obviously meant it.

Although those two simple words made me feel like crying, the still-trembling part of me wanted to lash out and say, *"But did you have to scare me to death like that? You could have guarded me just as well without letting me know you'd ever been nearby."*

But God had something to say to me about my ingratitude. *"Kim—or shall I call you Kimmy to remind you who's still in charge?—you asked Me to open your heart to Graham. Did you mean it or not? Here's your chance. I'm not promising you a second one."*

You know how to make a girl feel bad, don't You, Lord? I sighed.

"Graham, God may have asked you to come, but you didn't have to obey Him. By doing it, though, you've set a good example for me in my efforts to mature as a Christian."

I paused. No matter how sincere I'd been, my words probably sounded corny. Did I dare to try again? If this was the only chance God was giving me, I needed to. "I hope we get to know one another better while I'm here. I'm friends with everyone on the team but you, and I'd like to change that."

The only detectable response was the sound of muffled sniffling. If my words had somehow touched that strange old man, I could only pray that this evening's contact would be the first one, not the only one.

Before I could say anything else, though, he was gone. As the van pulled up beside me, Rob lowered the window.

"Where did he go?" I said. "Did you see him? He was right here."

"If you were talking to someone," he said, "he must have been a ghost. I could see you from a hundred yards away, and you were all by your lonesome."

I was too dumbfounded to explain. Maybe this was one of those things to keep in my heart and reflect on. The way Mary thought about Jesus' childhood words of wisdom after she and Joseph found Him in the temple.

"Get in, Kimmy. Let's go for a ride."

Rob drove another twenty or thirty yards up Red Cedar Lane and pulled into a visitor spot in the main parking lot. We followed him into a well-lit building that looked far too attractive to be part of a prison.

Racial stereotypes weren't the only kind.

"I learned something a few minutes ago when I called the warden—"

"You get cell phone coverage here?" Jo asked, her voice more chipper than it had been right after supper.

Ah. Maybe I was right.

Although Rob chuckled a time or two, his response was gentle. "Afraid not, Jo. That's why I brought the satellite phone on this project. Works anywhere in the world."

He must have seen the hungry—no, the starving—look on Jo's face. I couldn't think of a better word to describe it. "No free minutes on that thing, though, but I wouldn't mind letting you call home a time or two if you hold it down to five or ten minutes."

I forgot to breathe for a minute when Jo threw her arms around Rob and kissed him on the cheek. Not once, but three or four times.

Well done, Lord. You've already answered part of my prayer. I winked toward the sky as I drew a solid line between Rob and Jo on my imaginary relationship chart. I wondered if this would also make the line between Jo and me solid.

"Mr. Rob," Aleesha said. As uncharacteristically quiet as she'd been the last few minutes, I'd almost forgotten she was there. "What about in here?"

Rob looked at her as if she'd just announced she was a space alien.

"They have phones inside the prison. . ."

"Right!" The now-why-didn't-I-think-of-that look on Rob's face made me giggle. "Why don't we check with the warden? The office may have an 800-line he'd let you use in the privacy of somebody's office. I think he could rationalize a call home as facility-related."

Jo's transformation was nothing short of miraculous. She caught Rob off balance when she hugged him again, almost knocking him down.

"Kimmy," Rob said, "I know you've been worried about tonight"—*Rob, the word is* petrified, *but my prayer time has helped a lot*—"but I have some news that ought to please you. Some of what I told you earlier was wrong."

I searched his face for clues as I waited for him to continue. My heart rate had already begun accelerating, but more with hope this time than anxiety.

"The Red Cedar facility is a medium-security prison. Now, that is. It was maximum security when it first opened."

Come on, Rob. Spit it out. How is this supposed to make me feel better?

"Kimmy, we'll be leading worship with relatively minor offenders."

"Minor?" Had I heard him correctly? I could hardly believe how quickly God had answered that part of my prayer, too.

"Some of them are serving lengthy sentences, but you won't see any murderers, rapists, or animal abusers in the crowd. No one you should feel frightened of."

I was speechless.

"One other thing."

I raised my eyebrows in expectation.

"Warden Jenkins pointed out that the insiders have a great respect for women of all ages. They wouldn't be any more disrespectful of you, Jo, or Aleesha than of their own mothers."

I started squealing with relief. Before I knew what was happening, Aleesha was shaking me and talking excitedly. "You see, girl? You were worried over nothing. You should have spent that time and energy praying."

I smiled. I could hardly wait to tell her I had prayed. And to rave about what phenomenal answers God had already provided.

chapter thirty

Warden Jenkins met us at the visitors' desk of the administration building. As we introduced ourselves, he welcomed us by name. He would undoubtedly be able to address each of us by name for the duration of our visit to Red Cedar. I envied people who could remember names easily when I struggled so hard at times to remember my own.

"Do you know the insiders individually?" I asked.

God does, but you're not God. I don't know why that thought ran through my head. Maybe because the warden held the fate of so many men in his hands day in and day out.

"Kimmy"—*oh, no, you've already caught it from Rob!*—"I know most of them by name. Although my job requires a certain amount of that, I've gotten to know many of the men better than I have to. Family problems. Personal needs. Things like that. Allows me to live out my Christian witness on the job. I know the troublemakers and the most troubled far better than I do anyone else, though."

"Like in school," I said. "One of my favorite teachers used to say she could remember every exceptional student she'd ever taught—both the best and the worst."

"Same principle." He shook his head as if wishing it weren't true.

"Well, team," Rob said, "visiting with this fine Christian brother is good, but that's not what we're here for. He's already saved, even if he does belong to a different denomination than mine."

Aleesha howled with laughter, and that set off a chain

reaction among everyone within hearing distance. If only Mom could have known Aleesha. She loved to laugh. But I put an end to that.

Once we calmed down, Warden Jenkins took the floor again. "You all have your Form 106 Visitor Questionnaires? And a photo ID?" We three girls handed him our papers. Jo and I gave him drivers' licenses, but Aleesha handed him a passport.

I glanced at it. The picture showed the innocent-angel-look that had tickled me several times in Santa María. I couldn't keep from giggling. Aleesha grinned at me. She knew why I was laughing.

"Hmm," the warden said as he glanced over the paperwork and verified that we were who we claimed to be, "everyone is eighteen or older. No arrests or convictions. No points on your licenses, either. Good for you, girls."

Aleesha leaned over to me and whispered, "And why do you think I used my passport instead of my license?" We both giggled.

"Everything appears to be in order. I need to make a copy of your IDs—just a little extra protection for you. And for me, too. I had to get special permission to let you visit here on such short notice." I smiled at his modesty about the hoops he'd had to jump through. "Oh, I don't suppose you just happened to bring fingerprint sheets with you?"

He winked at us, but that didn't keep our eyes from opening wide. Even Dad and Rob's. A few butterflies flitted around in my stomach, but that was less obnoxious than nausea.

He couldn't have missed seeing our reactions. "We'll take care of that little detail before I walk you over to the building you'll hold your service in. While they're patting you down and checking you over with a metal detector, I'll buzz Chaplain Thomas and have him come meet you. He's supposed to remain with you throughout your visit."

Don't knock yourself out, Chaplain Thomas. We'd feel less inhibited without you.

"Larry," Rob said, "we told the girls a little of what you shared with us, but nothing about your, uh, specific. . . concerns." I thought he was going to say *suspicions.* "Scott and I thought having them keep an eye on Chaplain Thomas might prove helpful."

Warden Jenkins' demeanor didn't change. No signs of distress. "Good idea, Rob." He handed each of us a clip-on visitor pass. "Keep these on at all times. Without them, we can't let you out again. Guard them with your lives." He must have seen my face tighten. "Not literally, of course, but we can't let an insider get hold of one. He could use it to attempt to escape. Of course, we've never had an escape here."

My muscles relaxed again.

"Any questions before we go in?"

I looked at my purse. So did the warden.

"Oh, and you ladies won't be able to take your purses. Gentlemen, you might as well empty your pockets. Ladies, too, if you have pockets. These insiders can find the most ingenious uses for the least offensive-looking items. You can leave your things in my office. I promise they'll be safe. I'll be here until you leave."

Aleesha scrunched her forehead. I had no idea what she was thinking.

But the warden did. "Storing your things here is one step less complicated than using the lockers regular visitors use."

She nodded, apparently satisfied.

I took the Bible out of my purse. "What about. . . ?"

"Oh, Bibles are fine. But when they pat you down, they'll examine your Bible to make sure you're not trying to smuggle contraband."

He winked at us.

I remembered a kid in high school who'd gutted the inside of an ordinary looking book to make a hiding place for cigarettes and a lighter. He never had a chance to smoke in school—he couldn't find a safe place to—but he always had that book with him. He made me sick the way he boasted about beating the system.

I wouldn't be surprised to learn he'd ended up in some Georgia state prison.

After we deposited our valuables and invaluables in Warden Jenkins' office, he led us to an inside area near the prison building entrance. On the way, he explained that visitors like us didn't have to endure all the indignities of regular visitors, but he didn't elaborate.

A quick change of subjects caught me off guard at first. "One of my major concerns as a Christian," he said, "is that the separation of church and state might eventually interfere with church groups being able to do prison ministry."

"But it's voluntary, isn't it?" Jo asked. "Nobody *has* to attend our services."

"True." He sighed. "But where do we draw the line about what groups we allow to minister to the prisoners?"

"No Satan worshippers, huh?" Dad said. I started to laugh, but then I saw that he was serious.

"Can't you just have somebody monitor the services?" Jo said. "And make sure nobody teaches terrorism to the—?"

"Now, Jo," Dad said in his best Daddy-the-Reprover voice, "we can't go around accusing other religions of teaching terrorism just because we don't agree with their beliefs."

"Besides that," Warden Jenkins said, "you wouldn't believe what every inmate here teaches his cell mates and buddies about better and more effective ways to commit every imaginable kind of crime. Each one may come in with limited criminal skills, but he leaves with immeasurably more. If that fact weren't so tragic, referring to their interaction as cross-training might be amusing."

I shook my head in disbelief. He'd given me more to think and pray about than he probably realized.

"You've all read the rules," he said before turning to head back to his office. "Please obey them."

Rules? Had I read any? I couldn't remember even one of them.

The bored-looking matron who patted me down giggled when she discovered that my chain-link belt was the culprit that had set the metal detector off.

"I'm supposed to make you take that off, baby," she said after touching it. "You know, so I can make sure it's just a belt. But since you're friends with Mr. Larry, I think I'll skip that step."

I wondered what kind of disciplinary action a breach of procedure like that could result in. But I sure wasn't going to be the one to tell on her.

"Thank goodness," I told her. "I need it. My hips aren't big enough to hold these jeans up, and I'd prefer not to lose them. . . especially here."

The matron looked uncertain about whether to laugh or not.

"I told you you're skinny," Aleesha said. She knew I didn't mind the teasing nearly as much as I minded being skinny.

The matron took her cue from Aleesha and guffawed in a most unrefined way, one that reminded me of Sandra Bullock's Miss Congeniality snort.

"I can do that better," Aleesha whispered in my ear. "Great actor that I am."

"But this woman's not acting," I whispered back. "I'm afraid she really laughs that way."

About that time, a humorless-looking man of fifty swaggered in as if the prison belonged to him. Padded with so much fat that he didn't appear to need outerwear, he reminded me of a bear that someone had awakened prematurely from a pleasant state of hibernation.

"Greetings, Rev. Thomas," the matron said in a pleasant, cheery voice. When the chaplain failed to acknowledge or return her greeting, she made a vulgar gesture as soon as he turned his back. I felt like cheering her—the man had been *so* rude—even though I would never have made such a gesture myself.

"You're the five outsiders Jenkins interrupted my work about, huh?" Good thing the matron had addressed him by name since he hadn't bothered to introduce himself. Like his attitude wasn't enough of an introduction.

None of us bothered to respond to his warm, friendly greeting. I wondered if he'd always been that unloving. Maybe dealing with insiders for so many years had eroded his optimism. I could almost understand that.

But why hadn't he let God renew him—so he could once again rise on wings like eagles and fly? Or had he quit "waiting upon the Lord" altogether?

He gave each of us a lengthy once-over—especially us girls—accompanied by a frown that would have permanently shriveled every impossible-to-kill weed in my backyard. He didn't make any effort to shake hands or to welcome us. We were evidently one more cross he'd been forced to bear. An unavoidable interruption to his busy evening.

"I'm Rob White. We're here to conduct a worship service." The chaplain didn't waste time with common courtesies. "I've already told you no. Why did you bother coming back? You can't come in, and that's final."

Although Rob had warned us about this guy's attitude, I

thought he'd been exaggerating.

He hadn't been.

"Sir," Rob said in his most diplomatic tone of voice, "Warden Jenkins told us we *can* come in. We wouldn't have gotten this far without his permission."

"I don't care how you got here. You've got to turn around and leave."

Man! He wasn't budging an inch. Not a centimeter, a millimeter, or a hairbreadth.

I looked at Rob. Steam might not have been rising from his ears, but I suspected he was losing some of his cool. I'd already lost all of mine, and I could barely keep from saying something I knew I'd regret. This was definitely a time to defer to the wisdom of my elders.

Rob must have sensed my anger, though. He held his right palm the way he might have hand-signaled an obedience-trained dog to stay. I bit my tongue so hard it would probably be sore for days after that.

"Ma'am," Rob addressed the matron, "would you please call Larry Jenkins and tell him Rob White and his group need some help getting in?"

She glanced at the chaplain, who looked like a balloon that might explode at any second. Then she said, "Gladly," and punched in a couple of numbers on her phone. She didn't do a very good job of hiding her smirk.

Frankly, neither did I.

A few minutes later, we stood just outside the final gate. The guard who'd accompanied us from our security check looked at our visitor badges once more and wrote down the numbers.

"Inside," he yelled as loudly as if he weren't speaking into an intercom. His no-nonsense voice reminded me of the bailiff's *"All rise!"* on courtroom TV shows.

A moment later, the gate swung open. He nodded toward a short inner passageway. Not until the heavy steel gate clanked shut behind us did I notice that we had to pass through an inner gate, too.

While I didn't panic, I couldn't miss the fact that we were isolated from both the inside and the outside. For now—hopefully a very brief now—we were neither fish nor fowl. We weren't "in" prison, but we weren't free, either. We couldn't go any farther unless someone opened the inside gate, yet we couldn't change our minds and return the way we'd come unless someone bellowed, "Outside!" and reopened the outer gate.

I had entered the portal to a foreign world, and I wasn't sure how I felt about it. Maybe the prospect of involuntary confinement between the two doors should have frightened me more than it did. Chaplain Thomas would have preferred keeping us at that distance, but the warden had demonstrated his power over Chaplain Thomas, and that made me feel safe.

Safer, anyhow.

At orientation for the Mexican mission trip, I'd felt trapped by the hostility of the other kids and to some extent by Rob and Charlie's initial questioning of my irresponsibility. But God had liberated me from that feeling, and I was counting on Him to do the same thing now.

chapter thirty-one

"Wow!" I said when we got back in the van two hours later. What else could I say? Our visit to Red Cedar couldn't have been the more complete opposite of what I'd dreaded. I didn't want to leave, and I could hardly wait to come back the next night.

From the excited buzzing that filled the van, I wasn't the only one who felt that way.

"They're such spirited singers," Aleesha said. "That skinny, bald fellow hit some of the lowest notes I've ever heard anyone sing."

"And what about that big guy with a voice like a woman's?" I said. "If that was falsetto, it was the best I've ever heard. So sweet and pure."

"Oh," Jo said, "I talked to him after the service. They call him Hi because of his voice, but he spells it H-i like the greeting."

"Huh?" I said.

"Not *huh*," Jo said, laughing. "*Hi*. And you're right. That wasn't falsetto. Hi is a countertenor—a man who sings naturally in a woman's range. He told me he had a lot of voice training in college."

"You can tell," Aleesha said. "Even I can't sing that well."

"And that's saying something, huh, girl?" I poked her on the arm. "But college? How'd somebody like him end up here, anyhow?"

"The same way all of the insiders did," Jo said. "He broke the law. He didn't say what he'd done, and I didn't ask."

"But Hi *is* a Christian, right?" I said.

"Since he was twelve. I did ask that."

"And he still did something *illegal*?" I'd naively assumed that Christians didn't become lawbreakers and that the worshippers at Red Cedar had all come to know Jesus after being locked up.

"'Let whoever is without sin cast the first stone,'" Aleesha quoted. "Every one of us is capable of breaking the law if we give in to a sufficiently serious temptation or let our guard down for even one brief second at the wrong time. The most sincere repentance won't erase the damage, whether our activity has been illegal or not. Neither will it free us from the appropriate punishment."

At the mention of punishment, my stomach jolted big-time. While I'd tried not dwelling on the way my mom's death made me feel, I could never escape the feeling of culpability for long. Aleesha had described my situation too well. I'd given in to the temptation to try calling Mom instead of being patient, and no amount of regret on my part was going to bring her back. I couldn't imagine ever being free from guilt over that.

"You girls have made some mature observations," Dad said. "I'm proud of you."

"Me, too," Rob said. "Aleesha, I knew you were a good singer, but you're a great preacher, too."

At first, I thought he'd referred to her monologue as Mary the mother of Jesus, but then I caught on that he was talking about what she'd said about Christians and criminals.

"Kimmy, I've never heard you sing before, but you're terrific. You picked just the right hymns, too."

"You can thank Aleesha for that," I said, trying to hide my frustration. "Every time I opened my hymnal to something *I* liked, she leaned over and said, 'They won't know that one.' But if you want to praise something I *did* do, I came up with the idea of asking for requests."

Aleesha hooted. "Girl, you and the insiders have different tastes for sure. But they loved your a capella solos."

"Yours, too."

"I hate to interrupt this meeting of the mutual admiration society," Dad said with a chuckle, "but how do you think my talk went over? I didn't notice anyone asking to go back to his cell while I was speaking. . ."

"I doubt they had that option," Rob said before anyone could answer Dad's question. Although the darkness hid Rob's face, we couldn't have missed the smile in his voice.

"Mr. Scott," Aleesha said. She sounded more wound up than usual, and that was saying a lot. "That talk of yours was something else. I watched those insiders while you preached, uh, delivered your meditation, and nobody looked bored or restless."

"Aleesha's right," Jo said. "They nodded in agreement—"

"And they *amen*ed all over the place," I said.

"Many of them had tears in their eyes at one part of your message or another."

"And didn't all ten of them respond to your invitation?" Rob said.

"They wanted to rededicate their lives," Dad said. "I was thankful for that, but I wish someone had made a first-time profession of faith."

I wasn't used to hearing my dad sound disappointed. I'd never thought of him as a potential failure. Or as someone who'd ever need his confidence bolstered. I still had so much to learn about him.

"Maybe nobody needed salvation." Aleesha's comment seemed to help Dad a little, but still. . .

"You wait," Rob said. "Now that those ten know what we're doing, I'll bet we have twice as many men tomorrow night. I have a feeling communication is better among the insiders than among the staff. At least the insiders don't have an official bureaucracy to hamper them."

Laughter filled the van.

"Jo," Aleesha said, "you speak Spanish pretty well, don't you?"

"I took it from eighth grade all the way through twelfth."

"She's great," I said. "If we'd had her in Santa María, I wouldn't have had to read the Gospel of Lucas."

Rob and Aleesha knew I wasn't serious. The trip probably wouldn't have been nearly as successful if Jo had read to the villagers instead of someone who didn't know how to pronounce Spanish. My ignorance had generated ever-increasing interest as various villagers taught me to pronounce their heart language correctly.

"Aleesha," Jo said, "why did you ask about my Spanish?"

"I was talking to one fellow who told me about a friend who'd wanted to come to the service. His English is pretty poor, though, and he was afraid he wouldn't understand much of what was going on. He's very shy because of that."

"Tell him to bring his friend," I said. "Jo will make sure he gets the full benefit of our services, won't you, Jo?"

"Please. I'll do my best."

"Sorry, but I can't," Aleesha said. I had a feeling she had a tease up her sleeve, but Jo didn't know her well enough yet to recognize the possibility.

"No. . . ?" Jo couldn't have sounded much more disappointed.

Aleesha spoke in her most serious voice. "I can't." Then she lightened up and giggled. "I already have."

I couldn't see what happened, but from the "ouch" I heard from Aleesha's side of the seat, Jo must have given her a playful thump.

No one spoke for a while, and my mind went back to

Aleesha's comment about crime and punishment. God had forgiven me for my mom's death. I believed that with all my heart and soul. But how could I forgive myself?

In Santa María, I'd been concerned about Geoff's inability to forgive himself for his sins. What I couldn't remember was how he finally conquered that problem. I wasn't sure exactly when his self-forgiveness occurred. Not unless. . .

Could it have happened that last night when he came and apologized? Had my spoken forgiveness been the thing that freed him?

Oh, great. My stomach started turning inside out at the realization I was in desperate need of the one thing I couldn't have.

Mom's forgiveness.

chapter thirty-two

"Kim? Kim!"

Jo was shaking me like an apple tree she wanted to get every last piece of fruit down from. I rolled over on her hand without realizing it, and she jerked it out again as quickly as she could. Aleesha grabbed the flashlight from Jo's other hand and beamed it away from my eyes.

"Kim, are you okay?"

Jo, have you always been this stubborn and persistent? I yawned in her face with middle-of-the-night breath. "Trying to. . .wake up."

I don't know if she understood my mumbling or not, but I desperately needed to finish waking up. This nightmare had been the worst one yet, and it still had me trembling. Along with Jo's efforts to wake me.

"Kim, speak to me. What's wrong?" Jo wasn't giving up. "Were you having a bad dream or what?"

Aleesha looked at me, but the shadows hid her expression. I had no doubt it was a mixture of concern over my nightmare and sympathy for my having to endure Jo's inquisitiveness.

"Maybe she doesn't feel like talking about it, Betsy Jo." She drew *Betsy Jo* out in a convincing Southern drawl. As if addressing Jo by her full name hadn't been an adequate warning to hush.

Her teeth shone extra white in the dim light, making her resemble an angry wolf baring her fangs to protect her young. Maybe she didn't mean to come across that heavy-handed, but—if Jo's defensive scowl was any indication—that was how she took it.

"She's *my* friend." Jo's tone of voice reminded me of Anjelita's reaction to the other children in Santa María when they got too close to me without going through her. "My *best* friend."

She looked at me for confirmation, but this latest nightmare had drained me too much to worry about who was whose best friend, much less to respond.

She looked at Aleesha and pointed her thumb at me. "She wouldn't keep anything from me." Then she shifted her eyes back to me. "Would you? Go ahead. Tell her, Kim."

I blinked. I couldn't take Jo's babbling until I finished waking up, and I was still trying to fight my way out of the creepy never-never land that held me as completely captive as if a fifty-foot, woman-eating plant were sitting on my stomach.

"Jo," Aleesha said and then stopped. From her tone, she might have been a mother about to address a selfish, petulant child. "What kind of person is more concerned about secrets than about a good—a best—friend having another horrible nightmare?"

Aleesha, I hope you didn't say what I think you said. Expect problems if you did.

Jo couldn't have looked more shocked if somebody had slapped her in the face with a live flounder.

"You're just jealous because Kim and I are better friends than the two of you."

I might have been struggling to gain control of my consciousness, but I was alert enough to recognize that Jo's comeback was totally-off-the-wall inappropriate. I was shocked; I'd never heard her express such jealousy and possessiveness.

Did she think her lifelong role as my guardian angel gave her the right to take control of my life? Perhaps even to try living her life through mine?

Aleesha was undoubtedly rolling her eyes. Since I couldn't see her face clearly, I assumed Jo couldn't, either. That was a good thing.

Not that I gave two cents about Jo's feelings right now. Her attitude had angered and hurt me—just as it had when she failed to come over right after Mom's death. Forgiveness was the last thing on my mind.

So help me if she didn't do a double take before Aleesha or I could respond.

"Another horrible nightmare?"

No! Why did you pick now *to pay attention to Aleesha?*

"What's she talking about, Kim?"

"She. . .Aleesha knows that I've had a couple of nightmares recently." I didn't want to discuss it; but the can of worms was open, and I couldn't wiggle the lid back onto Pandora's box to save my life, to mix clichéd metaphors rather pathetically.

"But you didn't tell *me* about them." Jo sounded like she was going to start crying.

No, I didn't, and I'm not going to now.

She didn't wait for an answer. "Has this been happening just since Terri's death?"

Why can't you say "Miss Terri" like Aleesha? I hate it when you refer to my parents by their first names, especially since Mom's death. But that's not relevant.

Not as relevant as her being so on-target that I couldn't hide a guilty expression.

"So you knew. . . ?" Jo said to Aleesha. I hoped I didn't detect a catfight brewing.

I puffed a little sigh of relief when—instead of saying anything else to Aleesha—Jo looked out the window and started talking in a low voice. To herself? Maybe. To God? Uh. . .

"She told her dream to. . ." She mumbled the last couple

of words, but I doubted that it was a compliment. Nope. Definitely not talking to God.

She seemed to have forgotten for the moment that Aleesha and I were still there. "Kim told Aleesha about her nightmares, but she didn't tell her best friend."

Then she came back from wherever she'd been lost in space and looked at me again. "So, what was your nightmare about?"

What? I guess you weren't paying attention when Aleesha said, "Maybe she doesn't feel like talking about it."

"Which one?" I pictured Jo as the Phantom of the Opera and me as Raúl. We were dueling over Christine's fate—the continued privacy of my dreams—in a fight to the death. Although I feinted unpredictably to fend off her jabs, I was wearing down fast.

My question appeared to catch her off guard. "The first, uh, no, this one. . .uh, how many have there been?"

I gave up. I couldn't hold her off any longer. I just hoped she wouldn't say anything to Dad.

"Three." Maybe if I left out the pertinent details. "In tonight's, I dreamed it was Good Friday. The crucifixion was going on. I had a better view than the people with front-row seats, although—"

"Huh?"

"You might say I was on stage. I was one of the thieves being crucified with Jesus."

"Oh."

Aleesha didn't usually remain quiet very long, but I sensed her stillness. She was like that when listening intently, and that habit was comforting. I was counting on her ability to read between the lines. And on her prayers while I continued.

"Anyhow, the other thief had been talking to Jesus. He'd asked for salvation, and Jesus told him he'd have a place in God's kingdom that day."

I sighed. *Do I really have to tell you the rest?* Too late to back out now.

"Instead of cursing Jesus like the other thief at Jesus' actual crucifixion, I asked for redemption, too.

"But instead of giving me the assurance He'd given the other thief, Jesus looked at me and laughed. Oh, how He laughed. He never would have laughed at any repentant sinner that way in real life, but that doesn't matter in a dream. Then He said, 'Don't you see that sign above your head?' I couldn't angle my head well enough to read it. 'It details your crime,' Jesus said. 'Your unforgivable sin.'

"I kept pleading with Him. I repented of every sin I could think of, and that took hours, but at the end I was no better off than at the beginning. Jesus had already forgiven me for all of those piddly sins, but my own personal unforgivable sin hung over my head like a guillotine, and I knew there was no hope.

"Even though I was high in the air with breezes blowing all around, I could feel the fires of hell burning closer and closer. The smell was so rancid I started coughing. I couldn't stop. The devil was trying to grab me. He couldn't quite reach me, but he was getting closer each time he swung his arms toward me. In another few seconds, he would have been close enough. That's what you helped wake me up from."

Aleesha dropped down beside me, and I put my head on her lap. She understood what I'd meant and how real it had seemed. She stroked my hair while I sobbed endlessly.

Jo's face was one gigantic question mark. She must not have known what to do. It was too late for her to try to hold and comfort me the way Aleesha had done. The chances of her understanding how terribly that dream tormented me were slim, and she didn't stand the slightest chance of comprehending its significance.

"I need a breath of fresh air," I said before grabbing my coat and pulling it on over my nightclothes. I slipped into my furry kitty-cat slippers and opened the door.

Since Jo had never tolerated cold weather well, I didn't think she'd follow me. That was my plan, anyhow.

Sure enough. "Take care you don't freeze out there," she said before lying down again as if nothing had happened.

I caught a motion from Aleesha—four wiggly fingers flashing in my direction. She'd join me as soon as Jo went back to sleep.

I couldn't see my watch, but I doubted that three minutes passed before the door opened and Aleesha came outside. We went inside one of the units we'd already cleaned and painted. The inside temperature must have been thirty degrees warmer than outside, even without heat. We sat down on the floor and turned off our flashlights.

"Kim," Aleesha said, "that friend of yours is one sick puppy."

"I don't know what's wrong with her. She's never acted this way before."

"Has she ever had emotional problems?"

"She's a teenage girl," I said. "She has hormones. Why?"

"Something's bugging the daylights out of her."

"You, maybe?" I wasn't trying to be funny. "Our friendship? The way she was talking—"

"Those things are too obvious, Kim. They've been that way for months now. But this is new. I wonder if something's happened to her since we've been here?"

I shrugged. "Like what?"

"I don't know. Bad news, maybe? But she sounded so happy in the van. So enthusiastic. She'd done a one-eighty from the way she acted at supper, and now she's done another one."

"What should we—?"

"I'm going to talk to Mr. Rob." Aleesha turned and headed for the door.

"He gets up early." She stopped and faced me again. "You can catch him then."

"I'm going to talk to him *now*. I'm not sure this can wait."

chapter thirty-three

Graham O'Reilly stood in the doorway of his apartment, gazing in the direction of a sunrise that had yet to appear. His arms and legs were lost in a pair of red flannel pajamas that billowed like sails in the early morning breeze, making them look big enough to fit a man three times his size and propel the heaviest of the old-time clipper ships.

Perhaps they'd been a gift. From someone who didn't know how small Graham was. He surely hadn't purchased something so ill fitting for himself. That sleepwear made him look thinner than me, if that was possible. But at least I didn't look gaunt.

I wondered if he'd lived a particularly hard life. I couldn't imagine ever getting to know him well enough to find out.

Graham wore no robe, and I tried to keep from wondering how he kept his pajama bottoms up. Gross! I didn't want to imagine a strong gust of wind suddenly whipping them to his knees.

"Morning, Graham," I said as I pulled my coat together in the front and started fiddling with the zipper. "Aren't you freezing?" I almost felt guilty for wearing such a warm coat when the chill had turned him such an icy blue.

My hands felt so numb I couldn't fit the ends of the zipper together. I put my mittens on, but then I couldn't feel what I was doing. I took them off again. Even those few seconds of warmth had helped, though. I zipped my jacket all the way to my mouth without any further problem and pulled the hood over my head. I didn't care much whether it messed up my hair or not.

I didn't pull the drawstring, though. A too-tight hood might keep me from hearing this too-soft-spoken man. If he ever returned my greeting, that was.

He took his time, and when he finally spoke, he barely moved his lips. "Like Paul. Content whatever."

I had to think for a few seconds before remembering what I'd said, and I interpreted his answer to mean he was comfortable in the cold. Or accepting of it. Or maybe just unwilling to complain about it.

"Thank you again for walking me down Red Cedar Lane last night." I hesitated and then added, "Even if I didn't know you were there." I chuckled gently to let him know that hadn't bothered me.

"Young ladies. Not out alone. Not after dark."

I started to say, *"You shouldn't have worried. I would have been fine by myself. I know some major self-defense moves. Besides, nobody else was out there."* But something told me he would have disagreed strongly in his nearly wordless way, and I didn't want to start even the smallest of disagreements with a man I was determined to get to know better.

Maybe even to like, to enjoy, and to appreciate. And for more than just his exceptional cooking skills.

"I suppose not," I said with what I hoped was enough conviction to avoid provoking a reprisal. "I needed to pray, though, and that was the best place to do it."

"I know."

Something about his tone sounded. . .strange. Mysterious. Unsettling.

And *what* did he know? That I'd needed some private time with God? He must have overheard me tell Dad that. Or had he learned from his own experiences that Red Cedar Lane was a good place to pray?

"I like to be by myself when I pray," I said.

"In closet." Okay. So maybe he disagreed about Red Cedar Lane.

I stood there watching my breath and pondering the applicability of his statement to someone like me who was spending two weeks in a place that didn't have closets. I suppose I could have prayed in one of the units we'd already cleaned out, but why fret about Graham's admonition, anyhow? The man was obviously a bit too conservative for my taste.

"You. Pray aloud." Huh? How did he. . . ?

But, of course. He'd walked beside me almost the whole way from the two-lane road to the first building on the prison grounds. He'd heard me praying. He knew everything I'd prayed about. Including. . .

"I pray out loud whenever I'm by myself."

"Never alone."

"I meant whenever I'm alone with God."

He didn't respond. His eyes were on the sunrise, which was just starting to paint the skies above the mountains to the east. As far as I could tell, he hadn't taken his eyes off the horizon since I came outside.

"Gorgeous sunrise," I said. Although the brilliant colors erased the stark darkness of the mountains and made me feel like falling to my knees in worship, I needed to entice Graham to talk. "I guess you've seen a lot of sunrises in your lifetime. You're what—sixty, sixty-five, seventy?"

Now that I saw him this close in daylight, he looked more like seventy-five or eighty.

"Seventy. I think."

"I think" should have raised a flag, but I was too busy making a rough estimate of the number of sunrises in seventy years of life to dwell on it. He'd lived through maybe 25,000 sunrises—if I could still do some basic math without a calculator.

But before I could try to impress him with that figure, he

spoke again. "Long time, no sunrises."

"What? You mean the sun hasn't risen on a regular basis for a long time?" Nobody would be strange enough to say something like that. Not even Graham.

"Haven't seen."

"Why not?"

He didn't say anything at first.

"Now see. Six months. Seven."

Huh? He hadn't answered my question, but apparently he hadn't seen any sunrises until a few months ago. At the rate this conversation was going, I hesitated to question him further for fear it might slip from first gear back into neutral. And ultimately into reverse.

I decided to take one more chance. "Is there a reason for that?"

He seemed to hesitate. Actually, he looked like he wanted me to shut up, leave him alone, and let him enjoy the sunrise in solitude.

"Yes." He didn't offer to explain, and I'd already used up all the chances I dared to take. I wished Aleesha had been outside with me. She was better at probing than I was. Not that I thought she would have learned any more from Graham than I had.

"Jo troubled," he said.

Oh, were you hanging around outside our unit last night eavesdropping?

"You troubled," he added.

Continuing to focus on the sunrise, he missed seeing the flush that flooded my face. How did he know that? And how much did he know?

"I troubled. Same you."

I nodded, but he didn't see me.

"Guilt. No escape."

I wanted to run away. I didn't need some pathetic old man to confront me about my guilt. I already understood it far better than I wanted to, thank you very much.

But I forced myself to say, "Uh-huh."

What was he trying to say about my guilt? And how did he know about it?

You dummy. He overheard your prayer. You prayed aloud, and you covered every concern under the sun. You prayed about the prison ministry. You prayed about Jo. You prayed about your own guilt. He must have even heard you praying about—

"Guilt. Stays forever." A tear trickled down his cheek, and I wondered how he would react to a hug.

There's bad timing, and there's worse timing, but Aleesha's arrival outside before I could respond to Graham or hug him was the worst timing of all. I felt like I'd just started making a connection with him, even though I'd never spoken with anyone who was so difficult to talk with or who raised more questions than he answered.

"Having fun, you two?" Aleesha said. "Where's your robe, Graham? Aren't you afraid of being arrested for indecent exposure?"

Although he appeared to ignore her at first, his head jerked—possibly involuntarily—somewhere in the middle of Aleesha's greeting. I wondered which word had been the trigger.

I thought about motioning for her to leave Graham and me alone, but I changed my mind. The spell—such as it was—had been broken.

"So how does Rob look in the middle of the night when he hasn't had a chance to put on his makeup yet?"

Although Aleesha giggled at my question, Graham's expression remained unchanged. Passive. Unemotional. I no longer had his attention—or his interest.

"Cook now," he announced before turning around and

opening the door to his apartment. He shut it behind him before either of us could open our mouths to say good-bye. Had he realized that Aleesha and I needed to talk, or was he simply not in the mood to put up with our silliness?

Probably the latter.

"Rob looks the same during the night as he does during the day. Ugly as the soles of my feet."

She was teasing, although nobody listening to our conversation would have known it. We'd once agreed that Rob was reasonably good-looking for someone two long generations older than us. Besides, Aleesha didn't consider any part of her body to be ugly. Not even the bottoms of her feet. She believed in a bumper sticker that read, *My body is the temple of God, and God doesn't inhabit imperfect temples.*

"So, what about. . . ?" She pointed her head at Graham's apartment.

Part of me was dying to tell Aleesha about my conversation with Graham, yet it seemed too personal and private. Although he hadn't said more than a hundred words to me—maybe not half or a fourth of that—and I'd understood the words without always comprehending the meaning, I felt like he'd revealed something of himself.

I might not have understood what it was. But it was something he might not want me to share with Aleesha.

"I'm not sure whether I chipped the ice a little bit or broke the pickax trying. Either way, it's gonna be slick going."

Her narrowed eyes and wrinkled brow sent a clear message: *"Keep trying, girl."*

I nodded and smiled. I might still have to tell her about the conversation with Graham, but I wanted to figure out what he'd been talking about first. "Now, what about Rob. . .and Jo?"

Aleesha looked around to make sure Jo wasn't lurking within earshot.

"Mr. Rob was really concerned about her when we first got here. And working with her yesterday morning was apparently, uh, difficult. But he'd seen so much progress by the time she got involved in last night's service that he assumed she'd turned the corner. He thought she'd be fine from that point on."

"Didn't we all! She was as enthusiastic as you and me in the van last night. She sounded like the old Betsy Jo—from before Mexico. And I heard her mumbling in Spanish when we first got back. I guess she was warming up for that Latino fellow. I hope he comes tonight."

"Be that as it may, Mr. Rob was amazed to hear about Jo's reaction to your nightmare. Amazed, did I say?" Aleesha chuckled. "The poor man was shocked speechless."

I ignored her. "Does he have any idea what's wrong with her?"

"Not exactly. But he told me she had borrowed his satellite phone for ten or fifteen minutes."

I scratched my head. "I'd been curled up in my sleeping bag for a while when Jo came to bed, and she was quiet when she came in. I wondered what was going on."

"So does Mr. Rob," Aleesha said. "He said her eyes were red and raw when she brought the phone back."

chapter thirty-four

The scent of coffee filled Graham's apartment. That same nutty blend I'd enjoyed the morning before, though I still couldn't figure out if it was hazelnut or southern pecan.

"Good morning," I said to Jo as she entered the dining room. When I smiled and started to give her a hug, she grabbed my arm and pulled me into the living room.

"Kim, I acted a little weird last night. I am *so* sorry."

"I've reset my wrongness counter to zero," I said. She couldn't have looked more baffled if I'd just sprouted eagle wings. "Whoops. I didn't tell you that part of my experience in Santa María? That means *apology accepted.*"

When I opened my arms, she gave me a half-smile, and we hugged as if nothing strange had happened during the night.

"Anything you want to talk with me about, Jo?" I said when we broke apart.

Her right eye twitched a couple of times. *Is that a nervous reaction to my question, Jo?* Maybe not. It stopped as soon as she shook her head.

Jo, you may not want *to talk, but the more you resist unburdening, the more you probably* need *to talk.*

I didn't waste time trying to remember whether I'd picked up that bit of wisdom from Aleesha or Mom. The two wisest women in my life so far. Present and. . .past.

"Did you get to call home last night?" I couldn't think of a less conspicuous way to prompt Jo for information without sounding nosey. "We were so late leaving Red Cedar you didn't get to use one of the office phones."

"Uh-huh." But not a word about the satellite phone or the call itself.

"Were your parents glad to hear from you?"

"Uh." She spoke so softly I could barely hear her, and her response was one of those "uhs" that could have meant either "uh-huh" or "uh-uh."

What possible reason would Mr. and Mrs. Snelling have had for *not* being pleased to hear from their daughter, though? Their only child, in fact. Had her mom picked last night to ream her out over the phone for coming on this trip against her wishes?

Of course, Jo had called home sometime after 10:00 p.m. Pacific time. She'd probably awakened her parents from a sound 1:00 a.m. Eastern Standard Time snooze.

Maybe they had a right to be less pleased than they would have been at an earlier hour. Especially if she didn't bother to explain about cell phone coverage and not having access to a phone at a more appropriate time.

I decided to take my inquiry one level deeper. If it didn't yield results, I'd quit for now. "And how are the two of them?"

She didn't answer. Not in words.

The dam holding back a potential flood of sobbing might not have broken yet, but it sprang a noticeable leak. Jo's eyes glistened with moisture that confirmed that her parents were all or part of the problem. I was dying to find out what, but not even the best of friends could have asked anything else under those circumstances.

Had someone been in an accident? Had the house burned down? Was someone seriously ill? Had Mr. Snelling lost his job? Had Jo's parents been. . . ?

Had they been fighting? I'd often wondered about their relationship, especially after some of the things Mr. Snelling said—and especially what he didn't say—when we asked his permission to bring Jo to California.

If the Snellings had been fighting, I couldn't blame her for not wanting to say anything. She couldn't disguise the frightened look on her face, though. She knew I'd figured it out. Some of it, anyhow.

She stared out the window for a number of seconds. The sky's early morning glory had yielded the stage to a layer of clouds that hid the sun completely, even though sprinkles of sunlight spotlighted the distant mountains.

Jo looked at me again. "We'd better get back to the dining room." Her voice might have said, "*Breakfast must be ready now.*" But her eyes pled, *"I know you care, but you can't help. Please don't ask anymore."*

I resisted the temptation to reveal my frustration. Instead, I let my mouth relax in a friendly smile. We walked arm-in-arm back into the dining room. Just as I'd expected, everyone was busy eating. Scrambled eggs. Mmm. Topped with cheese. Graham had also cooked a pig-load of thick-cut bacon. And a good-sized bread tray full of biscuits that had to be homemade. When had Graham found time to do all of that?

"Have a seat, girls," Rob said. "Graham said he made these biscuits especially for the two of you. Fact is, he wouldn't let the rest of us have any until you got here and ate your fill."

Huh? Especially for the two of us? The two people he knew had problems? I wondered if I looked as dumbfounded as I felt.

I smiled at Graham and thanked him, but then I almost fell off my chair. He gave me a slight smile. Barely perceptible, but still a smile. Was he using those biscuits to invite Jo and me to join him in some secret society?

Or should I say a society of secret-keepers? It seemed as if the three of us wouldn't admit our problems even to one another, and yet we seemed destined to share at least some of one another's pain.

I don't know if Dad or Rob paid attention to what was going on, but Aleesha did.

"You have a good talk with Jo?" she asked quietly while we looked for a starting point in our first unit of the day.

I spent a couple of minutes pondering my answer.

"Not a good talk?"

I must have given her a defensive look.

"You groaned. That's why I assumed things didn't go well."

Oh.

"Sorry about that," I said, throwing my hands up in the air. "That's because this room is the worst one yet." Aleesha looked satisfied with my explanation. And why not? I'd told her the truth—as far as it went.

"She didn't tell me anything," I said. "Not anything specific."

I felt funny talking about Jo. Like I was breaking a confidence by admitting we'd even had a conversation. But Aleesha had seen Jo pull me out of the dining room to talk about something, so I didn't fret long.

I decided not to say anything about the Snellings, though.

"She apologized about last night," I said.

"She apologized to me after breakfast, too. Maybe she'd worn herself out too much to deal sanely with your nightmare."

"Sure." Her suggestion sounded better than the whole truth. That being upset about her parents had worn her out. And probably kept her from sleeping.

But why would one call affect her so severely? Had the Snellings been arguing while they were on the phone with Jo? I couldn't imagine Mr. Snelling doing that, but Jo's mother. . . she might not have given him any choice.

"Aleesha," I said about the time we'd cleared the room halfway, "maybe I should work with Jo this afternoon. You know, to see if I can learn more."

She nodded. "I was going to suggest that."

"Good. I'll—"

"And would you consider telling her about your guilt problem? She might be more willing to confide in you if you confide in her first."

I could feel my face reddening. "I hadn't thought about it." I wasn't sure I wanted Jo to know the details, but trying to keep things from her was a never-ending juggling act. Besides, Aleesha might be right. Maybe one confession would lead to another.

"Are you afraid she'll flake out and tell Mr. Scott?"

I *knew* I moaned that time. "She might." Did I dare to take that chance?

"There are worse things than your dad finding out, you know. As well as you two get along now, I think he can handle it."

Aleesha and I couldn't have been more completely on opposite ends of that opinion.

I dumped a handful of unused nails into an empty bucket and listened to their pings ring like gunshots. Then I climbed up on a sawhorse that reminded me of a wooden rocking horse I'd had as a kid. And of the mess-tent table supports in Santa María.

I looked at Aleesha. She was laughing her head off.

And why not? She had enough padding to sit on a sawhorse for hours without getting sore and enough sense not to do it.

"So how do I beat this guilt?" I asked. I faked a smile and feigned lightheartedness. "Share some of your street smarts on the subject, and I'll pay double your normal rates."

I didn't fool Aleesha any more than I fooled myself. She knew better than to take my cheerfulness at face value.

She didn't usually wait for an invitation to dispense free advice, but she'd apparently been holding back a sermon this time. I just hadn't realized it.

"Girl," she said, "you've come to the right place."

"To the source of all street wisdom?"

I didn't expect anything substantial or earth shattering. Not now. If Aleesha had known how to get rid of my guilt, she would've told me the cure long before now. If anything, she'd made a conscious effort to keep reminding me of it.

"Uh-*uh*, girl. God is the source of all wisdom—period—and He doesn't take kindly to competitors. Not even when they're ultra-talented drama and theater majors who specialize in my kind of modesty."

I cackled. Aleesha wasn't conceited. Not really. But sometimes I had to remind myself of that. She was just, uh, extremely conscious of how special she was and not the least shy about making sure other people knew it, too.

"I meant Red Cedar is the right place for you to be. I don't think God brought you here just to help complete this hostel."

I nodded and uh-huh-ed before responding. "He must have meant for me—for all of us—to touch lives in the prison ministry, too."

"I'm not disagreeing, but I believe God has plans for helping you deal with that Season of Pebbles you're going through. You've been suffering grief. Guilt. Fatigue. Nightmares. Now don't go getting paranoid and start looking for a new problem under every rock in your path. Fact is, though, more pebbles may lie in your path, and God may not plan to lead you to victory quite yet. But maybe it'll happen here."

My sigh could have started a tsunami. "I sometimes think God decided to go bowling and positioned me as the headpin."

"You don't really mean that."

I thought I did, but Aleesha seemed determined to set my thinking straight—fast.

She shook her head. I could tell from her expression that

the thoughts boiling in her brain were about to steam their way out to me. Although I wasn't in a mood to be preached to, maybe God could use one of Aleesha's sermons to alter my view of the circumstances.

"So maybe it's the devil who's bowling," I said. "Aren't you going to remind me that a father doesn't give his children bad gifts? And neither does God."

"He's the giver of every good and perfect gift," Aleesha said with the power and conviction she'd undoubtedly used in preaching to our teammates in Santa María. "And nothing bad comes from Him. Our hope is in Him. Remember what the apostle Paul said? Everything eventually works for good to believers who stay in the center of God's will. That's the Aleesha Jefferson translation of Romans 8:28."

I nodded enthusiastically. I'd drawn encouragement from that verse in the past, but I needed to believe it even more now. I couldn't let my guilt drive me over the edge. And yet could I stop it?

chapter thirty-five

Working with Jo that afternoon might not have provided any useful insights—we rarely spoke, in fact—but we got a lot done. At first, I was afraid my fatigue might return, but I didn't dwell on it. Aleesha's little sermon had warned me not to give in to the power of suggestion.

Nonetheless, after the first twenty minutes of strenuous effort, I was huffing and puffing, ready to collapse. Rob had told me to take a break whenever I needed one and not to worry about it. Although I knew he was right, I felt funny about it.

But I did it anyhow. Seated with my back against a wall, I lifted a bottle of cold water to my lips.

I watched Jo for a couple of minutes while she worked around me. No wonder I already felt worn out. I'd been trying to march to her beat, but she wasn't marching. She was running so fast nobody could have kept up. Not even Anjelita.

I'd never thought of Jo as a high-voltage gal. If anything, I'd considered her a tad lazy. But that word didn't fit her now. Had she somehow "caught" the energy I'd lost? As silly as it sounded, that was the best explanation I could come up with.

When I got up again, I felt better. I did what I should have done all along: I worked at my own pace. That not only kept me productive for the next three hours without pooping out, it also gave me a chance to observe my old friend more closely.

Why and how had she become this proverbial house on fire?

I got my first clue when I looked at her mouth. Maybe I wasn't good at interpreting body language, but my vision was

20/20—corrected with contacts—and I could see her gritting her teeth.

What did that signify, though? Determination? Maybe. I'd have to ask Aleesha the next time she and I were alone.

Even if I was right, though, why was Jo so determined? We weren't on a do-or-die schedule like completing the villagers' houses before the start of the rainy season.

And we weren't competing with Rob, Dad, and Aleesha, either. I didn't count Graham in the noncompetition because he didn't participate in construction activities. Even if he had, he took his time doing everything—not just in responding to repeated efforts to get him to talk.

Then I noticed Jo's eyes. The expression "shooting daggers" came to mind. She looked like she wanted to mutilate and destroy every piece of trash she picked up. She *threw* unused nails into the galvanized bucket, knocking it over several times.

I don't know where she got the momentum to do that. What had sounded like single gunshots when I dropped nails in the bucket resembled semiautomatic fire the way she propelled them. I made a point of looking at the bucket when Rob came by to empty it. It would never hold a liquid again.

And the usable leftover materials? By the time Jo dragged a piece of perfectly good plywood to the wheelbarrow in the doorway, she splintered the sides and knocked two corners off three times out of four.

Halfway through the afternoon, she began muttering. I thought she was talking to me, but she wasn't even looking in my direction. I maneuvered a little closer without being overly conspicuous.

She kept her volume low, but I could pick out an occasional word. Like *mother*, *rotten*, and *deserted*. Before long, her muttering turned into a growl of sorts. I never saw her take a breath, but the growls continued incessantly—like an emergency siren.

I wanted to help her, but. . .

"Jo?" She turned to look at me, but she didn't stop moving. After watching her purposely throw a couple of good tools into the trash pile, I almost chickened out of saying anything.

"Yeah?"

Hmm. Not the most receptive response she could have given. Especially since it contained more than a small hint of hostility.

She must have seen me draw back defensively. "Sorry," she said. "I'm not in the best of moods."

I wasn't about to tease her by saying, *"I could tell."* I could have done that with Aleesha under similar circumstances, but never with Jo. I was just glad I wasn't the one who'd upset her.

Lord, do I take a chance?

I could almost hear an audible voice saying, *"Go for it, Kim."*

"You want to talk about it, Jo?"

She threw a hammer across the room. *Oh, my!* Rob was not going to appreciate having to repair that wall.

I took that as her answer and didn't say anything else to her that afternoon.

Lord?

The little voice spoke again. *"I never said she'd talk with you. But making the effort was part of My plan. Obeying Me is always the right thing for you to do."*

The next time I listened to that little voice—at least in relation to Jo—I was going to ask for a suit of body armor. Nope, bad idea. It might be bulletproof, but that wouldn't make it Jo-proof. She'd find a way to put holes in it, too, just like she'd done with the nail bucket.

Rob walked in around 4:45. "Suppertime, girls." He grinned. "Unless you prefer to keep working."

To my amazement, Jo dropped the piece of two-by-four she had in her hands, smiled at Rob, and then beat him to the door. She must have finished working out her anger—at least for the moment. But would it—like my nightmares—come back to haunt her some other time?

Rob looked at the hole in the wall, and he squinted at me. I shrugged and shook my head as if I hadn't seen it and didn't know anything about it.

But he didn't buy it. I hadn't expected him to.

chapter thirty-six

I hated the idea of tattling on Jo, but when her attitude—her anger—made her purposely damage the very property we'd come to put the finishing touches on, I wondered if I had a choice.

I crossed my fingers behind my back the way a little kid might do when lying. "Rob, would you believe I tripped and fell against the wall?"

"You, Kim? I know you're a klutz, but you'd need a wrecking ball to do that kind of damage." He wasn't smiling.

So I explained. I had to. I talked as fast as I could so Jo wouldn't notice our delay in coming to supper and think we were talking about her.

During the time she'd been so enraged, she probably wouldn't have cared. But now. . .how could I be sure what mood she was in or how quickly it would change?

Before entering Graham's apartment, Rob asked me to keep a close eye on Jo. I would've done that, anyhow.

I wanted to do some serious praying before the evening worship service, though. How could I. . . ? Sure, why not?

"Jo, want to walk down Red Cedar Lane with me instead of riding in the van?" I gave a slight head shake to Aleesha. *No, I don't want you to come.* "When we first got here, you said you wouldn't mind a walk like that. It's a great place to do some silent praying." Not that I expected Jo to be talkative. "Besides, Graham doesn't think it's a safe—or at least not an appropriate—place for a gal to walk by herself."

Jo looked at me. With caution, maybe. Not fear. Wasn't one

just a more advanced state of the other, though?

"He's wrong, of course, but he'll never let me hear the end of it if I don't take somebody with me this time."

Jo started cackling. "Our Graham?"

"Maybe not in so many words." Jo laughed even harder. "The man has a voice, you know. He just about talked my ear off this morning while we were watching the sunrise." Having a little fun at Graham's expense wouldn't hurt anything, especially if he didn't know I was doing it.

"Sure, I'll walk with you, but I don't feel much like talking."

"Fine. I was serious about praying."

So we headed across the two-lane road after asking Rob to watch for us along the way. I had an extra-good prayer time— silent for Jo's sake—and she didn't say one word until the first prison building came into sight.

Then she slushed into melted gelatin.

"Kim, I felt so useless last night." That was the last thing I would have expected to hear Jo say. "I can't sing solos or do drama. Reading the Scripture doesn't take any talent. I'm no good at this prison ministry thing."

I hugged her. "Girl, the way you were loving on those guys. . ." Uh, maybe not the most appropriate way to describe Jo's interaction with a bunch of male prisoners who've been deprived of female companionship for a while. "The way you were talking with them. . .and listening was special. Listening is so important."

"You think?"

"I know." I was preparing to fake it, but the Holy Spirit came to my rescue before I got tongue-tied and tangled up in my explanation. "Do you think those fellows enjoy being locked up?"

"You even have to ask?" She started giggling.

"But they're Christians, aren't they? The ones who came

to our service, anyhow."

"They claim to be."

Duh. I'd forgotten that some of them might be pretending.

"So, when they can't be with their families, who do they most likely want to hang with? Who would they be most comfortable with?"

She didn't have to think long. "Other Christians, I guess."

"And who are we—you, me, Dad, Rob, and Aleesha?"

"Other Christians." Her smile was radiant. "And they're probably confident we don't have any hidden agendas."

I gave her an attagirl hug. "So what were you thinking about on the way over here?"

"I was practicing Spanish in my head. I haven't used it since graduation, and I want to be ready for that one guy's friend this evening."

"I wish I knew all the Spanish you know." I paused. "I wish I knew all you've forgotten since graduation."

She giggled. "And I wish my pronunciation sounded as authentic as yours." She turned her head to look back down the road. "I wonder where the fellows are."

"Don't let Aleesha hear you call her a fellow," I said before bursting out laughing. "She can outman any man I've ever met."

Seen in the glow of my flashlight, Jo's look of shock fed my sense of humor, but I tried to keep from laughing at her. "She's not. . . ?"

"No, not *that*." And so much for not laughing at Jo. "I meant she believes she can do anything a man can do and do it as well or better."

Audible relief puffed out. "Aleesha thinks she can father a child?" she asked with a smirk that made me giggle.

I was thankful to hear the old sparkle back. Maybe I'd get mine back sometime, too—for longer than an hour or two at a time.

"No way. And she doesn't plan to marry till she's too old to have kids."

"That's a thought."

"Jo, I've got to ask you something. Please be honest. How do you feel about 'people of the darker persuasion,' as Aleesha sometimes describes herself?"

"Huh? I've never thought about it. They're okay. Some are good, some bad. Just like us people of the 'lighter persuasion.'"

"So you don't think of yourself as racially prejudiced?"

"Good gracious, no! Why would you think that?"

She sounded genuinely surprised. And not the least defensive.

"Girlfriend, Aleesha thinks you are."

Jo's breathing started to accelerate and grow louder.

"She doesn't just think it; she's convinced of it. She has this built-in prejudice detector and she claims you registered strong the day the two of you met."

Quick breathing gave way to a raised voice. "That's crazy. I..." She stopped for a minute. She calmed down before speaking again. "Can I count on you not to tell her something?"

I nodded, although I don't think she saw me.

"I admit I wasn't too happy when I heard what good friends the two of you had become. But it didn't have anything to do with race. Although Papa told me he'd met her, he didn't say one word about her color. I didn't discover that part until I met her, and I'd started disliking her long before that."

I narrowed my eyebrows.

"Her showing up for Terri—Miss Terri's—funeral made me look bad. Not that I didn't deserve it. But then when she became a permanent fixture at your house, my jealousy went a little overboard."

"A little...?" I tried to say it gently.

"Okay, a lot. I've been praying about it, though. Constantly. And I've been trying really hard to accept Aleesha."

As a friend or just as a person? "But last night. . . ?"

"Forget about last night. Please. I'd never seen anyone have a nightmare like that, and I was so terrified I honestly didn't know what I was saying. But God reminded me of it first thing this morning. I could hardly wait to apologize to both of you."

What a relief! I'd rather think of Aleesha's smell detector as being wrong once than believe one of my best friends was prejudiced toward the other one. Jealousy was bad enough, but at least Jo was working on that problem.

"While we're talking about sensitive issues," she said, "what about those nightmares? Last night's wasn't the first one. Aleesha let that slip. But you haven't said a word to me about them. Aren't we good friends anymore?"

Oh, man. I'd be happy to tell you anything about any of my worst real-life experiences. But that? Don't you have enough on your mind with your parents' problems?

"Jo, of course we're still good friends." I hugged her. "You're one of my two very best ones, and you always will be."

She began sniffling.

"And would you consider telling her about your guilt problem? She might be more willing to confide in you if you confide in her first."

Aleesha, hush!

"Because of that, I'll be honest with you. I'm not comfortable talking about my nightmares. I'd just as soon Aleesha didn't know about them, but that was unavoidable. I suppose continuing to keep you in the dark isn't fair, though. But if I tell you, you can't keep any secrets from me, either. Okay?"

She narrowed her eyes. I waited maybe thirty seconds. Thirty tense, wordless seconds.

"It's very important—extremely important—that you don't tell Dad, either. He and I have gotten so much closer since

Mom's death, and I'm afraid this might hurt our relationship."

I waited another fifteen or twenty seconds. She still hadn't responded. So I took a chance that her silence signified her commitment to mutual secret-sharing.

"I've had three nightmares. The first one came just before my fatigue problem started. I dreamed—"

A horn interrupted my confession. Rob, Dad, and Aleesha.

I didn't know whether to be relieved about postponing my explanation or frustrated at not getting it over with.

chapter thirty-seven

Reaching the large conference room where we held services was a breeze that night. We still had to undergo the normal security procedures, but at least we knew what to expect. And not only was Chaplain Thomas waiting for us, but he also acted maybe one-tenth pleasant.

"Who says God doesn't perform miracles anymore?" Aleesha said while "Chappy"—I'd started referring to him that way when he was out of earshot—passed out hymnbooks for us. Our laughter got so out-of-hand he stopped what he was doing and looked at us. I felt horrible when he saw us staring at him.

But Aleesha won the prize for pulling that fat out of the fire. As rotund as Chappy was, that metaphor fit, uh, quite snugly.

She waved at him as if we'd been trying to get his attention. I'm still not sure how she pulled it off—I was preoccupied with watching him watching us—but somehow she got him laughing, too. Who but Aleesha could wordlessly "tell" a nonexistent joke across a good-sized room?

"Greetings, you all," Rock said in a mock Southern accent that sounded as fakey as the ones I would never get used to hearing at the movies. Yet I couldn't keep from smiling at him for doing it.

"Not Rocky," he'd told us the first night. "I call myself Rock after Simon Peter, and I'll beat up the first person—insider, guard, or outsider—who calls me anything different."

As gentle-spirited as he seemed to be, I was 50 percent confident that he was teasing and an additional 25 percent hopeful that he was at least exaggerating.

Like the previous night, he carried a Bible under one arm. What a contrast between tree trunk-sized muscles and the frail-looking holy book that bore signs of years of constant but reverent use.

"Guess we'll have to work harder to scare you off, huh?" Rock said. If anybody ever typified ear-to-ear grinning, it was him.

Although Chappy frowned at Rock, the rest of us gave him a hug. Even the guys. Women and children aren't the only ones who thrive on that kind of affection. Chappy frowned at *us* after that—presumably for *lowering* ourselves to show a Christian brother some love.

Maybe someone in his position couldn't afford to get too close to the prisoners. Physically or emotionally. Maybe remaining neutral was important. I couldn't say. But I couldn't see how a Christian chaplain could distance himself from them spiritually.

He didn't ignore them totally, though. Every few minutes, he singled out an insider and took him to the far corner of the room for a few minutes. But I was too busy trying to out-sing those rich-toned, high-spirited, highly Spirited men to pay much attention.

Repeating my hymn selection process from the night before, I took requests. "Amazing Grace." "Victory in Jesus." "The Old Rugged Cross." "In the Garden." These fellows could out-sing the congregational singing in any church I'd ever been in. Had anyone ever recorded a best-selling album in a prison?

I was about to announce prayer time when somebody yelled out, "Hey! It's almost Christmas, ain't it?" So we went through the first stanzas of six or seven familiar carols without using the hymnals. I sang "Away in a Manger" as a solo, but the insiders sang along. That was fine. They couldn't help it. Christmas carols weren't meant just for listening to.

About the time my voice started giving out, Aleesha did an a capella version of "O Holy Night"—all of our music was a capella—and I was so thankful I'd already done my solo, because hers was so. . .I couldn't think of a word *big* enough to describe the impact it made. Tears of joy and appreciation filled almost every eye, including mine.

Chappy still wore that stone-faced look, though. Maybe he was unhappy that we'd prolonged the service by singing so much, but I didn't care. We hadn't come to Red Cedar for his benefit. He was supposedly already a mature Christian.

Rob had led the prayer time the night before, but he didn't realize he should have offered the insiders a chance to pray aloud, too. Since Rock hadn't been shy about giving him the scoop afterward, Rob asked him to open the prayer time tonight and to let all of the insiders have a chance to pray.

When people did that at my church, the first person usually prayed so long nobody else wanted to chance running the service overtime by praying, too. But that wasn't the case at Red Cedar. No one was rushing to end these services.

Rock took his time, and he prayed with such power that the room echoed with choruses of "Amen!" "Praise God!" and "That's right!"

My stereotypical thinking flared up that night. I'd expected the African-Americans to demonstrate that kind of approval, and they did. But so did the Caucasians, the Asians, and the Latinos.

The Latinos? Uh, the Latino. Singular.

Yes, that one fellow brought his friend, Alfredo, and Jo was translating for him. I hated to open my eyes while somebody was praying, but I had to see how that was going. He and Jo were standing head to head. Under different circumstances, they would have made a cute couple. He looked maybe a year or two older than her.

The insiders focused their prayers on one another's families, salvation for specific people, what they perceived as the declining state of our nation, international evangelism, and everything else under the sun. They confessed their sins, and they didn't hesitate to admit being guilty of the crimes that had put them in prison and to ask God's richest blessings on their victims.

And how they prayed for God's forgiveness.

Alfredo's prayer came last. He sounded scared to death. "God, keep us safe. Help us to get out and find work. Amen."

Maybe he didn't realize he didn't *have* to pray. Or maybe he was just nervous about praying publicly in a group he hadn't been part of before. Either way, I couldn't convince myself that his "us" didn't just mean "me."

I was glad Jo translated his prayer into English for the rest of us, though. I grinned at the thought of what Paul had once said about speaking in tongues in worship and the importance of having an interpreter present.

I joined Rock at the back of the room for Dad's talk. We had a good view of people in front of us—especially Jo and Alfredo.

I could tell from the way Jo would look at Dad and then turn and whisper to Alfredo that she was doing okay with her translating. But then I got so engrossed in Dad's message— who would have thought a quiet English professor could be such a captivating speaker?—I quit paying attention to Jo and Alfredo.

Until I heard a giggle that couldn't have had to do with the message. I looked at Jo and Alfredo again. They were whispering. Although I kept my mind mostly on Dad's talk, my eyes remained on Jo and Alfredo. I tried reigning in any judgmental thoughts, but I couldn't. Jo and I had outgrown—or should I say we'd been forced to outgrow— that kind of behavior during childhood.

I had, anyhow, and I thought she had, too. But when I heard a giggle I recognized as Jo's, I felt the red creeping into my face. She was the one who should have been embarrassed.

Here we were, strangers in a "foreign" land, among people who needed to see how real we were, and Jo was acting like she was on a first date with a new guy. I might have been mistaken, but she appeared to be flirting with him. I hoped I was wrong.

The service no longer held my attention. Especially after I saw Alfredo put his arm over the back of Jo's chair during the prayer that preceded the altar call. She didn't protest when he let his hand dangle far enough to rest on her shoulder. He took it off fast enough when he heard the amen, though.

Jo, you'd better be careful.

chapter thirty-eight

O nce again, I was outside with Graham waiting for the sunrise. Although the temperature didn't feel as cold as yesterday's, he wore a thick-looking robe this time. Maybe he'd realized that the presence of three teenage ladies required a little extra modesty.

But the tranquility of the setting captivated me so completely I quickly forgot about Graham.

"Kim, we need to talk."

Man, you made me jump!

"Sorry, sweetheart." Dad kissed me on the cheek. "Good morning, Graham. Would you excuse us, please?"

The old man didn't respond, but the prospect of losing my company appeared to affect him. Sadness? Not exactly. But there was something about the look in his eyes. . .

"What's up, Dad?" I asked as he led me across the road to Red Cedar Lane. I half-expected him to say something about Jo's irresponsible behavior last night.

As talkative as everyone had been coming back the first night, last night had been the complete opposite. Nobody seemed interested in reviewing the service. I couldn't speak for the others, but I was too upset about Jo and Alfredo's conduct. I would discuss it with her as soon as I could, but not in front of everyone else.

But maybe Dad wanted my opinion about it.

"I don't know how to bring this up," he said, fiddling with his hands as if searching for lecture notes and finding he'd forgotten them.

"Oh, that's okay." I proceeded with my assumption. "Jo and Alfredo made quite a spectacle of themselves last night, didn't they?"

"Uh." He paused. "If you say so."

You didn't even notice them?

"That's not my concern this morning, though."

So much for my assumption.

"Kim, I know about the nightmare you had on the plane."

"You. . . ?"

"I put two and two together." How he'd figured it out didn't matter. My heart rate rocketed into triple digits at the realization that he knew more than I wanted him to know.

"I hoped you would tell me about it. Especially now that we've developed such a close relationship—one that should lead to greater trust."

The heat I felt radiating from my face could have turned a marshmallow to goo. I didn't need Dad to make me feel worse. I was already tripping on guilt rather than prancing on pebbles.

"Have you had more than the two I know about?"

His voice was compassionate, not angry. He was concerned, not curious. I needed to reassure him, even if it meant telling him the whole truth. Well, almost all of it, anyhow. If I hadn't been so scared that admitting my guilt in Mom's death would turn him against me, I would have told him months ago.

But I couldn't take that chance now. I needed my daddy's love more than ever. Not his hatred, resentment, or condemnation.

"I've had one more nightmare since we got here." I licked my lips and looked around for the sunrise. But I couldn't see it where we were walking. I hoped that wasn't a sign.

"Kim. . . ?" He looked like he was weeping inwardly over my pain.

I had to tell him.

"The fatigue may have gone away, but. . ." I proceeded to tell him about each nightmare. I omitted details that would make him aware of my guilt. Without them, though, the dreams probably didn't make a whole lot of sense, and I was afraid he might ask for clarification.

Tears ran down both our cheeks. I felt a partial sense of relief.

"I wish you'd told me sooner." Although he sounded disappointed, his voice didn't contain a hint of condemnation. I started breathing easier.

Hopeful that he wouldn't push for more information, I forced myself to say, "I didn't want to make you feel bad."

Although he had that *but that's what dads are for* look in his eyes, he remained silent for a few more seconds. "I understand that you feel guilty about something. Does it have to do with your mother's death?"

My stomach began hosting a world championship boxing match. Along with the Super Bowl and the final game in the World Cup. And they were all going on at the same time.

"Did Aleesha tell you that?"

If she had, would I be able to trust her again? Who else could it have been, though? Not Jo. She didn't know. And all Rob knew was Jo had gone berserk after the dream I had night before last.

"No, not Aleesha. Not Rob, either."

Come on, Dad. Don't lie to me. It had to be Aleesha. Who else. . . ?

"Graham mentioned it."

"Graham? You have *got* to be kidding." I might have drawn that last sentence out to twice its normal length in disbelief, but my words shot out machine gun style after that. "What did he say? He doesn't talk much, and he isn't the least clear in saying anything. What does he know about my feelings, anyhow?" My reaction was undoubtedly a mixture of amazement, frustration, and defensiveness.

But Graham *did* know the truth. He'd overheard me praying on the road the first night we went to the prison, and he'd commented about my guilt yesterday morning.

So I'd been knocking myself out to discredit an impeccable witness. *Sorry about that, Aleesha.* But that's how desperate I'd been to hide the truth from my father.

Dad smiled, and I relaxed slightly.

"You shouldn't feel guilty about your mother's death," he said as if words alone might cure my problem. "You couldn't have prevented her death, even if you'd been in the car with her. It's taken me awhile to accept that fact for myself."

"Dad— "

"It's like suicide."

I gave him a strange look.

"Family and friends punish themselves for failing to see it coming and not doing everything they might have done to prevent it. Caregivers experience the same kind of thing. If they'd just been a little more attentive to their ailing parents, couldn't they have prevented that fatal massive stroke?"

So you think I feel guilty for not being able to prevent *Mom's death? Just keep believing that, and we'll both feel better.*

No, I realized a moment later. Only Dad would feel better. I still had to live with the guilt.

I didn't notice that we'd turned and started heading back to the hostel until I noticed my shadow walking slump-shouldered in front of me. It looked as if it might have been trudging through deep mud, and each tiny footstep appeared to zap more of what little strength it had left.

Was that really me?

I looked at Dad to get my eyes off the ground. I hoped he

might think of some bit of wisdom to make everything right again, but he didn't seem to have anything more to say. I faked a smile in his direction. I couldn't blame him for doing what he thought he should do.

He couldn't help with the real problem, though—not unless I told him the truth about it. That wasn't about to happen. Not if fixing one problem would create an even worse one.

Still, maybe this talk had been a step in the right direction. In one small way or another.

We stood at the edge of the two-lane road waiting to cross. Two cars were visible, and that made two more than I'd seen the several days we'd been at the hostel. One turned beside us into Red Cedar Lane. The driver waved. She probably worked at the prison.

The other car was maybe fifty yards farther back. We could have crossed safely if we'd rushed, but since Dad has always been cautious about crossing streets, we waited.

I watched as the Honda Accord drew closer. I could see a cell phone in the driver's left hand. I couldn't see her mouth moving, though, so I assumed she was listening. When she was about twenty feet away, her car swerved unexpectedly in our direction.

I heard myself screaming and felt Dad jerking me out of the way.

chapter thirty-nine

B aby girl," Dad said as he looked into my eyes, "we're going home today—tomorrow at the latest."

"Today," I said. "No reason to wait until tomorrow to go back to the hostel."

The ER doctor had said I didn't have any real injuries. Dad wouldn't let me ask about the driver who'd been using her cell phone when she lost control of the car. That was okay.

Under the circumstances, I didn't want to know. What I'd just gone through had been too much like viewing my mom's accident in retrospect, even though I hadn't actually seen this woman take her Honda for a flying leap into the field.

I did learn that she didn't hit a tree, though.

"I can hardly wait to get back and start painting. I don't know why all of you had to come over here to get me checked over." *Huh? Graham, you came, too? That was sweet of you.* "Fact is, I don't know why you brought me here. That car didn't hit me, and you've wasted the whole morning."

Dad's face disagreed. So I managed a weak grin. "You saved me, Pops."

Had the doctor given me something for the pain in my shoulder? Dad jerked me out of the way pretty hard, didn't he? Surely Dr. what's-her-hair had medicated me with something strange, though. Strange and potent. I'd never called my father 'Pops' before. Not even in fun.

"I may have saved your life, but you started screaming like a madwoman *as soon as you realized what had happened,* and you didn't stop until the doctor gave you a shot." That question answered. "And *that* is why you're here."

A madwoman? Uh, bad choice of words, Dad. I'd already been worried that this guilt might drive me insane.

"Am I screaming now, Dad?" I almost said Pop again. I felt half normal and half loopy. I guess that still added up to loopy. Like a woman not being just "half-pregnant" at four-and-a-half months.

"No, and I'll gag you on the plane if you start up again." I loved his cute grin, but I didn't like what he was saying.

"On the plane? You said we were going back to the hostel."

"No, Kim. *You* said that. I called Dr. Lancaster while the ER doctor was examining you. He said to bring you home."

"No! What does he know? He's here and I'm there. Whatever."

Dad was pretty smart for a fortyish-year-old father. He didn't argue with me.

"We'll talk about it later—when that shot wears off and you're 100 percent rational again."

That was the last thing I heard for quite some time.

The smell of steak, fries, and—*yes, Graham!*—homemade rolls woke me up. I wished we could take him home with us. At least we'd eat well and he wouldn't wear us out by talking too much.

Home? No. We weren't going home. Seems like Dad said something to me at the hospital about going home, but I must have dreamed it. We still had a week and a half to go on this project.

"Hello, sleepyhead," Aleesha said with a grin. "Fine construction worker you are, lazing the day away in bed."

In bed? I looked around. Huh! I wasn't in my sleeping bag. Was this. . .was I in Graham's bedroom and Graham's bed? Must be. None of the units had beds yet. Besides that, the temperature was comfortable. I definitely wasn't in one of the units.

"What. . .time?"

"Suppertime, girl. Did Mr. Scott jerk your nose out of joint or just your arm?"

My arm? Uh, had the ER doctor even mentioned that? I'd probably been too out of it to feel her fix it. Ah, but the resulting pain was what that loopiness-inducing medication was supposed to kill.

Things were starting to come back to me. While nobody else was around, I told Aleesha about my discussion with Dad about my nightmares and the assumption he'd made about my guilt.

"Just let him think that, girl," she said. "Sometimes the whole truth doesn't edify anyone."

I'd never heard anyone rationalize a half-truth so biblically before.

When Jo stopped by a few minutes later, Aleesha and I cracked up.

"Wha. . . ?" she said in irritated protest.

"You must not have passed a mirror on the way in," I told her.

"You didn't think you were white enough?" Aleesha said. "You must have *bathed* in paint this time."

A look of confusion appeared on Jo's face. She might have thought we were exaggerating, but she couldn't have covered herself more completely if she'd filled a bathtub with white paint and jumped in with all her clothes on.

Aleesha found a masculine-looking hand mirror on Graham's chest of drawers and handed it to her.

I had to give Jo credit. A month earlier—maybe a week earlier—I would've expected to see a fiery red blush showing through her fine new vanilla coating, but she cracked up, too, and that got all three of us going.

"What in the. . . ?" Dad said as he walked in. "Oh, the three of you. . .together." That apparently explained everything.

He might not have realized it, but this was probably the closest Jo, Aleesha, and I had ever been. Maybe we'd even become three best friends.

"Dad," I said as soon as I could quit laughing, "you didn't say something in the ER about going home, did you?"

His mouth straightened from a smile to a father-knows-best look that was far too serious for my taste.

"We'll go." Aleesha motioned to Jo, who'd already started getting up off the edge of the bed.

"Don't leave me, guys!" I said. I shot them a desperate look.

"You girls may stay," Dad said. "Kim, your reaction to that accident this morning was off-the-scale. Dr. Lancaster agrees. We don't have any choice about taking you home and back to see him."

Jo's mouth twisted slightly, but I didn't make any effort to figure out why.

"Dad, I'm fine now. We had that great talk about my guilt this morning, and I know how supportive you'll be now that you understand. I love you, and I appreciate everything you've done for me. I couldn't ask for a more wonderful dad."

Dad couldn't see Jo's gag-me motion behind his back, but I almost broke out laughing at her. I'd never dared to try wrapping him around my little finger before our relationship improved, and I hadn't wanted or needed to since.

At least everything I'd said was true, even if my motive was less than pure. But he didn't seem to have been paying attention.

"Since I promised to take care of Jo, she'll have to go home with us. I've talked to Aleesha's folks, and they don't mind if she stays to the end."

I was ready to hop out of bed and start pacing at breakneck speed, but I didn't. "But we'll be letting Rob down."

"I discussed our situation with him. He shared some relevant news. We've been so much more efficient than he expected, he doesn't have enough work left to keep us here a second week. So we would've been heading home in four more days, anyhow."

"What about the cost of changing our unchangeable tickets?" A logical appeal to a man's money sense was worth a try.

"No good, Kim. I factored in that kind of expense when I budgeted for this trip. I wasn't 100 percent confident you were up to coming, so I actually paid more to get unrestricted tickets so we could make penalty-free changes if we needed to."

That man hadn't missed a trick. Maybe I should have had dozens of my own left, but I didn't. I was about to use the last one I could think of. It was drastic. Drastic. Almost certain to fail. Moreover, I wondered if I had enough courage to make the effort.

Aleesha could have done it easily enough. But I wasn't Aleesha.

"Dad, you remember when you and I asked Mr. Snelling if Jo could come?"

"Of course."

"Do you recall what Mr. Snelling said?"

"About. . . ?"

"About Jo's age?" Jo's face lit up. She knew what I was doing, but Aleesha still wore a blank look. She hadn't been at the Snellings' house with Dad and me, so she didn't know what I was up to.

"He said. . ." Dad must have had a lightbulb moment. "You rascal!" As serious as this discussion had been, he actually laughed. "Are you trying to tell me I can't *make* you come home because you're eighteen now?"

Aleesha not only joined in the laughter but also gave herself one of those *"Now why didn't I think of that?"* slaps on the forehead that made her head sound empty.

"Dad, I respect you almost as much as I love you, but this is my life we're talking about. You're trying to protect me, but I don't need protecting. Not like I did when you snatched me out of harm's way this morning, anyhow. I'm not fighting you. I'm just asking you to let me grow up and make this decision myself."

Jo and Aleesha both applauded. Rob had shown up sometime during this discussion, and he gave me a thumbs-up. And—lo and behold—Graham stood in the doorway wearing a smile so slight that I was the only person who could have recognized it.

Then again, I'd always claimed I could see cats smile.

"Okay," Dad said. "Looks like I'm outvoted. But if you have any more nightmares—I'm counting on you to be honest with me—we're going home that day if I have to tie you up and throw you in the suitcase. You understand?"

I nodded. Although I'd won the battle, had I won the war? How could I keep from having another nightmare when I hadn't been able to prevent the second and third ones?

I couldn't very well go without sleep for the rest of the week. *Nothing like a little extra pressure, huh, kid?*

chapter forty

After supper, I needed a break from the, uh, older adults. I hated to admit it, but sometimes I had trouble thinking of Jo, Aleesha, and me as adults. It wasn't "them and us" with Dad, Rob, and Graham, though. Not in a hostile way, but talking with them longer than a few minutes at a time reminded me that we lived in completely different worlds.

We probably belonged to a different animal species, too. If the men would just hibernate for a few years while we girls caught up, that would help to level the mountain between us.

"You two want to walk to Red Cedar with me? Those men"—I did a Vanna White sweep in the direction of Dad, Rob, and Graham, who were busy with their own conversation at the other end of the living room—"aren't very good at girl talk."

"Maybe not, honey, but I *love* hanging with those old men and listening to their wisdom."

Who won the World Series in 1964—and how—was wisdom?

While the men might not have appreciated Aleesha's "old men" reference, they would have warmed to her sincere appreciation.

"Mr. Rob and Mr. Scott are the best. You know what, though?" She didn't pause long enough to get a reaction. "I'm a great judge of character. Right?" No pause there, either. "But I'm still not sure about Mr. Graham. There's something about him."

"He's okay," I said, suddenly shy about admitting I'd grown rather fond of him. *Graham, why did you just look at me that way? We weren't talking loud enough for you to hear your name.*

But I couldn't argue with Aleesha's statement. Graham was just as much a mystery now as the day I met him. One I doubted any of us would ever solve.

"So, ladies, are you walking or not?"

"It's fun, Aleesha," Jo said. "Count me in."

"I guess I can stand a little girl talk, although I prefer woman talk. I'll have to go. You might talk about me if I don't." Aleesha snorted, Jo and I giggled, and the men looked at us and rolled their eyes.

"Let's go," Jo said as she grabbed her coat from the back of the sofa and started putting it on.

"What's the rush?" I said just before she reached the door. "The service doesn't start for another hour, and we don't need but twenty minutes to walk there."

Dummy! We need more time than that for what I want to discuss.

Jo broke out in a bright blush. Ah! That's right. Alfredo. Was she hoping to talk with him before the service started? Did she expect him to be waiting for her? We needed to discuss my concerns before their relationship got out of control.

Trembling and perspiring profusely in spite of the cold night air, I kept drawing back rather than setting my foot on the road.

"Here," Aleesha said, holding out her right hand. "Close your eyes, and I'll guide you across." Her powers of observation equaled her sensitivity. When Jo gave her a quizzical look, Aleesha said, "That woman's accident this morning. Kim doesn't want to see where it happened."

We'd barely made it to the other side of the two-lane road before Aleesha started talking. "Jo, why *did* you want to come over here so early?"

Although we all carried lighted flashlights, the shadows hid Jo's face.

"I. . .hate to rush," she answered. She couldn't have fooled a deaf and blind person with that excuse.

"Then why are we walking so fast?"

Until Aleesha said that, I hadn't noticed that we were zipping up Red Cedar Lane as if we were Olympic runners and Jo was slightly in the lead. This was no casual stroll. Aleesha seemed to be waiting patiently for an answer that never came. I decided to give it a shot, but I'd try a different approach.

"That Alfredo is pretty cute, isn't he, Aleesha?" I reached over and squeezed her shoulder in the darkness.

"My word, yes." Aleesha's exaggerated enthusiasm would have made a statue jealous. "If I didn't have to wait for him to get out of jail, I'd set my sights on him. I still might."

I heard a thud up ahead of us, followed by the crash landing of Jo's flashlight and the sound of batteries rolling all over the asphalt.

"You okay, Jo?" I said.

"I. . .I tripped." I shone my light where she'd bent over to pick up her flashlight parts. "Over my own feet."

"And it didn't have anything to do with Kim's mention of Alfredo. . . ?" Aleesha asked.

"No." From her tone of voice, she wasn't enjoying this conversation. "It was *your* comment."

"Ah? You're kind of sweet on that fellow, aren't you?" Aleesha might have intended to be more subtle, but even she wasn't a good enough actor to pull it off on an occasion like this.

Silence.

"I'll take that as a yes," Aleesha said.

"There are other issues involved," I said, "but I'm most concerned about your behavior during the service."

"I know that's right," Aleesha said.

Although I couldn't see Jo clearly, I could tell she was facing us.

Dad had once caught a possum in one of those animal-friendly traps. When we stayed away from her, she was just mean and ugly, but if we approached the cage, she opened her mouth defensively and bared the most ferocious-looking set of teeth imaginable.

I wondered if Jo was looking at Aleesha and me that way now.

"Nobody minds the talking when you're translating hymns and prayers," Aleesha said as if aware we weren't going to make any progress unless we helped Jo out of the corner we'd backed her into.

"Translating the message is especially important," I added. "Alfredo is lucky—"

"Blessed," Aleesha said.

"He's blessed to have somebody as talented as you to help him worship. But you two were getting a *little close*"—I purposely drew out those last two words—"during Dad's prayer last night." Aleesha's coat swished as she turned in my direction. She must not have known about that.

"I didn't do anything wrong, and we weren't disturbing anybody." Talk about a defensive tone of voice.

"No one but me maybe," I said.

"And why didn't you have your eyes *closed*?"

We're just trying to keep you out of trouble, Jo.

"The two of you were chattering pretty loudly during the message," Aleesha said in a tone that—for her—was neutral. "I don't believe you were translating the sermon and discussing it, too."

"If it's any of your business, I was. . .witnessing to him."

"And he thinks the Gospel is *amusing*?" Aleesha said. Neutrality had given way to bluntness. Anyone lying to Aleesha should expect major repercussions.

Dead silence.

Although Jo shot out ahead, leaving us by ourselves for a few seconds, we ramped up our speed and got close enough to stay maybe ten feet behind. She was huffing and puffing, and I suspected she was pouting as much as breathing hard from exertion.

Aleesha raised her voice to a level the insiders could have heard. "Miss Kim, I don't think Miss Jo is happy with me." Her tone had a slight lilt. Like she didn't care what Jo thought.

"You think?" I played along. "Why's that?"

"I don't think she likes hearing the truth."

"The truth? And what truth is that?"

"That I love and treasure her as a friend, but I have to step in and speak my mind when my friends act like they have a limited amount of good sense."

You know I'd never dare to talk to Jo that way. Just be careful.

"So you're speaking the truth in love?" Although that was a biblical concept, I couldn't remember the actual context. Didn't it have something to do with correcting Christians who'd strayed from the straight and narrow? If so, I'd worded my question in a more appropriate way than I realized.

"I'm trying to. But since Jo's not paying attention to me, I'll have to share it with you instead."

"Go, girl."

"I'm not too sure I'd take the affections of a fellow I met in prison too seriously."

"How come?"

Jo couldn't have shut this discussion out if she'd stuck her fingers in her ears.

"He probably hasn't been around a woman in ages. Any woman would probably look good."

"And anyone as cute as Jo would be an even better prize." No need to be completely negative.

"I'd say 'desirable target' and not 'better prize.' None-theless, if that woman isn't very experienced. . ." That statement flattened the nail head. Jo hadn't dated nearly as much as I had.

"If she doesn't have your street smarts about men, you mean?"

"Right you are, Miss Kim. She may think she's picking out a ripe watermelon"—I barely kept from cracking up—"but she can't be sure because it's locked inside a glass case where she can't give it a proper thumping."

I tried to keep from smirking while waiting for Aleesha to continue, but I couldn't.

"A gal can't be too sure what that watermelon's like inside until she can check it out more closely. Can't do that until somebody unlocks the case."

"Are you saying he may not be what he seems to be?"

"He may be perfectly ripe and fine. Or he could be rotten to the core. Or somewhere in between. I don't know. Wouldn't do to let a good friend pick some potentially rotten fruit because she isn't sufficiently cautious, though."

Aleesha, no! I said to be careful. I think you've gone a little too far.

But it was too late. She'd already said it, and Jo took off running.

Aleesha and I didn't even try to catch up. Our concern was no match for her anger.

chapter forty-one

"Forget being friends with Aleesha," Jo said as we began working on the next-to-the-last unpainted unit. I hoped she didn't expect *me* to feel that way. "She butchered my feelings last night. Treated me like I don't have any sense at all."

"In matters of the heart, any woman can, uh, lose her perspective." Definitely eggshell-walking time. "But she loves you. She just wants to protect you."

"Yeah, sure. It's not like I'd marry Alfredo the second he got out of prison."

"When is that? Do you know?"

"He's in for another seven years." She answered the next question before I could ask it. "And, no, he didn't say what he's in for."

I decided not to suggest that he might have committed rape, assault, or some other violent crime. After all, he was in a medium-security prison for less dangerous offenders. Still, seven years would be a dreadfully severe jail term for failing to pay a couple of parking tickets.

"I'll be glad when Aleesha goes home and it's just you and me again. You understand, accept, and respect me."

"I do, Jo, but I said some. . .things last night, too."

"That's okay. I forgive you."

How could I tell her I meant everything I said and wasn't sorry? I didn't need or want her forgiveness. I just wanted one of my two best friends to come to her senses and remain friends with the other one.

"I wouldn't have said it the way Aleesha did—"

"How can you stand being friends with someone who's so blunt and outspoken?"

She may be that way at times, Jo, but that's not the issue.

"She says what she thinks," I said. "You don't have to wonder where you stand with her. That's better than having a friend who's always talking about you behind your back."

"Not in my book, girlfriend."

I kept my sigh as quiet as I could. Jo wasn't thinking straight, and I wouldn't have much chance of changing her mind.

Time for a change of subject. "Thank you for not chatting last night at inappropriate times, by the way."

"Sorry about the night before. You were right about that."

"*We* were."

"*You* were. You singular."

"I'll have you know I kept my eyes closed during the prayer time." I winked at her.

"Thanks."

If I ever wrote about our experiences at Red Cedar, I'd have to edit that conversation down to basics. It went on and on like that forever.

"What do you think of that mountain?" Jo said, throwing the last shovelful of dirt on the previous topic.

Duh, Jo. Mountains are everywhere here. "Which one?"

"The one back of the hostel. The locals call it Tabletop Mountain."

What locals have you met? Graham? "I've never paid attention to it. I enjoy looking east toward the sunrise."

"But those mountains are too far away to climb." She laughed, and the tension that had my stomach in knots earlier finally loosened its grip. "This one's right outside our back door."

I stepped outside, looked behind the hostel, and then came back in.

"I see why it's called Tabletop. And you want to climb it?"

Such. . .ambitious ideas from a girl whose mom hadn't let her cross the street by herself when there wasn't a car in sight? Then again, maybe that's why she wanted to make this climb now.

"I asked Rob about it," Jo said. "He's climbed it. Graham, too. They both say the climb's not hard, but it's easy to get lost up there. Rob has written directions and a map. Got 'em off of the Internet, he said."

I laughed.

"You want to go with me, girlfriend?"

"I'll have to think on that one. Any bears up there?"

"All kinds of wildlife, Rob says."

Hmm. Not sure this would be my glass of soda. I might be able to face a bear if he wasn't very big, but not an uncaged possum.

"Let me know, Kim. Your dad says we're not leaving till Monday, and we won't do any work on Sunday."

"We'll still do a final service, won't we?"

"Sunday night."

Before I could say anything else, Aleesha came flying in. The look on her face was something to behold. I couldn't tell if it was fear, anger, or both.

"Jo. . ." Aleesha sounded like she was warming up for an attack. What in the world. . . ?

"I'm not talking to you, Jefferson," Jo said, turning her back on Aleesha

"You'd *better* talk to me." I'd never heard Aleesha so upset. "Where is it?"

Jo turned halfway. "Where is *what*?"

"The letter."

"I don't know what you're talking about."

I didn't know whether Jo was telling the truth, but it didn't matter. I couldn't make heads or tails of their argument.

"That Chaplain Thomas. He called Mr. Rob. Told us not to come back. Said the warden agreed."

My stomach felt like I'd just dropped to the ground in one of those free-fall amusement park rides.

"What are you two talking about?" I hoped my tone was exasperated enough to force an immediate answer from somebody.

"Jo. . ." Aleesha could barely get the words out. "She brought a letter out of the prison for Alfredo."

I narrowed my eyes and stared at Aleesha. She couldn't have been more serious.

"Yeah, Jefferson," Jo said. "A letter to his lawyer. I told him I'd mail it for him."

"Thomas saw you. He reported you to the warden."

"So? It's not like I was helping Alfredo break out."

"You really don't get it, do you?"

I didn't get it yet myself, but I had a nagging memory trying to break through the recesses of my brain. I'd read the rules when we got back from our first night's service. Hadn't they said. . . ?

Jo shrugged.

"It's against the rules to mail a letter for an insider. For all you know, you *could* be helping him plan an escape."

"You don't know Alfredo like I do," Jo said before slopping a big glob of paint against the wall. She stood there watching it drip without making any effort to spread it.

I didn't have to wonder whether she would've preferred giving Aleesha a good coating of white instead.

I was surprised that Jo had broken the rules, but I wasn't incredulous or even angry. I was too concerned about the fact the warden was punishing all of us. If we couldn't get back into Red Cedar, this trip would be a partial waste.

Construction was worthwhile. Even the limited amount we'd done. But interacting with the insiders—sharing with the real believers and witnessing to the ones who might be faking their Christianity—was our real purpose in being here.

If Jo's stupidity cost us that ministry, I wasn't sure I'd be in a rush to reset my forgiveness counter.

"Why's the warden punishing all of us?" I asked.

"Mr. Rob didn't say. Jo, you didn't mail that letter yet, did you?"

"I haven't seen a mailbox around here." Bitterness and sarcasm were a nasty mix. "Have you?"

"Mr. Rob has an appointment to talk with the warden this afternoon. He'll plead for forgiveness."

"Fat chance of that," I said. "Even a good Christian brother like Warden Jenkins has to obey the rules of his workplace. Especially somewhere like Red Cedar."

"That's why Mr. Rob asked me to get the letter. We'll give it back and show him we've all learned a lesson—no harm done."

"You think the warden's going to let me back in?" Jo said. "Not if he's that much of a stickler for those dumb old rules." An eighteen-year-old ought to have a more mature whine than that.

"You might be surprised," Aleesha said with a hint of kindness I couldn't have managed right then.

"He'd *better* let me back in. I can't leave without seeing Alfredo again." The quality of her whine was going downhill fast.

My parents used to sing a folk song that had been popular during the 1960s. Actually a protest against the Vietnam War, which was going on at the time, it had a line that went, "When will they ever learn? When will they ever learn?"

I was beginning to wonder the same thing myself. About Jo.

chapter forty-two

G od must have understood Rob's reason for asking me
to accompany him to see Warden Jenkins, but He
didn't explain it to me. I couldn't have been more terrified if
somebody had thrown me in the cage with that nasty possum—
only to have the ferocious critter look me in the face and start
licking its chops. Or maybe start foaming at the mouth.

"Rob. . .Kim." Although Warden Jenkins shook hands with
both of us, his greeting wasn't nearly as pleasant as it had been
on our first visit. His tone sounded more formal. He pointed to
two ordinary straight chairs, and we sat down.

Oh, man! We're in for it. . .

"Thank you for seeing us, Larry. I—"

"I'm sorry if I seem out of sorts, but I've just gotten off the
phone with my boss. He's not a Christian, and we have major
differences of opinion about how to run a prison. As if that's
not enough, he likes to micromanage. Need I say more?"

Oh, great. We'd come about a problem we didn't have
much hope of solving at a time that couldn't have been worse.
From the look in Rob's eyes, he had the same fears I had.

"We can come back later," Rob said. *Yeah, after missing
tonight's service.* "But I did bring Alfredo's letter—"

"Oh, that?" he said. "You didn't need to make a special trip
for that. Jo can give it back to Alfredo, and that will square
things. She just needs to remind him she's not permitted to
mail anything for him."

Huh?

Rob puffed up a little, and I hoped he wouldn't say

anything rash. "We've been worried to death ever since we learned that Jo broke one of the rules."

The warden waved his hands in a crisscross motion. "No need. She didn't break that rule on purpose." *You just keep believing that, Warden Jenkins.* "We all make mistakes, and Jo's was nothing major."

Man! Is the warden this easygoing every time one of the insiders messes up? I'll bet those guys really like him.

"Then why all the to-do about it?" Although Rob had managed to keep his tone calm, I'd rarely seen him more aggravated. "I mean, having Thomas tell me you weren't letting any of us come back. . ."

"Is *that* what he told you?" The warden cleared his throat. "No wonder you're upset." His threatening look dissolved into a smile of amusement. "If that had been the case, I would have told you myself. I don't let my employees do my dirty work. Nor do I ask them to."

"You mean it's not true?" I blurted out. Very seldom had I felt like cursing since breaking the habit in Santa María, but now was one of those times.

"What did you tell him, then?" Rob asked. He didn't appear to realize he was grinding one palm with his fist. Like he was getting ready to hit somebody. And that somebody was *not* the warden.

Warden Jenkins chuckled. "I thanked him for his report on the breach of the rules and said I'd ask your team to reread them."

Rob and I looked at one another and then at the warden.

"Why—?" I said.

"Why would he. . .bend the truth like that?" Rob said at almost the same instant.

"Your presence seems to threaten him. I think he's afraid somebody's going to tell you what's going on. Or what I think is going on."

Rob must have noticed my eyes narrowing.

"Larry, Kim doesn't know about that."

Warden Jenkins leaned back in his chair, crossed his legs, and looked into my eyes. "Are you a trustworthy young lady, Kim. . .Kimmy?" My eyes must have opened to the size of classroom-sized world globes, especially when he added, "And how sneaky can you be?"

You can't possibly want me to do more than just keep an eye on Chappy, can you? Please ask me to do something safer. Like kiss a rabid possum on the nose.

I made myself maintain eye contact. "I hope I'm trustworthy." Although I was trying to speak up, I could barely hear my own voice. "As for sneaky. . .I am a woman, sir."

Aleesha would never let me hear the end of it if she found out I'd made a statement like that. Especially to a man.

"Good. Now, have you noticed anything strange going on with Chaplain Thomas?"

"Besides Chappy's negative attitude toward us and his seeming lack of a living relationship with God through faith in Jesus Christ?" I felt like a preacher for a second there.

"Chappy?" He chuckled. "He deserves a nickname like that. You've made a good start. Sounds like we're on the same wavelength." His lingering smile dimmed and then disappeared.

"Actually, sir, I've noticed that he uses the worship services to speak individually with some of the insiders. I wasn't aware of it the first night, but I've been watching him ever since. The men don't seem to enjoy those private conversations. They look—how should I say it?—ill at ease. Perhaps even scared. I can't tell if it's worse when he calls them over or when they return to their seats."

"Excellent observations, Kimmy." Rob nodded in agreement. "You couldn't have done better if you'd known what to look for."

I held my palms out in a *"So what's going on?"* gesture.

"Won't it hurt Kim's objectivity if you tell her now, Larry? Power of suggestion might make her see what she's looking for instead of what really is."

"I'll have to take that chance, Rob." The warden uncrossed his legs and leaned across his desk as if he were about to confide the location of the Holy Grail. "Kimmy, we've become suspicious that Chaplain Thomas is abusing his position."

I couldn't have felt more confused.

"Let me be more specific. You're familiar with blackmail and extortion?"

"Not personally." I probably blushed. "I know what. . .I know what they are, I mean." My twisted tongue threatened to take over. "What do they. . .what does that. . .what do those things have to do with him? And me?"

"I believe. . .Chappy has been using blackmail and extortion to obtain money from the insiders." The warden's voice was kind. He hadn't meant to embarrass me.

"Money, sir?"

"The insiders have accounts here. Outsiders can send money for incidental expenses; the insiders also earn a pittance for the jobs they perform here."

"Enough to make extortion worthwhile?" I couldn't imagine such a thing.

"You'd be surprised. Don't forget the number of men Chappy meets in his day-to-day work. He's free to come and go as he pleases. He can interact with anyone—Christian or not. A little bit each from a number of men over a long period of time adds up. He's probably accumulated a small fortune."

Daddy, where are you? Can't you protect your baby girl from learning that the adult world is just as corrupt now as it was in Noah's day?

"If you know he's guilty of these things, why haven't you fired him. . .or arrested him or something?"

The warden hadn't said how long this behavior had been going on other than "a long period of time."

"We want to, but we don't have enough evidence."

"Then how did you learn about it?"

"An insider smuggled an unsigned note to a guard during mealtime when no one was paying attention." He handed me a photocopy of it. I glanced back and forth between the warden and the paper. "Whoever slipped it to the guard may or may not have been the actual author. None of the insiders would want to be accused of snitching—not even on a prison employee."

Because of the note's size and distinctive background pattern, I gathered that the original had been written on a paper napkin. I could see wrinkles, too. As if the sender had passed it along as an inconspicuous piece of trash.

"Chaplain. . .extortion. . .our money." I read aloud. "That's not much to go on, is it?" Anybody with a grudge against the chaplain could have written a note like that. Especially a non-Christian or a member of some group that opposes Christianity.

Warden Jenkins touched the Bible that occupied the left front corner of his desk and traced the printing with his index finger. I hadn't noticed before that he was left-handed.

"I take matters like this quite seriously, and I've done everything within my power to verify this accusation. Or to refute it. I'm not assuming Chaplain Thomas's guilt. This is still America, but—unfortunately—this accusation makes sense."

Rob eyed me with an *"Are you okay, Kim?"* look. I let my eyes respond, *"I don't know."*

"I've tried to become friends with the Christian insiders," Warden Jenkins said, "but they won't talk to me. Not except in a superficial way. I can't blame them. Even though they accept me as a Christian brother, that doesn't change the fact that I'm still the warden."

"So what do you want Kim to do?" Rob said. "She and her friends are leaving next Monday, so there isn't much time."

"We'll leave even sooner if I have another nightmare." I couldn't keep the inner pressure from exploding into spoken words. What a brilliant red my face must have turned when I realized how silly my outburst had probably sounded. "Uh, don't ask, Warden. But please pray I don't have another nightmare while I'm here. Seriously."

"Of course, Kimmy. That's the least I can do for you." He jotted something down on his desk calendar and put a big asterisk beside it. "I won't forget."

Peace I hadn't known since before my father delivered his ultimatum about going home bathed my soul and body. Had Warden Jenkins just prayed for me? That wouldn't have surprised me. The Bible said the prayers of a righteous man accomplish much, and he struck me as a righteous man who did an excellent job of serving God in a very unrighteous atmosphere.

"About helping. . ." He scratched his head. I wondered if his job had given him all those gray hairs. "At prayer time, why don't you pray out loud, too? Ask God to deal with any situations at Red Cedar that aren't Christlike. Maybe that will get some of the insiders thinking."

"Thinking and maybe ready to talk?" That sounded easy enough. But who would they be willing to talk to?

"Maybe express an interest in learning more about the men. Say something like, 'If you want someone besides your cellmate to talk to for a few minutes, just let me know. . .'"

Our team had talked with the insiders quite a bit, but always in groups.

"You think I'm qualified to help that way?"

"You seem to be a good listener, Kimmy."

"But is that safe, Larry?" Rob said. He sounded concerned. "I know this would still be within sight of the group, but. . ."

I hadn't considered this assignment to be dangerous. . .not until now.

"Male prisoners respect women of any age more than you can possibly imagine. Few men hate their own mothers. Kimmy won't be in any danger. And if an insider should request a private talk away from the worship service, we'll schedule it so my wife sits in on it."

"But will anyone even ask to talk with me with Chappy present?" I said. "I mean, if he's holding something over their heads, he's undoubtedly watching to make sure they don't talk at length with any of us. Especially not one-on-one."

"Hmm. Maybe it's time for me to tell Chaplain Thomas that he's done a great job babysitting you folks, but you're doing fine now and I don't need him to keep an eye on you any longer."

"Will he buy that?" Rob asked.

"He will when I tell him that's an order. Direct disobedience would simplify things. Between that and the way he lied to you and purposely misrepresented me—I'll document all of that in his personnel record—I could justify severe discipline. Read that any way you want to. But if he's guilty of the things we suspect, I'd rather see him spend the next few years of his life as an insider."

Boy! Was I glad this man and I were on the same side.

"Let me ask this, Kimmy. Are you free to come here during the daytime if an insider wants to talk with you then?"

I looked at Rob. "Ask my boss." I winked at him. "He schedules my time."

"We can spare her for something like that," he said.

After saying our good-byes, Rob and I walked to the office

door. Warden Jenkins had one more thing to say, though.

"How's Graham O'Reilly doing? I heard about his job at the hostel. Please give him my regards. He's the best cook we ever had. And a great guy. If anyone ever deserved his freedom, it's Graham."

chapter forty-three

I shook my head. For the hundredth time since I started giving Aleesha the report about my visit with the warden, I realized that—even if the warden hadn't requested me to leave Jo out of the loop—I wouldn't have had much choice. She wasn't objective. She trusted Alfredo—way too much.

That was too bad, because she would have been the incredibly perfect person to involve in this investigation. I didn't know enough Spanish to talk with Alfredo. But Jo did.

Alfredo would have confided in her. He wouldn't have had to worry about anyone who didn't speak Spanish overhearing him. She could have found out whether he had problems with the chaplain. . .and whether he knew of other insiders who did.

But she wouldn't simply have asked questions. She would have told Alfredo about the warden's suspicions, thinking she was doing something good. And he might have taken that information right back to the chaplain, enabling him to cover his back and avoid getting caught.

So the warden wanted me to try talking with him.

"I barely know any Spanish at all," I protested.

"That's okay. My wife is reasonably fluent. We'll arrange for the three of you to meet together."

The problem was arranging to talk with Alfredo without automatically putting him on the defensive. Warden Jenkins didn't have any suggestions about handling that.

"Girlfriend," Aleesha said after I finished giving her the lowdown, "what in the world have you gotten yourself mixed up in this time?" Before I could respond, she added,

"Sounds like bad TV."

I shook my head. I'd watched more than my share of reality shows before Santa María, but now I felt like I'd gotten trapped inside one.

"Aleesha, let's pray."

We knelt on the drop cloth and joined hands. "Lord God," Aleesha said, "we praise You for who You are. You know the number of hairs on our heads and the thoughts inside. You know we constantly fail You, even though You never stop loving us, and we beg Your forgiveness for each sin. But You also love each of the men in that prison. You love even the most unrepentant insiders as much as You love the two of us. We pray for the ones who already belong to You, and we pray for salvation for those who don't."

Aleesha's prayer was picking up momentum, and—even though I often had trouble praying along with someone else's prayers—my spirit was in sync with her every word. "We pray for Chaplain Thomas. Whether he's guilty of extortion and blackmail or not, we don't know. But You do. And You know whether he's even one of Your children. Lord, please do whatever is best for Your kingdom, and use us in whatever way You desire to bring about a suitable solution. The solution that suits You, that is. . ."

When she paused, I took over.

"Father, each of these men is precious in Your sight. Help us to inspire the believers we've been worshipping with, and use us to reach the pretenders. It hurts us deeply to imagine that Chaplain Thomas might be abusing his position in such a harmful and illegal way. Help us to find the truth. We admit we don't like the man, and we ask Your forgiveness for that. It's wrong for us to hate somebody You love."

I knew I was taking a chance, but I felt led to add this to my prayer, "Lord, please be with Jo. She's lived such a sheltered life that she's far too susceptible to people like Alfredo. Father, please give her some of Your insight into what we see as the foolishness of her actions, and help her not to be hurt in the process.

"Heavenly Father, You know how much I treasure both Aleesha's and Jo's friendships, and it hurts me to see the way they avoid one another. Please unite them somehow."

Although Aleesha didn't release my hand, she lessened her grip until we were barely still holding hands. I must have hit a raw nerve. I wasn't trying to, though. I just wanted God to solve a relational problem I couldn't touch on my own.

I didn't feel led to pray about my guilt or my nightmares, although thoughts of them had haunted me throughout the day. I'd come to California hoping that helping others would alleviate those problems, and it had done a reasonably good job on the symptoms. But it hadn't solved any of the real problems. The guilt would come back full force when we got home again and I found myself in the midst of everything that reminded me of Mom.

Oh, no. . . Aleesha had begun praying again while I was off in la-la land, and she just paused. Had she been praying about her and Jo? Would I dare to ask?

"Heavenly Father," I said, "please bless Warden Jenkins and help him in his efforts to administer Red Cedar in a Christian manner. And please help Graham to be as free in spirit now as he is in body."

Aleesha squeezed my hand.

"In Jesus' name, we pray. Amen."

"Amen."

Aleesha didn't waste any time trying to satisfy her curiosity. "What's this about Graham and freedom, girl?"

I couldn't keep from laughing at her. She'd probably squeezed my hand to end the prayer just so she could ask that.

"Warden Jenkins didn't say much. Just something about giving his regards to Graham and Graham being the best cook they'd ever had and Graham deserving his freedom."

"And you didn't ask for details?"

I hoped Aleesha was teasing. "I'm not you, you know." I giggled. "Is that something a woman of the darker persuasion would have done?"

She started laughing, too. She knew I didn't believe anything so silly.

"Nope. Only pushy white girls do that."

I knew she didn't mean that, either. Our ability to exaggerate and laugh at our racial differences never ceased to amaze me.

"Seriously, though"—her eyes pled with me to fulfill her curiosity—"that's all he told you?"

"He didn't 'tell' us anything."

"Are you going to ask him?"

"Him? The warden? I should think not."

"I wouldn't, either. I meant Graham. The two of you have been getting tight. I've—"

"You know I don't drink," I said with a giggle.

"You know what I meant. I've been watching you and Graham. Before you know it, you're going to be an item—another Jo and Alfredo."

When Rob heard us laughing, he stuck his head in the door. He looked from one of us to the other. He didn't have to say anything. Just as Dad had done a day or two earlier, he shook his head as if seeing us together was all the explanation he needed. After he left, I held up my left hand. "Isn't it beautiful?"

"What's that, my dear?"

"My engagement ring. It's made of two carrots—the edible kind—no diamonds."

"My! One of a kind. I would have expected him to give you

an onion ring, though."

"Ah? Onions are forever, aren't they?"

"The smell is. So's the aftertaste."

I guffawed. "I know you're right about that, girl."

"Seriously, though," Aleesha said, "aren't you curious?"

I exaggerated a quizzical look.

"About Graham, not carrots and onions."

"Of course I am. How long Graham was at Red Cedar. What he did. What his life was like in there. When he got out. All sorts of things I'd like to know."

Aleesha nodded.

"But he deserves his privacy. No way I'd ask Graham personal questions like those. It's none of my business." Then I noticed Graham standing in the doorway. He slipped away before I could say anything.

chapter forty-four

Tension had off-colored the worshipful atmosphere at the prison that evening. Among our team, anyhow.

Jo resembled a paranoid fish in a very small glass bowl the way she kept looking around in every direction. She probably wanted to see who was watching her and Alfredo. And for good reason. All four of her teammates were.

She had returned the letter to Alfredo, but—judging by his unperturbed look—she didn't tell him about the conflict it had created. He looked cool and calm about the whole thing—like Jo's failure to get away with mailing it didn't surprise him. But when she wasn't watching, I saw him tear it into tiny pieces and sprinkle them on the floor.

Aleesha seemed to keep her eyes glued to Jo and Alfredo from the instant they greeted one another until the moment he left to return to his cell. Her distrust of those two was probably as obvious to everyone else as it was to me.

Not that I blamed her. But her attitude was an ongoing reminder that our team had serious relational problems again. I was afraid nothing short of a Red Sea miracle would make things right.

Although Rob seemed to be watching Jo or the chaplain most of the time, I periodically caught him looking at me.

"Kimmy," his eyes seemed to say, *"you asked Larry to let the chaplain attend one more service so you could pay more attention to which insiders he talked to. You thought that might give you a chance to single a couple of them out and inquire casually about their talks with Chaplain Thomas. I'm*

praying for you, girl."

Chappy started with Rock that evening. Ten minutes.
Rock looked tense when called over. He was scowling when he
returned to his seat.

Then Hi, the fellow with a woman's singing voice. He
looked scared at first. Terrified at the end. Twelve minutes.

But I thought I was seeing things when he called Alfredo
over.

Did that mean Chappy was sufficiently fluent in Spanish
to communicate with Alfredo? Or was Alfredo's English less
limited than we thought?

Inadequate English was the reason he hadn't attended the
first service. Although his friend wouldn't have had any reason
to lie about that, I could easily imagine somebody like Alfredo
keeping his English fluency a secret. What an advantage to be
able to understand the other men without their knowing it.

Oh, man. Now I understood why Rob expressed a concern
about my seeing things. Just because I expected to.

Come on, Kim. You're here to help lead in worship.
And tonight you're supposed to share your testimony with
these thirty-some insiders. You can keep an eye on Chaplain
Thomas without straying totally out of a worshipful mood,
can't you? Ha! I guess not. You'd have to get in a reverent
mood first.

"Kimmy wants to share with you now," Rob said from the
podium.

Whoops. That time already? *Lord, I'm counting on You.*
"Hello, fellows."

A robust variety of greetings came at me like handfuls of
confetti from every part of the room. I heard one lone wolf
whistle, followed by a painful "Uhhh!" Somebody must have
given the whistler a good jab in the ribs.

"That Kimmy is a lady." Loud amens followed Rock's

comment. He didn't need to add, *"So treat her like one."* Although he appeared to be addressing the fellow next to him—I got the impression he was a newcomer—he didn't drop his volume when he continued. "You haven't been here so long you've forgotten what a lady is, have you?"

He shook that basketball-sized fist in the air as a warning for all the men to treat me with respect. Those super-sized arm muscles looked bigger than ever. Then he looked around as if daring someone to disagree with him.

Once the clamor of agreement settled down, Rock looked at me. "Miss Kimmy, the floor is yours again."

"Thanks, Rock, and thank you all, men."

Although I was eager to start, my carefully planned testimony no longer seemed appropriate.

Lord, please give me the right words. . .

"When I asked for a chance to tell you what Jesus means to me, I planned on talking about how I used to be a spoiled, self-centered, middle-class girl who grew up in a Christian home, became a Christian a few years ago, and has done a lot of growing up—spiritually, anyhow—during the past six months."

I gasped for air. "My word! Did I really say all of that in one breath?" Light laughter.

"But now that I've just told you that much about myself, let me tell you what God is doing in my life right now." Murmurs of approval.

"Wow!" I said. "I haven't had this much attention from a fine collection of men since"—I scrunched my nose—"uh, since ever."

The men cheered. They seemed to accept and appreciate my sincerity. They *were* fine men. They hadn't lost that quality just because they'd made bad decisions that landed them at Red Cedar. From what I'd seen of this group, I couldn't imagine that any of them would become repeat offenders when they got out.

Not any of the real believers, anyhow. I had my suspicions about which of the men might be goats trying to pass themselves off as sheep, but I couldn't be sure. I lacked a God's-eye-view of their hearts.

"When I first learned that my friends and I would be doing prison ministry while working on the hostel across the road"— *You do know about that, don't you? I can't break the flow to explain now if you don't*—"I was delighted. But you know what killed my joy for a while?"

I looked around. The men were hooked on my words. Even Chappy glanced at me a time or two.

"You're going to laugh at this, but I'd assumed this would be a ladies' prison." The men grinned and pointed at one another. One guy stroked his beard and shook his head. "When I learned it wasn't, I was scared to death. Terrified. I was sure I'd be a lamb among wolves. Nothing personal against the fellow who gave me the wolf whistle a few minutes ago."

Chappy actually laughed at that.

"Yes, I was certain you were all a bunch of murderers, rapists, and animal abusers."

Smiles all around. "Not us, good sister," one gray-haired gentleman said.

"I'm glad I was wrong." Smiles again. "I believe God brought me here to minister to you. If I didn't have a living relationship with God through faith in His son, Jesus Christ, I couldn't do this. I wouldn't care about any of you. I'd still be living that selfish life I used to live."

Heads nodded.

"I admit it. Until not too long ago, I would've been the first to say, 'Serves them right. They're just a bunch of criminals. Throw away the key.' But I don't feel that way anymore. God has reminded me that He loves each of you just as much as He loves me."

A number of eyes glistened. Several men shouted, "Praise the Lord!"

"From what I've learned about God's way of looking at things—I don't claim to understand it—the worst sin any of you has ever committed is no worse in God's sight than the most insignificant wrong I've ever done. I hope that makes sense. I just mean sin is anything that separates us from God, and it's all equal in His sight."

A sniffle here and there. Nodding. Uptight looks relaxing. Smiling.

"I don't believe everyone in this room is a Christian. My friends and I will be going home on Monday, and I don't want to leave without knowing that each of you has the same kind of relationship with God I have. I don't want to see any of you miss out on the victorious life God wants you to live, and I don't want to arrive in heaven and find any of you missing."

Oh, Lord! You've kept those words pouring out of me without my having to think about what to say next, but where do I go from here?

God answered in an unexpected way.

"Men," Dad said. "You've heard my daughter, and let me assure you she wasn't exaggerating about what she used to be like. . .or about what she's like now." The pride in his voice tore me up. "Kim—Kimmy—wants to chat with any of you who want to talk with her. About spiritual matters. . . or personal ones. Anything. Just get her attention after the service when she's not with somebody else. If there's not time to talk to everyone who's interested, we'll make special arrangements for her to visit with you at another time."

A number of men stopped by to chat with me about one thing or another, but nobody said anything about the chaplain. I couldn't help noticing that some of the men kept glancing at him with apparent apprehension. Like they wanted to talk about something they were afraid to bring up.

We stayed later than usual that evening. Until I'd finished talking with some of the men one-on-one. But I was no closer than before to learning anything that would help Warden Jenkins.

As soon as we got outside, Jo held me back while Dad, Rob, and Aleesha headed for the van. "Be right there," she yelled. Then she said something to me, but she spoke so quietly I couldn't hear her at first.

"What, Jo?"

"Alfredo wants to talk to you privately. As soon as possible."

chapter forty-five

Y ou shouldn't go with Kim to talk with Alfredo," Aleesha told Jo. "In fact, you can't."

I was beginning to regret making the effort to get the two of them into the same room. What had started as an attempt at reconciliation was turning into a verbal brawl. My cats at home sometimes spatted and played at fighting, but Jo and Aleesha didn't act as domesticated as my pets.

"And why not?"

"He probably wants to talk about you."

Although I agreed with Aleesha in principle, her response struck me as unusually, uh, catty.

"Sorry. I didn't mean it that way. Really." She must have seen my look of disapproval. "We don't know what he wants to talk with Kim about, and he might feel inhibited having you in on the conversation. It's probably not about you, but it's apt to be personal. You don't want to make him uncomfortable, do you?"

I smiled. Who but Aleesha could turn such a blunder into something so sensible and do it so easily?

"But he doesn't *know* you, Kim." Jo didn't even bother looking at Aleesha. "He's comfortable with me. He'd probably freeze up and not talk without me there. Besides, who'll translate?"

"The warden has arranged for a neutral interpreter," I told her. "Someone who doesn't have any personal interest in what Alfredo has to say and who'll also serve as a guard." I thought *guard* would cause fewer objections than *chaperone*.

Jo might not have growled aloud, but Aleesha and I had

obviously failed to convince her that her absence would be for Alfredo's benefit. How I was dying to tell her, *"Jo, there's more to this than you realize. If I dared to tell you what, I could let you come and translate, but I can't take any chances. Not my idea. Warden's orders."*

Instead, I said, "That's what Warden Jenkins is insisting on. He's the one who says you couldn't come. Blame him if you want to blame anybody."

"You just don't want me to visit my boyfriend," she said as she stormed out of the room.

Huh? I don't know which shocked me more—Jo's lack of understanding or the fact she'd openly referred to Alfredo as her boyfriend.

"That went well, don't you think?" Aleesha said. "I thought she'd be upset about not going with us."

That bit of extreme silliness broke the tension Jo's reaction had left in its wake, and we cracked up laughing. Once we settled down again, I realized what Aleesha had said.

"You're not going, either, you curious critter." I grinned at her.

"I'm going with you in prayer," she explained.

We hugged.

"Time to go," Rob yelled from the doorway.

He and I didn't talk much in the van. We both realized I was facing a far different ministry challenge from anything God had asked me to do in Santa María. I tried praying about my specific concerns for this conference, but my prayers kept coming out as, *Help me, Lord. Help Alfredo. Help Mrs. Warden Jenkins.*

Over and over and over again until we arrived at Warden Jenkins' office.

I knew Rob was praying, too. He was that kind of Christian man.

"Kimmy, this is my wife, Laurie."

"Hello, Mrs. Jenkins." I started to shake hands with her, but she hugged me instead.

"I'm Laurie. We're all members of God's family. No need to stand on formalities."

As nervous as I was about the meeting with Alfredo, my mind went berserk in a weird kind of way. "Or to sit on them, either."

Warden Jenkins shook his head in mock disgust, but Laurie and I started giggling like a couple of young girls.

"Anytime you two are ready, I'll send for Alfredo."

I hadn't noticed it before, but the warden liked to refer to the insiders by their first names. I'd never seen that in a prison movie. Must have been part of letting his Christianity show on the job.

He picked up the phone and punched three buttons. "Hello? Jenkins here. Please send Alfredo Rodriguez down to the infirmary. The doctor wants to check on his allergies."

He looked at Laurie and me. "I assume he's allergic to Chaplain Thomas. The non-Christian insiders could make big trouble for Alfredo if they had an inkling he'd requested a conference with Kimmy. It would look. . .suspicious."

Laurie and I looked at one another. This was still a prison after all, and I'd only seen one side of prison life. A very small side. And an unusually tame one.

Warden Jenkins paused at the infirmary door and inserted an electronic card key.

"Kimmy, I let Laurie know what this is all about. We've both been praying for you."

He shut the door behind him. It didn't have an inside handle. I could never design a prison. I wasn't sufficiently cautious or suspicious.

Laurie put her hand on mine. I'd begun trembling. So much depended on this meeting. I couldn't imagine how many people the chaplain's crimes had affected. Then again, I needed to remind myself I had no right to assume that Chappy was guilty. I needed to ask God's forgiveness for that sin as much as for any other.

I heard a click at the door. Someone had inserted a card key. I tried to see the guard who'd walked Alfredo to the infirmary, but the door shut too quickly.

Poor Alfredo had big sweaty places under both arms. He looked wild-eyed. Terrified. Didn't he know why he'd been brought down here? If the warden had fooled Alfredo by handling things this way, he would certainly fool anyone who would give Alfredo grief over it.

Then he saw Laurie and me. I'd never seen anyone go from terrified to jubilant quite so quickly. All smiles, he pumped my arm up and down until I thought it would either fall off or produce a roomful of fresh well water. He did the same with Laurie.

"*Buenos días,*" I said. "*Mi español no es bueno.*" *Hello. My Spanish isn't good.*

Laurie took my cue and spoke to him in his native tongue.

"No worries," he said. "I speak more better English than I let know, but it isn't so well, either."

Thank You, Lord!

"Sounds like you don't need my services," Laurie said. *Don't desert me.* I'd forgotten she was present partially as a chaperone.

"Don't go, Señora," he said. "If you are a Christian."

"I am."

After a few pleasantries, I could tell that Alfredo was restless to get down to business.

"What did you want to talk with me about, Alfredo?" I asked.

He didn't answer. The anticipation was making my stomach churn, and I thought my heart was going to jump through my throat. Could the problem be worse than the warden suspected?

"Alfredo. . . ?"

He removed something he'd been carrying under his left arm. *Huh*. . . Maybe he'd been reading it when Warden Jenkins called for him.

"Will you. . .tell me how. . .how to. . .become a Christian?"

chapter forty-six

I couldn't stop myself. I threw my arms around him. I'm afraid I startled him at first.

He handed me a *Santa Biblia*—the Bible in his heart language. I recognized the familiar-looking red paperback. It was identical to the one I'd read aloud from and left behind in Santa María.

"It belongs Jo," he said. "She told me read it."

I didn't even realize she'd brought it with her, but I spent a quick moment thanking God she had.

"I begin reading, but not all words understand. Teachings not. . .not how I live."

What should I say? Not a problem. Alfredo didn't pause long enough for me to respond.

"Jo told me start *Lucas*. Have read *Nuevo Testamente*. All of. I am good reader."

"Fantabulous!" I said.

After cocking his head, his eyes questioned me before he said anything. "I do not understand. My English not so good."

"The word I used means terrific! Wonderful! It's a combination of *fantastic* and *fabulous*." No need to confuse the issue by admitting that *fantabulous* probably wasn't a real word.

From the way he narrowed his eyes at me, a vocabulary lesson was not high on his priority list. That was just as well. I didn't want anything to sidetrack him from making the most important decision of his life.

"You help me become Christian, yes?"

Laurie looked at me with tears in her eyes. "Will we ever!"

"Yes." She and I had spoken at nearly the same time.

I looked at Laurie Jenkins. Since she was probably thirty-five years older than me—maybe more—and a far more mature Christian, she'd undoubtedly had more experience in leading a person to Christ.

"Do you want to do this?" I mouthed to her.

"You go ahead, Kim. I'll pray for both of you. Let me know if you need help, though."

I don't know what I said to him. But from the things he told me, he already had a good grasp of repentance, faith, and forgiveness. All I needed to do was fill in a few gaps.

Once I felt confident that he knew what he was doing, I told him about the sinner's prayer.

"Yes!" he said. "I am sinner. Want to pray that. But I do not. . .I do not pray before."

"That's okay, Alfredo. You'll just be talking to God. He's here in this room with us."

"He is insider?" he asked with an all-too-serious look. Then a smile broke through. "Joke."

"He is very much an insider," I said. "Although He stays here all the time, He's not a prisoner. And He stays everywhere else at the same time." Aware that I'd probably confused him, I clarified. "God is everywhere in the universe at the same time."

"That I hoped."

"You said you've never prayed before. . .maybe I forgot to mention that I'll say the words of the sinner's prayer, and you repeat them after me. But don't do it unless you really mean them."

"Ah? That is good. I mean them."

And so we prayed.

"Dear Jesus," I started.

"Dear Jesus," Alfredo repeated.

"I am a sinner."

"I am a sinner." Pain and sincerity in Alfredo's voice brought quick tears to my eyes.

I swallowed hard and continued the prayer, pausing for Alfredo to repeat the words after me. "I confess my sins to You. . .and ask Your forgiveness. . ."

After a soft *amen*, Alfredo beamed. "God forgives me. I am clean. God is my *padre* now. He wants good. Red Cedar bad before, but I not Christian then. Good I not still outside."

I could barely see Alfredo. Too many tears blocked the way.

I'll never stop believing that God put additional words in my mouth. "Alfredo, God will continue to forgive you, no matter what you have done in the past, but you must confess your sins daily—those things you do that displease Him—and ask His forgiveness. Then you must try never to do them again."

I hoped we wouldn't bog down now with something like *"But what happens if I do those things again even though I try not to?"* We'd have time to disciple him a little bit before going home.

"That prayer. . .that sinner's prayer. . . not confess all my sins. Must do now."

He threw himself facedown on the floor—did the New Testament say something about praying prone, or did he instinctively recognize that position as the best demonstration of his humility?

Laurie and I knelt beside him, and each of us took one of his hands, but reaching down like that was awkward. So we prostrated ourselves, too, one of us on each side of him.

He began listing the sins in his life, beginning with the one that landed him in prison. Statutory rape with a number of different young women. Maybe that should have shocked and horrified me, but his plea for God's mercy was too moving for me to be the least judgmental.

Next he confessed petty crimes he'd never been caught or

punished for. As he begged for God's forgiveness, he spoke of wanting to make things right. He would talk with the warden and tell him about those other crimes. If he had to spend more time at Red Cedar, so be it. That would give him time to try to win other insiders to Christ.

He must have prayed for thirty minutes as he asked forgiveness for what seemed to be the major sins in his life. Then he moved on to the minor ones. I fought to keep from laughing when he admitted grabbing the muffin from a new insider's tray that morning at breakfast.

"Jesus, I will try do right thing. I will tell him I am Christian now. I am sorry. Give him my bread three days show I am change."

Oh, man! Have I ever met such a sincere new Christian?

"Señorita Kimmy, must talk now of sin someone else. Against me. Against others. Will you permit?"

chapter forty-seven

A nd he was specific?" Warden Jenkins said.

"Quite. He has good reasons for hating the chaplain."

"But he's afraid to go public with his knowledge?"

"Not exactly afraid. Alfredo has taken his Bible reading seriously. He said if Jesus could forgive the people who put Him to death, he should forgive the chaplain. He feels strongly about that."

"So he's not going to cooperate?"

"I didn't say that, sir. I agreed that forgiving the chaplain was *one* of his Christian responsibilities. But I believe I convinced him that protecting other people from the chaplain is *another* one."

"Good approach. So he *will* cooperate?"

"If we can find one additional witness. Alfredo doesn't want to be the only man to file a complaint. He doesn't want Chappy's future to rest in his hands alone."

Warden Jenkins shook his head. He appeared to be fighting back a frown. "So near and yet so far."

"Yes, sir." I hadn't seen him look so serious before. Not even after the unhappy phone call from his supervisor a day or two earlier. "Hmmm." He traced the writing on the Bible cover with his forefinger. "But he's willing to testify if someone else does?"

"If and only if. I think he's read in the Bible that a man can't be convicted of a crime unless two witnesses agree."

"And if there's only one and he's a convicted felon. . .and the accused is a respected professional. . . ?"

I didn't answer. As frustrated as he sounded, I got the impression he also understood and respected Alfredo's point of view.

He spent several minutes jotting down the things I'd told him. I couldn't help noticing that his handwriting looked like the stereotypical doctor's writing—completely illegible. Periodically, he asked me to repeat something or clarify a detail. When he finished, he looked up.

"Kimmy, don't be offended, but I'll have to ask Laurie the same questions I've asked you. Even though we can't convict Thomas on hearsay, it's important to have stories that match in every detail. Unfortunately, because of Laurie's relationship to me, her testimony will automatically be suspect. Quite possibly inadmissible in court."

Good grief! Are you saying we didn't accomplish anything?

He must have noticed my frustration. "No need to fret, Kimmy. You've made a major breakthrough today. Now we *know* the man is guilty. I don't need a second victim to confirm that."

"But you'll need one in court, won't you?" I said.

"Sometimes I think you must have watched too many years of courtroom dramas on television, young lady. But additional witnesses in this case—whether one or twenty—would help tremendously." He paused and then sighed so pathetically I wanted to hug him.

"But at least you have one," I said. "That's a start."

"Even though he won't talk with me as long as he's the only one. . ."

"What are the chances some other insider will step forward?"

"I can't say. I can't even guess. The grapevine here is the speediest one I've ever seen. Despite our best efforts to keep your talk with Alfredo private and confidential, you can be sure the other men in his cell block already know he didn't come to the infirmary to talk to a doctor about his allergies today."

"He's not in any danger, is he?" I'd feel worse than horrible if I'd endangered him by meeting with him.

"From other insiders? I doubt it. Because everyone believes he barely speaks English, they probably think he doesn't understand much of what's going on. He'd be wise to keep it that way."

"But now that he's a Christian, he wants to convert his whole cell block."

His eyes seemed to plead, *Please don't question me.* "He'll be very wise to keep his knowledge of English to himself—at least until this situation has been resolved."

"And what about Chaplain Thomas?"

"What? Will he hurt Alfredo? Not likely. If he suspects anything, Thomas will probably steer clear of him for a while. That's not to say he won't warn his other victims to keep their mouths closed around Alfredo."

"I can't believe the power he holds over those men. Can he really use his position to affect their release?"

"A bad report on his part may not extend their prison time—not except under unusual circumstances, and I know of only one of those—but if he reports that an insider has become a Christian and that he's seen x, y, and z signs of a complete change in him, that goes a long way with the parole board."

"So he's swinging a two-edged sword. . . ?" I was catching on.

"Hmm?"

"If the men give him what he wants, he eventually gives them what they want. And if they don't, he threatens to add bad things to their records."

"Not exactly. He just withholds his support. That's more effective."

"Oh, of course." What had I just thought about *catching*

on? I was wrong. *This is all too much for me. I just want to go home. Not to the hostel, but back to Georgia where life is normal.*

But things wouldn't be normal there either, though. My guilt would confront me every day and night for the rest of my life. But at least I wouldn't have to worry about the insiders at Red Cedar.

Who was I trying to kid? I couldn't quit caring about these poor guys any more than I could quit praying for the salvation of the villagers of Santa María.

"You ready to go back to the hostel?" Warden Jenkins asked.

I let a slight moan slip out.

"I know that's right," he said.

I laughed. "Now you sound like Aleesha."

"Good. I wanted to make you laugh. May I give you a ride?"

"Thanks, but I need to walk. Maybe it'll help me forget some of my concerns."

"I wish something would help me do that," he said as he began walking me to the door of the Administration Building.

"Warden Jenkins, we're overlooking the obvious."

He looked at me.

"Prayer. That's what I'll do on the way back to the hostel."

He looked like he wanted to smile, but couldn't. Like maybe he was all prayed out.

I hugged him and started my walk down Red Cedar Lane. This would be the first time I'd walked from the prison back to the hostel. It felt odd. Unnatural.

I wondered how Red Cedar Lane made insiders feel upon their release. Did it make them joyous over their new freedom? After all, it led away from a wasted part of their lives. Or did it frighten them? For many of the insiders, it probably represented an unknown passage to an equally unknown future.

As much as I might want answers to those questions, I wasn't likely to get them. Even though I wasn't responsible for what went on inside the prison, I felt a great sense of responsibility toward the insiders—especially my Christian brothers.

I started praying for each one of the ones I knew by name. Hi, the countertenor. Rock, the Simon Peter wannabe. And Alfredo, the new convert.

Before I could get any farther, I heard a car pull up behind me. I didn't bother looking at first—probably somebody headed home from work—but when the driver beeped and pulled up beside me, I glanced at him.

No! Not Chaplain Thomas. And he was lowering the front passenger side window.

"Miss Hartlinger," he said, "you shouldn't have to walk back to the hostel."

"Chaplain Thomas, how good to see you." Oh, man! I hadn't lied like that since who knew when. Why hadn't I limited my response to *"Chaplain Thomas. . ."*?

"Why don't I give you a ride? It's on my way, you know." He laughed as if he'd made the greatest joke in the world. I didn't.

Of course the hostel is on the way, Chappy. Red Cedar Lane dead-ends there.

My stomach began churning with apprehension about being out there alone with the man, although I didn't think I was in any real danger. Visitors, delivery people, and employees drove that road in both directions all day, so he would be foolish to do anything to me when someone was almost certain to pass by at the wrong time.

Has the prison grapevine informed you of my talk with the warden? If so, remember that he's aware of my general whereabouts. He's sure to call Rob after a while to ask if I've made it back safely. If you do anything to me, he'll know who the likely culprit is.

But if the grapevine had been silent, Thomas couldn't be positive I'd been to the prison. He might suspect it, but he couldn't assume I hadn't just been out for a walk in that direction. Especially since I wasn't that close to the prison complex now. No, I decided, he couldn't have been sure what I'd been up to.

I could hear Chappy drumming his fingers on the steering wheel in impatience. I guess he was still waiting for an answer. "I'd rather walk, thank you. It's a beautiful day."

"Clear, sunny, and thirty-three degrees may be beautiful, but not for walking."

"My down jacket is quite warm," I told him.

"I won't take no for an answer." He smiled—oh, what a fakey-looking smile—before leaning over and opening the passenger door.

I hesitated. Should I take a chance? I hated being rude, even to someone I had less than no respect for.

"I don't bite, you know."

I know nothing of the kind.

But going with him seemed safer than continuing to argue. After "accidentally" dropping a glove on the ground as a clue if I suddenly disappeared, I climbed in and closed the door. He pressed his power lock button. I pretended to examine the fancy door paneling while trying to unlock my door.

I couldn't.

I hadn't felt so closed in since the first night, when we were in the no-man's-land between the outside and the inside of the prison building. The click of the car door lock had been quieter, but it had the same effect on me as hearing the gate closing shut behind me.

"See, Miss Kimmy? No danger from me."

I thought about those self-defense moves I'd learned in

high school. I hadn't practiced them in a while. Now I wished I had.

"Did you have a good visit at Red Cedar today?"

No, I'm not going to confirm that I was there. But I'll make you suspicious if I don't respond.

"I always enjoy my visits to the prison, chaplain." There. Nothing specific.

"Especially today, huh? Alfredo Rodriguez told me the two of you had a real good conversation in the infirmary."

chapter forty-eight

"B ut he didn't hurt you?" Aleesha said.

"If he even touched you. . ." Although Dad had never been my image of Mr. Tough Guy, each word exploded with such violent thunder that I was thankful to have him on my side.

As shaken up as I'd been by the time I got out of Chappy's car and ran inside Graham's apartment, the last thing on my mind was keeping anything from my team. My good friends. My best friends. My family.

I hadn't noticed at first that they were eating an early supper. I broke out crying as soon as I saw them and knew I was safe. I wasn't consciously trying to attract support, but boy! did I get it. I'd never received so many hugs at one time, and I needed every one of them.

I filled them in on the story of Chaplain Thomas and his insistence on giving me a ride. I also told them what he'd said about talking with Alfredo. That meant nothing to Jo and Graham, but Rob, Dad, and Aleesha understood Chappy's implications: *You can't do anything around here without my knowing it, and you can't trust Alfredo. I've got him under my thumb, too.*

I didn't tell them I didn't believe Chappy, though. Not after witnessing Alfredo's conversion. If he'd faked that, he was a better actor than Aleesha could ever hope to be.

I didn't say anything about my visit with Alfredo, either, although everyone but Graham knew that's why I'd gone to Red Cedar. Considering Graham's ability to park silently in open doorways, I wouldn't have been surprised to learn that he already knew about that, too.

"No, he didn't touch me," I responded to Dad's statement. "He'd be wearing a fresh set of claw marks all over his hands and face if he had, and I'd have Rob on the satellite phone with the police right now."

"I'm going to phone Larry," Rob said. "He needs to know about this. Intimidation alone may not land Thomas in the pokey, but it's more ammunition to use against him."

Jo didn't ask what in the world we were talking about. Not at first. She just stared at Rob in wide-eyed wonder. I'm afraid we'd all forgotten that she wasn't in the loop. And that she wasn't supposed to be.

Graham wasn't, either, but he wasn't in a position to do any harm. Or was Jo still a potential problem? I couldn't think clearly anymore.

But then she began firing questions at me. Very pointed ones. "What are you talking about? What's this with Chaplain Thomas? Has he done anything to hurt Alfredo?" Her voice was a cross between rage and worry.

Her third question seemed safe enough. *Fine. Be more concerned about Alfredo than about me.* "He was doing great when I talked with him awhile ago." *Okay, Kim, don't let your expression change now. Don't let your eyes betray concern about whether he's still all right.*

"None of us likes that chaplain," Jo said, "but why are you accusing him of intimidation?"

Jo, haven't you been listening?

"Something happened this afternoon and— "

"To Alfredo?" Her tone was near-frantic.

I might have had a one-track mind, too, if I had a romantic interest in someone in that prison. Maybe I could distract her with good news.

"He's fine, Jo. I already told you that." I paused

strategically. "He's better than fine, in fact."

"Huh? What?"

"Jo, your, uh, friend became a Christian this afternoon. The chaplain apparently found out about it and—for reasons we don't understand—he isn't as happy about it as we are."

There. Close enough to the truth.

"Alfredo became a Christian? You led him to Christ? You should have let me do that!"

Aleesha's face was clouding up. Each of Jo's outbursts seemed to darken her frown a bit more. I motioned for Aleesha to stay calm, but she didn't notice. Either that or she preferred to ignore me.

"*You* are the most selfish person I've ever met," Aleesha said. "White, black, or plaid."

Jo looked like somebody had just slapped her.

Aleesha didn't wait for a response. "Here Alfredo has made a profession of faith—the most important decision in his life—but are you happy about it? No. Any normal person— normal Christian, that is—would be thrilled to hear such good news. But you? Uh-*uh*! All you seem to care about is who gets the star in her crown for it."

Dad had excused himself a number of minutes earlier to polish his message for that evening. If only I'd gone with him. Away from these two squabblers.

Rob wasn't in the room now, either. He'd taken the satellite phone outside. He didn't have to listen to this, and I envied him.

And Graham was. . .somewhere. Probably somewhere nice and quiet. I couldn't help grinning at the thought of that frail-looking old man trying to referee a fight between Jo and Aleesha.

"You're crazy!" Jo said. That was mild compared to what I'd expected her to say. "If you'd let me go to translate this afternoon, I would have been the one who led him to Christ."

I hoped Aleesha wasn't going to waste her breath saying any—.

"I wasn't the one who stopped you. I told you this afternoon the warden wanted an impartial translator."

No, girl, don't pay any attention to that.

"Impartial?" Jo actually quieted down. Instantly. I could almost see the wheels spinning, but I couldn't tell what gear she was in. "Now I *know* something strange is going on."

Duh. You just figured that out, did you? Where were you when Rob asked us to keep an eye on the chaplain's interaction with the other men? I mentally slapped myself on the mouth for thinking such unkind thoughts.

"So what's going on?"

Jo wasn't looking at Aleesha. She was looking at me, and I knew that look. She expected an answer, and she wasn't going to settle for baloney when she wanted steak.

Although her question was the one I'd hoped most to avoid, I would have done almost anything to keep her from yelling at Aleesha anymore. Or provoking Aleesha to yell back. An online-chat friend in Australia once described people who can't get along as being like cheese and chalk.

Nothing could have described Jo and Aleesha more perfectly. Thank goodness Aleesha hated violence, and Jo had never been exposed to any.

But, Lord, how do I answer her?

"Something bad is going on at Red Cedar." As soon as I said that, I knew I'd said too much. I had to keep going, though. "Alfredo isn't guilty of any wrongdoing. He's one of the victims. One of possibly many victims. The warden asked me to talk with him and—"

"Alfredo asked to speak with you," Jo said. "Remember? I'm the one who told you."

She might as well have accused me of lying. I'd never

known her to act so irrational. I still needed to corner her and find out what was going on with her parents. Especially if it was affecting her like this.

"The warden wanted me to find out if Alfredo was a victim or not."

Jo still didn't look satisfied, but at least she didn't argue. And she shocked me by not asking what he was a victim of.

"He brought your Bible to our meeting. He's read the whole New Testament. That led him to ask how to become a Christian."

I glanced over at Aleesha. I could almost see her biting her tongue to keep from saying, *"Why didn't he ask you that, Jo? Didn't he think you knew?"* As much as I didn't want her to provoke Jo further, I couldn't have blamed Aleesha.

"Oh."

Jo sometimes took longer than Aleesha and me to catch on to something, but she was no dummy. Based on experience from our long friendship, I knew she was processing this information to see whether it fit with her concept of the truth.

"Hello, girls," Rob said when he came back inside. His cheeks were a nice rosy red. So was his bald spot.

"Cold outside, Mr. Rob?" Aleesha said.

He nodded.

"It's been hot in here."

"I could tell. Girls, we need to pray for tonight's service. Then it'll be time to leave."

Rob went to get Dad. We formed a circle, but when Jo discovered she'd have to hold hands with Aleesha, she changed positions and got between Dad and Rob. Our prayer time was quite intense as we prayed around the circle. Whether Jo had gotten over not being the one to lead Alfredo to Christ, I couldn't say, but she was eloquent in praising God that it had happened.

We were putting our coats on when Graham came through the front door. He handed the satellite phone to Rob. What a shock. I couldn't imagine Graham knowing somebody's phone number, much less calling it. But that wasn't any of my business.

Graham shocked me even more when he got in the van with us. He hadn't gone to any of our services before, and I couldn't imagine why he'd chosen to attend now. I thought it strange he hadn't brought one of his many Bibles with him, though. He seemed like the type of Christian who would.

His failure to come to the service seemed even stranger. I couldn't imagine where he'd been. Although he was waiting for us at the van when it was time to leave, I couldn't believe he'd spent the last two hours there.

But what had he been doing?

chapter forty-nine

Jo, we need to talk," I said.

She and I were doing some outside painting, and no one else was close by.

"Did you hear me?"

She started crying silently. I set my brush across the top of a paint can and approached her.

"You haven't been yourself the whole time we've been here," I said as gently as I knew how. "I don't mean that critically."

I could see from her pained expression that talking about her problem would be excruciating. I considered telling her about my guilt problem first, the way I'd originally planned to do.

But now wasn't the time for that.

After another sniffle, she managed to start talking. Just a word or two at a time at first, but then she picked up speed. She seemed to realize she'd been holding this in way too long.

"Kim, I'm so sorry. It's just. . ."

Please help her, Lord. Let her know how much I love her. How much I care.

"My parents are getting a divorce."

The look I pictured myself wearing now couldn't have begun to express the shock I felt inside. Jo took my hands in hers. I looked into her eyes, and we both broke out crying.

"I didn't think your parents were getting along well, but I had no idea things had gotten this bad."

"They have."

"Are they going to counseling?"

"My mother moved out, and she's living with some

twenty-five-year-old guy."

No nightmare this time, Dad. This one's real, and it's not mine.

"When. . .when did you find out?"

"On the phone that night after our first visit to the prison."

"No!"

"Oh, you don't know the half of it."

I couldn't imagine anything worse, but I was wrong.

"Papa and I found out at the exact same time."

The horror I felt was so indescribable I could only respond with tears. "He and I were talking on the phone that night. Mama came in the room and told him everything. Since she hadn't noticed that he was on the phone, she didn't realize I could hear everything she was saying, too. Can you disown a mother?"

I couldn't tell if she was trying to be cute or not. . .trying to cover up her grief with a bit of whimsy. But whether she had been or not, I snorted once, and soon we were both laughing as if we'd been in the world's greatest mood.

It didn't last.

"What. . . ?" I had a million questions, and I didn't know which one to ask first. And which ones not to ask at all.

"So that's why I've been playing the female-dog part all week."

The female. . . ? Oh.

That also helped to explain why she'd been so quick to latch on to Alfredo. She was desperate to grab hold of some sympathetic male while she was so far away from her papa, and Alfredo had been in the right place at the right time. I wondered if she'd told him about her mama and papa.

"Don't tell Aleesha, though. I hate her."

Could this soap opera get any worse?

"She doesn't like me. She doesn't understand me. She doesn't respect me."

"You don't think she'd be more sympathetic if she knew the truth?" A long shot, but what else could I say?

"Ha! She'd probably accuse me of driving my mama away."

Whoa there, girl. What are you really trying to say? What Aleesha might accuse you of or what you're accusing yourself of? This was starting to sound familiar.

"It's not your fault, Jo. Every kid whose parents split up thinks it is, but it's not. It never is." I knew that was true. Everyone knows it's true. Everyone but the kids.

The half-painted exterior wall paid as much attention to my statement as Jo did. "I could have been a better daughter. I could have been less demanding. I could have been more obedient."

And I could have avoided calling Mom when I knew she was driving in bad weather.

"Jo, you wouldn't feel this way if you'd been at home when you found out. She would have told you in a nicer—at least a gentler—way, don't you think?"

Mom would have been nice about forgiving me. That hit me in a way I hadn't thought about before. I'd been despondent because she *couldn't* forgive me, but I hadn't given her credit for what she *would* have done if she'd been able to. When had Mom ever failed to forgive me for anything?

She loved me with all her heart, and people who love forgive. But what about Dad?

Could he forgive me for what I'd done to Mom? Did he love me that much now?

Now? What am I talking about? He's always loved me that much. He just hasn't been good at showing it until recently. Oh, man. He and I need to talk.

Jo remained silent while God inserted that realization into my brain like coins into a drink machine. She somehow sensed that she shouldn't interrupt. How thankful I was for that.

"You okay, Kim?" she asked. Her voice sounded steadier than before.

"Better than okay." I started crying again. But from joy. And relief.

"You asked if Mama would have been nicer in person?" I nodded. "I have to believe so. She's still my mama."

And I had to hope Dad's forgiveness would come unhesitatingly if I ever dared to tell him. He was still my daddy.

"Are you better now?" I asked Jo.

She smiled.

"Can you excuse me for a few minutes? I need to talk to Dad."

But I still couldn't tell him everything.

chapter fifty

Jo asked me not to say anything to Aleesha about her parents' marital problems, and I honored her request, even though it made—or should I say it kept?—things unnecessarily tense. I explained to Aleesha that Jo's problems were so serious we should ignore the way she'd been acting, but that didn't seem to lessen her hostility any.

The two of them didn't talk in the van going to that evening's service. They walked through the door to the Administration Building at the same time—as far apart as the width of the doorway allowed; neither was willing to yield to the other. I followed several feet behind, shaking my head at their childish stubbornness.

Although Alfredo appeared to be as thrilled to see Jo again as she was to see him, all he could talk about was his conversion to Christianity, which he obviously found even more thrilling than he did Jo's company. She didn't seem to mind, though, until he turned most of his attention to the two other Latino guys he'd brought from his cell block.

Their conversation was lively. *Y tan rápido.* And so fast. Even if I'd been perfectly fluent in Spanish, I couldn't have followed it. Judging from Alfredo's animated look, his friends must have asked why he'd start acting so different after a single two-hour visit to the infirmary.

Although Jo looked mildly jealous when he sat between his two buddies rather than beside her, she couldn't have missed seeing his newfound joy or criticized him for wanting to share it with friends. I don't know whether seeing him witnessing to those other two guys made the trip to California worthwhile for her, but it did for me.

I was in an exceptionally worshipful mood that evening. Probably more than at any time since Santa María. The singing buoyed my spirits higher than ever, and the songs reminded me what an awesome God I served; the prayers reminded me that God was truly in our midst, and the message spoke to my needs in a special way. How could Dad have known what I needed to hear? Only the Holy Spirit could have arranged a "coincidence" like that.

Yet a shadow seemed to hang over the other worshippers. The insiders knew we'd be leaving on Monday. Maybe they were already grieving our absence the way the villagers of Santa María had done when we were preparing to go home. Yet I didn't think our departure would be a problem for these guys. They were probably more accustomed to people coming and going than I would ever be.

I'd never asked Warden Jenkins whether Chappy held services for the men, and I couldn't imagine what they would have been like. He seemed like the sort of man who'd purposely pick all unfamiliar hymns and preach the longest, dullest sermon possible. No way he could have drawn these men out the way the Holy Spirit had done through us. Not unless he'd been a more. . .righteous and caring person.

Maybe his presence was part of the problem that evening. Brother Larry probably hadn't told him tonight would be the last of our services he'd attend. Chappy called the men out one at a time just like before. And he had the nerve to smile at me every time he did. Like he'd won a major battle and wanted to rub my nose in his victory.

No wonder our team shared a concern that our leaving probably meant handing the lambs back over to the wolf. Such precious lambs, and such a very big, very mean, very greedy wolf.

No one asked to talk with me one-on-one that evening. If I knew Chappy half as well as I thought I did—if he was like one of the bad guys on TV—I wasn't the only person he'd tried to intimidate. He must have done an effective job of it, too. His very presence was enough to put all of the men in an *"or else"* silence.

Thank goodness, we wouldn't have to deal with him the last two nights.

On Saturday, we finished everything that needed doing at Welcoming Arms, although I doubted that any of us felt the same sense of success and completeness about our prison ministry.

"Get in or walk," Jo said to Aleesha when she slowed down to fasten her coat.

"What?" Aleesha said. "You can't wait another few seconds to see *him* again?"

"Get lost," Jo said. What kind of snake could have acted more deliberately venomous?

"Children, children." They stared at me as if I had three eyes.

Aleesha's attitude toward Jo really disappointed me. I'd always admired her ability to charm her way through any circumstances, but Jo seemed to bring out the worst in her. And vice versa.

But I still loved both of them oodles and bunches. And I prayed that—someday—they'd come to love each other just as much.

Everyone was unusually quiet when we got into the van for our next-to-the-last drive up Red Cedar Lane. I didn't know why Jo, Rob, Aleesha, Dad, and Graham were so silent, but I was too caught up in prayer to waste words on small talk. We didn't have much time left to finish disposing of an unworthy chaplain, and our hope of succeeding shrunk more with each passing second.

Although Chappy's absence from the service would promote a more positive atmosphere than the night before, I didn't have much hope that anyone would talk with me tonight. How I prayed I was wrong. I didn't want to leave our new friends in worse condition than when we came.

Nobody had spoken during the ride to the prison. As we got out, Graham leaned over and whispered something in a voice I could barely hear. "No worry. Almost over." I couldn't imagine what he was talking about. Maybe just his way of saying we'd soon go home and put the Red Cedar experience behind us.

As if I could have done that.

As soon as we walked in, I could sense that something special was going on. The excitement stopped just short of exuberance. The insiders seemed to expect something. They reminded me of little kids on Christmas Eve.

Then I noticed Warden Jenkins waiting for us. He'd never come to one of our services. He probably didn't want his position to interfere with our interaction with the insiders. The men acted glad to see him, though. They shook his hand as if he'd become their hero, and Rock shocked the daylights out of him with a huge brotherly hug. Unlike the last time I'd seen Warden Jenkins, he was smiling. . .and laughing.

What in the world had happened?

"Before these good folks lead us in worship tonight," he said to the little congregation that had grown to nearly forty, "I need to address an issue I've been concerned about since I first learned of it."

I looked around. Sure enough, the chaplain wasn't there. I was dying to cheer about that.

He grinned at his audience. "The Red Cedar grapevine is the most efficient one of its kind in the world. It could easily replace the Internet." I heard several chuckles. A number of the men nodded in agreement. "Sometimes you men learn about things I've done before I even *decide* to do them." The room exploded in laughter, which soon gave way to whoops and applause. "So let me tell you the facts before the grapevine distorts them." He paused and looked around the room. "Judging by your faces, though, I think the grapevine has beaten me to it again."

More laughter. And many additional cheers.

"The news of the hour: Chaplain Harry Thomas has been arrested on a number of serious charges. If convicted—and there's not much of a chance he won't be—he may join you here for much of the rest of his natural life. . .without pay, I hasten to add."

The men whistled, hooted, and hollered. They clapped, and they stomped, and I was as loud and enthusiastic as any of them.

Warden Jenkins looked embarrassed. Or perhaps mildly bothered. I couldn't tell which. Maybe he hadn't expected a group of Christian inmates to cheer over somebody's arrest. Or maybe he felt frustrated that someone in his position couldn't properly join in the cheering. He must have been dying to.

"I'm not 100 percent sure who your next chaplain is going to be, but I have an idea. I promise you he'll be a Christian, though. I'll make sure of that personally." Man! That was a strong statement. Before the men could start cheering again, he continued. "When I look at all of you, I thank God that these good people"—he pointed to each of our team members—"have done such a wonderful job of ministering to you. I intend to keep these services going. Not every night like this, but on a regular basis. If I can't find any people from my church who're willing to make the sacrifice of time and gas, I'll do it by myself."

Now the men were on their feet, moving forward as one humongous tidal wave and clapping him on the shoulder. The guards uncrossed their arms and instinctively touched the handles of their pistols, but they crossed their arms again almost as quickly. If this was a prison riot, it was a first-of-its-kind—a desirable one.

"Men, I hate to interrupt this wonderful adulation, but I think these folks want to begin a worship service."

As I headed for the podium, a hymnbook in my hand, Graham touched my arm. "Over now. Said no worry."

How could he have known?

chapter fifty-one

Act 3

I t was late when we got back to the hostel that night. I'd
fallen asleep in the van.

"Girl," Aleesha said as she shook me, "Mr. Rob and I
carried you in from the bus at Santa María and put you in your
new sleeping bag, but you've gained weight here. Get up and
get inside."

She was right about the weight. I'd done some hog-wild
eating between the time of my unexpected instant recovery
and our departure for California. Enough to gain back what
I'd lost while I was sick. I'd probably gained six or eight new
pounds eating Graham's cooking. Pounds that repulsed me
almost as much as my memory of Chaplain Thomas.

One unfortunate aspect of having a small build—aka, being
skinny—was the inability to be selective about where extra
weight ended up. I'd never found the paunchy look to be very
flattering, and I'd seen enough rotund, bare midriffs to have
something to base my opinion on.

But I'd never expected to end up looking that way myself.
Oh, well. I wouldn't get to enjoy Graham's cooking much
longer. Or Aleesha's, for that matter. I'd lose that weight fast
when I started eating my own cooking. I hoped I wouldn't kill
Dad with it, though.

Kill Dad. . . ? Uh, not funny.

⁓

When I woke up the next morning—was it Sunday already?—
sunlight was streaming through the windows I'd done my best
to clean the day before and still left streaky. If Aleesha had let

me sleep in again and made me miss breakfast, I was going to give her what-for when I caught up with her.

But when I unzipped my sleeping bag and sat up, I saw body-sized bulges in the other two sleeping bags. Huh? I was awake before Aleesha? I'd never let her live that down.

The memory of bedtime the night before was a distant patch of fog in my less-than-wakeful condition, but I vaguely remembered Rob saying we wouldn't need to get up at any given time. He was rewarding us for getting the hostel ready for the building inspection by not planning any Sunday activities. Not even an informal Bible study or a worship service. We'd hold one at Red Cedar tonight, and he said that would be good enough. He knew how truly tired we were, although our fatigue was probably more emotional than physical.

He'd also mentioned something about going to church in town with Larry and Laurie. The round-trip would take about two hours. So he'd be gone almost all day.

We probably disappointed him by declining the invitation to keep him company. Not even Dad wanted to go, and that must have seemed strange. Those two men had grown almost inseparable during the course of the week.

Oh, and hadn't Rob said something about Graham having ham-and-cheese quiche in the fridge, ready for us to microwave when we got hungry?

Yum. Let's try for pound seven. Or will it be pound nine?

Graham must have been getting used to us girls. Just before supper the day before, he'd invited us to move back into his spare room (I cleaned his windows in appreciation). I think he was concerned about us continuing to camp in an unheated unit, although—truth be told—we'd been quite comfy in our sleeping bags. Nonetheless, having easy access to the shower and being within scenting range of food cooking made his offer one we couldn't refuse.

I slipped into the cleanest of my grungy work clothes. Graham had a small washer and dryer, and I was planning to use them once everyone was awake. Otherwise, I'd be plenty stinky and dirty flying home the next day. Filth had never been a normal part of my feminine charm.

I hoped the sound of the microwave dinging itself off wouldn't wake Aleesha or Jo. I wasn't worried about Graham. He'd undoubtedly gotten up at dawn to watch the sunrise. Not a bad habit for someone who didn't mind getting up that early, but I still couldn't understand why it meant so much to him. I'd probably never find out.

I knew what Jo planned to do later. She'd been after me to climb Tabletop Mountain with her, and last night I declined what I hoped would be her final persistent invitation.

I was an outdoor girl when it came to riding in my convertible with the top down and sunning at the pool or the beach, but I didn't believe in voluntary physical exertion if I could avoid it.

Worthy projects like the litter cleanup campaign in Santa María and cleaning and painting the hostel were rare exceptions, yet I'd taken on both projects willingly and cheerfully.

"Why don't you ask Aleesha to go with you?" I'd asked Jo tongue-in-cheek.

She'd answered with a sharp snort that left no room for doubt. Her attitude toward Aleesha hadn't improved.

The quiche was so yummy, I had a second helping. Graham always cooked enough to feed all of the members of a good-size church. I didn't know what he did with the leftovers; he never served them to us.

"Fatty, fatty, two by four, can't get through. . ."

I looked up from my almost-empty-again plate to see Aleesha grinning at me. She bent over, and I hugged her without bothering to get up. She plopped down in the chair opposite me.

"You going climbing today?" she asked.

I smirked. "Are you?" I said. "I heard you asking Rob for directions."

"I'd planned to, but I think I'll curl up somewhere and read. I have such a reading list for next semester I'd better start on it now."

"Sounds good."

Aleesha loved reading as much as I did, although assigned reading was iffy and depended on the subject. She was antsy to get the lower-level required courses out of the way and focus on drama and theater.

I set my fork down and leaned back in my chair, hands folded over my satisfied belly. "I don't know what I'm doing today."

"Hmm. You must have been asleep when your dad said something in the van about climbing Tabletop."

"Really?" I didn't think Dad was any fonder of physical exertion than I was.

"The two of you together."

I gasped.

"What's this?" Aleesha said of the sheet of paper that was sitting on her placemat. "My name's on it. Now who around here would dare to use my name in vain?" She chuckled, picked it up, and unfolded it. "Oh. Directions for climbing Tabletop Mountain. Mr. Rob must have left this for me."

"Now don't you feel guilty for making him go to all that trouble for nothing?"

"Here." She handed me the paper. "Why don't you give this to Mr. Scott?"

I wrinkled my brow slightly.

"Just in case he doesn't have directions yet."

"Thanks." I folded the paper and stuffed it in my shirt pocket as if I'd meant it.

"Hello, girls," Dad said as he joined us at the table. "All ready for some vigorous mountain climbing today?"

His chipper mood made me think once more about his reaction to Mom's death. Sure, he'd done plenty of grieving—I'd only been aware of some of it—but why had he started acting so cheerful so soon? Denial?

I enjoyed having him that way, but still. . . Add that to my list of things I'd probably never know.

"Not me, Mr. Scott. I'm going to cozy up with a book. Maybe two."

"You even have to ask, Dad?"

He kissed me on the cheek. "How soon will you be ready then?"

What? Had my sarcasm lost its edge? "You. . .you're serious?"

"Of course. It's a beautiful day outside. We can work off those extra pounds. . ."

No! Don't tell me even my unobservant dad can see my weight gain.

"I have another reason, Kim, I need to talk with you about something important, and a peaceful mountaintop would be an appropriate place to do it."

"You're not already engaged to somebody else, are you?" I felt super-dumb for asking that, but it was the first thing that popped into my head.

"You don't *mean* that, do you?" The shock in his voice made me feel like kicking myself all the way back to Georgia. "I haven't even *looked* at another woman since your mom died. Or since we started going together, for that matter. No one can ever take her place."

I turned to look at Aleesha, but she wasn't there. Leave it to her to slip away quietly from somebody else's private conversation.

"No. Just a silly thought." *Silly thought nothing. If I'd thought about it first, I never would have said it.* "Sorry."

He smiled and then shrugged. Or maybe he shrugged first. I couldn't tell. "So you'll climb Tabletop with me?"

"Sure. Anything to spend quality time with my favorite dad. By the way, I've got some directions Rob left here for Aleesha." I pulled the paper out of my pocket, but he waved me off before I could finish unfolding it.

"We don't need that. Rob gave me directions several days ago."

At the rate I was going, I was going to wear that paper ragged just from taking it in and out of my pocket.

But that was okay. Today was going to be a perfect day.

chapter fifty-two

The way looked easy. Until we walked around the left prong of the U to the back of the hostel, that was.

What we hadn't seen from the front was a small lake of fallen rocks that made the first milestone in the directions look fifteen miles away rather than merely fifteen feet.

The rocks varied in size from pebbles—not more pebbles!— to stones that were heavy enough Dad and I would've had trouble lifting them together. Even the smallest ones appeared to have sharp edges, though—edges I wouldn't have wanted to tackle barefooted. The uneven layering made the surface dangerously unstable to cross.

Once we started trekking across, we discovered how unstable *unstable* could be. Memories of my experience in the Skyfly terminal of San Diego International didn't help. And we hadn't even reached the base of the mountain yet.

Before we'd gotten halfway across, my abdominal and leg muscles screamed at me for straining so hard just to maintain my balance and remain upright. Although I was wearing my good sneakers—I hadn't thought to bring anything more appropriate on this trip—I could almost feel blisters starting to form on the bottom of both feet. Thank goodness, I wasn't going to cross this more than once.

Ugh! Plus the return trip.

"I don't guess you want to give up, do you?" I said. I was only half-teasing.

"Do *you*?"

That's when it struck me that I actually *wanted* to make

this climb. Even if it killed me. So I wasn't very athletic. That was no secret. But I didn't want my father to think of me as a quitter.

I shook my head. "We're in this together, old man." I giggled, trying to imagine what kind of face he'd make at my comment.

Rob's directions weren't just good; they were excellent. Not counting having to cross those fallen rocks, that was. But truth be known, he probably hadn't climbed Tabletop since the rock slide. He would have noted it in the directions or provided an alternative starting place if he'd realized.

Our climb wasn't bad, but getting lost would have been a cinch without those directions. Fortunately, the landmarks Rob described were right where they were supposed to be. I hoped they'd be equally recognizable on the way back.

How dumb would we feel if we reached the top without problems and got lost on the return trip? The descent wouldn't be something to attempt in the dark, even with a considerably more powerful flashlight than the LED penlight I had in my coat pocket.

I noticed several sheer drops just yards from our path. *Path*? Calling our walkway a *path* was like referring to a migrant shack as a luxury hotel. The area was thick with underbrush, and many times we couldn't see what we were about to step on—or into. I shivered periodically at the thought of accidentally waking a hapless snake. A very poisonous one.

I could just see Dad trying to haul my body down the mountainside. Maybe he'd slip me over one of those steep drops and pick up what was left when he got back down. What would that hurt if I'd already died of snakebite?

We hadn't seen much wildlife yet. Just a few boring birds that didn't even have the decency to greet us in cheerful song or the courage to protest our invasion of their territory with squawking. We assumed a few furry little critters might be crawling around nearby or watching from hidden places and wondering who these idiotic intruders were. I tried not to consider the possibility of larger animals.

Why fret, though? I trusted Rob; he wouldn't have blessed our climb or given Dad the instructions if it hadn't been safe. I also trusted Dad; he had the patience to follow those directions implicitly. I trusted God even more, though; He'd created Tabletop Mountain, and it belonged to Him.

About an hour and a half after leaving the hostel, we found ourselves six feet from the top. Most of the climb had been fairly easy going—like climbing a steep hill—but these last six feet were the longest, steepest six feet I'd ever seen. Straight up. Were we supposed to climb a six-foot cliff face with our bare hands? Maybe those rocks at the base of the mountain had once been stair steps leading from here to the top.

"Look about five feet to your left," Dad said. "Rob doesn't say anything about it, but that spot looks like it has a couple of potential handholds."

"Uh. . ." I looked where he was pointing. "Right there?" I didn't want to admit I couldn't spot them.

"Uh, tell you what, baby girl."

"What, Dad?" Was a sense of defeat one phase of caution?

"Looks like we'll still have to pull ourselves up the last foot or so. Not much danger of falling far, though. I'll go first and then pull you up."

I would've thrown my arms around that man in a major hug if I could have done it without losing my balance. I did the best I could to move aside and allow him access to the handholds he thought he'd seen. He took a deep breath. I think he was almost as petrified as I was, but at least he didn't let on. He probably realized his terror would be catching.

Why does the advice *Don't look down* always make

a person want to do just that? If Dad had dropped me, I wouldn't have fallen far, but this terrain was rugged. Rugged enough to lack a soft landing spot. I could see myself breaking my right arm all over again. Or maybe both arms this time.

Dad grunted as he pulled me up inch by inch. Small slivers of rock fell past my head, bounced off our launch point, and landed somewhere yards below while I dangled like someone in the sweaty hands of a first-time trapeze artist. How small and harmless my Santa María pebbles seemed in retrospect.

"Good thing you're a lightweight," Dad said as he pulled me over the top. He held me steady while I stood up and got my footing.

I was up! On top. Alive and ready to sing "Climb Every Mountain" at the top of my lungs. Even if I couldn't remember many of the words.

"Let's move away from the edge, Kim." He didn't have to suggest that more than once.

The view a safe fifty feet away from the edge was. . .I'd say *breathtaking*, *majestic*, or *grandeur-iffic*, but those words wouldn't begin to describe it. I could see miles in every direction. Mountains to the east of me, mountains to the west, and more to the north and south. Some of the taller ones already wore a cap of snow. Or maybe leftovers of the previous winter's snow. Between the mountains were valleys the late fall hadn't totally browned and rivers that zigzagged like pieces of ribbon someone tossed in the air to see where they'd land.

"This place is something else, isn't it?" Dad said.

I hadn't even looked at the ground I was standing on. I already understood where the name Tabletop had come from, but now it made even more sense. We were standing on a plane maybe two hundred yards in each direction. But what was that I saw growing. . . ?

"Prickly pear," Dad said before I could say anything. Same kind of cactus Santa María had such an abundance of. . .the kind that had ringed the girls' sleep field. . .and Rob and Charlie had somehow magically used for fuel. "Rob told me about these. Birds must have flown here from some area where prickly pear abound. They'd feasted on edible parts of the cactus and ended up with cactus seed in their digestive systems. Then they flew over this mountain, and some of the seeds fell when they—"

"TMI," I said, cackling at the enjoyment my normally prim and proper father had demonstrated in telling this tale. "Too much information. I get the idea. But it's weird that the only other vegetation on top is tall grass."

"You've got me on that one."

We explored the top and looked out in every direction. The climb might have exhausted me—it had been steeper in some places than in others—and I was afraid those blisters on my feet weren't imaginary, but I was so glad Dad talked me into coming. I never lost my sense of awe at the view, and I'd probably already filled up half of my four-gig SD card taking pictures.

"I wonder if we'll run into Jo today," I said.

"Hmm. Maybe, but what I wanted to say is for your ears only. For now, anyhow. Guess I'd better go ahead and tell you before Jo shows up."

Dad pointed to the ground as if offering me a cushioned seat. I couldn't recall the last time I'd abused my back and legs so much, but I'd definitely earned the right to yelp at touch-down on the hard ground. I couldn't imagine being able to move the next day. Or to stand up again today, for that matter.

I unfastened my shoes and took off my socks. Sure enough, I had silver dollar–sized blisters on the soles of both feet. The kind that squish miserably when walked on.

Dad sat down beside me and smiled. He looked at my blisters and shook his head sympathetically. "You'd better take it easy on those feet, baby girl."

Did I have a choice about using them to get back down? I might have been petite, but I was too big for a piggyback ride.

"I'll bet you've been wondering about my reaction to your mother's death." I couldn't imagine the shocked look on my face. "I'm more observant than you think."

"Dad. . . ?"

Are you telling me that you've known how curious—no, how concerned—I've been? No wonder you didn't want Jo around now while we have this talk.

"I've struggled with guilt every day since your mother died. I should have been with her when she drove to the airport to pick you up." He sighed. "I wanted to be there to meet you, too."

"But you were in a meeting with the president of the university. . ."

"Yes, and that meeting was quite important." I nodded my encouragement. "One of the most important meetings I've ever attended." He yanked a blade of grass—it was so tall he didn't have to stoop to do it—and started wrapping it around his index finger and then unwrapping it again. Over and over. Like he was winding and unwinding his thoughts.

What are you so nervous about telling me? Come on, Dad. Just spit it out. I considered myself one of those rare young women who preferred to start at the bottom line of a story and then work backward. I liked to fill in relevant details that way rather than move step by torturously slow step from the beginning to the conclusion. I hated keeping my listeners in suspense. Or leaving them in boredom.

A lone blast of cold air gusted out of nowhere in particular as if God was saying, *"Listen to him."*

"Kim, I told Dr. Cutshaw I planned to resign from the university. . ."

"What?" My mouth dropped open. Dad had been in a tenured position longer than I'd been alive. An educational professional didn't give tenure up on a whim.

"How would you feel about having your middle-aged father attend seminary and prepare for the ministry or some other full-time Christian vocation?"

chapter fifty-three

Meanwhile, back at the hostel...

Where is everyone? I asked myself as I looked around the room. Kim's sleeping bag was empty. So was Aleesha's. I went out in the hall. Graham's bedroom door was closed. He wouldn't still be asleep—not this many hours past sunrise—so maybe he was reading. Or perhaps he'd gone mountain climbing. The day looked perfect for an outdoor activity.

I wandered into the kitchen, my stomach growling loudly enough to echo throughout the apartment. It seemed like it, anyhow.

Nobody there, either. Maybe Kim and Scott had changed their minds and gone with Rob to Larry Jenkins' church. And—thank goodness—still no sign of Aleesha. I'd been hoping for that. Counting on it.

I checked Aleesha's place at the dining room table. Sure enough, the directions I'd addressed to her were gone. Since she'd said something last night about getting off to an early start today, she was probably well on the way up Tabletop Mountain. Trying to follow my bogus directions and going farther astray with every step, that was. By the time she realized how hopelessly lost she was, she'd be so terrified that she couldn't help shedding some of that know-it-all self-assurance that fooled everyone else into thinking she was the cleverest person on the face of the earth.

I'd show everybody that *I* was the clever one by following some duplicate directions and rescuing her. Maybe I should leave her out there all night first. How angry would Mr. Scott be if Aleesha made the group miss their flight by going out by herself like that and getting stupidly lost?

I'd be the hero. And Aleesha would show her true colors— no racial prejudice intended—as a foolish, sniveling victim. She would have to show me plenty of respect after that. That's all I wanted. Aleesha's respect—at the cost of her ego.

The outside door opened and closed. "Yo, Graham," I said. "You're not out mountain climbing today?"

"Too cold."

"Too cold to go outside and watch the sunrise?" His habit of doing that tickled the life out of me. I—on the other hand— hadn't risen to watch the sunrise a single day that week. A little extra sleep was more important.

"Not *that* cold. Never that cold."

Even though Graham had apparently felt comfortable asking me for help that one time, we hadn't grown any closer. Maybe if Rob had let me help him. Oh, well. Too late now.

I liked the old fellow okay, but I hated trying to talk with him. Those short, choppy sentences—rarely complete ones at that—made communication tedious at best. Interpreting them required too much guesswork. He didn't seem very willing to open up, either, and I detested having unfulfilled curiosity.

"Have quiche. Heat up."

I didn't wait to hear that suggestion a second time. Using a red plastic pie server, I slid a good-sized hunk onto a paper plate and licked the utensil. Mmm. But before I could finish yanking a paper towel off the roll to put over my food in the microwave, Graham handed me a round plastic cover.

"Use this. Lasts forever. Saves trees."

I decided not to argue that plastic was an oil-based product and needed protecting more than a replaceable tree. After all, he'd been right about the microwave cover being reusable and lasting forever. The pie server was the same, too.

"So Kim and Mr. Scott went to church with Rob after all. . ." As certain as I was of that, I didn't bother putting a question mark at the end of my sentence.

"No."

"They didn't?" I suppose I sounded surprised, but not incredulous.

"Not church."

Graham, do I have to tickle this information out of you? I shook my head. "So where are they?"

"Climb. Tabletop. "

My growling stomach had been loud, but it was nothing compared to the volume of my response. "They what. . . ?"

Graham's bedroom door flew open, and Aleesha came bounding out, a thick book in one hand. "What's wrong, Jo?"

I purposely gave Aleesha what would have been one of those over-the-glasses stares if I'd been wearing glasses. "I thought *you* went mountain climbing."

"Changed my mind. I needed to do some reading." She waved a dictionary-sized book at me. "So what were you screaming about? A mouse run across your toes?"

I ignored the sarcasm. "But you *can't* be here." If I was starting to whine, I didn't care. "The directions on the table. . .the ones for climbing Tabletop Mountain. . .the ones addressed to you. . .they're gone."

"Yeah, sure, of course they are. When I changed my mind about going, I gave them to Kim. She and Mr. Scott were going to use them. They left, uh. . ." Aleesha glanced at her first edition Mickey Mouse watch. "They left here nearly two hours ago."

My first yell might have been loud, but it was nothing compared to my second one. If any furry little critters lived close by, my bellow surely sent them scurrying from the hostel and scampering up the mountain as fast as their little legs could carry them.

"They used *those* directions?" In my uncontrollable frenzy, I almost broke out crying. "No! Everything's messed up. *You* were supposed to. . . Never mind. Come on. We've got to find them."

I grabbed Aleesha's hand and pulled her toward the door.

chapter fifty-four

The downward trek from the top of Tabletop Mountain wasn't terrible, but it was just as steep as the trip up had been. Dad summed it up as only a quick-witted English professor can. "Although falling down a mountain is faster and easier than climbing one, the survival rate isn't nearly as good."

We chatted more on our descent than we had on the way up. I wasn't nearly as out of breath. Anxious—or *eager*—to hear more about Dad's plans, I was happy to stay quiet and do most of the listening.

His story came in bits and pieces.

"I'd been wrestling with God about this call to the ministry for a number of months. It's not that I opposed the idea, you understand, but it seemed like such an impractical undertaking at this stage of my life. . .

"Even though I hadn't heard about your activities in Mexico yet, your willingness to go helped me understand my own call more clearly. Especially when you didn't run home crying after breaking your arm. That *really* made me stop and think. . .

"Your mom was as supportive as any woman could have been and more so than most. I miss her more than you'll ever know. No one—man or woman—could have given me the prayerful guidance she did."

So I'd totally misinterpreted his happiness in the days and weeks following the accident. I couldn't see his private grief. Or his guilt, even though Aleesha had told me about it. All I saw—and failed to recognize—was the peace, contentment, and especially the joy that came from saying yes to God and trusting Him to take care of the details.

In spite of Mom's death.

We stopped walking for a few minutes. Both of us needed to cry. He'd just told me how happy Mom had been when he finally made the decision she'd been praying for. Only then did she tell him how many years she'd been praying that he might receive a call like this. Convinced that he was in the wrong place doing the wrong thing, she'd patiently waited for God to plant that seed in his heart rather than chance going against His will by suggesting it herself.

Dad's university had a theological seminary. "Is there any other kind?" I asked.

"Private schools are sometimes called seminaries."

Oh.

He'd hoped to get a master's degree and maybe even a doctorate—he already had one in Medieval Literature—on an accelerated part-time basis. But that would have required him to take courses during some of his classroom hours. And that's why he'd made the appointment with the president of the university.

"God's attention to details blew my mind," he said. "Like during my meeting with Dr. Cutshaw. . ."

"Scott," Dr. Cutshaw said on the afternoon of Mom's death, "your call to the ministry means you will eventually leave us. As much as I hate to see that happen, that choice isn't really yours."

Dad didn't respond. Not in a mood for someone to try talking him out of his prayerfully made decision, he was thankful Dr. Cutshaw understood.

"Do you realize tenured professors can take classes here at no cost?"

"That's one reason I want to attend seminary here," Dad told him.

"Let's make things a little easier for you," Dr. Cutshaw said, jotting a few notes on a nearby legal pad. You don't mind if I give your lower classes to a few of the instructors who need the experience, do you?"

"Of course not, but—"

"Don't worry about the money, Scott." He paused. "You're long overdue for a sabbatical. Why don't you take one next school year and work on your Masters of Divinity full-time? You can probably finish in six semesters including summer sessions."

He proposed that, *Dad. . . ?* And I thought God had worked some major miracles in Santa María.

We started our descent again. My squishy blisters were bugging the daylights out of me; my sweaty socks weren't helping. "So Mom knew you'd made your decision. But did you get to tell her the great news from your meeting with Dr. Cutshaw?"

Dad stopped. His face clouded over. Had we missed a landmark while we were busy talking? "I phoned her while she was coming to pick you up, but she didn't answer. I ended up leaving the news in voice mail. . ."

I could barely speak at first. "Dad, she was—"

"I know. She was listening to voice mail when she lost control of the car. I—"

"Dad!"

"I know, Kim. I was responsible for your mother's death. I really believed that. At first I felt guilty for not driving Terri to pick you up, but that was silly. Then I realized she wouldn't have used her cell phone while driving if I hadn't left a voice mail."

"But she *would* have." I could barely hold my own emotions in check. "I left voice mail for her, too."

I felt as if I'd just begun to emerge from a long, steaming hot bath. Maybe I wasn't sparkling clean yet, but at least I could tell Dad the whole truth now. That I didn't feel guilty for not being able to save Mom—he'd just assumed that was my problem—but for killing her. I told him my nightmares again, but this time I filled in the details I'd purposely omitted before.

Dad appeared to be somewhere off in space for a few seconds, but then he started chuckling. Softly and slowly at first. Then they built up speed and volume.

I furrowed my brow and nearly started crying at his horribly inappropriate reaction. But what I really didn't get. . .he looked relieved. Like Neil after confessing his failure to help me with Spanish in Santa María.

"We've *both* felt guilty about the same thing, if I can describe it that way. . .when *neither* one of us was guilty."

"Neither one?" I couldn't believe what he was saying. Or how positive he'd sounded. "How can you be so sure of that?"

He laughed again, and I started to burn.

"I don't find this at all amusing." I was starting to regret making a confession. *"Give him a chance to explain,"* God's still, small voice prompted.

"When I got Terri's phone back from the police—they returned it just a few days before we left to come here—I got curious." I could feel my eyes narrowing. "So I checked her voice mail."

Unable to look him in the eye, I watched his lips as he continued. "She'd already listened to both of our messages. I know that because she *saved* them. She was apparently dealing with somebody else's message when she hit the slick spot on the road. That message distracted her, not yours or mine."

So many thoughts hurled through my mind I almost

missed hearing Dad add, "Terri probably wasn't even driving when she listened to our voice mail. The credit card bill showed a gasoline purchase a moment or two before the accident. I made a trip to that service station. The accident scene is about half a mile away. I'm convinced she listened to our messages at the gas station and was just starting to listen to the other person's message when she pulled on to the interstate. It still showed as unread because she hadn't done anything with it yet."

"Who was that message from?" I wasn't sure I wanted him to tell me.

"I don't know. I deleted it without listening. I didn't want to know whose message had contributed to Terri's death. Not because we would have any right to blame that caller, but sometimes ignorance is blissful beyond description."

I couldn't possibly describe my sense of relief. I almost giggled, though. The devil might have used technology to make us feel guilty, but God one-upped him by using the same technology to free us from our guilt.

We resumed our downhill trek. My blisters had broken without my realizing it. Yes, the soles of my feet would be painful for a while, but that was better than having to keep walking on the squishies. Just as grief over Mom's death would continue to hurt.

But at least now I could live free from guilt.

"Dad, I love you."

"I love you, too, baby girl."

"I can't tell you how proud I am of you."

"For what?"

"Just for being who you are—a wonderful husband, a fantastic dad."

"God gets the credit. He set a great example as Jesus' Father."

"You know what? Mr. Jefferson—"

"Aleesha's dad?"

"Uh-huh. Yes, sir, I mean. He says Christians sometimes go through a series of severe problems. Taken as a whole, they seem insurmountable. He calls it a Season of Pebbles."

I described my experience at San Diego International.

"And you've been experiencing one of those Seasons, haven't you? I can't tell you how sorry I am. If I'd understood your guilt—what was really behind it—I would've told you about the voice mail as soon as I found out about it. Truth is, I was afraid it might make you feel worse."

As much as I felt like crying, I couldn't do anything but sigh. I wouldn't accomplish anything by complaining about needless suffering. Besides, it was my fault, not his. If I'd trusted him enough to admit my guilt, maybe he could have helped me even before discovering the truth about the messages. We could have helped each other. Everything—everything but the fact Mom died—would have been so different.

"That's okay, Dad. I've been learning to rely more completely on God and not let bad circumstances nibble away at my faith. Aleesha says unshakable faith enables us to 'prance on pebbles' instead of falling."

I whistled a couple of lines from "Victory in Jesus." He remained silent. Maybe he was thinking about the beauty and aptness of the prancing metaphor. Or maybe he was praying.

I began singing that glorious final stanza from "It Is Well with My Soul." I'd heard that the author wrote it after his entire family drowned at sea. What faith.

Dad hadn't said anything else. I started singing again. . .a different song.

"All those who wait upon the Lord shall have their strength renewed.

They will walk and not get weary and run, but not
run down.
Yes, they'll walk and not get weary and they'll run,
but not run down.
They'll walk and not get weary and they'll run, but
not run down,
And they'll rise up on wings like eagles and fly.
They'll fly. Yes, they'll fly. They will fly."

Then I did some joyful and thankful praying.
Dad and I must have been more preoccupied on the
way down than we realized. We reached the bottom of the
mountain and crossed the span of fallen rocks without
noticing how sharp and slippery they were. I didn't know what
walking on water felt like, but we must have floated across the
rock slide.
Or did we *prance*?

chapter fifty-five

I shouldn't have been surprised at the good things that had taken place during our stay in California. After all, God had been in charge. Not us.

He'd helped us deliver a number of insiders from the claws of the devil himself (I couldn't help thinking of Chappy that way, and I didn't feel guilty about it). He helped us lead several men—including Alfredo—to Christ. He helped us to lead many of the insiders to greater levels of commitment. And if those things weren't enough evidence of God's power, He convinced me to quit feeling guilty about Mom's death.

But healing still hadn't taken place between Jo and Aleesha, and that remained heavy on my heart.

"Dad," I said as we walked around the building to the front of Graham's apartment, "this has been such a great week. . .a magnificent week. . ." My tone of voice must have betrayed my hesitation.

"But. . . ?"

"Jo and Aleesha are further apart than ever."

"I've been praying for them."

"Me, too, but I feel like I ought to be able to draw them together."

"I know what you mean, baby girl. One of the hardest parts of growing up is accepting the fact that some things are beyond our control."

I reached over and squeezed his hand. He turned the doorknob with his other hand and gave a "ladies first" bow.

"Hello, Graham," I said.

Dad glanced around the living room. "Where are Jo and Aleesha?"

"Climb mountain. Together. Look you. Go wrong way."

We understood the *what* and *where* parts easily enough. What took five minutes of hard labor, though, was deciphering the fact that Jo thought our directions were so bad we'd end up miserably lost. Figuring out *why* Jo thought that proved impossible.

"That doesn't make sense, Graham," Dad said. "Rob gave me these directions earlier in the week."

He handed Graham the paper. After glancing at it, Graham said, "Correct. Goes to top. Some good. Almost safe."

Of course, it's correct, old fellow. We wouldn't have made it to the top and back again if these directions had been bad. You're spot-on about "some good" and "almost safe," too. I could've lived without those rocks at the base of the mountain and that final push, uh, pull to get over the top, though.

"Not best way. Hard. At bottom. At top."

Now you tell us, Graham.

I looked at Dad and rolled my eyes. *Why'd you ask Rob for directions and not Graham?* Then I started giggling. Would Graham have written directions the same way he talked? If so, we might never have reached the back of the hostel.

Dad appeared to be deep in thought, and I didn't want to disturb him, but I'd just had a lightbulb moment. I stuck my hands in the pockets of my down jacket. Nope. Not there. I unzipped it and pulled the paper out of my shirt pocket.

"Aleesha found these directions at her place at the table this morning. Her name was on the paper. Since she'd changed her mind about mountain climbing, she gave them to me. But you already had directions, so we didn't need these."

Dad reached for the paper. After reading a sentence or two, he shook his head. "Nothing like ours."

"Aleesha assumed Rob had written those directions. But if he didn't, who did?"

Dad handed the paper back to me.

I looked at it for the first time and gave a low growl. "Jo's handwriting."

"Why would she. . . ?" Dad said and then stopped.

"Wait. Jo told Aleesha to get lost the other day. You don't suppose she decided to make sure it happened, do you? To get Aleesha literally lost, I mean."

I hoped I'd have all sons when the time came. Girls could be too catty, too vengeful, and too hard to figure out. I knew plenty about that last characteristic. I didn't understand myself yet, and I couldn't understand Jo, either.

"I can't imagine her doing something that *dumb*," Dad said.

I narrowed my eyes in disapproval. He might as well have cussed.

"I know, Kim. We always taught you not to use the word *dumb*. Well, I'm sorry, but if she did something this dangerous, it was *dumb*."

My head bobbed in agreement. "But shouldn't we do something about Jo and Aleesha?"

"Why bother? When they reach the top and don't find us, they'll come back down."

"But they'll use the wrong directions, too, won't they? I mean, they'll have to if they want to go the way they think we went."

Dad was speechless. He reached out for the directions, glanced at them and sighed, and then passed the paper to Graham, who looked over them briefly.

"Bad," he said. "Dangerous. Go after."

"Oh, great," I said. I didn't share Graham's sense of urgency, and I really didn't feel like going back outside, much less climbing the mountain a second time that day. Would my feet blister again? "We're both exhausted."

"Starving, too," Dad said.

I started to say "Mmm" in agreement, but my stomach growled so loudly I didn't bother to.

Graham walked to the refrigerator before we could ask for his help, pulled out a variety of sandwich fixings, and busied himself making us some lunch.

"At least we have bad directions to follow," I said. "Let's just hope and pray we can find our way back—assuming we locate Jo and Aleesha."

"The insiders will have to understand that I used my message preparation time to rescue two foolish and vengeful teens. Tonight's message is special. I've been working on it all week, but it's not finished."

Duh. We'd been back five minutes, every muscle in my legs and back was screaming in protest against a return trip up the mountain, and we hadn't even sat down yet. I remedied that mistake first—or would God view it as a sin of omission?—and Dad followed my lead. I'm not sure I sat down in the usual sense as much as I let every part of my body ooze into the chair. I hoped I could get up again. I was afraid I'd morphed into a human jellyfish.

Whipping up a pair of sandwiches for each of us took Graham only a couple of minutes. One was bologna and mayo, the other peanut butter and jelly. Both on healthy, whole grain bread. I smiled our thanks when he handed us our lunch.

My blessing for the food was extra short, but—even so—I noticed Dad had already taken a bite out of his first sandwich. A huge one.

After practically swallowing our sandwiches whole, Dad and I looked at our empty plates and sighed. The food would perk us up some, but we still weren't in the best shape for going back out. Although Jo and Aleesha might not be that far up, they'd been gone. . .how long? Graham hadn't said.

Long enough to get into trouble, though. Serious trouble. My face probably had as many worry lines as Dad's.

Graham handed each of us a bottle of water. Dad opened his and started to drink. I was glad I wouldn't become a forty-something for a number of years. In the warmth of Graham's apartment, Dad fell asleep with his lips still around the mouth of the bottle.

"Kimmy. We go. He sleep. He prepare. When wakes."

What choice do we have?

"Leave note?"

Now why hadn't I thought of that? I searched the room for paper. No luck. "Have paper? Pen?" I said to Graham. *No! Am I starting to talk like you now?*

He disappeared in the direction of his bedroom and returned with a spiral-bound notebook and a ballpoint pen.

Graham and I—I scratched out "and I"—*Graham, Kim. Up mountain. Need find girls.* If I was going to talk like Graham now, I might as well write like him, too. Like he talked, anyhow.

Outside again and feeling nourished and refreshed by the water and the sandwiches, I started walking toward the familiar field of fallen rocks.

"No," Graham said, putting his hand on my arm to restrain me. "Easier way."

Bless you, Graham.

He pointed to Jo's paper, which said something about starting at an area seventy-five feet to the left of the rock slide. Had she unwittingly made the beginning of her misdirections better than Rob's? Of course, he hadn't known about the rock slide.

Graham seemed to know Tabletop Mountain better than most people know their spouses after years of marriage.

I wondered if he'd grown up in the area. I decided to ask. Knowing Graham, I'd get one of several possible responses. . .

- A yes or a no
- A grunt that could mean either yes or no
- A response that didn't seem to answer the question
- A response I'd die of frustration or old age trying to figure out
- No answer at all

I was betting on. . .one of them. Any one. I giggled at my indecision, and Graham turned and looked at me. Whatever his family background, he must not have grown up in a household of females.

"Did you grow up around here, Graham?"

"No." Hmm. That was the least expected response.

"You know this mountain so well."

"Climb often. Since. . ."

I looked him in the eye. Not harshly. Not impatiently. I didn't care how hard he was to communicate with. He was precious in God's sight, and I'd grown to love him, too. He turned and kept on climbing. After scrambling to catch up, I gave him a big hug. Although he seemed hesitant to accept it, he didn't struggle to break free.

"Graham, I love you."

I couldn't see if he was crying. The tears in my eyes blurred my vision too much.

"Love. . .Kim." Then he hugged me back.

chapter fifty-six

Somewhere else on the mountain...

I gasped as a sudden gust of wind blew the unfolded paper out of my hand. "That's it, Aleesha. We were lost before. Now we're *really* lost."

"That's what we get for following bad directions. Where'd you get those, anyhow?"

"You don't want to know. But ours was a duplicate of the ones Kim and her dad were using."

"You make me exercise like this, get me lost and almost killed, and then you won't answer a simple question?"

"It'll just make you mad, Aleesha."

"I'm already mad. What kind of spoiled white girl trick is this, anyhow?"

"Hey, what'd I do to deserve that?"

"To deserve what?"

"Being called a 'spoiled white girl.'"

"I didn't call you that. I just said a climb like this with what you knew were bad directions *seems* like the kind of thing a spoiled white girl might do."

"Oh."

"You ought to know by now I'm no racist. If I'm superior, it's because God made *me* that way. As an individual, not because of my color. And what if I had called you some kind of white girl? You *are* one, aren't you? You don't have some other skin color hidden under all that makeup, do you?"

"All what...?" I touched my face. "No, of course not. I mean yes, I am."

"Then I'd be accurate calling you a 'spoiled white girl' if you were spoiled and if name-calling didn't go against my principles. Which it does, I hasten to add."

"Whatever."

"And *whatever* is the origin of those directions? I'll just get madder if you don't tell me."

By then, we'd climbed up on a flat rock that overlooked the steep, so-called pathway we'd just come up. And down. And around and around.

Although we were only a third of the way up the mountain, I felt like I'd been climbing all day. We'd probably circled the mountain three times by now without going one foot higher.

"I don't want you mad at me, Aleesha. Not any longer. I don't like it."

"That works two ways, girl. I don't like having you mad at me, either."

"Truce?"

Aleesha nodded and held her right hand up palm out while I stood there with my hand outstretched. She compromised and bumped knuckles with me, and we both giggled.

We sat down on the rock several feet apart. Facing one another.

"So I can be honest without making you angry?" I wasn't about to take any chances.

"If I haven't bit your head off yet, I *probably* won't."

"I can take that as a promise of self-restraint?"

Aleesha shrugged. "Whatever." Was I imagining things, or did she wink?

"Do you remember when I told you to get lost?"

"Uh-huh." Aleesha wrinkled her forehead in a way that made her dark skin look especially ominous.

Do I dare to continue? "Did you believe I meant it?"

"I believed you were angry."

"Did you expect me to make good with my threat?"

"That was no threat. Not even a promise. You were letting off steam. I understood that."

"So you didn't expect me to send you up Tabletop Mountain with a set of made-up directions hoping to get you good and lost?"

"I am not angry." Aleesha said in a slow, strained tone of voice with a break between words. "I am not angry." That time went a bit faster and louder. "*I* am not *angry*." Her voice hadn't reached shrill yet, but it did the final time. "*I* am not angry!"

"You're not?" Kim always said I had a tendency to take things too literally at times. I took a chance this wasn't one of them. "Then I don't need to apologize for purposely getting you into this mess? I mean, God's punishing me by letting me get hopelessly lost, too."

"And what's He punishing me for, girl?"

That one got me. I didn't respond for several seconds. And then not for another several seconds. "For stealing my best friend and not understanding how I felt about it."

Aleesha leaned forward on one arm. She resembled Rodin's *The Thinker*. If *The Thinker* had been a female sitting on a rock instead of a man who looked like he was sitting on a—

"Kim is big enough for both of us," she said, bringing me out of my gross, mental comparison-making.

"She is not," I said instinctively. "She's super petite. We couldn't even both hug her at the same time."

Whoops! Am I being too literal?

"Haven't you ever heard of a family hug, Jo?"

"A group hug, you mean? Of course, but my parents and I have never had one."

"Humph! What kind of family do you have, anyhow?"

I could barely keep from tearing up. "I'll tell you about that later."

"Okay. But back to family hugs. . .group hugs. You think any two people even try to hug the same person—all of that person, I mean?"

I shrugged.

"The answer is no, my dear Miss Jo. So a three-way hug—ergo, a three-way friendship—among you, Kim, and me ought to work great. Each of us gives up a little bit of Kim, plus we get part of each other, too."

"That makes sense. You really are. . ."

"Go ahead and say it, girl. 'You really are smart.'"

"I wasn't going to say that."

"Huh? What then?"

"I was going to say, 'You really are just as lost up here as I am, aren't you?'"

We both started giggling.

"I don't know where Kim and Mr. Scott are," Aleesha said, ignoring my question. "But I have a feeling they don't need our help nearly as much as we need theirs."

"So what do we do?"

"Let's look for a path over there You see where I mean?" Aleesha pointed to a slight opening between two bushes.

We slid down from our rock, and I sprinted toward the bushes with Aleesha close behind.

"It goes downhill," I said. "Shall we?"

"If you want to see Alfredo one last time before we go home, I'd suggest trying it."

Aleesha broke out into a rambunctious version of "Victory in Jesus" as we began what I hoped would be our final downward trek. I was so enthralled with her singing I stopped for a moment to listen.

And Aleesha was so caught up in her own singing that she rear-ended me. "Better get those taillights checked out, Jo."

When Aleesha got to the chorus, I joined in. Although

I'd never been much of a soloist, I was great at making up harmonies for practically any song. Tenor or alto.

Although the trail ran downhill for a little way, we soon reached a decision point. Once again, which way?

"Lord, show us the way," Aleesha prayed. "The right way. We can find the wrong way on our own." She cocked her head skyward as if expecting God to shout detailed directions or maybe issue a small pillar of clouds for us to follow. "Guess He wants us to use our heads this time," she said when God failed to offer any visible or audible help.

After flipping a coin, we checked behind one unlikely looking bush. Sure enough, not only was the way visibly clear for a number of yards, but it also went downhill at a gentler slope than the short path we'd just run out of. Feeling encouraged and, uh, victorious, we resumed our singing.

When we reached the next decision point, we climbed up on a rock to rest.

"So tell me about the life of a famous actress-to-be," I said.

"They say *actor* now regardless of gender. And since I've already done some acting, the 'to-be' part doesn't fit, either. I do have a life, though, but you need to tell me about the life of a middle-class Juliet first."

We chattered on like a couple of squirrels for thirty or forty minutes. We did some deep sharing. Sharing and bonding like we'd never done before. And we prayed together again.

"We really need to find the next part of the way down," Aleesha said. "It's mid-afternoon now. I wouldn't want to be up here after dark."

"I see one possibility." Pointing to my left, I said, "There."

Aleesha pointed the opposite way. "There's another." Everything else in sight was clearly too steep or too rocky to climb down.

We scrambled down from our perch and moved carefully

to the first small opening. Pulling several branches aside, we found ourselves gaping at a steep drop just a few feet from where we were standing. I inhaled a nervous gasp as Aleesha pulled me away from the bush and let the branches snap back into place.

"We would have been on an undesirably fast track down if the ground had given way while we were standing so close to the edge," Aleesha said. The perspiration on her face glittered in the sunlight.

I don't know when I'd ever breathed so hard. Although I hadn't come anywhere close to falling over the edge, I'd never been in such a dangerous position. How could I have been. . . the way my overprotective mother had always treated me? The same mother who had just deserted my father and me to go live with a younger man.

"Maybe the other one. . . ?"

We hadn't moved two feet when Aleesha held her arm out to stop me. "Do you hear that?"

"What?"

"Be quiet for a minute."

I listened hard. I finally heard it. A rustling sound. Moving. Coming closer.

"Kim? Mr. Scott?" Aleesha's voice came out just above a frightened whisper. Nobody responded. The noise stopped for a few seconds, but then it resumed.

"Come on, Kim," I said. My voice was so shaky I hoped I could be understood. "Trying to scare us isn't very nice." We heard a slight movement in the underbrush several feet from where we were standing. Was the wind blowing some branches or. . . ?

"Are there any bears up here?" I said. "Or wildcats?"

I wondered how my mom would react to the news that a wild animal had eaten me while I was out mountain climbing, but my thoughts focused more on how painful being eaten alive would feel. I fell to my knees and barfed. Big-time.

Aleesha and I raced to see who could scramble back up the rock first. I wished I'd had an eye in the back of my head so I could guard my back. I half expected an elephant to tiptoe through the bushes. "Do you suppose we'll be safe here?" I asked while we scooted as far back on the rock as we could.

"I don't know."

"What if"—I shuddered at the thought of our unknown adversary—"what if it can jump this high?"

"Or climb." I threw my hand over my mouth. "That's how *we* got up here. We'll be goners."

The branches parted slightly. I couldn't hear Aleesha's screams. I was too busy screaming my own head off—at the first sight of a pair of furry black feet.

chapter fifty-seven

"Miss Kim," Graham said while waiting for me to catch my breath. We were almost a third of the way up, and my feet, legs, and back were killing me. If I had any new blisters, I couldn't feel them over my variety of other aches and pains. "Your guilt. Okay now?"

"Yes, thanks. I had a great talk with my dad. Seems we both felt responsible for my mom's death this past August, but everything turned out okay. He learned she wasn't listening to either of our voice messages when she lost control of the car."

He gave me the strangest look. I should have realized he wasn't a cell phone kind of guy. Not that my response would've made sense anyhow.

"My guilt," he said. "Not okay."

Huh? I had to think for a few seconds about what he was trying to say. That's right. He'd said something to me last week about guilt. His and mine, but he hadn't said anything else since.

Sure, Graham was on the odd side, and he was a bit somber even for someone who must have lived a mighty tough life, but what could that harmless old man possibly feel so guilty about? And how was I supposed to answer him? What did he want me to say? *Lord?*

"Not okay. Not now. Not ever."

"God can forgive anything," I said. After just four months of anguishing over unnecessary guilt, did I really think I could make Graham feel better with four simple words? He was a Christian—probably had been one a lot longer than I had—and apparently quite a student of the Bible. He already knew about God's willingness to forgive. And His desire to.

Then, too, I was comparing grapes and grapefruit. I'd finally learned I hadn't done anything I needed forgiveness for. If not for that, my guilt would still be plaguing me, and I might have ended up feeling as hopeless as Graham. While I couldn't imagine Graham doing anything terrible, he might have earned his guilt. And he might have suffered with it a lot longer than four months.

"God forgives. Dead person no."

Piecing those words into something coherent took only a few seconds, but I wasn't sure I'd done it correctly.

"God can't forgive a dead person?"

He shook his head no. His mouth tightened in frustration—like a non-English-speaking immigrant who's desperate for help and can't make himself understood.

"God can forgive, but a dead person can't?"

He nodded.

The pain on his face kept me from laughing at the obvious truth of his statement. Besides, I thought I understood what he meant. I'd recently wanted—I'd needed—my mom's forgiveness, but she was no longer able to give it to me. Was that where Graham was coming from?

"Somebody has died, and you need his forgiveness?" The mist in his eyes answered my question. "I don't get it. Did you have a falling-out with someone who died before you could ask his forgiveness?"

He looked away. I hoped my bluntness hadn't scared him into silence, but he was the one who'd started this conversation. And he'd chosen the topic. Did he want me to listen to a confession of some kind? *Graham, I can't forgive you for something you did to someone else. But I can still listen. I have two ears.*

Using the same prompt Aleesha once used on me—the one I'd recently used on Jo—I said, "The time you don't feel like talking about something is probably the time you most need to." That sounded. . .it had felt like the right thing to say.

Graham turned to face me, although he didn't look me in the eyes. "Miss Kimmy. You safe."

"Of course I am, Graham. I'm with you, and you know this mountain forward and backward, top to bottom. I couldn't feel safer if I were sitting on your living room couch."

"Not hurt. You."

"No, I'm not hurting." I stretched and purposely let out a painful moan. "Except for a body full of worn-out muscles, I couldn't feel better."

"No. Not hurt you."

"Oh, you're not going to hurt me? I wouldn't think so." I thought for a moment. I'd been dying to tell him this, but I'd been too much of a coward. Maybe the time had come. "Graham, I'm—I hope you don't mind—I'm adopting you as my grandfather. I never knew my own granddad. I need one sometimes, and you're the one I've picked."

The hardness on his face softened, and he wiped his eyes on his coat sleeve.

"I'm serious," I said. "I'll send you birthday and Christmas presents. I'll—"

"Hurt someone. Old." I must have looked confused. "Old hurt."

Why was he ignoring what I'd just said? My words had obviously moved him.

"You hurt somebody else?" Although I was getting better at understanding him, I couldn't imagine where he was going with this.

He hung his head. I could barely hear him say, "Kill."

"What? You killed somebody? Like in a war? You were

a soldier?" *You're too old for Iraq or Afghanistan. Vietnam,*
maybe? I read about that war in school.

He shook his head.

"In an accident? You killed someone in an auto crash?"

He shook his head again. I'd never seen such tension in
one man's face. He finally got it said, though—"Killed. Anger."

I hope my mouth didn't fly open as far as I'm afraid it did.
"You killed someone in anger?"

"Prison. Thirty-five years."

You were incarcerated for thirty-five years? No wonder
you treasure every sunrise now.

"You've been out six months?"

He nodded. "Six. Maybe seven."

The pieces were falling into place now. He'd remained in
the area because he didn't have a family or a home to return
to, although I was just guessing at that. Maybe he didn't have
enough money to go elsewhere. I couldn't imagine he'd be
eligible for Social Security, since he hadn't worked in thirty-
five years. Getting a non-strenuous job that provided a place to
live must have been a real blessing.

Who could blame him for staying away from our services?
What man in his right mind would want to set foot in that
place again after such a lengthy incarceration?

But if that was true, why had he come with us in the van
those two times? What did he do the first time while we were
worshipping? He hadn't stayed in the van; we saw him get
out. And why attend last night's service after avoiding all of
the ones that preceded it? Or should I have been wondering
why he didn't come to the earlier ones?

If questions had been pizza, I couldn't have forced down
one more bite. Yet I had little hope of getting answers.

Graham looked at me with eyes that begged for attention.
I hugged him, and he hugged me back. When we broke apart,

I looked in his face. "Graham, I still love you, no matter what you've done or why. I always will."

We fell into one another's arms then, and the tears fell like a cleansing spring shower.

We continued talking as we resumed our search for Aleesha and Jo. I learned—a few words at a time—that Graham had been one of ex-Chaplain Thomas's intended victims. One of the few who hadn't caved in to his threats.

Graham's integrity had cost him dearly, though. When he was eligible for parole fifteen years earlier, Thomas waged a dirty campaign to keep him behind bars. Telling one lie after another, Thomas insisted that Graham was still very much a threat to society, and the parole board bought it. Every single incredibly false word of it.

Graham didn't blame them, though. After all, who would have questioned the integrity of a highly respected professional like Chaplain Thomas? Fine, moral, upstanding man that he was. . . . Despite his broken manner of speaking, Graham's sarcasm shone through clearly.

At the time of Graham's release, he wanted to go straight to Warden Jenkins. But he'd become friends with Alfredo, and Thomas threatened to keep Alfredo in jail forever if Graham squealed on him. Graham was a faithful friend. For Alfredo's sake, he pretended to remain silent.

But just before leaving, he managed to smuggle an anonymous note to the warden on a paper napkin. When he learned through us that the warden was looking into the matter, he experienced an exuberant sense of relief. He liked and trusted the warden and knew he would do the right thing.

Only when Graham learned that the warden needed corroborating testimony to put Thomas away did he feel safe coming forward. He didn't realize Alfredo's testimony was what he'd corroborate. It turned out that Graham had first ridden with us so he could meet secretly with Larry Jenkins.

"You two must have had quite a talk," I told him. He actually laughed. Silently.

But then his face fell again. He described his problem with guilt. It reminded me of mine, though mine was minor in comparison. Bad enough over the years, it intensified at the time of his release.

He was a completely different person from the man who'd entered prison thirty-five years earlier. He'd accepted Christ and received God's forgiveness early in his incarceration.

He started building the library of Bibles, commentaries, and good fiction we'd seen on his bookcase, using every scrap of money that came his way. Money Thomas did his best to take away from him. He read and studied everything he could get his hands on. He might have had difficulty communicating verbally, but he was literate and quite intelligent.

Only at the time of his release did he realize he'd felt good about being in jail; he'd deserved that punishment. But his newfound freedom felt undeserved. After all, he'd deprived his victim of his earthly freedom—permanently. And because his victim had been a non-Christian, Graham had cut him off from all chance of becoming one. He'd not only killed the man but also sent him to hell. And that's what he'd been struggling with.

I was beyond hopeless about how to help. His heavy-duty sin had grown an unhealthy crop of heavy-duty guilt. Even though his body no longer suffered the restraints of a physical prison, he was still a prisoner of the consequences of his sin and the horrible feelings associated with it. Would he have to endure them forever as part of his punishment?

I had to say something, but what? *Lord?* "Graham, I can't say I know how you feel. I thought my guilt over my mother's death was bad, but it was nothing compared to yours. And mine went away when I found out I hadn't done anything to feel guilty about. But yours. . ." I couldn't find a way to say it diplomatically. "I think I understand why you feel the way you do."

His chin dropped to his chest. I'd never seen anyone look more like giving up.

Then that still, small voice whispered to my soul. *Thank You, Lord!* "Are you familiar with 1 Corinthians 13?"

"'Tongues men, angels. No love, no good.'"

"That's it. Do you remember one of those verses talks about love not keeping a record of wrongdoing?"

He nodded.

"You believe God loves you, don't you?"

His eyes were already misting. "Yes."

"And you've asked God's forgiveness for your sins, haven't you? Even the murder?"

He nodded again. "Asked. Begged. Received."

"So don't you think He's forgotten all about your sin? I mean, He's got the most perfect love possible, and elsewhere in the Bible God says He puts the memory of our sins as far as the east is from the west."

He nodded. He looked at me as if his future depended on my words. If I'd thought I could help him on my own, I would've been seriously wrong. But these words were God's, and they clearly applied to him.

"So how do you think you make God feel by continuing to remind Him of your sin? Don't you do that by dwelling on your guilt?"

"Not good."

"So how can you please Him?"

"Forget. Forgive self." He stopped. He could barely speak when he continued. "Can't."

"Do you want to, though?"

"Yes."

This conversation seemed more important—or at least more intense—than any I'd ever been part of. I didn't know what God would do with the words He'd given me, but I'd obeyed Him, and that was the most I could hope to do.

"Let's stop and pray." I pulled off one glove and held out my hand.

He looked at it a minute before taking it.

"Do you want me to start?"

He turned his eyes upward in affirmation.

"Then you can pray, too, if you want to."

I'd just closed my eyes when I heard the sound of singing. Loud singing. "Victory in Jesus." Aleesha was belting out the old hymn, but. . .wasn't that Jo singing with her?

They didn't sound that far away.

chapter fifty-eight

The singing stopped.

"Jo? Aleesha? Where are you?" I probably yelled loud enough to be heard all over Tabletop Mountain and across the way at Red Cedar as well. Maybe I should've tried that when we first started searching. Aleesha could've sung loud enough to answer back.

"We don't know," Jo said in a pitiful voice.

"Where are *you*?" Aleesha sounded more upbeat. Almost brave. Or was it just her well-practiced bravado?

"Graham and I are on our way. Stay where you are. Keep singing, and we'll find you."

"Be careful, Kim," Jo said. "Several wild animals have cornered us. We're up on a rock where they can't reach us."

"At least we hope they can't," Aleesha added. She didn't sound quite as brave as she had a moment earlier.

Before Aleesha could finish speaking, Graham—he really did know that mountain from top to bottom—was speeding toward the sound of their voices.

"Sing," he said. They started singing "It Is Well with My Soul." I wasn't so sure they meant it.

"Wait for me, Graham." I'd felt brave enough when we were walking side by side or one in front of the other, but watching him disappear in the undergrowth left me feeling fearfully inadequate. I could just see myself getting lost while he finished finding Aleesha and Jo. What a horrible new meaning that would give to the concept of "left behind."

He stopped and waited for me to catch up. I brushed on by him.

"Careful," he said. "Wild animals."

Whoops. I'd already forgotten about Jo's warning. I waited for Graham to get ahead of me again.

"It is well. . .it is well. . .with my soul. . ." Aleesha and Jo sang. Jo's alto couldn't have sounded sweeter if she hadn't been terrified. I'd have to tell those two how harmonious they sounded despite their mutual hostility.

Five minutes later, Graham stopped and turned to me. "Bushes. Other side."

"Kim," Aleesha said, "we're trying to scare them off, but these beasties aren't moving."

"I think they like us," Jo said. No matter how calm her voice had sounded while singing, it was quivering now. And not with the vibrato of her singing voice.

Graham handed me a broken tree branch to use as a club. He took a knife out of his pants pocket and opened it.

"They're my friends, Graham. I'm scared to death, but please let me go first." He stepped aside. "I'm coming through now," I said as I started brushing my way through an extra-bushy thicket. "What kind of—?"

Before I could finish my sentence, I tripped over a hidden tree root. When I looked up, I found myself face-to-face with the biggest, meanest looking possum I'd ever seen, and it had the nerve to bare its ugly little teeth at me as if I'd had the courage or the desire to hurt it.

No, Lord! Couldn't you have given me a raccoon? Or a deer? Even a wolf or a bear?

At least I still had enough presence of mind to poke my tree branch at her. She didn't waste any time scampering off in a different direction. Graham reached down and helped me up. Whew. Close call. *Thank You, Lord.*

Wait, Kim. Jo told you, "several wild animals." What else. . . ?

"No, Kim. Not now. Stay back!" Aleesha yelled as if my

life depended on it.

But it was too late. The skunk had already sprayed me at close range before scurrying off on his merry little way.

Thank goodness, my mouth had been shut. A rarer occurrence than I would want to admit. I wondered if skunk spray was poisonous.

At least I'd been wearing sunglasses. I don't know what the spray might have done to my eyes. I pinched my nostrils with my right thumb and middle finger, but I could still smell it.

No wonder. It was on my fingers, and some of it must have gotten inside my nose, too. Yuck!

I turned to Graham. "You okay?"

"No problem."

He'd been behind me. Far enough behind that I apparently took the brunt of the attack.

"Girl, you stink!"

Girl? When had Jo started talking like that?

I looked up at the top of the rock. Jo and Aleesha stood tall in the sunlight with their arms linked together, and they were both giggling at me.

"That's a fine way to treat your rescuer," I said. "Maybe we should just leave you two here."

"You can try," Aleesha said. "But we'll just follow the stink home."

Home? Oh, man! Smelling like this in the otherwise fresh air of the mountainside was bad enough, but I doubted whether my teammates would let me come inside Graham's apartment now. I'd feel guilty to try.

Although I pictured myself sleeping outdoors and burning my sleeping bag before leaving the next day, I forced those thoughts out of my head for the time being.

Graham started leading the way back down. Jo and Aleesha stayed close to him, but they made me follow at a distance. Whenever they changed direction, they signaled before moving on.

So I was "left behind" after all. How I wished I could leave my *odeur d'skunk* behind, too.

Dad and Rob's raucous laughter almost made me angry, but at least Rob was willing to approach me. He led me into the farthest unit from Graham's apartment and explained what we needed to do.

But first, he asked Graham to scout around—check the project supplies as well as his own—and find a quart of 3-percent hydrogen peroxide, a quarter cup of baking soda, and a teaspoon of liquid soap. Dishwashing detergent preferably. He cautioned Graham not to mix the ingredients together yet, because the resulting concoction would lose its potency quickly. It should be mixed immediately before use.

"Skunk spray contains mercaptans," he said. "The solution we're going to make—I'll leave out the boring details—neutralizes them. You'll need to get undressed—"

I must have given him a horrified look.

"Don't worry. I'll be outside. Feel free to lock the door."

Of course he'd wait outside. Who'd want to be trapped in this unit with me and my glorious stink?

"Your dad's bringing you some clothes. We'll dispose of the ones you're wearing. Scott's orders. Too much trouble trying to de-skunk both you and them."

Oh, man. Could things get any more complicated? I wondered how skunks stood being around each other.

Graham knocked and then came in.

"Peroxide no. Tomato juice."

Oh, man! I disliked tomato juice more than any other kind. How was drinking it going to help? What? No glass? Was I supposed to drink all of it—directly from the can?

He set everything down, rubbed his eyes, and almost ran back outside. If he thought *his* eyes were burning, he should have been wearing my share of the stink. Maybe this was an instance of "turnabout is fair play." I'd suffered no guilt compared to Graham's, so he'd suffered no stink compared to mine. What in the world was my inner voice babbling about!

"Hmm," Rob said. "Juice'll be messier, but it'll do."

So I don't have to drink it? Thank You, Lord. I touched the twenty-eight-ounce can. "This is freezing cold!"

Rob's look was priceless. "You want me to microwave it?" He would have done it, too. He was that kind of man.

I shook my head.

"So here's what you need to do, Kimmy. Get undressed after I go outside. Open the door just enough to throw your old clothes out."

"Even my jacket?" I'd really grown attached to that coat. Actually, as cold as the temperatures had been this past week and as much as I'd depended on that jacket, it had probably grown attached to me.

"*Especially* your jacket."

I frowned at first, but managed to emit one weak laugh before he continued.

"Combine the ingredients in the bucket using a paint paddle." When he saw my questioning look, he held one up.

"Oh, a wooden paint-mixing thingy," I said, trying to be cute. Acting cute while stinking so badly I couldn't stand being around myself wasn't the world's easiest thing to pull off.

He shook his head and smirked.

To pay him back, I said, "I thought you said 'a paint *palette*.' "

He rolled his eyes. "Here's a clean rag. Dip it in the solution and start sponging yourself off all over. Keep it away from your eyes, though. Personally, I'd also avoid your nose, mouth, and, uh, other sensitive body parts."

I rolled my eyes at him that time. "And when I'm done?"

"You need to leave it on for about five minutes."

In this unheated room? Brrr. "And when I'm done?" I repeated.

"Knock on the door and I'll hand you a coat. . .Graham has a spare."

Unless it was as big as his pajamas, it should fit fine. I just hoped it would be long enough. Long enough for a shorty like me? Now *that* was worth giggling at.

"And you think I'm going to Red Cedar this evening dressed that way?" I wasn't going to miss that final service if I had to wear my skunk scent at 100 percent full strength.

"Calm down, Kimmy. After you treat yourself with that solution, you'll do a thorough scrub-down in Graham's tub."

That's a shower, Rob. Graham doesn't have a tub. Men!

I didn't like the sound of these instructions, but what choice did I have? Although some of the insiders had objectionable odors of their own, none of them smelled as horrible as I did. Would they all back away or maybe leave the room when they caught their first whiff of me? Or were they so hungry for a taste of the outside world that even a skunk scent would bring back "sweet memories"? If so, I felt sorry for them.

I followed Rob's directions, and then I must have spent twenty minutes in the shower. It took that long under a stream of steaming hot water for me to thaw out. If I hadn't run out of hot water, I probably would have stayed there forever. Or at least until suppertime.

When I came out of the bathroom, dressed in the cleanest of my dirty clothes—oh, no! I hadn't gotten to do any laundry yet today—Rob took a whiff.

"Much better, Kimmy." He came closer and took another whiff. "Tell me something, though. . ."

I didn't like the look on his face, and I had a feeling I wouldn't like what he was going to say, either. "Did you use that tomato juice concoction on your hair before washing it? It still smells a bit like skunk."

Kim-Kimminy, Kim-Kimminy, are you having a good time on your day of leisure?

chapter fifty-nine

I don't know if God was angry at His world the day He created skunks, but I was slightly miffed at Him for protecting them in such an obnoxious way. Why couldn't He have just dressed them in camo fur? Wouldn't they have looked precious with those little splotches of brown and green, black and tan?

On second thought, that wouldn't have worked. Hunters would have made them extinct by using their pelts to fashion masculine-looking fur coats. Extinct? That was the ticket.

I sighed. No, not even I would want to see those little critters become extinct. . .

I was going to draw the line at returning to step one and doing the tomato juice thing on my hair. Fortunately, I didn't have to. Graham couldn't find any more juice. Everybody would just have to tolerate a little bit of Cologne d'Heavenly Scent.

I'd gotten so much exercise in the previous five hours that every muscle in my body screamed *no!* at the prospect of more. So I don't know why I gave in and agreed to walk to Red Cedar that night—unless to promote team unity and to keep Rob from having to lock me out of the van. His threat had sounded far too serious.

Graham offered to accompany me. His heroic rescue of my friends—I couldn't have done it without him—hadn't miraculously transformed him into a fluent speaker of any known human language, but I'd come to understand his way of talking far better than I used to.

"Go, too" was perfectly clear.

I assumed from the Bible he was carrying that he planned to attend tonight's worship service. The final one. I expected it to be emotional for our team and for many of the insiders as well. As much as we'd shared together, they might not grieve our leaving, but I hoped they'd at least miss us for a while.

Larry Jenkins joined us in the meeting room. He gave both of us a big hug. "Graham." He stopped as if reconsidering what to say. "Mr. O'Reilly. . ." I gathered he was trying to show respect for his elder. Or perhaps to acknowledge Graham's well-deserved status as an outsider.

"Graham," the old man said as he held out his hand. "Graham."

"Only if you call me Larry," the warden said.

Graham nodded, but he didn't say anything. I'd rarely heard him address anyone by name—maybe never—and I couldn't believe he'd ever even *think* of Warden Jenkins as *Larry*. He was from an older—a different, a more courteous—generation.

I couldn't imagine how it would feel to be on friendly terms with a former jailer after so many years of incarceration, but he didn't show any signs of nervousness or resentment. Perhaps their bond in Christ was stronger than I'd realized.

The rest of the team showed up a few minutes later. Alfredo and Jo rushed toward one another, but—spotting Larry—they slowed down and shook hands instead of hugging.

The warden smiled at them. "Maybe all you two want to do is shake hands, but I want a hug." At that, he embraced the two of them simultaneously and then pulled away, leaving Jo and Alfredo in one another's arms. I wish I had a picture of the astonished look on Alfredo's face.

Warden Jenkins saw it, too. He winked at Alfredo, who then broke into the biggest grin imaginable. Alfredo whispered something in Jo's ear, and she started smiling, too.

At first, I was too busy watching the lovebirds to notice anybody else. But when I looked around, the number of worshippers had already grown to eighty-some—double the high attendance record of the previous night—and they were still trickling in.

Regulations required one guard per some unknown number of insiders—even in a medium-security prison—and most of them looked uncomfortable about being there. Their eyes never stopped moving—here, there, and everywhere—and I could appreciate their apprehension. Nobody in that room was going to make trouble, but the guards couldn't safely make that assumption or—pardon the pun—let their guard down.

I saw curiosity in the eyes of several guards who hadn't worked any of the previous services. But whether newcomers or repeat visitors, the guards were more of a captive audience than the insiders. Their presence was a job requirement. I hoped Dad's talk would touch them.

I waved and smiled at Mr. Gray and Mr. Hudson. Gary and Ray. Rumor had it they'd traded shifts with some other guards to be with us every night. They'd sung as freely as if they hadn't been on duty, but they kept their eyes open during prayer time. I was thrilled to see them again tonight.

When things settled down, I led in singing Christmas carols without bothering to pass out the hymnals. One of the guys who'd come for the first time last night brought a guitar with him; from the battered looks of the old Gibson, it had lived a long, hard life—probably much like its owner.

I was glad he'd brought it. Although I'd heard that Christmas carols weren't as easy to play by ear as regular hymns, he was so good I didn't notice any wrong chords, and I was apt to be conscious of things like that.

I asked Mr. Guitar if he wanted to do a solo, but he passed.

"These fellows have already heard everything I know. They'd start a riot if they had to listen to me again."

At the word *riot*, the guards stood up straighter and touched the handles of their guns.

"Just joking, man," the guitarist said to the nearest guard. "We're here to celebrate peace with a capital P." It took awhile for the guards to ease up again, though.

Although our routine called for prayer time next, the warden asked if he could speak to the men first. "I have more news for you." He looked around the room. "But doggone it, put me in front of a group of people and I feel like preaching." He paused, and a spattering of laughter filled the room.

"Preach if you want to," Rob told him.

"You can have my time if you'd like," Dad said. Although he'd planned a special message for tonight, he was obviously sincere about his willingness to give it up.

"Don't mind if I do, Scott, but I won't use all of your time." The men eyed one another with surprise. "Some of you men have been here as long as I have." Looking around the room, he called off a couple of first and last names. "Some of you have been here longer." He named several more. "To you, I've been 'the man' who holds a major part of your life—the world you currently occupy—in the palm of his hands. That's true only to an extent, though. Somebody bigger than me holds your entire life in His hands. Mine, too."

Every eye focused on Warden Jenkins. I could tell from their nods and smiles that a number of insiders in that room knew exactly what he meant. Perhaps most of them.

"That 'person' is God."

"Amen!"

"You tell 'em, brother."

"Praise the Lord!"

"I know that's right."

Once the affirmations calmed down, he continued. He talked a lot about sin and breaking God's laws and Jesus being the ultimate forgiver. He said Jesus was the ultimate innocent victim, too. He'd been arrested on trumped-up charges even though He'd never committed even the smallest sin, much less an actual crime. And He'd received the death penalty without the pretense of a fair trial.

Oh, man. How was Dad ever going to preach after an address like this one? He'd spent hours trying to pack all the ammunition he could into this final message. But what could he hope to accomplish now?

After a few more key points, the warden sounded like he might be winding down. "I mentioned that God holds me in His hands. He knows how this prison affects me. Sure, I'm free. I can leave here every night and go home. But I'm not free to leave my concerns about you at the gate."

Although he looked wearier than I'd noticed at first, he smiled as he removed his hands from the podium and straightened up to full height.

"Men, I've tried to run this prison by Christian principles. But the State of California—and I'm not criticizing the government—doesn't permit me to do everything I'd like to do."

He laughed and shook his head. "Brother Scott, you said you didn't mind me preaching, but you've probably changed your mind by now."

Dad smiled and shook his head.

"Sometimes my long-ago seminary studies take hold of me like wind in a sail, and I keep on navigating across a rather large ocean instead of returning to port."

"No problem," Dad said. He must have recognized that the men needed to hear a sermon like that—from someone who understood them and their circumstances far better than he did.

The warden smiled like a farm boy bringing the cows in for the night. "The truth is. . ." He hesitated, touched the podium for several seconds, and then removed his tie with an awkward jerk. "The truth is I didn't come here to preach tonight. I came to make a resignation speech."

Loud murmurs reverberated throughout the room. I was as shocked as anyone.

"I've resigned as warden, but I'm not leaving Red Cedar." Every forehead furrowed as one. I held my breath. "Did you fellows know I started my career in the prison system as a chaplain?"

Many of the men looked at one another with "*Did you know that?*" "*No, did you?*" written all over their faces. I probably did, too.

"I promised that your new chaplain would be a Christian."

I'd expected to hear more choruses of "Amen!" "Praise the Lord!" and "I know that's right." But the men were still too much in shock. I think we all knew what might be coming; yet until he actually said it, nobody dared to assume it. Or to hope for it.

"I figured the best way to keep that promise was to transfer into Harry Thomas's position. I just received the approval before coming in here. Men, I'm your new chaplain, although I'll have to serve double duty for the next few weeks."

Cheers broke out all over, along with whooping, hollering, and stomping. Men jumped to their feet, and a number of them bounded to the front of the room to give their new chaplain a clap on the back and a hug of approval.

The guards touched their gun handles again. They couldn't have looked much more befuddled. What was going on? They'd probably never witnessed a nonviolent prison riot before.

chapter sixty

Prayer time was extraordinary.

Alfredo's prayer meant more to me than any of the others. Not because it was elegant. It wasn't.

But what a contrast between this prayer and the one he'd faked earlier in the week before becoming a believer. Tonight's prayer couldn't have been more genuine and heartfelt. And it wasn't the least selfish in words or tone.

I prayed for Jo while Alfredo prayed. Despite the fact that his English was better than most of the insiders realized, he must have felt more comfortable praying in Spanish. Jo appeared to have an unusual amount of difficulty keeping up with the translation. Maybe because his prayer moved her. Or maybe because she knew she wouldn't see him again after tonight.

How my attitude toward Alfredo had changed. Just as he himself had changed. No matter how critical I'd been of Jo's attachment to him before, my concerns had finally melted away like snow in bright sunshine.

Had she been smart? Probably not. Had she been human? Very much so. Had she demonstrated the finest of Christian love toward Alfredo? Absolutely.

Rock ended the prayer time, and Dad stepped up to the podium. He looked at somebody—I couldn't see who—and gave a slight nod.

Huh? Graham? Why was that sweet little man moving slowly toward the front of the room, and why didn't Dad act surprised?

"Friends, brothers in Christ, fellow forgiven sinners, Mr. Graham O'Reilly has asked to address you. He didn't say why, and I probably wouldn't have understood him if he had." Everybody cracked up. Everyone but Graham, who put his hands in front of his face in an apparent effort to hide his reaction. "But when somebody as quiet as Graham wants to talk, the Holy Spirit must have gotten hold of his tongue."

The men started laughing again. Laughing and cheering. Most of the guards and all but the most recent arrivals at Red Cedar knew Graham well. Him, and his abbreviated manner of speaking.

"Are you speaking in tongues today, O'Reilly?"

"Didn't know you had it in you, Gra-hambone."

"Found any good recipes since you got out?"

"When you coming back to cook for us again, man? I'm losing weight eating the new guy's cooking."

"I know that's right. New cook's pretty careless. I hope we don't end up with him in the soup."

"Not more than one finger at a time."

More laughter. High-spirited, good-natured laughter. I couldn't keep from smiling at the antics. Their camaraderie was something I hadn't expected, and it made me feel good.

Even Graham smiled that time. Maybe not the biggest smile his mouth was capable of, but a smile nonetheless. Dad stepped aside so Graham could stand behind the podium, but Graham waved him off.

"Too small," he told the insiders. "Can't hide there." Dad smirked, and the rest of the men started laughing again.

"Inside before," Graham said. "Not happy. Outside now. Not happy. Pray often. Pray much. Warden preaches. Graham listens."

Every eye in the room was watching him. Even the guards appeared mesmerized. No wonder. I doubted that many insiders came back to visit after getting out. From what I'd observed so far, Graham had been more popular than I'd realized or suspected.

I could hardly wait to hear more. I hoped his old friends would be patient with his slow and troubled shorthand way of talking. Oh, but of course they would. They'd probably gotten used to it during the years they'd been locked up together.

Graham looked up at the ceiling for a few seconds, as if appealing to God for help. He didn't appear to be nervous, though. From my spot in the middle of the room, his eyes seemed to have an *"It's all in Your hands now, Lord"* look.

I didn't understand it, but as soon as he looked at the insiders again, his face looked twenty years younger, his smile grew huge. . .radiant. And he began speaking.

I mean *really* speaking. In normal-people talk. Not short, choppy nonsentences, but complete sentences, whole paragraphs, and what would soon add up to complete, coherent pages. *If I'm dreaming, Lord, don't wake me till it's over.*

I could have been witnessing Jesus' healing of some biblical character. Not one of the special few He brought back from death. Not a man born blind. Not a leper Jesus made clean again or a paraplegic He enabled to walk. But the restoration of Graham's ability to speak was 100 percent as miraculous as anything I'd read about in Scripture.

I wasn't the only person in the room suffering from shock. At first, I heard only a few murmurs here and there. But as more people realized what they'd just witnessed, their jubilation grew and spread in such intensity that the room filled with shouts of "Halleluiah," "Praise the Lord," and "It's a miracle."

Graham stopped speaking. Nobody could have heard him over the sound of eighty-some men rejoicing and praising the Lord together.

If the guards failed to understand what happened earlier, what were they thinking now?

"Friends," Graham said when things quieted down some. I could almost picture him glowing like Moses when he came off the mountain with the second set of stone tablets. "Friends, I can't explain what's just happened, but I can tell you it's from God."

Amens from nearly every mouth in the room. Affirmations louder than before—if that was possible. He waved his arms like a windmill that couldn't decide which way it was supposed to turn, and the crowd settled down. From the looks on their faces, they were more anxious than ever to hear what their old friend had to say.

"I'm not a violent man—not normally—but I killed another man in anger. Living with myself after that threatened to tear me apart emotionally. I lost my ability to talk normally the moment the jury foreman read my guilty verdict aloud in court. When the judge asked if I understood the verdict, I answered, 'Understand verdict. Guilty. Be punished.' Tonight is the first time I've spoken normally in over thirty-five years.

"Talking like that wasn't a choice, but I had to decide whether to reveal my secret or not. Even though I could have obtained psychiatric help, I didn't want word to get out. I faced a lengthy sentence, and I vowed to speak as little as possible.

"I became a Christian early in my time here, and that changed my whole way of looking at things. I asked God's forgiveness for my crime, and I believe He heard and forgave me. But I couldn't forgive myself. To this day, I believe God has always wanted to deliver me from my affliction. He just wanted me to put more trust in the power of His love and forgiveness.

"Instead of resenting my incarceration, I almost enjoyed it. I knew I deserved it. When ex-Chaplain Thomas blocked my early parole, I secretly rejoiced. I didn't deserve to get out. So when I reached the end of my sentence, I knew I didn't deserve my freedom then, either. I may have been harmless to society, but I couldn't undo the damage I'd done."

He stopped and looked around the room. From the anguish I saw on a number of faces, these men could relate to his predicament.

"I had no family to go home to. My wife divorced me years earlier, and we didn't have children. My parents died while I was inside, and I didn't have any siblings. Completely destitute, I appealed to Brother Jenkins' church for help, and they took care of me after my release.

"When they decided to build the hostel to house the less affluent of your visitors, Brother Jenkins invited me to become the manager. That kindness was one more thing I didn't deserve, but I was grateful for it.

"Little did I know that this group of missionaries—they came last week to put the finishing touches on the hostel— would have such a profound influence on me. They found me strange. I overheard them talking about it more than once."

A smattering of laughter. Thank goodness, Graham didn't look in my direction. I was glad Jo was looking elsewhere, too. I didn't want either of them to watch me break out in a blush to beat all blushes.

"I deserved to have them talk about me that way, though. In my guilt, I had become. . .truly strange. Freedom amplified my guilt and deepened my feelings of worthlessness."

He wiped his eyes with the back of his hand and cleared his throat. "Don't be shocked when I tell you I toyed briefly with the idea of killing myself. Inescapable guilt had grown that serious. But I knew suicide would leave a mess for someone else to clean up, and I couldn't depart this earth with that on my conscience, too."

What might have been a concerned reaction started instead with a chuckle here, a snort there, and a snicker somewhere in between. Soon that tiny snowball of humor rolled downhill and ended up a meeting room–sized ball of hilarity.

Graham looked at Dad when the men quit laughing. "Brother Scott, I apologize for taking up so much of your time. I'll sit down now if you want me to." Grumbling. Loud protests. The men wanted to hear more.

Even so, they respectfully gave Dad their attention when he stood up to respond.

"Brother Graham, like the sermon Chaplain Jenkins gave"—four or five men interrupted with applause—"yours is probably more relevant than mine."

Graham twisted his face in disagreement, but Dad kept going. "You have great value in God's eyes, my friend, and you have great value in ours. Let's hear everything God wants you to share. We don't have anywhere we need to be now."

"Especially not back in our cells," Rock said. That cracked everyone up. Even Graham.

"Around midday yesterday," Graham said, "I learned that my Christian sisters, Jo and Aleesha, were somewhere on Tabletop Mountain. Probably lost. I've come to know that place from base to peak and back again, and I offered to help— no, I insisted on helping—Miss Kimmy rescue them."

Somebody in the back row gave him a thumbs-up.

"Along the way, she told me how much she loved me. She said she wanted to adopt me as a grandfather." I couldn't tell if he'd paused for a few seconds to collect his thoughts or to enjoy the memory of that special moment. "But she also told me I displeased and dishonored God by holding on to my guilt."

I knew he'd paid attention to what I told him, but hearing him refer to it now. . .I couldn't believe it.

"Kimmy"—he looked at me—"Kimmy probably doesn't know how much she helped me. She made me see that my guilt was as great a sin as any other. One I needed to repent of. I talked to God about it last night, and tonight I've found freedom. *Real* freedom. 'The truth shall set you free,' Jesus said. He wasn't just talking to hear himself talk."

chapter sixty-one

A breakout occurred at Red Cedar Correctional Center that evening, but not a single insider attempted to escape. It didn't make the late evening news on television or the early morning edition of the newspaper, even though it deserved that kind of attention and more.

Perhaps I should have described it as an *outbreak* rather than a *breakout*.

God's Holy Spirit moved among the insiders like nothing I'd ever seen. His Spirit might have ignited the fire with Warden/Chaplain Jenkins' sermon, but He used Graham's testimony to fan it into a sizeable flame. Despite forty-five minutes of heavy-duty listening, the men insisted that Dad speak. They were raring for all of the spiritual food the evening might provide. It would provide extra fuel for God's fire.

"I'm not going to use the special talk I prepared for tonight. I wanted to make it the high point of my messages to you men, but God had different wants from mine. . ."

Grins appeared on most of the men's faces, and Rock and Hi chuckled. The true believers in the room understood that man's plans were far inferior to God's. And they were always subject to change—whether forced or voluntary.

"God told me to scratch that message. I could use it elsewhere. He said to share the plan of salvation instead. Many of you don't need to hear it, but some of you do.

"I'm not here to 'scare the hell' out of you," Dad said in a quiet, understated voice that made his use of the word *hell* even more amusing. Although he never talked that way, it seemed proper in this context. "What I want to do is keep you *out* of hell."

"This joint is hell!" one of the men shouted. Several others grumbled in agreement.

"Then let this be a lesson to you," Dad continued. "Hell is real, and it makes the most atrocious prison in the world look as pleasant and enjoyable as your living room at home. Everyone who hasn't accepted God's gift of salvation is already destined to go there. In His eyes, everyone is guilty. Automatically guilty. That's what the Bible says."

"Not my grandmom," a voice chimed in. *Huh? One of the guards?* "She's no Bible-toting, churchgoing Christian, but she's a saint, anyway."

I prayed for Dad to handle the interruption in the godliest possible way.

"Many fine, well-intended nonbelievers spend a lifetime doing good deeds, and it seems like they should be able to waltz their way into heaven. No waiting in line."

"That's her," the guard said with a smile.

"It doesn't work that way, though, friend. Everyone has sinned. You, me, your wonderful grandmother. Sins are equal in God's sight. Has she ever been angry or held a grudge against someone?"

"Of course."

"Then she's sinned. That's the same to God as killing Him."

"But she's just being human," somebody said from the other side of the room.

"She is, and that's why no human being is good enough in God's sight. Even a single sin makes a person unacceptable to God."

A few of the men fidgeted, while others leaned forward and closed their eyes. Dad—actually the Holy Spirit—was getting through to them. To some of them, anyhow.

"On the other hand, many people refuse to believe that God can forgive the terrible things they've done. Some of you may fall into that category."

Dead silence.

He started looking around. A moment later, he caught my eye. "Kim, would you sing that song. . . ? I can't recall the title, but it's the one about not being good enough or bad enough. . ."

I nodded. I knew just the one he meant. Standing up where I was, I bowed my head and closed my eyes. I don't know why. It just seemed like the right thing to do.

I began singing. I'd never done this song a capella except in the shower. I don't know about the insiders, but I imagined angels singing backup with the most gorgeous harmonies.

> "What good can I do? What good can I say
> That's good enough to pay the Lord for loving me?
> There's nothing I can do. There's nothing I can say
> That's good enough to pay the Lord for loving me."

Mr. Guitar figured out what key I was singing in and started playing along. He couldn't have done a more effective job if he'd been playing that song all his life.

> "What bad can I do? What bad can I say
> That's bad enough to keep the Lord from loving me?
> There's nothing I can do. There's nothing I can say
> That's bad enough to keep the Lord from loving me.
> Well, what then can I do? What then can I say
> To thank the Lord for loving me?
> I'll do everything I do, I'll say everything I say
> In the name of the Lord who never stops loving me,
> In the name of the Lord who never stops loving me."

Although those fellows had always applauded when somebody sang, the Holy Spirit moved them and kept them from desecrating the awe-filled reverence that filled the room after the last notes faded away. I'd experienced perfect silence several times in my life, but I'd never known stillness like that.

Dad presented the Gospel plan in words a child could have understood—but he didn't talk down to the inmates. He didn't waste words with unnecessary embellishment, either. Not the way TV preachers sometimes do. God must have had him by the tongue, too.

He might have been assembling a jigsaw puzzle from the bottom up the way he laid the foundation of salvation and then built upon it word by word, concept by concept. Nonbelievers would soon see the completed picture of Christ crucified, raised from the dead, and offering forgiveness and new life to everyone who accepts it.

"Many of you are already Christians," he said. "I couldn't feel any more at home here than I do with the men at my own church. Faith, hope, and love—God's love—tend to do that to Christians. Believers, if something is on your heart tonight, please share it with your new chaplain or me. Then I want you men who need to make the eternally significant decision to become Christians to step forward."

I didn't notice the dozen or so men form the line to talk with Dad or Chaplain Thomas. They just appeared there. No pushing. No shoving. No signs of impatience. Only the sounds of sniffling broke the stillness, and that somehow made the atmosphere seem even more reverent.

I stayed in my seat and tried to keep from blubbering. I needed to pray. Some of the men in that room had undoubtedly pictured themselves as tough guys before coming to Red Cedar, and many of them had probably worked hard to maintain that image as insiders.

Even though God wanted to win the soul of every insider present, He wouldn't force Himself on anyone. Yet not even the toughest man in the room could have rejected the Holy Spirit's tugging that evening without a painful struggle.

Chaplain Jenkins had told them the Good News. So had Graham—in his own special way. Dad, too. While some of the men had undoubtedly listened with open ears and receptive hearts, others had hardened themselves to the message. Each man would have to make a decision—to accept Christ and live or to suffer both earthly and eternal separation from God. I was thankful for the rededications, but my most earnest prayers were for the men who had yet to reveal their decisions.

When the line of people making rededications got down to one or two, a sudden onrush of men headed to the front of the room and lined up behind them. Unable to ignore them and keep my mind on my prayer, I noticed that only a few men remained seated, and several of them had the strained, agonized look I'd always pictured Jacob having when he wrestled with the angel of God.

I felt sorry for the guards, though. Several of them looked like they had taken God's call seriously, too, but they couldn't respond while on duty. I made note of their names to give to Warden, uh, Chaplain Jenkins.

I'd never heard of a revival taking place inside a prison, but I spent one glorious evening of my teen life watching one insider after another break free from the captivity of sin in a meeting room at Red Cedar Correctional Center.

chapter sixty-two

The service was officially over, but spirits were still high. Anyone witnessing the interaction among the insiders, Chaplain Jenkins, Graham O'Reilly, and the members of our ministry team would have thought they were watching a Christmas family get-together. The only thing missing was food and drink.

Hmm. I started thinking about what had been going on at my home church tonight—actually three hours earlier. The Sunday night before Christmas was special because the choir presented its yearly musical. Several years earlier, our director started making the singers memorize it. Although they grumbled at first, they had to admit that the presentation sounded considerably more polished when they didn't have their faces stuck in their books.

Because I'd been suffering from fatigue when rehearsals for the musical began, I would have missed too many to sing in the choir tonight anyhow. I'd participated each of the four previous years, though. Although it wasn't going to be the same, I'd had my heart set on being there in the front pew.

But the way God worked things out, I didn't feel like I'd missed anything that night. I'd been among special Christian friends who were like family to me now. They'd blessed me with their prayers and their testimonies.

And who needed a well-blended church choir when we could enjoy the richness of men's voices—enhanced by the sweet sound of Hi's countertenor and the power of Rock's super-low bass—singing from their hearts as if they'd been the shepherds worshipping the baby Jesus in Bethlehem.

Unlike my departure from Santa María, when I didn't discover what my Spanish Bible reading had accomplished until the bus was well on the way back to San Diego, we'd *seen* results at Red Cedar. Plenty of them. Rededications. First-time commitments. And announcements with far-reaching implications.

Rock told me he felt called to the ministry. Maybe not as the pastor of a church, but doing some type of ministry where tales of his prison experiences would include his personal Saul/Paul conversion testimony. Maybe he'd enter the chaplaincy—if his prison record didn't prevent it.

Graham shared with the men individually how much he'd missed them. They'd been his best and only friends for a number of years, and he planned to slip across the road frequently to visit them. Even if no other outsiders chose to do a regular prison ministry, he would come back and assist the new chaplain.

In an effort to be truthful and honest with his fellow Christian insiders, Alfredo had made an announcement in passable English. "I speak English good. More good than I let on." I giggled at the wide-eyed look of shock on the face of the friend who'd brought him to the service.

Especially when Alfredo said in mock seriousness, "Be more careful what you say when I nearby." The guys poked each other good-naturedly as if to say, *"Now I can ask Alfredo what you really think of me—what you say about me behind my back."*

He also touched me in a personal way that evening. "Miss Kimmy, I can't thank you. What you do. For Jo and me. You do not approve. I am sorry—"

"Alfredo, I was wrong. About you. About you and Jo. I'm the one who should apologize."

"No, you right. At first I—how you say?—I made use of her. So good sit next to pretty girl. Pretend she mine. But she is friend now. Just like you. You brought me Jesus."

Good thing I'd had the forethought to bring several packets of tissues with me that evening. I was already halfway through the second one.

"Jo helped, though, didn't she? She gave you the *Santa Biblia.*"

"Sí. Both of you helped."

"Will the two of you stay in touch after we go home?"

"I do not know. I think I. . .am not worthy Jo." He sighed. Although he'd referred to her as a friend, his feelings obviously ran deeper than that. I couldn't believe he was going to give up on her that easily.

"Wait a second, fella," I said. "You aren't worthy of God's love, either. But He gave it to you anyhow." *Lord, please keep me from elaborating on that observation and making a simple point more complex than it needs to be.*

His face brightened. The most brilliant of Graham's sunrises hadn't been more radiant. "Have present. For you." He handed me something he'd been carrying under his arm. It looked like a Bible at first, but it wasn't. "A thank-you."

I smiled, took the hard-bound book from him, and looked at the cover. It was a well worn copy of Miguel Cervantes' classic *Don Quixote*. In Spanish at that. The language Cervantes wrote it in.

I opened it up, found the first chapter, and began reading aloud. "*En un lugar de la Mancha, de cuyo nombre no quiero acordarme, no ha mucho tiempo que vivía un hidalgo de los de lanza en astillero, adarga antigua, rocín flaco y galgo corredor.*"

What I wouldn't have given for a picture of Alfredo's mouth dropping open.

"Jo is right. You read *español* good. *Perfectamente*."

I didn't want to burst his bubble by admitting I only understood a handful of the words I'd read, and I couldn't even fit those together in a way that made sense. The villagers of Santa María had tutored me in pronunciation, not grammar and syntax.

"I learned to do that in Mexico," I said.

"Jo told me. The villagers. . .they teach you good."

I smiled at him. "You sure you don't want to keep this?"

He nodded. "Jo says you want to learn Spanish. For you to read. . ." He seemed lost in the search for the right words.

"For me to read when I learn Spanish well enough to understand what I'm reading?"

He smirked. "Sí. You do that."

"This is a precious gift, Alfredo. I wish I had something to give you."

"You give me God's love. Can I . .hug you, Miss Kimmy? Like brother-sister?" Instead of verbalizing a response, I hugged him.

"Pardon me, please," he said as he looked around at the rapidly emptying room. "Must tell good-bye Jo."

Considering how much Alfredo's farewell had torn me up, I couldn't imagine the effect it would have on Jo. Resisting the temptation to watch wasn't easy.

Staring wouldn't have been just morbid curiosity, though. If Aleesha and I were going to rebuild Jo's spirits afterward, I needed to see how badly she was taking it. I compromised by watching something a few feet away from them and relying on my peripheral vision.

I didn't move closer, though. Eavesdropping would be too great an invasion of their privacy. But Jo surprised me by talking with Alfredo for only a couple of minutes. They exchanged little scraps of paper—I assume with their addresses. Then she gave him a quick hug and a peck on the cheek.

After Warden. . .*Chaplain* Jenkins walked us to the parking lot, Jo pulled Aleesha and me to the side. "Anybody for a walk back to the hostel?"

"I'm worn out," I said, probably in a whinier voice than I realized. "Didn't we do enough walking today?"

"I think she wants to talk to us, girl," Aleesha whispered in my ear. "We're her best friends. Remember?"

"But sure, Jo." I said in a more positive voice. "It's a beautiful night. Let's do it."

We didn't start talking until Rob, Graham, and Dad passed us in the van. They'd spent a few extra minutes talking with Chaplain Jenkins.

"How'd it go, Jo?" I expected her to break out bawling any second now.

But she didn't. "Okay," she said.

I shone my flashlight on her face in disbelief. No tears.

"*Really* okay." She shone hers on mine. "Don't look so surprised." She laughed.

"Surprised, girl?" Aleesha said. "Try amazed. Stupefied. Dumbfounded. Thunderstruck. Not to mention we just plain don't believe it."

Girls' giggle time. In three-dimensional surround sound.

"Isn't anybody glad?" Jo said, trying to catch her breath after laughing so much.

"Yes, of course," I said.

"I was praying for you the whole time," Aleesha said.

I started to say, *"Then why are you so surprised that it went well?"* but changed my mind.

"Isn't anyone going to ask *why* things went so well?"

"Besides the fact I was praying for you, girl?"

As wonderful as it felt having the old Jo back, I was going to miss having Aleesha around, too—if she carried through with her plans to transfer to Howard University the next semester. Now that we'd finally melded into a Christ-centered, three-in-one, one-for-all-and-all-for-one fellowship, I knew of two people who were going to try their best to talk her out of going.

"Go, Jo," I said. "Don't keep us in suspense."

"Alfredo and I both admitted we'd been using one another from the start."

"You. . . ?"

"Used him?"

"I was so angry at Mama for what she'd done that I wanted to pay her back by doing the most dangerous thing I could think of."

"You mean besides getting me lost up on the mountain?" Aleesha's tone morphed in mid-sentence from a mild rebuke to a gentle tease.

"More dangerous than making you angry, Sister Aleesha. Trying to get romantic with an insider—or at least pretending I was. I wanted to call Mama as soon as I got home. Tell her I'd gotten engaged to a Latino I'd met doing prison ministry. Wouldn't that have put her in a tizzy?"

"That would've gotten *my* attention," Aleesha said. "You're sure you're not still young enough for your mama to spank?" Not a hint of a tease in her voice that time.

"Well, God didn't like my attitude, either, and He didn't like my leading Alfredo on, even though I was almost positive he was taking advantage of me, too. I knew what I was doing when I took that letter. I'd read the rules, and I hoped to get in trouble over it. Anything to hurt Mama a little more."

Aleesha and I didn't interrupt. If she felt the same way I did, we were both confused and concerned. Jo knew God disapproved of her attitude. She'd admitted it. But it sounded like Jo hated her mother. Maybe more now than before.

We didn't have a chance to ask, though. "Kim, Aleesha. . . when we get back to the hostel I'm going to borrow Rob's satellite phone."

"Calling your dad?"

"No. My mama."

chapter sixty-three

I couldn't believe Jo. Not the fact that she was going to call her mama. And not that she was going to do it this late at night. Since it must have been three or four o'clock in the morning at home, maybe she thought it would be fun to punish her mama a bit more by interrupting her sleep.

But Jo asked us to be with her when she called, and that floored me. "I'm going to put the call on speakerphone," she said. Maybe she wanted witnesses.

"Rob has Mama's number in his contacts. I was tempted to delete it, but I realized I might need it when I worked up the courage to tell her I never wanted to speak to her again." She paused. "I've never bothered to memorize it," she said before I could ask.

I groaned. Why in the world would Jo want Aleesha and me to listen to her and her mother have a shouting match over the phone?

I was jealous of Graham now. He'd gone to his room as soon as we got back and was probably already sound asleep. Rob and Dad were in their unit, undoubtedly unwinding from the evening's activities. Maybe discussing Dad's plans, too. Rob might not have had any seminary training, but he was one practical and insightful Christian. And he had the additional advantage of being older than Dad.

We could've called Mrs. Snelling from our room, but it was next door to Graham's. No matter how good he'd gotten at ignoring three teenage girls and their lively, endless noise-making, we didn't want to chance disturbing him with a phone call like this.

The living room was still too close, despite having a carpet that would have muffled the voices slightly. The kitchen and dining area were far enough away, but the tiled floor and variety of hard surfaces would probably have amplified the conversation.

We took a vote. No matter how much Jo detested the cold, outdoors won.

As long as we made our call outside the opposite side of the U from Rob's unit, nobody would hear us. I didn't know about Aleesha, but I hoped the just-above-freezing temperature would make Jo cut her conversation short. Graham's spare coat was warm, but not like my skunky down jacket.

Huh. Nobody had complained about my scent at the prison that evening. Too polite to, maybe. But I could still smell it.

If the cold wasn't enough reason to go back inside soon, the trip-and-a-half up and down Tabletop Mountain and the round-trip walk to the prison made my whole body ache more than I want to remember or try to describe. Not even learning to walk in high heels had been this painful.

If I had to stand up longer than a couple of minutes, my muscles would probably just say *"We quit"* and let me slither to the ground and freeze to death. I hoped Dad could get a refund on my unused ticket.

"It's ringing. Be quiet, you two."

Aleesha and I hadn't said a word since we came outdoors. Jo must've heard our teeth chattering, and I wasn't about to quit just so she could hear better. I couldn't.

"Hello?" Michelle Snelling sounded as sleepy as I felt.

Jo didn't say anything.

"Hello? This is Michelle Snelling. Who's calling, please?"

At least she was still using her married name. Of course she was. She'd still be a Snelling until she and Jo's papa got the divorce. I quit thinking about that and started wondering why she hadn't recognized Jo's name and number on her caller ID.

You are so dumb, Kim. Jo is using Rob's satellite phone, not her own cell phone. You'd expect Mrs. Snelling to recognize Rob's number?

"Mama, it. . .it's Jo."

Mrs. Snelling was quiet for a moment.

"Jo?" I could almost hear her scratching her head in confusion.

"Yes, Jo." Silence. Two loud yawns. Silence again.

Would I recognize my daughter's voice at first in the middle of the night if I'd been sound asleep for a number of hours? Yeah. I hope so, anyhow. But wouldn't introducing herself by a nickname I'd never heard before confuse me? Probably.

"Jo? Betsy Jo?" She sounded more alert now. And much more excited.

"Yes. . .ma'am."

"Are you all right? Is anything wrong? Where are you? Do you need help?"

Random questions kept rolling out like pebbles from my tote bag, and Jo didn't interrupt her to answer any of them.

I heard a sleepy male voice mumble something in the background. Oh? She was there with *him*? Of course she was. That's why she'd left Mr. Snelling.

End of questions. Jo's turn. "Mama, I'm still in California—"

"When are you coming home? This week has gone so slowly, and I don't know if I can stand having you gone for another seven days."

Hmm. Jo's whereabouts hadn't surprised Mrs. Snelling, and she knew about the timing, so her soon-to-be-ex-husband must have had a chance to tell her about the trip. And she'd probably let him have it for allowing Jo to come.

"Tomorrow, Mama. We finished up early."

"I'm so glad." Mrs. Snelling sounded completely awake now. "I love you, sweetie, and I've missed you terribly."

Do you actually believe that, Jo? If I were you, I'd probably say something evil like, "You mean you've noticed I've been gone?" or "You loved me so much you moved out on Papa and me?"

But she didn't. "I love you, too. . ."

Wow. I'm not sure I could have said that if I'd been in Jo's position. Aleesha moved closer to me. Her hand was just inches from my face. Maybe to cover my mouth if she needed to.

"Have you had a good time?" Mrs. Snelling asked. "No, I mean has your work gone well?"

"Wonderful. Thanks. Especially the worship services we've been doing at the prison across the road."

"I'm sure those women appreciated your coming."

"Uh, it's a men's prison, Mama."

Dead silence. "I'm sure the men appreciated your ministry."

Come on, Jo. I dare you to say something about Alfredo.

"We saw a number of insiders make first-time decisions." Jo's tone was a little, uh, maybe not curt, but slightly brittle. At least she was polite. *Good on you, girlfriend.* "It's been far too wonderful to try telling you about on the phone. Especially at this time of night."

"I'm looking forward to hearing every detail when you get home."

That's when I would have said, *"And where should I look for you when I get home?"*

I heard the male voice in the background again, but I couldn't make out what he was saying. "Betsy Jo. . .Jo—what a cute nickname. I like it. Somebody here wants to talk to you."

I could picture her handing the phone over to her young, scantily clad, uh, friend. What I couldn't imagine was why.

"Hey, Jo!"

"Papa! What are you doing there? Uh, I mean Mama. I. . .I don't know what I mean."

"Jo, your mama's come back home."

I could hear Mrs. Snelling in the background. "Where I belong. And am I ever glad to be home. Leaving your papa and pretending to move in with a younger man was the most stupid thing I've *ever* done."

Aleesha grabbed my arm and yanked me in the direction of Graham's apartment. Time to let Jo talk with her parents in private. The last thing I heard before we got out of earshot was, "I love you, Papa. And I love you, too, Mama. And I miss both of you so much."

chapter sixty-four

I was dead tired from going to bed so late, and my legs, feet, stomach, and back—plus body parts I couldn't even identify—were so sore I could barely wiggle, but nothing could keep me from getting up to watch one last sunrise with Graham.

When the colors finally showed, he turned to me and said, "Sunrise good." I knew he was just teasing by pretending to revert to guilt-speak.

"Sunrise very good," I replied.

We stood there together for probably twenty minutes. He put an arm over my shoulder, and I wrapped mine around his waist. We stood together as two beanpoles taking up the space of one average-sized human being.

I whispered in his ear, "I love you, Grandpa."

Graham couldn't come to the airport with us. The power company was going to do its long-awaited hookup that morning, and furniture for the units was scheduled for delivery that afternoon. He'd spend the next few days setting the rooms up in preparation for the building inspection later that week. Once the hostel passed inspection, Graham would receive an occupancy permit. He already had a backlog of people waiting for reservations.

During the van ride to Sacramento, Dad renewed a long-forgotten discussion.

"We still need to decide about a place to live, Kim. We talked about an apartment or a condo."

"It'd be crazy to *buy* something since you'll probably move elsewhere after you finish seminary."

"You won't be living at home forever, either." He steadied his eyes in a mock stern look. "And that's an order."

I laughed. "I don't know what my future holds, but I can't wait to go back to Santa María, and I want to be able to speak the language next time. The most perfect Spanish possible."

"I know that's right," he said, punching Aleesha playfully in the shoulder while still addressing me. "We don't have to move out of the house unless you want to."

"I'm in no rush."

"Folks," Rob said, "would you like some advice from a building trade professional? Not to mention someone who's done a lot of moving. . ."

"Go for it, Rob," I said at the same instant Dad said, "We're listening."

"Selling a house is like looking for work. Best time to do it is when you don't need to."

"Hmm?" Okay, but I didn't have experience looking for work. Just in avoiding one kind in favor of another.

"So you think we should. . . ?" Dad's voice tapered off.

"With the housing market the way it is now, I'd put that house on the market as soon as possible. Price it reasonably and then don't compromise. If somebody makes an offer tomorrow, great. If it takes two years, okay. Better to start a two-year wait now than in two years, when having an unsold house might be more of a liability."

"And if we sell it before I move out of town. . . ?"

"Get an apartment. . .with a month-to-month lease, if you'd like." Rob was so smart.

We didn't let him hang around the airport with us. He was going home for a long stay. He hadn't seen his wife in weeks, and he missed the grandkids, too.

"What's that saying Jewish folks use in parting?" he asked.

"'Next year in Jerusalem'?"

"That's it." He shook Dad's hand and then hugged each of us girls in turn. "See you next year. . .in Jerusalem. Or somewhere." Then he turned to me and added, "And you'll be fluent in Spanish by then, won't you?"

"I learn. I speak. Do good."

Rob was still laughing his head off the last time I looked back.

~

Rob's question about Spanish really made me hungry to get going on my studies. I could probably get into the local community college for the spring semester even at this late date, but I wanted to start studying sooner than that. My guilt and its various side effects had kept me off-course far too long.

I'd brought *Don Quixote* in my carry-on luggage. As if I'd be capable of reading it. I was dying to try, though. It symbolized what I wanted to accomplish. Maybe that's why keeping it close by seemed important.

I barely noticed Dad slip away from our gate and walk toward a small cluster of shops. I looked up when he came back, though. He was holding something behind his back. A chocolate chip muffin, maybe? I salivated and reached out with both hands.

"Not so fast, baby girl. Close your eyes." Even though it had taken eighteen years to become his baby girl, it still felt great. I closed my eyes, and he put a plastic bag in my hands. *A dozen muffins wouldn't weigh this much.* I barely managed to keep Dad's present from falling. I opened my eyes. What? A bookstore bag?

I must've hugged the daylights out of him for his thoughtfulness as the best dad ever. Who would have thought he'd buy me a Spanish grammar book and a Spanish/English dictionary—a big one—on the way home? I started picking out random words from *Don Quixote*, pronouncing them aloud, and then looking them up. Half an hour later, I put the Cervantes novel down and got out a clean sheet of paper.

Dad grinned. "You planning to write your translation of *Don Quixote* down?"

"Nope. Gonna try translating something into Spanish, actually."

"Oh?"

"Sure," I said as I winked at him. "The words to 'Victory in Jesus.'"

epilogue

Heading home from the Welcoming Arms Christian Hostel couldn't have differed more from leaving Santa María.

I'd left the northeastern California mountains by van rather than a flat portion of northwestern Mexico by bus. I was waiting to fly out of the Sacramento airport rather than San Diego International, and I was with Dad, Jo, and Aleesha and not by myself. I wasn't carrying, dragging, or kicking a leaking tote bag of pebbles, and I didn't sprawl out of control at my departure gate.

Although I'd lost the world's best mom before I finished getting home from Santa María, I'd reconnected with the world's finest dad on this trip. And I didn't just have the two greatest gals for my best friends, either. I had two best friends who were now best friends and *sistahs* with one another.

As we boarded the plane, I couldn't help smiling at the memory of Aleesha and Jo sitting on the rock singing "Victory in Jesus." Four disturbing months of prancing on pebbles had made me fall in love with God all over again. As one of the writers of Psalms said, "His trustworthiness is eternal."

I was at peace. The kind of peace the non-Christian world doesn't know anything about. Or understand. The kind only God can provide. And the kind that enables Christians to face the future with confidence.

I'm not saying I *wanted* anything else in my life to go wrong. Who wakes up every morning and asks God for a batch of new problems just so she can enjoy watching Him solve them? No sane person I've ever known, anyhow.

As far as I was concerned, my Season of Pebbles had lasted long enough. But at least it had given me new confidence in God's ability to sustain me whenever new troubles arose. I said "whenever" and "new troubles" because I'd come to accept the fact that growing up doesn't free a young woman from problems.

Neither does maturation cause them. Not counting hormonally induced challenges and the body's gradual breakdown as it starts its inevitable race toward old age and death, that is.

But growing up makes a young person more aware of how serious life's problems can be.

Thank You, Lord, for the peace I have in Jesus. He not only walked on water, but He also pranced on pebbles to show me how. How much more victory is there than rising from the dead and ascending to heaven forty days later?

I settled back in my seat and closed my eyes. My mind kept wandering in one direction and then another. I must have fallen asleep, though, because I nearly jumped out of my skin when a flight attendant leaned over and touched me on the shoulder.

"I'm sorry to bother you, miss, but may I speak with you? Privately."

I excused myself as I climbed out over the person in the aisle seat. Although Dad had exchanged our tickets easily enough, Skyfly had undoubtedly won an overbooking prize for that flight. I don't know the exact number of passengers they had to entice to take a later flight in exchange for a free future ticket, but I'd noticed at least five.

So the fact they had to seat the three of us in different sections of the plane was no surprise. As good old helpless, unhelpful Millie Q once pointed out, at least we were inside the plane.

"This way, please," the flight attendant said. Curious but unconcerned, I followed her forward. She sidestepped into the first food service area she came to and turned to face me. "I apologize for disturbing you, but several of your seatmates have complained about your. . .strong perfume."

Huh? I wasn't wearing any. Ah, but my hair still contained a small yet still odiferous hint of skunk scent. Had the people adjacent to me really referred to it as perfume, or was the flight attendant just being diplomatic? At least she hadn't sounded sarcastic.

No matter. I couldn't do a thing about it until Dad and I got home. We had hydrogen peroxide there, not cold tomato juice. I'd merely disliked tomato juice before Miss Nasty Skunk sprayed me. Now I hated it with a passion.

I hoped the flight attendant could understand my inability to get rid of the smell. At least she couldn't put me off the plane in midair or make me sit on a wing. Of course, she could put me in the cockpit to keep the flight crew awake. Or would the stink knock them out?

"I don't think it's bad at all," she said. "It's very unique, in fact. Is that what you use to catch fellows?"

I put my hand over my mouth to keep from giggling. Next thing, she'd be asking where—

"Do you mind telling me where I can buy some? I think my boyfriend would love it."

I put my other hand over my mouth, too, and I tried to physically force my mouth into a less tickled-looking shape.

"I got this at a place called Tabletop Mountain. It was readily available there. I didn't have any trouble finding it." Under my breath, I said, "Getting rid of it again was the problem." She apparently didn't hear that part.

"Oh, we don't have any of those where I live. Do you think they have it at any places I might be familiar with?"

Lord, I'm sorry, but I have to play this one out. And she's not even blond.

"Ma'am"—I looked at her name tag—"Charlotte, this scent is found easily in out-of-the-way locations on the outskirts of most towns and cities. Even the smallest towns. I don't know the place names, but they're apt to be called something Forest or Mount something. To tell you the truth, you're most likely to come across this scent when you least expect to."

Are you such a city girl you've never even been to the country?

"Oh, really?" Her face perked up so much I had to bite my tongue to keep from laughing. "I almost forgot to ask. What's the name of your perfume?"

"Eau d'Mephitidae," I said without thinking. Rob had taught me so much about skunks that the family they belonged to was burned into my brain for eternity. "It's most common on females who wear head-to-toe, white trimmed, black fur coats."

Her face fell. "That sounds too pricy for me. I don't get paid enough for fur coats."

"I couldn't afford it myself, but I received a substantial sample as an unexpected gift. In fact, the manufacturer's representative sprayed me without asking. Once this wears off, that's it. All gone." I started to add, *"And never again if I have my way,"* but I didn't want to burst Charlotte's happy little bubble by sounding too negative.

"I know you'll be sorry when that happens," she said.

"I can't begin to tell you how that'll make me feel. Variety is the spice of life, they say, but this is the spiciest scent I've ever worn. For variety, I'll try something more ordinary—more conventional—next time."

"Well, look, I'm really sorry about those old ladies and their complaints. They just don't understand how adventuresome we modern women are."

I wondered if I could make an explosive laugh resemble a sneeze. Probably so. This poor girl would believe anything. And if I'd told her the truth, she would probably have thought I was just teasing her.

"I promised to move you," Charlotte said, "but—as you've probably noticed—we don't have any seats left in economy. Would you mind sitting in an empty first-class seat we keep for emergencies? At no extra cost, of course. There's enough room between seats to keep anyone else from noticing your perfume."

I tried so hard to keep from squealing in delight that I managed a fairly convincing sigh. "Okay. If it'll make those funny old ladies happy." I hadn't paid attention to my seatmates' ages. Or to their gender, for that matter.

She thanked me profusely, helped settle me into my new seat, and brought me a fancy dessert dish filled with fresh strawberries and real whipped cream.

"Can I get you anything else?"

"I'm fine. Thank you."

She returned to economy, and I stretched my arms and legs. I couldn't have reached the seat in front of me if I'd tried.

Lord, feel free to let me prance on pebbles like these anytime.